Alex Manningley: Evil Rises

By R.J.Foster.

In loving memory of Peggy and Peter Gypps, and also of Paul Danter,

gone but never forgotten.

I dedicate this book to my wife, without whom this would not have been possible.

Prologue

Charles stared at the sign above the tavern; his heart was aflutter with the sensational beating that arose from seeing only his closest friends. The sign read 'The Adam and Eve'. He was unfamiliar with this establishment but he had heard that the publican within was renowned for rewarding those who served with the British Army. Charles considered that a good sign.

The delightful night air of the summer encased him in a cocoon of warmth as he peered through the windows to spot his fellows within. His final days at the Royal Military Academy of Sandhurst had been full of splendour and ardour in equal measure as he made the final push towards becoming an officer. He spied his comrades within, with whom he had graduated only that afternoon, and gave them a quick wave as he strode towards the heavy wooden and iron tipped door that led into the pub. The door opened with a creak that was usual of such an aged building and instantly Charles was reminded of the billets back in the grandiose halls of the officer recruitment centre.

The scent of alcohol permeated every orifice of the small dimly-lit room where the patrons could sit and enjoy a nice beverage and a pleasant conversation. It was not a smell that he was unaccustomed to and he delightfully sniffed the air to take in as much as he could; like a pig in filth he had always considered such places to be his environment. As his hard steel-toe capped boots walked across the rough wooden floor, with some difficulty due to the stick that it had procured from the various spilled drinks that had no doubt washed over it, to his companions he surveyed the pub and its inhabitants.

Behind the bar, rather obviously he thought to himself foolishly, stood the bartender. He was a rugged looking man with a roughly shorn beard and a haggard looking face. He met Charles' eyes and spotted the army uniform that he was wearing. Instantly his eyes lit up as he knew that he had another loyal member of her majesty's service within his tavern. The beer stained apron upon his front told Charles that his friends had been keeping the bartender busy for some time and so it was no wonder that he should be delighted to see another patron joining the ranks.

To his left he spied a small group, roughly similar in number to his own circle of friends that were present, of young women who were busy flirting with the men in uniform. A perk of being in the army, as Charles always saw it. Amongst them he noticed a beaming blue-eyed beauty with a smile on her lips as she examined the latest addition to the group of soldiers. His thoughts were momentarily lost on her before he returned her look with a wink, almost hitting his head on a low wooden beam in the process, and continued the walk to his friends. Charles had always been quite the ladies-man and so relished in the attention that was being given to him.

The only others that were present were an old couple who quietly laughed amongst themselves over their many years of experience. The man's wrinkles lifted as his lips drew back in a wondrous smile that the grey-haired woman could not help but resist as she too joined in on the mirth. For all his exploits Charles could not help but yearn for such a moment with someone that he truly loved. Alas, the experience had, as of yet, eluded him and he concluded to himself that he had plenty of time to find his soul mate. After all, he was still only twenty two years of age and had a long and plentiful life ahead of him.

His friends greeted him with a formal salute, much to everyone's aggravation as they were all of the same rank of Lieutenant, and shook his hand as they welcomed him into their camaraderie. Both Willis and Goodwin clasped him on the shoulder and pointed towards a pint glass full of the amber coloured liquid that all young men were fond of.

"My thanks." Charles spoke.

As was common when drinking with friends, their drinks did not last long as they took the rims of their glasses to their mouths and tilted their necks back to flow as much of the drink as they could down their gullets. The sharp tanginess of his drink, combined with the deep cold that only a freshly poured beverage could attain, was almost enough to force Charles to stop after a single mouthful. Yet valiantly he carried on until he could see the bottom of his glass. With a triumphant cheer he slammed the empty pint down upon the bar, causing the others glasses to shake.

The young wiry figure of Henderson was the last to finish as the soldiers applauded his effort but heckled his slowness. Knowing full well that Henderson would have to buy the next round, as was customary amongst his friends; Charles excused himself to visit the gentleman's. The bathroom consisted of two urinals and a single cubicle with two sinks opposing them. For a public toilet they were in a rather good condition, Charles thought to himself, even if the newspaper that was given for customers to read was a week out of date.

"July 18th 1993, I don't think that's right at all." He said as he laughed openly to himself and walked over to where the sink was placed within the small room.

Vain though it was he stood in front of the plain square mirror that sat above the neatly polished sink. He stared back at his own reflection and marvelled at how out of place his hair had become. Gently he pushed the ginger strands to the side to present the orderly appearance that he was so familiar with. His blue eyes had turned red and bloodshot from the exertion that he enacted upon them the night before as he had been unable to sleep due to the nerves of finally becoming an officer that morning. Before leaving he pressed the collar down on the hem of his olive green parade jacket, the standard number two uniform that all soldiers had to present when on formal parade.

He returned to his friends and saw that they had intermingled with the group of women that were also present. Nervously he noticed that the young brunette that had caught his eye once before was sitting with no-one to talk to as her friends were engaged in shallow conversations with his companions. A sudden shyness had overcome him and his legs refused to move as he stood, completely still, with his left arm propping him up against the bar.

"Charlie! Over here, you lemon!" Willis shouted across the pub.

Charles shook himself out of his timidity and walked over to the merged group with confidence in his step to redeem his earlier folly. The woman who held his affections looked up at him and smiled and suddenly his nerves returned again as his stomach twisted itself in knots like the mast on a ship. He sat himself casually beside her and struggled to get the conversation started as his friends abandoned him to pursue their own topics of discussion with their chosen women. As the words struggled to form he looked down anxiously and thought bitterly upon what her opinion of him must be.

"Hi, I'm Charlotte." She said to him as she noticed his plight.

Sheepishly he risked looking back up and met her eyes once more. "Charles…" This was all he could manage as he struggled to maintain his composure in her glorious presence. Thankfully she laughed playfully and the radiant smile caused him to disregard all previous stumbles. "My friends call me Charlie though."

"And do you have a last name, Charlie?" She politely enquired.

"Manningley." He courteously replied.

"That's a rather unusual last name." Charlotte joked as her smile filled Charles with glee.

"I like to think it makes me special." He answered with a laugh.

"I've noticed." She responded as she too broke into laughter.

Charles was amazed by the simplicity of it all. It had been so easy for him to connect with this woman, a person that he had never met before yet now seemed so comfortable in front of. His thoughts crept away from him and all his anxieties had been laid to rest. All of this because of Charlotte, he thought to himself. Charlotte, he savoured the name as it tantalisingly leapt around his thoughts like a merry marionette.

"Would you like another drink?" He found himself asking.

She nodded and so he made his way to the bar, careful to avoid the low beam this time, and asked for another pint of beer for himself and a rum and coke for Charlotte. He lightly chuckled to himself as he looked at what was happening to him. It was normally the case that he first had to imbue himself with alcohol before he could talk to a woman of her stature, and yet now it was the other way around.

He was happy.

Charles propped his arms up against the bar as he turned his back to the bartender to survey how his friends were doing. From the corner of his eye he noticed the old man looking at him and so he turned his attention to the balding figure. The man gave a wink and a smile as he pointed his thumb over to Charlotte and laughed heartily. His wife playfully slapped his shoulder and raised a hand to her mouth as she also giggled.

A sudden tap upon his shoulder caused Charles to turn around. The smashing sound of glass was all he heard as he realised his mistake. In turning around to see what was required of him he had knocked the drinks that the barman had brought for him onto the floor. With a flicker of slight annoyance the bartender scowled and grabbed a brush that he kept behind the bar.

"I…I'm so sorry." Charles stammered.

"Quite alright young sir." The barman responded. "Just see that it doesn't happen again. There's a small trough in the front garden if you want to wipe the alcohol off your shoes." He added with a smile.

"Thanks."

With the stains likely to ruin the smell of his shoes very quickly he set off outside to deal with the problem. Once more he opened the heavy wooden door and it gave a slight groaning at being forced to open. He had not noticed the ornate design upon it before but now he realised that a tree had been shaped out of black iron. Below it he could see two figures, which he assumed were Adam and Eve, with the latter clutching an apple in her hand. How he had not noticed this before he did not know, yet everything suddenly seemed more beautiful to him as he stepped outside into the moonlight.

It was a clear night and so the stars offered their warmth unto him and bathed him in their ever-glowing light. It was so magical, he thought to himself. Even the few wisps of cloud that remained in the sky were bending around the stars so as not to obscure their splendour. He spent so long just looking up at the night sky that he had completely forgotten about the stains upon his shoes. Charles cursed himself for being so absentminded and turned to the left where he noticed a small trough that was probably being used as a fresh supply of water for the local wildlife. The stains themselves left his boots with little trouble. The smell, however, still lingered as he lowered his nose to sniff.

"Damn." He angrily muttered to himself. In an attempt to calm himself down he uttered the phrase that his father had taught him and that he would one day teach his own son, should he be granted one. "To overcome anything, we must push all restrictions aside and focus on those we love." Unfortunately it didn't seem to help very much.

"Are you alright?" He heard a voice behind him call.

Charles was about to shout at the person for such a ridiculous question. As he turned around though he noticed that it was Charlotte that had called out to him. Her radiance combined with the beauty of the stars allowed his anger to flow out of him and his mind was filled with only her.

"Yes…yes, I'm fine." He replied with a smile. "I was just thinking actually…" His mind stopped him before he could go any further and stood, silently, looking at her with his mouth agape.

"You were thinking that you wanted to ask me out to dinner?" She suggested with a smile of her own that rivalled the light cast by the stars.

"Yes, that's exactly it."

The boom of the thunder and the patter of the rain pelting down upon them forced Charles and Charlotte to bolt into their new home as quickly as they could. Frantically he fumbled for his keys and opened the tiny door that led into their new abode. Jestingly, he extended his hand as if to hurry Charlotte inside so that she could attain some solace from the ceaseless howls of the wind. They both laughed as he slammed the door shut, as the wind was attempting to thrust itself inside their house and chill them to the bone. It had been a good night of celebration, now though they could truly relax with each other.

Before Charlotte, Charles had always been a social creature, desperate to sink his teeth into the flesh of conversation and chatter, even if it did not concern him, yet now all he wanted was to spend time with his beloved. The entirety of those present at their first meeting had accompanied them to the restaurant and the mixture of elation and embarrassment that had been shared between them had thrown the atmosphere into a black hole of awkward gesticulations and haphazard jokes. Still, he rarely got to see his friends, now that they had all been deployed, and so he was grateful for that at least and he knew that Charlotte felt the same. Now they had returned to their new residence he was aware that only one task remained for the evening. The lump in his throat caught any speech that he could make and so he contented himself instead with removing his coat and placing it upon the coatrack that sat adjacent to the entrance by the stairwell.

The small Victorian home had been a cheap sale that he simply could not ignore. The black wooden beams ran through it in typical design, giving the rooms an almost formulaic appearance that had latched itself onto Charles' sense of order and appearance. As he glanced through the landing and into the living room, that was adorned with photos of his time together with Charlotte, he knew that he was home. The kitchen was simple enough and the house only possessed two bedrooms, even the bathroom had the most basic of adornments. It had not bothered either of them though as they imagined snuggling on the black leather sofa together, in front of the open fireplace, watching television.

An entire year had passed since that fateful night at the Adam and Eve, a night that he relived every time he looked into Charlotte's aquamarine eyes. The magic of their meeting had never been lost on him, and he intended to prove it. As he riffled through his sopping coats many folds his anxiety began to take hold. He had not spent much upon the ring itself for he knew that it would not matter to Charlotte, she was like a rose that continued to blossom all year round, as he had delved into the deepest depths of her personality and revelled in ecstasy over her benevolence and tranquillity. Never had he met someone so enticingly altruistic as her, she would give all she could until her heart ceased to beat if it meant that she could help another person. Tonight though, was all about her.

Desperately he searched in the various pockets of his garment, hoping to find the small velvet covered box. His fears were alleviated as he felt the familiar brush against his fingers, the tingling of the material brought with it a kind of instilled calmness as he prepared himself for this frightful moment. He had always assumed that it would be done in a restaurant, as his childhood films had taught him, yet he could think of no better time than how they were now.

Still completely drenched he turned to his dearest love, who was trying desperately to warm herself against the archaic radiators that the house possessed. He wanted to savour this moment for the rest of his life. The acrid smell of damp upon the walls; the undying cacophony of rain hitting the windows as the wind pushed furiously against the foundations; the beauty of the woman before him. He captured it within his memory and pulled the box out, clutching it in his hand as though it would escape if he loosened his grip, even by the slightest of adjustments. Charlotte turned away from the radiator, her bedazzling smile still playing upon her harmonious face as she gently brushed a strand of cascading brown hair behind her ear. She instantly spotted the box in his hand and her smile broadened, the shining purity of her smile filled Charles with courage as advanced towards her and dropped onto a single knee. He could feel the perspiration building within him as he struggled to find the words that might adequately express his feelings.

"Charlotte…You are, without a doubt, the single most beautiful woman that I have ever met. Your hair is so outstanding, and your face so fair, that Aphrodite herself would bow in honour of your vivacity. Your body is moulded as though sculpted by God himself. Your eyes are bluer than the truest lagoon, and far deeper besides. It is your smile though…" He paused as he looked at the thing in question once more, completely taken in by the beauty of her smile as each tooth complimented the next with a pearly magnificence that dimmed even the brightest of lights. "It is that smile that has captivated me since the day that we met. Never, in my short life, have I experienced such a look…such a twinkle within someone that has so altered my life. You have given me strength when there was none to be had. You have consoled me when my world crumbled before my very eyes…" He pushed the thought of the letter that he had received aside, his orders did not concern him currently. "You are beauty incarnate. You are intelligence made flesh. You are humour…okay you're not quite that funny." She smiled at his quip as a single tear of joy rolled down her delicate cheek. "I am nothing without you. Would you do me the greatest honour that I can conceive of, Charlotte Abigail Jacobs, and become my wife?" Finally Charles opened the purple velvet container and revealed the jewel within. It was a simple band of Argentum silver with a singular diamond upon its head, a half carat's worth.

Charlotte was so overcome with emotion that she could not even muster the response that she desperately wanted to give. Still she fervently nodded as the tears poured from her eyes like a waterfall. As the ring was put upon her finger she raised a hand to her mouth in disbelief. It was a moment that she had dreamt of ever since meeting the young army officer, and now that it had arrived she was unable to respond.

Charles pulled her in close for an embracing hug to express his joy. As they pulled away, and as the rain suddenly begin to give way to the beautiful night sky, he cupped her fragile cheek within his hand. Longingly he looked into her eyes and moved his head closer to hers as their lips came together. With a final gust the wind died down as their lips met upon this perfect evening.

The monumental ceiling of the church towered above Charles as he glanced into its architectural grandeur. The flowers had been delicately arranged across the ends of the benches and sat in bunches of wonderful bouquets before the steps that led up to the altar. All in all it was a rather simple affair with relatively few lavishing adornments and only their closest friends and relatives present. Charles felt a twang of pity that his father could not be present to see this day, even though he knew that he would be with him in spirit.

Charles made a final check of his number two uniform to ensure that nothing was out of place for his and Charlotte' big moment. The collar had stubbornly refused to go down without a significant helping of starch and a hot iron. Still, he could not care less about the smaller details on a day like this. All that mattered was that the moment had finally arrived for him to wed his beloved. It seemed as if no time at all had passed since that night at The Adam and Eve, even if the bartender, who was present, seemed to have aged many years in this relatively short stretch of time.

As he looked around the church he knew that everything was exactly how they had imagined it would be. It was perfect. The figures in the stained glass windows were smiling down upon him, blessing him, as they too surveyed the scene that was unfolding in their presence. Many of his friends also had been able to make it. Although, regretfully Charles reflected, Henderson had not been able to attend due to mitigating circumstances. They had all mourned the loss of their friend and he could not help seeing the young officer's face every time he looked into the wave of people that were present. Charles pushed aside such negative thoughts and focused on his happiness. He felt as though his heart was about to leap forth from his chest and bellow his love for Charlotte from the top of the spire, like a great mountain bearing the call of an animal. His mother gave him a broad smile as she could upon seeing his elation.

The doors to the church suddenly opened to the right and the music began playing. This was the moment. Through the thick and heavy oaken doors, that churches so often possessed, came the figure of his father-in-law with a long white dress tailing to his side, just out of sight. As his betrothed calmly walked towards him he felt an unutterable serenity overcome him. It had always been known as the calm before the storm, yet he could see no storm in his future, there was only Charlotte and the never-ending bliss that she would bring with her. Like the tales of old, their own song would be immortal, lasting well beyond their years and down the lines of their descendants. Charlotte had only bequeathed him the knowledge that she was with child the night beforehand. No words could have adequately expressed the joy he felt when she told him, yet even that, the most jubilant of occasions, was overshadowed by the sheer pleasure he was experiencing in knowing that he was only moments away from achieving everything he had ever wanted in life.

As her father brought Charlotte around the corner, and onto the main stretch of the aisle, a new level of happiness arose within him. He had always considered Charlotte to be the most beautiful woman that he had ever known, and even by these lofty standards she truly looked divine. The dress was a simple, yet elegant, design. There was no ruff, very few examples of lace, just the shining purity of the brightest white coupled with Charlotte's natural radiance.

She beamed her majestic smile at him as she looked upon the familiar sight of his uniform. It gave her a feeling of solemnity as she looked into the distance at what their future would hold. Of course Charles would be given shore leave, as all members of the armed forces were, but still the thought of going months on end without seeing the man that she truly loved filled her with dread. Even so, little could stop her joviality as she walked, almost bounded, down the aisle. Her friends gave her crude winks and gestures that she had come to expect from them. They had always had a unique way of showing their cheerfulness, although Charlotte knew that they were happy for her, as any friend would be when they come across someone so magnificent that love is an inevitable occurrence.

The last few steps onto the altar seemed to take an age as the best man and bridesmaids all looked intently towards the priest. He was a middle-aged man that Charlotte had personally known for many years, as he was a family friend. His short, well-kept, hair and neatly trimmed beard gave him the appearance of a confidant. Not a single piece of his cloth had frayed or was out of place. It was perfect.

With one final step, and a gentle kiss on the cheek of his darling daughter, Augustus released Charlotte and she took her betrothed hands in hers. Once Augustus had resumed his seat, causing a minor nuisance as he struggled to remember where he should be seated, the service began.

"Dearly beloved…" Began the priest. "We are gathered here today to witness the union…"

The rest of the words were drowned out as she looked lovingly into her soon-to-be husband's eyes. It was love within them. Pure, brilliant and undying. The most basic of all human emotions, yet the one that set itself so deeply within them that to have it torn apart was nigh on fatal.

The service progressed quickly and, before either of them knew it, the time had come to give their vows to one another. Charles removed a small piece of card from his pocket before throwing it onto the floor, such was the level of confidence over the words he was about to speak.

"Charlotte, they say that chivalry no longer exists in the modern world, that to get married is almost always the path to a divorce…" He paused for a moment as the crowd laughed at his jape. "Yet when I look at you, into your amazing eyes or your munificent smile, I realise that there is nothing else I would rather have than your hand in marriage. There will, almost certainly, be times when we do not get along but, to quote my family words, to overcome anything we must push all restrictions aside and focus on those we love…" He was quickly silenced as Charlotte raised a single finger to her husband's mouth. It was her turn to speak.

She began where Charles left off. "To overcome anything, we must push aside all restrictions and focus on those we love. Remember them, for when you need them the most, they will help you find your way." It was simple, it was effective and it said everything that needed to be said. Charlotte had thought for a long time about her vows, and about how Charles' career would affect them. She had never considered herself a wordsmith, but as she looked deeply into Charles' eyes as they welled with joy, she knew she had done well.

"Wonderful…" The Priest continued. "Then do you, Charles Alexander Manningley, take Charlotte Abigail Jacobs to be your lawfully wedded wife?"

"I do." Charles responded instantaneously.

"And do you, Charlotte Abigail Jacobs, take Charles Alexander Manningley to be your lawfully wedded husband?"

"I do." She spoke as a solitary tear of joy rolled down her soft cheek.

"Then I now pronounce you husband and wife." He turned to Charles. "You may kiss the bride."

Charles wasted no time in leaning in to Charlotte and holding her closely against him as they kissed over the altar. Their first kiss as husband and wife. The crowd roared in approval towards the married couple as petals poured over them to celebrate their matrimony.

Charles looked once more at the sickening adverts that littered the sterile halls of the hospital. Charlotte had not wanted him to see the birth, fearing that it would turn him away from her, and so he had been reduced to sitting in the waiting room with all the other fathers-to-be. They were all pleasant enough, but nothing could interrupt his desire to be in the room to witness the birth of his child.

Awkwardly he paced up and down the corridor for some semblance of the midwife. Nothing came. The nauseating smell of the hospital deterred him from wandering too far into its depths. He found the whole concept of the hospital completely sickening. A place where life and death were intermingled. Of course he applauded the work that was done within its walls, but ever since the passing of his father, Alex, he had not been able to withstand the horrific nature of the buildings.

Their advertising was not much better. The poster that had caught his eye was one about the rise of brain defects in infants, hardly something that he wanted to think about. He considered them all to be scare tactics into getting people to live healthier lives, he was well aware of the manipulation presented by the government as the armed forces employed much the same techniques. He only had three months left on his shore leave, a thought that troubled him deeply. He would not even get to be with his son for the point at which he could recognise him as his father.

The Second Battalion of the Royal Anglian Regiment, known as 'the Poachers', were due to be dispatched, and his company were being sent to the Middle East to try and quell some of the more turbulent regions that the local forces simply could not cope with. Still, he took some solace in the fact that it would not be forever. Once his service was up he intended on taking a period of absence from the army, to be there for his son as he grew up. His father would have disapproved, having been a veteran within the army during the difficult campaigns of the Second World War. Although he did have an idea for something that Alex would have most definitely approved of.

His mind focused back onto his surroundings as a young woman pushed through the doors of the maternity wing and into the waiting room. The lime green walls behind her made Charles even more nauseated as he closed his eyes to cover the disgusting colour. Desperately he turned to the young woman, as did all of the waiting fathers, to see if the news she had been sent to deliver concerned him. Alas, it did not and so Charles congratulated the young man who had just become a proud father to a small baby girl. He could barely contain his excitement as he burst into tears of joy and pushed his hands to his beardless face to mask what he obviously saw as a sign of weakness. Charles gave the man a pat on the back in congratulations and sat down upon the crooked seats that were offered.

He longed to feel that great relief that the young man had just felt. Instead he was left with a great ache upon his entire being as his mind struggled to control his body from walking into the maternity wind and seeking out his wife. Desperately his legs tried to propel him forwards as though he were some kind of automaton and so he contented himself with gently bouncing his leg up and down upon the point of his foot. It did not help to suppress the curiosity within him but it did keep his body busy enough to stop him diving forth from his chair and flat out sprint towards his beloved.

Over three hours he waited as time and time again the nurses would come forth. Each time he dared to hope that his child had finally been born, and yet each time he was left with a bittersweet taste within his mouth. He was pleased for the men who had become fathers, and at the same moment he was greatly enraged that he was still waiting.

In the end he simply could not help himself as he pushed through the surprisingly light hospital doors as though it were some epic feat. He pressed into the maternity wing and pressed his face into every room that he could see, hoping against hope that his wife would be in one of them. Finally, as he came to the last room, he found her. Charlotte looked truly exhausted with sweat absolutely drenching her entire body. Her hair was matted and her breath came quickly as she attempted to restore herself. She smiled as she saw him and moved her eyes over to where the midwife was holding a small child within her arms.

It was then that he heard the very first cry that his son had ever let out. It was a small mewling, as if from a kitten, and he was instantly attuned with every sense of his child as he struggled to take in the world around him. Charles could not help but cry, for it was not a sign of weakness as the young father had thought of it, it was a sign of strength and attachment. What good is life if there is no-one to cherish within it? Charles thought to himself, and now he had two people to cherish until the day of his death.

Slowly, and with aching tiredness in each step, he moved towards his wife as the infant was wrapped in a warm towel and handed back to her. She looked at their child and gave him the same adoring smile that he had been graced with for years. They were truly a family now, something that he could protect and provide for. He determined then and there that he would never let disparity come between them and that he would always be there, whether immediately or distant, to guide and support them.

"Would you like to hold him?" Charlotte asked confidently.

"Of course…" Charles muttered as he approached their son with his arms outstretched.

Gently Charlotte placed the boy in his open arms and he lowered his head to examine his child. He was even more beautiful than he could have possibly imagined. His tiny body was still adjusting to the world and his hand clasped onto his father's little finger for some sign of support. As he twisted his head around to look at who he was grasping Charles was able to see the full beauty of his child. Although something peaked Charles' curiosity as he looked at his son.

"Why are his eyes green? Aren't they normally blue at birth?" He asked tentatively to the midwife.

The midwife shrugged and continued about her business of packing away all dirty linen from the labour. Charlotte gave him a reproachable look and Charles realised that he was being stupid. It made no difference to him what colour his eyes were, all that mattered was that he was alive and healthy. However, Charles still could not seem to help staring into his son's piercing green eyes that shone like emeralds. Both he and Charlotte had blue eyes, of some variety, and so it was certainly most odd. It did not bother him though and so he gently leaned in and gave his new-born son a gentle kiss upon his forehead, thus leaving his mark of love upon him forever more.

"You know…" He spoke as he turned towards Charlotte. "I have had an idea about the name…" He deliberately trailed off to see how she would react.

"I know you have." She smiled. "And I think it's a wonderful idea." She concluded as she beamed at him.

With a wide smile of his own Charles turned back to look at his son, and his intensely green eyes. "Alex Manningley, welcome to the world."

Chapter 1

The wheels of the bus grinded to a screeching halt outside the main gates of the school, leaving the same set of black tire marks on the ground that renewed itself every morning. One by one the children began to leave the vehicle and rhythmically walked towards the tall grey buildings that were darted over the school grounds, thus completing the absolute zombification of the pupils in the dull magnetism that was before them. For the remainder of the working day they would be subjected to the monotonous environment that the school offered. He didn't dislike school; rather, what he disliked was the lack of individuality that the teachers seemed to possess. History was the only subject that he truly liked.

After looking at his reflection within the mirror, at his self-decidedly average body; with short brown hair and nothing to make him stand out, with a heavy sigh, Alex made his way to the end of the bus and exited with all of the other children. The bus driver, an old, almost toothless, man gave him a fake farewell before speeding off back in the direction of the depot. Instinctively he looked towards the school sign, 'The Henbane Secondary School', and felt nauseous in knowing that his day would be filled with misery as soon as he crossed paths with Arthur Cressing.

Alex did not know why but the muscular sixth-former had taken a disliking to him, and, rather unfortunately, shared all of his subjects for A-Level, except for Psychology, but that was his least favourite subject anyway and so it hardly made the situation any better. Alex had hoped that, when their results had been posted the previous summer, Arthur would not have done well enough to get into the school's somewhat prestigious sixth-form. Unfortunately, that had not been the case and now almost every day was the same cycle of bullying and embarrassment. Alex had been a pupil with Henbane for over five years without incident, he had been able to keep to himself as he preferred, not now though.

Resigned to his fate, Alex began to walk towards the main entrance of the school with his rucksack slung over a single shoulder. Being in sixth-form meant that he was allowed to wear what he liked and so today he had come dressed in a simple arrangement of some trainers, a pair of light blue jeans and a smart-casual two layered shirt with a collar on the under layer that he purposefully put down over his top layer. His father had always taught him that appearance was everything and so he never allowed himself to look shabby in front of others for fear of what they might think, even though he was perfectly aware that the other pupils thought of him as an outcast and a freak. Alex reached for the pack of cards that he kept in the side pouch of his rucksack and pulled them out. He knew several tricks, all of which made him unpopular within the school, and practiced daily in his free periods.

As he fumbled to open the plastic cover that kept the cards safe they fell from his hands and spilled across the ground before him. Alex mumbled under his breath and bent down onto a single knee to retrieve the cards. The trodden in patches of chewing gum that spread across the tarmac made the ground an unpleasant sight as, with each retrieval, a new piece was revealed. Thankfully the smell did not match what could be seen and he breathed in the unique aroma that the blackthorn planted around the school offered.

The sudden sound of footsteps behind him would normally not trouble him, as even if people thought him weird they were still pleasant enough to help him in the situation that he was in; but he knew the sounds accompanying the rumbling could mean only one thing.

Desperately, and as quick as he could, he scrambled his cards together. Just as he went to pick up the last one he felt a knee between his shoulder blades and was pressed forward into the ground, which was still slightly damp from the deluge of the previous night. As his face connected with the hard surface he felt a slight burning sensation upon his cheek that told him it had been grazed by the impact. It was a feeling that he had grown accustomed to when around school and so it did not bother him as much as Arthur hoped it would.

As Alex pushed himself from the floor, with loose pieces of tarmac embedded in his face and un-styled brown hair, he turned his face towards the offender. Arthur stood with his usual troupe of thugs and laughed down at his victim. Behind them he could see another teenager who was deliberately shying away from the conflict to avoid any signs of confrontation.

"Need a hand there, snot-eyes?" Arthur jeered as he offered a hand to Alex.

For all of his faults Alex could still not come to distrust Arthur, nor anyone for that matter as he believed in the truly good nature of people. It was very rare to come across someone so lost, so desolate, that they were beyond redemption. His father had taught him that evil was like the solitary peak of an iceberg within an ocean, it never truly revealed the extent of someone's character, it was just the small area that could be seen by everyone. Everyone had it within them somewhere, the choice was in whether or not you use it. A defence mechanism he had called it, although Alex learned about such things in psychology and was certain that Arthur did not act the way he did to protect himself. Even still, Alex found it tough dealing with his bully but he still did not believe that Arthur had crossed the irreversible threshold that would send someone in a one way journey into ruin. Not yet. With this mentality he grasped Arthur's extended hand only to have it pull away as he was lifted halfway onto his feet. With another smack against the tarmac Alex found himself on the ground once more, this time with pain emanating from his rear.

"Why look so glum Manningley?" Arthur called as he continued to laugh with his friends.

Alex could feel the anger inside of him, but, as he had done a thousand times before, allowed it to cool within his mind instead of unleashing it upon the bully. Alex pushed himself to his feet and put the rucksack upon his shoulder once more, making sure to put the cards back where they were so that Arthur would not see them. The black haired youth was not fond of his magic tricks.

"One day, Arthur, you're going to understand what you did to me, and then you will live the rest of your life in emotional torment for what you were." Alex said calmly.

"Do you know what that sounds like to me?" Arthur questioned as he positioned his face less than a hair's breadth away from Alex's. "That you want to fight."

Alex stood looking into Arthur's piercing brown eyes as he felt the latter's breath flow over his face. "I wouldn't dream of it." Alex responded.

"Of course you wouldn't!" Arthur shouted. "Now, get out of my way, freak."

With a shoulder barge, another attempt from the bully to display his physical dominance over Alex, Arthur and his cronies moved off and into the school just as the bell rang to signify that first lesson would begin in five minutes. The loud clanging resonated in Alex's ears and he felt a great aggravation towards the device. As he focused his mind on drowning it out the noise came to a halt, much earlier than usual, and Alex began to walk towards the classroom for his first lesson.

Behind him came the familiar pattern of footsteps that he so often heard after a confrontation with Arthur. They were hurried steps, as the young man was running to catch up with him, and the heavy panting that grew louder, as the youth got closer, was enough to indicate, even without looking, who it was. Thomas Gordon, his best friend.

"Alex…" He struggled as he caught his breath back. "Alex, are you alright?"

"I'm fine Thomas. It would've been nice for you to help though!" Alex replied somewhat angrily as he stopped just outside the reception area.

"Against that lot?" His deep voice trembled at the very thought of it. With a slight tremor he pushed aside a strand of his short, dirty blonde, hair that had come across his face and ruined the windswept look that he had been trying to achieve. "They'd just pick on me too, you know how sensitive I am about my weight, well, about everything really."

Alex looked into the dark brown eyes that sat within his friend's sculpted features, he could not be mad at him for very long and his tough exterior crumbled. They had been friends since they were infants and he could not let a silly thing like cowardice come between them, especially on an issue such as Arthur Cressing, who was clearly of little concern in the overarching scheme of things. Thomas had always been the shy sort and so Alex saw no reason as to why that should suddenly change.

"I'm sorry Thomas." Alex said regretfully as he put a hand upon Thomas' shoulder. "I didn't mean to get angry with you; it's just getting harder to contain my emotions with Arthur." He explained in the hope of redemption.

"I know it is. You need to find a way of letting your anger out…" He paused before continuing. "Or your…powers…might come through again."

Alex shot him a warning glare; he wanted to avoid the subject altogether. Thomas opened his mouth once more to protest but instead thought better of it and gestured to the main entrance of the school, so that they would not be late for their lesson.

Thomas, having been with Alex for almost every step of his childhood, had witnessed first-hand what he was capable of. Ever since he was a toddler he had known about his ability, but that did not mean that he could control it. He had tried to when he was younger. Even the memory of that afternoon was too much for him to bear and so he locked it in his mind to save himself the pain of what he had done. Every time his emotions flared out of control he would let his gift seep out into the world and cause disruption and confusion. Luckily though, no one had been harmed because of it. Despite this, he fought desperately to keep himself under control at all times, for fear of what he might do should he fail.

The duo continued walking down the deserted corridor, as everyone else was already in their classes, with an eerie silence hanging over them due to the prior topic of discussion. In an awkward attempt to break the silence Thomas grasped a poster that was on the school's announcements board and checked over it searchingly, as if he were some kind of learned scholar attempting to decipher the riddles that the page held.

"Alex." He probed once he had finished reading the paper. "There's a talent show coming up! If you're interested that is?" Thomas asked sheepishly. "I could be your glamorous assistant." He added, chuckling lightly to himself as he did.

Alex allowed himself a small smile that betrayed his veiled contempt for his best friend at this moment in time. He extended his hand and read over the page with due diligence. He certainly couldn't say that he wasn't interested as the prize for the three winners was a trip to the Imperial War Museum in London, a place that he had always wanted to visit. At least it would get him away from Arthur, Alex thought to himself.

"It does sound quite good, but how would I win?" Alex questioned.

"Well, I was thinking you could use your skills…" Thomas replied.

Alex cut him off before he could finish his train of thought. "You know how I feel about using my abilities Thomas!" He whispered angrily.

"No! I didn't meant that!" Thomas responded frantically. "I meant that you could do some of your card tricks; they're really impressive." He added with a smile.

Alex smiled at his friend and gave a brief nod before setting off down the long and winding hallway that would lead him to his first lesson. Thomas gave him a mock salute and laughed as he ran off into one of the rooms that ran parallel to the hallway. Before A-Level he and Thomas had been able to pull through the slow agony of the day together, as they had shared the same classes, laughing and conversing throughout. Now though, they shared no subjects together and Alex's school days were filled with trial and torment. Even his most loved subject had turned into an hour of tribulation.

Still, with a reluctant step and a feigned grin, he walked towards the psychology room where he would spend the first two hours of the day locked in a room leaning about how people behaved and why they behaved in that manner. Alex was not a very social human and so he could think of little worse.

The day progressed slowly. Psychology, although Arthur free, had soured his mood from the very off with mentions of some awful examples of what humans are capable of doing to one another. They had learnt about a psychologist called Zimbardo and his awful Stanford Prison Experiment. Sometimes Alex wondered if the human race was too evolved for its own good. He preferred the way that animals sought out their lives. They had no purpose and no aim, they merely wanted to eat and be well until they died.

Then, during his third period, he had been tasked with analysing a section of the popular Shakespearian play Macbeth. That was all fine and well, as Alex was a fond reader of Shakespeare and enjoyed every line, except from that fact that Arthur had spent the entire lesson flinging paper triangles at his head from an elastic band. It had taken all of his restraint not to respond. Thomas was right, he thought to himself, his rage was becoming uncontrollable and he needed a way of releasing it without endangering anyone. For a split second he considered using his unique abilities in the talent show before immediately chastising himself for thinking such a stupid thought. He could not bring himself to do it, instead he would have to bear it for as long as he was physically able.

Lunch had been fine though. He and Thomas had gone to the local shop, which was little over two minutes away, and bought some snacks that they had devoured within half an hour. Now the day had come to an end and he was sitting in his final lesson of the day, History.

Alex looked around the blank canvas of the room. Over the course of the summer the entire school had been stripped of what little character it had and now there were no decorations or adornments, there was just the sickening cream coloured walls that seemed to possess a disgusting hue of grey.

Alex sat at the front of the classroom obediently taking notes as his teacher, Mr Barnes, went through the various slides. They had been learning about the intricate details of the Industrial Revolution for little over a month and, although he dearly loved History as a subject in general, Alex was beginning to find it very tedious. His pen twirled and swirled as swiftly as he could make it as he sought to record every piece of information he could before they moved on. His hand ached terribly from the force with which he was writing and he suddenly pulled his hand back and shook it to alleviate the throbbing. Alex had not realised that he had been so wrathfully writing. Every word that he had written had almost been printed across another ten pages of paper, such was the ferocity of his work.

He stole a rare moment to look towards the girl that he liked before glancing back at the board, as he did not want her to notice. He found himself instantly memorised by one of the figures on the slide. He was a young looking man, although still a few years older than Alex himself, with brown hair, much like Alex's, that was swept back and placed under a bowler hat. His high cheek bones and prominent jawline gave him the appearance of a man with a great deal of wealth.

Next to him stood a man with similar features, although with grey hair and a small allowance of stubble, which Alex imagined to be the young man's father. They were both clad in early twentieth century garb, which consisted of a black three-piece suit and a long black coat with fur ruffles. Above them was a sign which read 'Malum Metal Industries'. The photograph was from The Times and read 'Titans of Industry, The Malum Legacy continues', and it was dated to 26/05/1915.

"Sir, who are they?" Alex asked without raising his hand.

Mr Barnes, a slightly portly and jolly middle-aged man, smiled at his enthusiasm and was more than happy to respond, seeing as he shared Alex's passion for history. "The older gent is Peter Malum, the owner and proprietor of Malum Metal Industries, a very lucrative iron working company during the late Victorian age and the First World War."

"If he's so special, who come I've never heard of him?" Arthur called out.

"Arthur! Please don't shout out, raise your hand if you have a question." He glared at the youth before continuing. "You probably haven't heard of him because he died not long after this photograph was taken and his company fell into the hands of his son, Magnus, who led the company to ruin before shutting it down."

"Magnus Malum..." Alex whispered to himself.

"What's that Alex?" Mr Barnes asked.

"Nothing sir." Alex responded promptly.

Alex could not quite figure out what it was, but there was something off about the son, Magnus. His eyes; his mouth; the posture of his body within the photograph; his facial expression, everything made Alex cringe uncomfortably. It was like looking at a spectre, he was strangely fascinated and yet completely horrified at the same time. The man had probably been dead for quite some time and yet he captivated Alex like a snake charmer ushering him forth from his basket. As he stared at Magnus there was an almost palpable look in his eyes. He was staring deeply into his father's eyes and it was as if Alex could sense the emotions behind it. Rage; anger; loathing; and lust for power, for it was clear that he sought an end to his father.

"Sir, how did Peter die?" Alex enquired.

Mr Barnes gave him a searching look, it was almost as though he had completely forgotten what they were talking about. He arched an eyebrow as if completely oblivious. Alex pointed to the figure of Peter Malum in the picture and the teacher examined the photo for a moment before seemingly remembering.

"Ah yes, Peter Malum, owner of one of the great metal-works of the First World War." He responded jubilantly.

"I would like to know how he died." Alex replied patiently.

Mr Barnes clearly had no definitive answer as he continued to stare at the photo with great intensity. It seemed to Alex that he too had picked up on the pure malice within Magnus' eyes, although he did not arrive at the same conclusion.

"Well, he was an industrial worker in the early twentieth century, up north as well where conditions were particularly bad in these factories…" He theorised. "He was quite lucky to live to the age we see him at in this photo."

"Well not that lucky obviously." Arthur jeered.

"Arthur! Please don't shout out, raise your hand if you have a question." Mr Barnes exclaimed as he turned away from the board, and the photograph.

Alex was confused at what was going on. The teacher was in a state of amnesia. Every time that he took his eyes away from the board and focused on the class it seemed that he completely forgot what he was teaching. The pupils were not affected though, Alex mused, as they were all just as confused as he was. Once again, Alex found his eyes inadvertently shifting focus onto the evil figure on the board. The wickedness within him was astounding. Now that Alex looked at the photograph some more he thought he could detect a green glint within Magnus' eyes, although his eyes were glaring at his father and so it was hard to tell.

Under Peter's arm there was a newspaper that read 'Malum Metal Industries Owner Names Successor', a prototype for the title they actually went with. This only furthered the suspicion he felt towards Magnus and the death of his father, Peter. It seemed that once Magnus had been given what he wanted he wasted little time in disposing of the old man. Peter did not seem in bad health, as the picture showed it, and so Alex saw no other explanation.

Alex suddenly realised that he was judging the dead and so started to laugh off his deranged misgivings. Magnus had almost certainly been dead for over fifty years and he saw no point in furthering his ludicrous obsession with the man.

A sudden ringing bellowed into his eardrums that informed him of the end of the school day. Lackadaisically, as if given in to the tedium of the school day, every pupil raised themselves from their desks and sluggishly put together their belongings, like a zombie slowly rising from the cold earth. Arthur and his followers were the first to leave and Alex felt a slight relief that there would be no after school delights to dread, even if the bully gave him a sly wink that almost assured there would be more to follow the next day. They had not tucked in their chairs and so, with Alex being a strict follower of rules and customs, he set about methodically pushing the chairs to the brim of the desk to give the environment a regimented feel. His father had told him that a life without order is a life without direction and so he had always been conscientious in following the established set of norms, even if he did not approve of them. By the time he had finished his self-assigned task there was only Mr Barnes left with him.

As on a typical school day Alex packed up his belongings and began to make for the door, with the dull squeaking of the floorboards enunciating every step. Something stopped him though as he placed his hand upon the cold metal knob of the classroom door. His reflection in the glass showed the emerald tint in his eyes and he found himself compelled to turn around and voice his strange enquiries. Mr Barnes, who was busy looking at an article online a moment before, turned his eagle-eyed attention towards Alex, casually pushing his glasses to the bridge of his nose to show that he was very much still inclined to act as a teacher.

"Is there something I can help you with Alex?" He asked.

Alex hesitated for a moment. His concerns seemed completely outlandish and barely worth the amount of time he had spent upon them, and yet therein was the cause. Why had he spent so much time pondering this issue? Logically speaking it was a matter of no concern, considering that one of the subjects was no longer a part of the world. There were no words that could voice his opinions without sounding utterly preposterous. As he stared at his transparent reflection, the green tint still glowing bright, the answer came to him.

Without answering the teacher, and very much in a thought process entirely his own, Alex turned back into the classroom and stamped towards the smart-board that all classrooms had been equipped with. On it was still the image of father and son, murderer and victim as he saw it. Magnus' eyes were still drilling into Peter's skull, and within them the green flicker was still present in spite of the photo clearly having been developed before the time of the colour photograph. Gently Alex pressed his hands onto the green flicker to see if it was some kind of mark upon the board that had, however coincidental it might seem, matched up to the eyes of the killer. It would not remove itself though.

"Alex?" Mr Barnes asked once more.

"It's just…" Alex could not form the words to describe the extreme sense of trepidation he felt staring into the green abyss of Magnus' haunted eyes. "His eyes, they're green."

Mr Barnes laughed initially and brushed Alex aside to inspect the smart-board. He too attempted to scratch away the invisible marks. With each failing he scratched more determinately with the aim of finding the point at which it was attached to the board so that he might peel it off instead. Still his efforts were fruitless. Relentlessly he continued his assault upon the smart-board filing down his nails as he went until he also arrived at the horrific conclusion that something was amiss.

"But…" He stammered as though the great veil that had blinded him had now been lifted "That's…that's not possible. It must be some trick, somebody altered the picture…" He reasoned with himself.

Alex watched as Mr Barnes descended unto his computer and began rifling through the various pictures that the internet contained on the elusive figure of Magnus Malum. Every single one contained the same effect. A picture of Magnus standing next to a younger man, who was no older than Alex, dressed in a similarly disgusting black finery took Alex's attention. What was more intriguing though is that this young man also had the same green eyes that Magnus possessed.

"Who is that?" Alex asked his teacher.

Remarkably all of the other known pictures of Magnus, except the one with his father Peter, were of him and nobody else. He was a solitary man, which made it all the more fascinating as to why this young fellow was with him. Magnus was old in this photograph, at least a man in his late forties, and his greying hair and wrinkled face was indicative of the strains that had been placed upon him. He was haggardly to say the least, like some kind of Shuar tsantsa.

"At a guess I would say it was his son." Mr Barnes responded.

"With all due respect, sir, I don't think it is." Mr Barnes gave Alex an abashed look as the student questioned his teacher's wisdom. "They share almost no similarities in appearance other than dress…" Alex explained. "And if we look at the other picture…" He paused momentarily to bring up the picture with Magnus and Peter. "Peter does not share the same effect as Magnus, so it isn't a hereditary thing which means that this young man cannot be his son." Alex concluded feeling rather proud of himself for his deductive abilities.

"Well done Alex." Mr Barnes congratulated him. "If that is the case then I can honestly say that I have no earthly idea as to who the younger one is. If he is not Magnus' son then that would explain why the Malums are no longer around today." He pondered the situation for a moment. "In any case this seems to be the last known picture of Magnus, there's nothing further on him." Mr Barnes shrugged to indicate that he could not tell Alex anything else upon the evil looking man.

Dissatisfied and reluctant, Alex walked towards the door and took one last glance towards the image of Magnus. It seemed strange to Alex but Magnus' eyes seemed to be focused directly upon him like a painting in an episode of a spooky children's show. As he grasped the door handle one final thought occurred to him.

"Sir…" He spoke as he turned his head back. "What happened to Magnus Malum?"

His teacher looked seriously at him before answering. "Nobody knows."

Chapter 2

Once more the wheels on the bus came to an un-rhythmical stop, this time by the bus stop that sat only a short walk from his home. The pale foliage, or perhaps that was only how he saw it after such a dismal day, that surrounding his neighbourhood was indicative of his mood. Decaying and desolate, he understood their pain all too well. Even the weather seemed to register his mood as the sun had been blotted out by the unbroken grey mass of clouds that mocked his every waking moment. Alex realised that he was increasingly becoming more solemn as each day passed, and there was one person who was solely responsible for that. Arthur.

After the tantalising History lesson on the industrial revolution he had been cornered by Arthur and his half-wit band of thugs. They pushed and shoved him, taunting him over his 'special connection' with their teacher. Yet that was the kind of bullying he suffered day in and day out, that was not what fazed him. It was what he did after that had left him deeply troubled. As the bullies continued their unprovoked assault upon Alex they all suddenly found themselves unable to move, which allowed Alex to sneak away before releasing them from his mental grip. He had not meant to do it. He was not proud of it. Yet still it had happened and the horror of his loss of control from the day still haunted him as he stomped away from the bus before it drove off.

Thomas got off at the same time, since his house was only down the road from Alex's, and waved his friend goodbye. He offered a sympathetic smile at Alex as he left and skipped happily back towards his home. Alex wished that he could feel the same kind of joy that Thomas seemed to find, but he simply could not. Normally he was a happy person outside of school, the use of his powers had changed him though. He would not be able to forgive himself, at least not for a few days before all of the commotion had died down. Arthur had actually left him alone that day. Alex did not see that as a good thing as it meant that something had changed Arthur for the time being. He was afraid of Alex, and with their ringleader out of action so were the others.

Still brooding to himself he stopped and reflected upon his actions. The monotonous colour of the pavement underneath his feet sickened him as he looked down. There was no character in the world anymore, everything had a structure and a duty to fulfil, and nothing was left out of the new world order. Even the trees along the road, once so natural, were planted and clipped at regular intervals to keep the 'aesthetic' of the neighbourhood concurrent with every other suburb in every town across the whole country. Even the smell had become neutral, almost stagnant, under the oppressive scheme of normality. Alex had never seen the point in being normal, why be like everyone else when you can be yourself?

He took a deep breath to try and calm himself before he continued walking along the snaking pathway that led to his house. As always his neighbour, Mr Senest, could be seen through his window watching television whilst combing his hand through his long and bristly beard. He was a quiet man, since the passing of his wife, who always kept to himself and never troubled anyone. If he did see Alex he made no indication of wanting to talk to him as he continued to stare blankly at his television. Alex wondered if he even knew what was on.

Finally he arrived at the faceted white door that led into his home. Even his own house was not safe from the curse of normality. The windows were, typically, the same gleaming white of the door with little to distinguish them from those of everyone else. The red brickwork, which had once had ivy crawling across its surface, was now bare, nothing covered its shame. His father had cut the ivy back upon his last visit, he had always been the kind of man to expect everything to be in a regimented order; and so Alex reluctantly followed suit. It was a sight that he was used to seeing every day and so he made no fuss and brought his keys from his pocket. Compared to some, they were relatively simple with only a front and back door key attached to a simplistic metal ring that would hang loosely from his belt.

Accidentally he dropped the keys on the stone floor that led to their home. As he bent down to pick them up his eyes were drawn to the small plaque that was protruding from the ground. A sense of obligation overcame him as he hurriedly picked up his keys and moved towards the small headstone. He noticed that a small amount of moss was growing on the right side of the polished stone and that gleam from the brass plate on top had diminished. He could barely make out the memorial that they had laid out over half a decade beforehand. Affectionately he bent down and felt the ground, as if expecting some kind of response from the long since dead animal. Every time he witnessed the accident he could not help but wince. He had been young and foolish, but that was no excuse for what happened and he knew it.

As he struggled to hold back the flow of emotions that sat within him he walked back towards the door and placed his key within the keyhole. His family were already inside, his brother having claimed being ill for the entirety of the day and both his mother and sister finishing before himself. The usual humdrum of noise that accompanied them could be heard. His brother, Steven, would be selfishly guarding the television so that he could watch what he wanted, a trait that Alex found undoubtedly abhorrent. His mother, Charlotte, would probably be in the kitchen preparing dinner for them as they ate early to stop Steven ravaging the cupboards for anything and everything that he could find. His sister, Abigail, would be as quiet as a church-mouse. She loved to read and was just as skilled at it, if not more so, than both of her older brothers. The weekends, for her, were times of tranquillity and creativity as she read and would often note down an idea or two that she had for works of her own. Abigail was unbelievably perceptive for her age. Alex knew that there would be great things for her later in her life, and that thought always comforted him.

As he opened the door the familiar creak of its hinges alerted everyone to his presence. Steven, as always, let out a derogatory remark and continued to unenthusiastically lounge about on the leather sofa. Abigail was, as expected, reading silently at the oak dining table, riffling through the pages of a thick novel as if they were mere child's play. His mother tried to grab his attention, but he was in no mood to talk. He did not want his depression to spread like some kind of insidious disease amongst them; and so he retired to his room. The dull squeak of the stairs could not hide his intentions. In a strange way he almost wanted those closest to him to know his deep regret so that they might offer words of comfort. Yet they did not know about his special abilities, and he did not want them to. If they did then they might reject him, and then the people that mattered most to him would be gone. Only Thomas knew, back when he had held the folly that his powers were a good thing, and Alex wanted to keep it that way.

As he climbed the carpeted stairs he actually felt sanguine for the first time in a few days, even though it was at the prospect of being alone. That was also seemingly robbed from him as he heard Abigail quietly slip down from the dining table. He could almost feel her eyes sympathetically examining his lumbering shell as he mounted the last stair.

The short corridor at the top of the stairs splintered into three directions. To the left was the upstairs toilet. Despite the somewhat languid appearance of the door inside the bathroom was full of the newest innovations in hygiene, renovated by his father only a few months beforehand, that strained the eyes as glinting metal was positioned wherever you looked. To his right was his parents' room, the master bedroom of the house with all the trimmings of wealth, even though the rest of the house lacked this. There was also his sister's room, bursting at the seams with books on all manner of subjects, all relatively advanced for her age. Directly ahead was his own room, a simple room by comparison to the others that held his personal belongings. It wasn't much, but he could truly relax and do what he enjoyed within the confines of his abode. Behind him, up the stairs once more as they had had the loft converted upon the birth of his sister, was his brother's room which he rarely entered.

He had barely closed the ill proportioned door and laid down upon his single, double-pillowed, bed when the door was jarred by a gentle knocking like that of the wind timidly pushing itself upon a gate. Alex did not respond to the knock, he knew that he did not have to. Without any reply the door continued to open and the frame of Abigail's glasses came into view against the dim light of the corridor. Casually she seated herself upon his computer chair and began spinning upon its axis like a sail caught in a storm.

"What's wrong Alex?" She asked, although she already knew the answer.

He did not respond.

"Listen, Alex, everyone gets bullied, the only difference is between those who accept it and rise above it and those who allow it bring them down into the depths of depression." She explained to him as she had done before.

He had prepared his answer beforehand for such a debate. "And what if you are somewhere in between?"

"You can never be in between, you can change between the two but you will always be in one state or the other. I can't remember who said that." She concluded as she veered off topic to try and recall the information from her capacious mind.

Smiling, with his mood now tremendously improved despite the lack of conclusion from their debate, he lifted himself from his bed and sat on the edge of it with his palms gripping the wooden frame. He tilted his head towards his sister.

"You're far too intelligent for an eleven year old." He chuckled. "But that's not what's been troubling me…" He shifted his attention back towards the floor as he eyes began to burn bright, like the fire of Vesta, with the fear that he had instilled in himself. "I am afraid…afraid of what I can do when I let my emotions get out of hand."

"Well you know what to do then don't you?" Abigail said as she merrily hopped removed herself from his computer chair and made for the door.

"What's that?" Alex found himself asking as he continued to loath his abilities.

"Don't let your emotions get out of hand." She said with a smile. "Find an outlet, something to occupy your mind." She finished as she placed her delicate hand on the door, gave one last loving look to her brother, and left the room.

Alex removed his fixation from the ground and focused back onto his room. He allowed himself to smile as his sister's words sank in. He would join the talent show, he told himself, which would occupy his mind for the time being. With his mood heightened he decided to do the one thing he loved before dinner, writing. He turned to his computer, an old but reliable model, on and waited for it to load before opening the short story that he was occupying himself with. In it he poured his emotions into the story of the 'Machines that threatened to destroy the world', a concept which he had always found both enthralling and terrifying at the same time. He fastened the watch that his father had given him around his wrist so that he might time himself on how quickly he was working. It was an old face with an almost worn out leather strap that seemed to creak under the pressure of its age, like most things. He peered down at the antique and felt his mood soar even higher as he was reminded of the jovial features of Charles, his father.

He did not have very long to write, or at least not long enough in his own mind, as soon his mother called up the stairs to usher him to dinner. Why she could not walk up the stairs and politely ask him to come down was beyond him, but that was his mother in a nutshell. She was not the most tactile of people, often very blunt and to the point. Perhaps that was what his father saw in her, a reflection of Charles' own well-ordered and direct style of thinking and presenting oneself.

With a shallow grunt he put his monitor to sleep and replanted his feet upon the soft fur that covered the floor of his room. It was then that he realised just how hungry he was, not having eaten since breakfast. Unlike most teenage boys he never seemed to be able to consume the vast amounts that a great many of them enjoyed, but his voracious hunger was churning his stomach and producing some very odd noises, so he determined to fill his belly since he was now in a good mood. He almost bounded down the stairs with enthusiasm as the sweet aroma of his mother's dinner delicately hugged his nostrils and caressed them. It was like being serenaded by Dionysius.

The rest of his family, apart from his brother as he was still fixated upon the television, were already gathered at the dinner table. Dutifully Abigail put down her books and placed them underneath her chair as she sat patiently waiting for her brothers to arrive. She often presented herself as the perfect lady at the dinner table, as did his mother, but he knew that as soon as Steven managed to peel himself away from whatever drivel he was watching that they would devour what Charlotte had diligently prepared.

Abigail gave him a loving smile as he seated himself at the table in his usual seat. Even without their father present they still left his seat empty at the head of the table. Upon the oak table sat their dinner in three different varieties. In a simple glass bowl, complete with tongs atop it, was some salad that consisted of lettuce, rocket, tomatoes and cucumber. They had this almost every night and so he knew that it would be present regardless of the dinner that would accompany it. At the far end of the table, by Charles' decorative chair, was the dessert. His mother had placed a layer of cling-film around it so that no-one could indulge themselves without her knowledge. That too was relatively simple as it consisted of another glass bowl, but this time with a ladle inside it and a plethora of fruits, both common and exotic, within. It was all a part of his mother's 'new' diet. He had no qualms with her attempting to better herself, if that was indeed her wish, but he did hope that she would be able to stick to it for more than a week or two this time.

As enticing as all the accoutrements were to him, as he was very keen on fruit and, to a lesser extent, vegetables also, it was what sat in the middle that truly made his mouth water with excitement. A honey-roasted ham, still steaming from the process, sat before him, teasing him as the wisps of steam encircled them. Around its edge were some boiled potatoes, not Alex's favourite but he was hungry enough not to care. As he watched a piece of juice from the ham dribble down onto the plate he silently cursed his brother taking so long. It was tradition in their home to wait for everyone before beginning, although Alex supposed that that was simply good manners wherever you happened to be, and so they had to endure the agony of staring at their magnificent dinner for another five minutes before Steven joined them. With his brother's usual slump into his chair they began attacking their dinner.

Charlotte carefully sliced the ham into how much everyone wanted, leaving more than enough for sandwiches for the following day, which both Steven and himself were very happy about, and allowed them take as many potatoes as they liked. His sister and his mother tucked in to the salad as well, leaving the vast majority of the protein and carbohydrates to the two young men. It was a relatively simple meal, even though it required a good deal of preparation, yet Alex could tell as he lifted his first fork-full to his mouth that it would be something to savour. The intense smoky flavour of the boiled ham, which he also drenched in barbeque sauce, was almost enough to make him pass out from sheer pleasure. The potatoes too, plain as they were, seemed to be complimented well by the ham in that they offered the completely distinct flavour of fluffy potatoes that had been bubbled and marinated in a fine selection of herbs and seasonings.

There was almost no conversation as they systematically tore apart their dinner like a pack of wolves attacking a carcass. His mother gave a brief update on how their father was doing in his latest assignment, as she spoke to him daily over the internet or by phone, and Abigail commented on some new discovery about giant squids. Apart from that the table was devoid of any signs of civility. Alex found it amusing that, when everything is stripped away from them, they really were just animals.

When the main course had been demolished their mother unwrapped the fruit salad and gave a bowlful of the assorted fruits to everyone. Alex was slightly bemused at seemingly getting more melon than anything else, his least favourite fruit of all the options within the bowl, but still ate it anyway to sate his lust for further sustenance. When everything had been finished he pulled his familiar pack of cards from his jean pocket and placed them on the table, having been careful enough to leave space for his tricks. He removed the cards from their plastic covering and laid them out in four groups of four on the table, placing the others off to the side. It was one of his simplest tricks, but still one he enjoyed all the same as it required good memory skills.

Steven, rather reluctantly Alex thought, volunteered himself to take part in the trick. Abigail had already left the table to watch a documentary and his mother was already busy cleaning the plates in the kitchen, so he was left with no other choice. He allowed his brother to select one of the cards from the pile, careful to make sure he only pointed to the pile and not the card itself. Alex collected the piles individually, gathering the pile that Steven's card was in lastly so he knew that his card would be one of the top four when he drew them again. He laid them out once more with the piles re-arranged so that he could recognise each possibility in every pile. When his brother pointed to the pile his card was in Alex knew exactly which card was his, the king of hearts.

Prudently, he picked up the cards again, in the same order for the piles, so he knew for certain that his brother's card was the fifth card in the deck. As he laid them out for a third time, face down on this occasion so he could not see the cards, he pinpointed the location of the fifth card and asked Steven to systematically remove piles until it came down to just his card. When he revealed his card Steven looked bewildered, still unaware after years of having the trick done on him, and Alex smiled at his simplistic success. He had learned that trick from his father when he was nine years old, and that had been what had given him his passion for the sleight of hand tricks that he now prided himself on. Regardless, and if everyone else berated him for such trickery, he found enjoyment within it.

"You're such a loser, Alex, why don't you spend your time doing something normal instead of sitting in your room and weeping about being a spineless coward!?" Steven insulted him.

"Says the one whose life revolves around a screen!" Alex shouted back.

"How's that book going Alex? Any good? Or, like the rest of your life, is it doomed to misery and failure?" It was a well-placed jibe that was spoken with just enough softness and ferocity to tip Alex towards the edge.

Alex struggled to maintain the swirling vortex of emotions that were inside of him. The unbroken rage within him was twisting at his guts like a hurricane, having returned from earlier with a sinister vengeance. He could feel the urge to use his abilities, as he had against Arthur and the others, but he could not reveal himself to his family. Even the slightest notion that he was different from them would drive his loved ones away from him, and then he would be truly alone.

With an explosive grunt, as he slammed his fist against the table and forced his chair back against the wall with a loud smack, he stormed outside into the back garden. As he pushed his way through the kitchen, with his mother seemingly oblivious to the argument that had erupted instantaneously like Mount Vesuvius, he could actually notice his eyes glowing green with the emotion within him. The cool night air was enough to temporarily sooth him but it did not stop the fury that sat within. His mind was screaming at him to let it out, to uncage the hidden potential within him. It hurt, so much so that Alex clasped his hands around his head and fell to his knees in a desperate struggle to maintain control. As he rubbed his eyes and took his hand away from his face he remembered that his father's watch was around his left wrist. It gave him solace. Such a simple object was able to calm his demons and relax his soul. It almost seemed ridiculous to Alex that he had gotten so angry.

The world was pleasant to him again. The sweet smells of the night, the jasmine of the neighbours' garden, the petrol-like scent of rain that was soon to fall, were no longer annoyances. The hooting of the owls did not seem so irritating, nor did his brother's jabs. Everything was so minute, and yet so important. Every detail, from the craters of the moon to each blade of grass and everything below, was harmonious. One thing complimented the next and transformed his viscosity into tranquillity. He closed his eyes and visualised sweet memories of him and his father playing football in the same location. He was never very good at it, but that did not matter. Charles' words of encouragement and love were enough to forgo any insufficient skills. It was a blissful memory from a time in his life when there had been no worries.

He continued spooling through the memory, as he could often do as his memory skills were very almost photographic, if not completely. His dog, Muffin, a silly name but one that he remembered with great fondness and sorrow, attempted to chase the football with his short legs. The long ears that typified his species bounced as he enjoyed the freedom offered to him by his masters. The beagle was a happy reminder of the pleasure that Alex was capable of feeling. Not everything was doom and gloom after all.

Yet, almost as though his subconscious had developed a path of its own to follow, like when the wind carries a leaf down a winding path, the memories changed focus. The first few frames were happy, with Alex playing cheerfully with his faithful companion as he gently forced the tennis ball that Muffin was trying to retrieve into the ground. The dog tried to remove it with his canine teeth but was unable to as the young boy continued to exert his powers into it for his amusement. Muffin barked at the ball, being unaware that it was Alex that stopped him achieving his aim, and wagged his tail happily as he planted his features into the ground and patiently waited for the tennis ball to be released.

Young Alex was curious about his powers and was only just beginning to understand them and what they meant. He would change the face of the world, yet he would be an outcast. He would be the pinnacle of evolution, and so completely and utterly alone. He could destroy any who opposed him, and yet doing so would necessitate the destruction of all. He had power, but his power was exactly what made him feel so powerless. Still, Alex thought as he looked towards the happy dog, it was worth investigating.

With only a brief moment's hesitation he imposed his will upon the canine. He could see everything that Muffin was seeing, and in such a way that he could still move about himself unhindered. Curious to learn more, Alex called to the dog who twisted his vision towards the young boy. It was like looking into a mirror, except the mirror could respond. Desperately Alex tried to stop the memory, but it persisted. The young child tested his abilities a bit further, physically controlling the dog's movements. The canine was still very much in control of its own mind and was seemingly enjoying the strange sensation of its limbs moving without its accordance.

Young Alex could see no reason to stop and so continuing manipulating Muffin, exerting slightly more energy with each passing moment. The dog was still reasonably complacent and so he forced everything that he could into him. For a few more moments everything was fine. Then Muffin stopped walking. He let out a casual whimper and sat down on the floor.

Alex realised that something was horribly wrong and so he released his grip on his friend and walked over to check on him.

Alex was now fuming with the exertion he was putting into stopping the memory. It would not cease. His younger self approached the dog, who was lying as still as he had been for the past minute with no signs of recovery. Even though the situation was clear enough Alex still expected some kind of redemption. All he wanted was for Muffin for to move, to twitch, or to show some kind of life. There was nothing. As he leaned over the beagle and pressed his face to the floor he could see the last bit of life leaving Muffin's eyes. They were sad, and scared for what may happen next. Even after what Alex had done to him he still seemed to look lovingly at his master, a symbol of forgiveness that made it all the worse for Alex, as his eyes glazed over and his life ebbed away from him like the gentle retreat of the tide upon the beach.

Alex was silent, simply not knowing how to respond. The emotions within him had reached a standstill. Anger over his actions fought bitterly with the deep regret he felt and the sadness over the loss of one of his closest companions. The still corpse of his dog suddenly took over all emotions other than the last as his green eyes began to well with tears. An uncontrollable grief came over him. He sobbed heavily and let out a sharp scream so piercing that his family ran out of the house to see the young boy cradling his puppy.

The memory abruptly ended and Alex was left staring into the same patch of grass, with his knees soaked from the dew of the evening. He softly touched the ground, as he did with the plaque, to try and draw some kind of connection with his deceased pet. It had always been, and was now also, as he felt his anger leave him and the urge to use his powers subside, a blunt reminder of why he should never use his powers. Under any circumstances.

With his levelheadedness now restored he walked back inside the house, with Charlotte still not recognising her son's internal plight, and up the stairs. He had only one goal on his mind now. Shutting the door to his room, and locking it, he pulled a piece of fine quality paper from his shelf and an envelope from his drawer. He would have a lot to talk about this time. With his problems about to be transformed into a letter he felt a sudden sigh of relief as he wrote the words 'Dear Dad'.

Chapter 3

He glanced over the familiar penmanship that circled artistically around the crumpled and stained parchment. Despite the markings it was a high-quality paper that had the thickness and balance of an ancient scroll or papyrus. Before even reading the first sentence he knew exactly which one of his children had sent the letter. The strange linking of the letters told him that it was his eldest Alex that had sent him this letter.

Alex had always been fond of traditional styles, a trait which he had studiously observed from his old-school father. Even though Charles preferred it this way he still could not help feeling some semblance of guilt over not seeing his son face to face. Modern technology allowed him to do so with his wife and his other children, yet Alex remained acutely reserved. He had always been worried about the insecurities of his child, and he feared that this latest letter would not tend to those fears. Somewhat lackadaisically, he brought the paper closer to his eyes. He did truly love all of his children deeply, since the first moment he saw them. Yet, considering Charles was in an active warzone in Afghanistan with desert around and civilians to protect, he did not feel that he had the time or the effort to address his son's issues. There were bigger things at stake. Or so he thought.

His interest peaked as he began reading about a mysterious figure who had possessed the same unusual eye colour as his son. The troubles of his son, and his bully Arthur, evaporated from his thought. Ever since the day he was born Charles had been curious about his son's eye colour, believing it to be significant in some manner, although he was not sure how. Both he and Charlotte had blue eyes, as did his other children. This character, Magnus Malum, seemed to have the same eye colour. Charles wondered if it was some kind of biological defect, or advantage. His suspicions were raised even further when he read that Magnus' father did not have the same eye colour as his son. It was almost like a direct parallel that had somehow occurred another one hundred or so years later.

Charles placed the letter back upon his rickety metal table. The canvas of his leather tent shuddered a little under the light winds of his surroundings. Being a Major he had the advantage of holding one of the more luxurious accommodations that were afforded by the British Army. Even still, it was not as homely as he would've liked. The canvas of the tent was stable enough to cool him during the day, but the evenings were cold when the icy winds picked up and carried the chilling breezes over to him. It was as though Jack Frost himself was paying him a personal visit each and every night. The interior was typically adorned in a military fashion. His bed, although a double in size with an extra pillow, was the basic stretch of material that you would expect to find in an army camp. He had a wardrobe, probably the most extravagant piece of furniture in his quarters, which was made from very basic slabs of balsa wood, a completely unsuitable material for the job. Everything else was used for his job. Maps, radio's, a pile for his dirty gear to be taken at the end of each week, a pile of clean gear at the end of his bed (placed there in the morning, every morning). There was very little of the comforts that the inhabitants of the western world had come to expect, except a very small television that only picked up channels one and two. He took some solace in the fact that he could still watch his favourite shows about time travelling and cars.

The substance of the letter that his son had given him was completely harmless, yet as he glanced over towards the entrance to his tent he could not help but think that there was something insidiously sinister about the situation. Things were more convoluted than they appeared, yet he did not know why. Charles brushed the thought aside as a preposterous notion not worth the merit he was giving to it. This man, Magnus Malum, had been dead for over half a century. He choose instead to focus his thoughts upon the problems that Alex was having with his school's bully, Arthur Cressing, since they were the main source of concern for his son.

It seemed to Charles that Alex was allowing this bully to control him. Alex was not weak, by any standard of the word, and so he could not understand why he was being so submissive to this other child. Even when he was younger he had possessed the same fire and tenacity that Charles himself embraced, the kind of passion that could warm the heart and kick the backside. It had been the death of their young dog, Muffin, which had changed his son. They had always been particularly close and the loss of such a dear companion had hit Alex hard, as he had always blamed himself for simply being present when the dog unexpectedly died of some sort of cardiovascular problem. It was the only explanation after all as there were no signs of trauma on the corpse.

Charles decided to deal with this as he always did, by encouraging his son to resolve the issue with his own methods, but remembering that he would always be there to help Alex should he desperately need his aid. Of course, Charles would have a quiet word or two with the parents of Arthur Cressing when he returned from his latest tour of duty. Until then though, Alex was by himself.

Charles turned the paper over, simply unwilling to find another piece, and drew out the pen that he kept within his pocket. It was only a simple biro and so the penmanship would not be anywhere near close to what his son's was, but that did not matter. What mattered was the message. It would be a message of hope, a sign that it never truly left us no matter how dire the circumstances might appear. A message of opportunity, the chance to grasp what he could and use it to put the bully in his place, by any means necessary. Above all though, it would be a message of love to remind his son that even in dark times there is always a shaft of light to guide us back to those who matter to us.

Yet barely had he put to pen to paper when his Lieutenant, Cassandra Williams, stomped into his quarters and kicked sand over the foam flooring with her affirmative halt. Before he could even turn around he knew that something was the matter. The two were firm friends after all and a casual meeting between the two of them was common. This formal entrance told Charles that something was amiss, and he had a horrible feeling that it somehow linked to his son's letter.

"Lieutenant Williams reporting sir!" She shouted from her expansive lungs.

"Come now, Cassandra, there's no need to be so apprehensive when it's just us. I told you that before." Charles responded with a slight annoyance.

"Apologies sir, you know this is not my usual way with you, but something urgently requires your attention." She blurted out, almost in a panic.

"Very well, I suppose my son can wait another hour or two. What is it?"

"Something you need to see sir, we can't explain it." She responded.

Charles, now palpably annoyed, turned to face his subordinate. Every time he looked upon her he could not help being reminded of one of his teachers. The comparison was frightening. Her cropped black hair did not so much flow as it did sit, somehow self-styled without the aid of a brush, upon her fine features. Her chiselled features told of a very ruthless nature within her, a trait that he was yet to see for himself, and her dark brown eyes made looking directly at her very difficult for he always felt as though he was staring into some deep recess within space, an untouched schism. She, like himself, had become a young officer, but she was only just starting her career whereas Charles hoped, nay, prayed, that his was winding to a close.

"Very well." He sighed with an obvious lack of elatedness. "Let's go see what this is all about then, shall we?" He extended his hand towards the heavy flaps of tent to signal the move to the outside.

Cassandra obligingly moved out into the unbearable heat and humidity of their surroundings. For a moment, Charles actually considered leaving the matter to his lesser so that he could return to the relative cool of his quarters. He chided himself for such a thought and continued the long walk to wherever it was he was being led. Such thoughts had recently started creeping into his mind, like a snake amidst long grass, and were leading him astray from his duties. It was a sign, a sign that he was nearing the end. He had loved the army his entire life, it was all he knew, but now, he was finished with it. This would be his last tour of duty and Cassandra, young as she was, was to take his place.

"So what is it that's so important as to disturb me writing to my eldest?" Charles asked.

"Writing?" Cassandra retorted with a snide smile.

Charles merely raised an eyebrow towards his sarcastic friend for she was well aware of how he communicated with his eldest son. She reacted with another grin and continued guiding him to their destination, it was almost as if she hadn't heard the question. A regular officer might chastise such a blatant disregard for authority, but he knew that it was nothing deliberate and so spared her the punishment.

As they moved away from their small base, although in truth only considered small when compared with Camp Bastion, they could see the jovial locals going about their daily rounds with safety and impunity. Charles could not help but feel proud of what he and his soldiers had achieved over the region. When he had arrived the terrorist cells of the area had already retreated but they had left an imprint of fear within the locals. After the skirmish of three months past though, the locals had taken to their new regime as if it had lifted a great pressure from their weary and laden shoulders. He was not sure if he agreed with controlling another country's population, but he was protecting the innocent and that was all he ever wanted to do.

The scars of the skirmish were still with him, a harsh reminder of the bitter realities of war. When he was growing up the memories of World War Two were still fresh within the minds of the adults and they were quick to tell anyone who would listen the horror's that conflict wrought upon a man's body, and upon his soul. Yet that had not deterred him, in fact, it had done the opposite as he strove to ensure that such atrocities were never revisited upon mankind. The human race was quick to judge, yet they often forgot that blame never belonged to one party alone.

Charles looked down at the fresh scar upon his forearm, the result of a fortunate misfire that he had had which only led to a grazing wound rather than a serious injury. He could still recall the dreadful cacophony of battle, the hideous orchestral performance of machinery as bullets whizzed through the air, each one possessing the capability to take a man's life and deliver him swiftly into the arms of God. Even the smell, the acrid stench of heated metal colliding with flesh, leaving entrails in its wake, was a foul memory. It had not been his first taste of battle, far from it, but he desperately wanted it to be his last.

As he blinked he could see the streets themselves changing into that horrific battlefield. The macabre image of craters in the streets and holes in the walls was only a small portion of the atrocities that mankind had placed upon itself that day. The locals were screaming, desperate to escape the symphony of carnage that was upon them, hoping beyond belief that it was all some kind of act and that everything would right itself. His own troops, trained warriors, were left stunned by the cataclysmic violence. He could not bear to remember the grislier details and so he decided to dwell no further on such awful memories. As he opened his eyes once more, all within the same split-second that he had blinked, the natural order had been restored. The bullet holes still riddled the walls like some kind of surrealist painting, but everything was normal.

The people conversed happily with each other, completely ignorant, or at least impervious, to any kind of threat that might decide to visit them again one day. Several of the people cheered the Major and his Lieutenant as they strode past them, one old lady even came and patted Charles on the shoulder. It was a common enough occurrence. She was regarded as the leader of this small community, a kindly old woman who hailed the army as saviours. Even if others disagreed with her opinions they did not voice their own out of respect for the resplendent female.

Several of his troops were patrolling the junction before them that led out of the community and onto the small dirt road that twisted for miles towards the next settlement. Even though the threat had largely been eradicated they still had to be vigilant. The sergeant amongst them halted his squad and ordered them to salute their superior, as the man himself also did with an exasperated sigh. Whether it was from the tediousness of formality or the exhausting heat, Charles could not tell. Ever the man who acquitted himself with honour and dignity, the Major walked up to them to provide a more human element to their regimented daily lives.

"Morning gentlemen, and ladies, at ease…" They relaxed their fixed posture. "How are we all feeling this morning?" He asked casually.

They all responded with different answers, creating a kind of squabbled response that rendered Charles unable to reciprocate. The sergeant looked angry at this inaudible reaction until he saw the calm smile upon his superior's lips.

"Slow down there…" Charles said with a slight chuckle. "I'll just assume that you're all fine and dandy, except you…" He continued as he pointed to one of the three men in the front row, who suddenly became quite nervous. Charles burst out laughing and so did the squad as they realised that they had been had by their superior. "Calm down lad, I'm only teasing. A fine specimen like yourself ought to be alright with such wondrous conditions as these…" He said with another smile. "It marks a change from the kind of rubbish weather we're used to back in Britain anyway, eh?"

"Yes, sir." The youth responded, still somewhat embarrassed about being singled out by the Major for his awful jest.

"Have any of you heard about whatever this commotion is?" Charles asked politely.

They all shook their heads, each one afraid to speak for fear of angering their senior officer. Yet it was not Charles they should've been afraid of as the sergeant reprimanded them for not answering the Major directly. Charles gave a simple hand gesture to suggest a more delicate touch to the non-commissioned officer before moving away and continuing back down the path to his objective.

The road they travelled upon could barely be considered such as they moved away from the cobbled tarmac surfaces and onto the sandy strips that signified an end to the settlement. Sometimes the men would do physical training around the deserts and so Charles surmised that they must've just happened to stumble across whatever it was that they found. There was no big mystery to solve here, it was a simple matter of lost and found, albeit if no-one knew it was lost or was trying to find it.

Cassandra seemed to be scanning the environment around her, her thin frame allowing her to rotate without trouble so as to examine as much as she could. Her breath was shallow and her eyes seemed glazed, as though she was not truly present. It was almost as if she was in some kind of coma, but was still conscious. Charles watched her for a moment to see if something was driving this strange behaviour, but he could not decipher anything. She was like a clean plate, everything wiped from her.

"Is everything alright Cassandra?" Charles asked delicately.

There was no response from his Lieutenant, her eyes remained fixed upon the point they had been settled on for a few moments, as if they had found their target. Her posture, also, was as rigid as a piece of metal, standing completely straight without the usual slouch that everyone carried with them under such conditions. Day after day, for months on end, they exerted and pushed themselves to the absolute limit and slept no more than five hours every night. A small amount of slouching was to be expected, in fact, Charles encouraged it so that a few could find some form of respite whilst under the vicious regimes of the armed forces. Indeed, Cassandra, with her wiry frame was often one to take what opportunities she could to rest so that she could be refreshed later on.

Charles said nothing for another minute or two, as he was still convinced that there was something motivating her odd behaviour. Yet further and further they crept into the desert with no sign of their destination or of Cassandra snapping out of whatever had entranced her so skilfully. She was only the puppet, Charles wanted the puppeteer.

"LIEUTENANT WILLIAMS!" He shouted at the top of his lungs as moved in front of her to halt her.

Cassandra seemed to snap out of her trance as she saluted the Major as though nothing had happened. "Yes, sir?" She responded inquisitively.

"You do not know why I yelled at you Lieutenant?" He enquired.

"No sir." She responded innocently

Charles did not want to embarrass his Lieutenant and so quickly thought of something to ask to save her, and himself, any misgivings. He grasped in his mind for a moment before thinking of something plausible. "I simple wanted to ascertain as to how you have knowledge of whatever it is the situation is." He replied coolly.

"Oh, I was running with that new squad that came in last week when one of them fell over and uncovered it. It left quite a nasty bruise on his ribcage." She explained honestly.

"Very well, was he taken to the infirmary?" Charles asked.

"No, he refused to go sir, said he would be fine." Cassandra replied.

"Alright then, did you get a good look at whatever it was?" He probed as he continued his line of enquiry.

Cassandra opened her mouth to reply again, but something stopped her. Her expression was vexed as she clearly struggled to recall the event. Quizzically she continued for a moment before answering. "I don't remember sir…" She said with an obvious tone of worry.

"Don't worry Cassandra, I'm sure it's just fatigue." He reassured her with a smile. "Shall we continue?" He said as he extended a hand to usher her forward, just as he had done an hour or so beforehand.

Charles hoped that Cassandra had taken his words as genuine. He did not want to upset her as he believed he had found the culprit to her strange behaviour. Anyone who entered the armed forces had to be screened for any history of illness within their family, including mental illness. Charles knew that her mother had suffered from Huntington's Disease, and now Charles believed that her daughter had inherited the affliction. Although he had never seen Cassandra writhe, or even twitch, involuntarily before, he thought to himself. He shut down any doubts from his mind as he arrived at the conclusion that there was no other logical possibility, and yet still his mind continued to lean back towards that name. Magnus Malum. Why though? Charles pondered, what made him so important that he could occupy the minds of the living in death?

The Major pushed such nonsensical thoughts aside as he considered the course of actions that would need to be taken. Obviously Cassandra would need to be tested for the disease. If she was found to be positive then it could ruin her entire career, perhaps not immediately but certainly within a few years if the signs were beginning to show now. She was certainly within the right age bracket for the disease at thirty-two years of age. The thought of losing her saddened Charles deeply for she had been his second for over two years now, and they had become firm friends in that time. She knew of his deep internal struggle over not being with his family and she had helped him through some very difficult times, and there was nothing he could do to help her.

Magnus Malum. There it was again, that nagging thought that kept invading his mind. He could not push it away. Forcefully he drove the thought from him, or at least he hoped he had, as they arrived at the artefact in question. From far away Charles could not make out much of it, all he could see was a piece of black metal that stood out from the monotonous gold coloured sand. It alone was the only thing worth looking at for miles around them. He could tell that the new squad was thinking the same as they simply could not take their eyes off of it. There was something about it that willed Charles towards it, it almost gave him pleasure to gaze upon its magnificence. It was only a piece of metal though and Charles could see that, but he did not want to believe it. There was something deeper to it, something that he could not quite explain. Still, he needed to appear composed in front of his troops and so collected his thoughts and stored them away so that he could approach the subject with the appropriate attitude.

Gingerly, having been shaken slightly by his lapse in mental judgment, he advanced towards the object. As he neared it though it was almost as if the troops could sense that Charles could not see in it what they saw. One of the squad, a young female with dusky skin and dark hair, gave him a searching look, as though she didn't even know that he was her superior. Charles had read of such situations before, when troops turned on officers. He was not sure of what he had done wrong but did not wish to anger his soldiers for fear of his own health. He resolved instead to deal with them when they got back to the camp and had a bit of rest, he imagined the heat of being out in the open desert all day was quite exhausting, especially so for new arrivals.

Almost as though the young woman had sense his thoughts, she drew out her poncho from her rucksack, used when sleeping out in the open, and covered a part of the metal with it. The others followed suit and Charles just watched in amazement, and fear. When the piece had been completely covered they tied the pieces of fabric together with cables and hoisted it into the air.

"Right then, let's move back to the camp. I imagine the Colonel will be interested to see what you've found when he makes his next visit from Bastion." Charles dared not to say more, for the consequences could be too severe.

They moved back the way he had come with great zeal, so much so that Charles found it difficult to keep up with the impressive pace that they were setting. Whilst he did not go on as many runs with the troops as he used he was still a physically fit man, probably in better shape than half of the squad that were now twenty paces away from him. Cassandra, thankfully, did not seem to share their enthusiasm and had recovered from whatever bout of sickness she had suffered earlier in the day.

"What is wrong with them today?" She asked.

Charles did not respond, he merely smiled empathetically. The Lieutenant seemed completely unaware that she had been just as clouded in thought earlier. The Major revised his view that whatever was affecting her was Huntington's Disease, unless every member of the squad also had it which was an extreme unlikelihood. His hypothesis had shifted now towards a more simple explanation. There were two possibilities. Either, it was the exhaustion from the severe heat that they had been experiencing lately, as was probably the case considering it was mid-spring, the time when ultraviolet light was at its highest and so the risk of heat exhaustion was also, or sun-stroke. Charles could definitely see that as a very real possibility as a bead of sweat fell down from his forehead and rested on his nose, creating an uncomfortable itching sensation. The other option was that there was some kind of infection spreading around the camp, most likely through the water supply as it was all acquired from the same source. The likelihood of this though was not high as the locals seemed completely tranquil, as they always did, and they shared the same fountain.

He did not dwell on the matter further, believing that either scenario could be solved by a day or two off for those affected. Undoubtedly that would create some slack but Charles was more than prepared to fill in the rest himself, after all he never had to experience the roughness that the privates went through. Cassandra was very nonchalant also as they continued walking, as though she had forgotten her previous enquiry. Charles surmised that she was just trying to keep up appearances for the troops, should any of them notice that something was off.

As they were walking back through the town, his soldiers still a few paces ahead of him, the kindly old lady strode out of her home once more. She stopped in front of the troops, curious to see what they had found. With a gentle flick she withdrew a sharp knife from her hand and sliced open the cables that were holding the fabric in place, revealing the black metal underneath. Without hesitation the squad dropped the object and took out their weapons, aiming them towards the woman with obvious intent to harm, or kill. Charles rushed in as quickly as he could, screaming at his soldiers to put their weapons down. They would not listen. He could think of little else to do other than to shoulder tackle the nearest of the soldiers to the ground. The jerked movement caused the others to focus in on their Major, their attention momentarily snatched from the artefact. The young female who had warded him away from the metal earlier pointed her SA80 at her superior before a flicker of recognition came across her features and her violent intentions crumpled, along with the others it seemed as they looked sheepishly away from Charles.

Charles quickly scrambled to his feet to set his soldiers in order. "WHAT THE BLOODY HELL DO YOU THINK YOU'RE DOING!?" He did not wait for a response. "I don't know what is going on with you lot but I will ensure the safety of everyone, both military and civilian, by any means necessary!" He continued.

Cassandra, who had simply stood gobsmacked throughout the whole scene, moved towards her Major to reinforce his authority. Charles wondered though if she could be trusted, especially if she seemed to have whatever illness his troops had acquired. Gently he flicked off the sand from his jacket before continuing with his tirade. He could not inflict any physical punishment on them and so he chose to give out a financial one.

"Each of you will have one month's pay deducted!" The outbursts occurred immediately. "I DON'T GIVE A DAMN WHAT YOU THINK ABOUT IT!" He screamed at the very top of his voice. "The punishment for threatening an officer is far more severe than that! So, head back to camp and wait in the mess hall. When I return you will be placed under armed guard until the Colonel arrives to judge your full punishment. You are dismissed!" He hissed the final statement.

Words could not express the anger he felt towards them. Cassandra could see it as well as she began to escort the soldiers back towards the camp. She seemed noticeably less annoyed than himself. Charles held the one closest to him, the dusky skinned female, back for a moment with a gentle hand placed upon her shoulder. She clearly expected further punishment to be issued, as she had been the one to threaten him. Her body shook almost uncontrollably with fear. Charles had no such intentions though.

"You're one of the new recruits right? What's your name?" He asked as he turned her around to face him.

"Sir, I don't know what happened...I'm so-"

"Save it, you're in trouble regardless of your intent, there's no way around that. I asked for your name, not an apology." He reiterated. He was in no mood for pleasantries.

"Private Atiqa Wazid, sir." She replied cautiously.

"So you speak Pashto I take it?"

"No sir, I can understand it but I have difficulties speaking it."

"Well, I need you to tell me what that lady is saying." He said as he pointed towards the old lady who effectively ran the town. She was muttering quietly and pointing at the metal which was now rested on the ground. She looked worried.

Private Wazid listened in to the woman. She was hesitant at first, clearly unfamiliar with her family's language. Her dark hair was brushed over her ear in some failed attempt to understand the words more clearly. Eventually though, through much perseverance, she seemed able to decipher the words. She turned towards her superior and looked him in the eyes.

"Well, what does it mean?" He asked irritably.

"Evil."

Chapter 4

It had been another day of various doldrums. He had not even been able to focus on his favourite lesson, and he had paid no attention to the subject of his affection. Thomas had noticed his apathetic response to the world and had probed him for information, but Alex could not give the reason as to why he was so withdrawn from the usual activities of the school day as it was ridiculous to even contemplate. Yet he did ponder over it, in fact he thought about a great many things.

First and foremost he thought about the strange aura of mystery that surrounded Magnus Malum. He could not explain why he was so prominent in his mind but the long since deceased businessman seemed to have permeated his every waking moment. There was some unexplained mystique about him. Why had no one been able to discover what happened to such a high-profile individual? His father's company had been one of the driving forces behind the British war efforts, and so its importance had been well established. Magnus, though, had let it fall into ruinous decay before dropping off the face of the earth. Then there were his eyes, that deep green that was exactly the same as his own. It was not hereditary. Perhaps it represented some kind of defect, Alex thought to himself. That would mean that Alex possessed the same defect, would he suffer the same fate as Magnus as well?

Any moment that was not preoccupied with the otherness that surrounded Magnus was taken up by his struggles with Arthur Cressing. His bullying had become far worse since

Alex had begun to battle back, not that Arthur could feasibly explain that Alex was actively retaliating. His imprudent use of his powers had incited a new wave of torture, both mental and slightly physical, that Arthur was now inflicting upon him. His campaign of spite had reached an all-time high two days past when he had successfully turned half of the school against him by making him seem like the villain of the situation. Those who actually knew Alex believed that he was not as Arthur had portrayed him. The bully had told the school that Alex had been nothing short of vindictive in seeking to make Arthur's life a misery. Apparently Alex had been constantly belittling him about his intelligence which had greatly depressed the manipulative young man. Of course Alex had done no such thing, in fact he tried to stay away from Arthur as much as possible. The unwarranted tidal wave of abuse that had followed had made Alex retreat completely from the world at large. Despite Alex trying his best to maintain his resolve it was not working. Arthur was winning. He had swapped his physical dominance for mental superiority, and the results shockingly swayed in Arthur's favour.

So much time had been taken up by the mental anguish within him that he had not been practising for the talent contest, which was now only one day away. Luckily, having done it for most of his life, Alex was naturally gifted with tricks and so did not need the practice. Still, one or two of his illusions had not been used for a long time, as he had been preoccupied with other matters, and so he thought it best to rejuvenate them. Mechanically, he pulled the foiled packet of cards out of the left pocket of his school rucksack and placed them upon his knee. For once, probably due to the abuse that he might receive, he hesitated. Cautiously he looked around the bland appearance of his sixth-form common room. There was almost no-one within it as everyone, barring those dozen or so that did A-Level History, was in lessons. Thankfully, as Alex surveyed the grey walls that lacked almost any adornment whatsoever save for a few posters advertising universities, Arthur was not present.

He did not live far from the school and so he was likely using the time to do whatever activities that he preferred to do outside of school. Still, there was a small group of students sitting at the other end of the common room. Alex decided to continue anyway as he did not care what they thought about him. They all called him a freak anyway.

He pulled the cards close to his face to examine their condition. He had had this pack for little over a year and they were already beginning to crumple from frequent use. Some of the corners were fraying and bent over giving the pack an unregimented look that was displeasing to the eye. Patches of dirt, and gum from when he dropped them on the floor previously, marred the laminated surfaces. They were still usable though and so he began to imagine as though he was performing the card opposite a volunteer. In his mind they had picked a card which Alex then placed back into the pack before shuffling. Deliberately, he pulled the wrong card out from the pack before doing so again to make it seem as though he had got the trick wrong. Alex slammed the table and produced the card. Obviously he had chosen the card himself but he could guarantee that the end result would be the same when he did it at the talent show.

Luck seemed to be on his side as Thomas strolled in from his lesson, which had ended ten minutes early, seeing as the next period did not start until then. His best friend smiled at him as he walked over to the back end of the common room, past the pathetic excuse for a kitchen which barely contained any functional equipment, where Alex was seated. He yawned out of boredom and dropped his bag down next to his friend. Thomas could see that Alex was practicing his card tricks and his interest immediately picked up. Alex found an amusing thought in teachers performing tricks as well to make some of their more difficult students keen to learn again.

"You alright?" Alex asked Thomas as he stared at the pack of cards.

"Yeah, I can't take geography anymore though." He sighed. "All we learn about is 'human geography', I want to know about earthquakes and floods and all of that stuff."

Alex smiled. "Well, if you would've done GCSE geography then you would've." He chuckled to himself. "In fact you should count your blessings that they're letting you do geography at all."

"Blessings?" Thomas laughed sarcastically. "I certainly won't be doing that at university, unless the weather becomes a bit more interesting around here."

Alex ignored his friend and continued playing with his cards, shuffling them in his unique fashion. Thomas was mesmerised by the vague illusions that Alex created. It would normally take years to master such techniques as those that he knew, yet it had always been like second nature to him. Alex assumed that both his powers and his near perfect memory were probably the reason he had been able to pick up these skills so quickly. He remembered when he had first seen a street performer do the tricks. He had been a small bearded man with a green jacket that clearly did not need the money he gained from hustling people. The sweet smells of the seaside still clung to his nostrils as he recalled the line of buskers along the beachfront that performed their various trades. Alex had watched the man no more than four times before asking to do it himself under the heat of the midday summer sun. He had done it perfectly first time. Alex was only young at the time, only eight years old, and the memory of the busker snatching the cards back and claiming that the sun had been in his eyes was one that filled him with a strange mixture of sadness and joy. Typically, as all children were, he had been upset at being shouted at by an adult. But he had also been overjoyed to realise the potential he had.

He had been so consumed with the memory that he had not noticed that the period was almost over, and he had been shuffling his cards for at least a minute or two. Thomas was staring at him blankly, his eyes not really focusing as they seemed to glaze over his smart-casual shirt as if he had a stain upon it. His eyes snapped back into focus as he realised his friend had recovered.

"Ah, back with us are we?" He asked.

"Sorry, you know how I get." Alex replied.

"Yeah I do…" Thomas paused before asking. "So, are you going to do that trick for me?"

Alex raised an eyebrow inquisitively. "You've seen it a hundred times…"

"Yeah, but I still don't get it." Thomas responded with a laugh.

"Well, I recently saw a new one on TV that I could try on you?" He suggested.

"Sure thing." Thomas retorted with active enthusiasm.

Alex allowed his friend to pick a card, the eight of clubs, out from the deck and then he himself chose one, the jack of spades. Gently he placed Thomas' hands on top of each other with the card sandwiched between them. Equally as delicately he placed one of his hands, with his card underneath, on top of Thomas' and moved it slowly in a circular motion. With a simple click of his fingers the trick was done. In his hand Alex held the eight of clubs. Thomas opened his hands and his face twisted in an amazed expression with his faced extended and his mouth completely agape. In his hands was Alex's jack of spades.

"What!?..." Thomas said in a state of complete stupefaction.

Alex merely laughed to himself as Thomas tried to work out the various mechanisms behind the trick. He rejected every theory that his friend put to him and each time they became more convoluted and outlandish. In truth the magic behind the trick was rather simple, but Alex would not tell Thomas for that would ruin the unexplainable attraction that it held.

"How did you do that?" Thomas asked as he desperately tried to pry information from him.

"Why would I tell you?" Alex replied as he continued laughing to himself.

The other pupils began to pour in from their lessons as Thomas slumped back into his chair full of childish contempt. Alex knew that he was not really annoyed, it was just his way when he did not get something that he wanted. He had been the same since they were very young, especially when he discovered Alex's powers and became immensely jealous at not having powers of his own. Alex fondly remembered the superhero duo that they had come up with, taking bed sheets from the clothesline and tucking them in at the top of their shirts to give them a cape. They had even pulled underwear over their trousers in a kind of childish homage to the somewhat laughable superheroes of the sixties and seventies. Manningleyman and Gordonovich had been their names. Two enemies who had come together as friends to fight small scale crime. Alex smiled at the memory for it had been when he was truly oblivious to all the negative aspects of the world, of which he considered there to be many.

For every darkness though, there was light, Alex considered himself to be one of the last candles in a world increasingly covered by the black abyss that humanity seemed to spew forth at every opportunity. Muggings; murders; chemical and nuclear warfare; starvation and greed, and gluttony. They were all threatening to snuff out the good in the world. That is why Alex did his very best to be as unresponsive as possible when Arthur made him his target. As he watched Arthur saunter through the sixth-form doors he hoped that he would be able to continue his pacifist stance against Cressing's tyranny. Arthur may not have crossed the line into evil, but he was certainly getting closer with each encounter.

"Alex?" Thomas piped up. "Why don't you show that trick to everyone?" He asked with that same childish glee that he often possessed as he bounded up from his chair, which would've made him lose his light blue jeans had it not been for the fact that the top button had somehow caught around the loose fabric of his basic t-shirt. Before Alex could even protest, his best friend called across the common room.

"Everyone!" He shouted, against his usual shy nature. "You need to see this trick that Alex has learnt, it's so cool!"

The response was as Alex had anticipated. Nobody seemed to move as they all glanced towards the clock, realising that the next lesson was only a minute or two away. Alex let out a sigh of relief, he was glad that for once the listless nature of teenagers had made them ambivalent at best.

"What were you thinking Thomas?" Alex asked as the other pupils shifted uneasily, some still uncertain to take the first plunge that would drive others towards him.

"You told me that I need to stop being so shy!" Thomas hissed back.

"Yes, but I didn't mean for you to become quite so impulsive." Alex responded.

"Sorry, I thought you'd want people to see it. The talent contest is tomorrow so this could be your chance to get people rooting for you!" Thomas exclaimed with enthusiasm.

"I suppose..." Alex conceded. "But it doesn't matter anyway because no-one wants to see it."

Just as he let the words fall from his mouth he saw Arthur Cressing continue his determined walk towards him. Clearly he was not bothered about being slightly late for his lesson. "Come on then snot-eyes..." He started. "Show me the trick."

Like traditional sheep, the other pupils followed in Arthur's wake, careful not to overstep the social boundaries set by their 'leader'. Cressing pushed himself directly into Alex's face, letting him know who was in command of the situation. Alex was reluctant to perform the trick, purely because it would spurn Arthur, but he knew that the bully would give him little choice; and Alex did not want to use his powers for any reason. Reluctantly, he fanned out his deck in front of Arthur. The bully looked at the pack of cards as if there was some trick already within them, Alex could not blame him as his recent use of his powers had made Arthur very jumpy around him. In fact, it had made him more aggressive as he had clearly felt the need to reassert his dominance. In the end, after much deliberation, Arthur picked a card with almost the entire sixth-form watching with eager anticipation. It was almost as though they were watching some kind of spectacle, a kind of battle between David and Goliath. A much less interesting battle than the one of legend.

"Could you show it to everyone please?" Alex politely asked, fully aware that the answer would be less than cordial.

"Why would I do that freak?" Arthur responded in a quick burst of anger.

Alex sighed with irritation. "So that the others can see it."

Arthur, his face turning slightly red from the social embarrassment of his obliviousness, showed everyone his card, the king of hearts. Alex laughed internally at the irony of his chosen card. Arthur's close friend, and once his own, Simon examined the card to check for any kind of concealments, it was almost like some kind of shakedown. When the lanky teen declared the card safe he gave it back to his master, who was then instructed by Alex to place the card firmly between his hands. He did not seem to take kindly to being instructed but he did as he was bade for the benefit of everyone else. Alex imagined that he desperately wanted the trick to go wrong so that Alex could be further humiliated in front of his peers, thereby continuing Arthur's Cold War against him.

Alex picked his own card from the deck, the easily recognisable ace of spades, and placed his hand on top of Arthur's. He could already tell that the reaction he would get would cause a great deal of laughter and malice. As expected, Arthur retracted his hand in horror.

"Did you see that?!" Arthur cried. "He tried to hold my hand…" The pupils laughed, although not genuinely. "What's wrong snot-eyes? Wasn't your Daddy there to hold it for you?" He smirked.

Alex instantly felt his blood boil. Arthur, having known his family through his own parents, since they had been at the same schools since their education started, was well aware that his father had not been present for most of his life. It was sore for Alex, and yet at the same time that thought of physical contact with his father seemed unnatural to him. It was bad knowing that Arthur could still find ways to torture him, but it was worse realising that the bully had revealed a harsh truth. Desperately, not wanting to display his gifts, Alex stifled his rage, smothering it with the common decency required to act accordingly in front of his classmates. A witty repost occurred to him as the pupils laughter was beginning to subside. He decided not to use it though. He did not want to drag himself to the kind of base humanity that Arthur was exhibiting.

"It's part of the trick." Alex assured Arthur. He was about to leave it there but he couldn't help having a small dig back at his tormenter. It was a kind of healthy subversion for his anger that he believed stopped it channelling into his powers. "Not that you'd understand that." He muttered under his breath.

"What was that?" Arthur asked back in hush, but unmistakably wrathful, tones.

"Nothing." Alex said with a hand gesture to wave it off as he placed his hand back upon Arthur's.

Alex continued to rub Arthur's hand, despite the sniggers and chuckles, and snapped his fingers to indicate the conclusion of the trick. The sun suddenly pressed itself through the window and hit both of them in the eyes, blurring their vision and the final part of the deception. As it cleared, just as before, Alex held Arthur's king of hearts within his hand and, with a mixed sense of confusion and trepidation at proving 'snot-eyes' right, Arthur revealed that he held Alex's. The pupils all gasped in astonishment, their puerile lives having never experienced such wonder. Thomas looked around to the others with a knowing look, the kind of expressions that said that he knew it would be good and they should have believed him, and his face beaming from ear to ear. Everyone was in awe of Alex and for once he felt one of the many splendours that life had to offer. The applause and adoration of his audience made him feel such elation that he could not even express his joviality. He smiled and held his hand up to acknowledge the congratulations of his peers. It seemed that he had won back some of those that had turned against him, although he wasn't sure if it was worth it for such fickle individuals.

Arthur and his cronies were the only ones not cheering. The bully realised that his smear campaign was failing fast. "How did you do that?" Arthur asked, clearly bitter with his defeat.

"It's not about the logic behind everything. It's about the experience." Alex replied quietly as he continued to intake the applause that was emanating from his 'friends'.

With Alex distracted by his fanfare Arthur grabbed him by the throat and pushed him back against the wall, creasing Alex's shirt and pulling it up with him to reveal the small of his back. He made no attempts to hide his wrath. Another wave of gasps from the sixth-form informed him that they knew Alex had never been the one to blame. Yet Arthur's stranglehold over them, couple with Simon's role as the enforcer, ensured that they did nothing to stop the bully as he continued to press his hands into Alex's throat. They were all cowards, a common trait of humanity, which then retreated away to their lessons to leave Alex at the mercy of his bully.

With a quick surge of courage Thomas bolted into the path of Arthur. Yet the villain understood his surroundings well; perhaps his naturally aggressive nature had made him more attuned to such attacks. He forced his elbow backwards into Thomas' chest. His best friend crumpled to the floor and clutched at his chest, his eyes already welling with tears even though the pain would not have been that bad. It was more of a reaction to the whack.

"Stay there Gordon!" Arthur spat. "You can watch this!"

Instantly Arthur's followers gathered Thomas to stop him squirming away. Arthur cocked his fist, ready to strike, but he obviously had not noticed the green glow in Alex's eyes.

Arthur flung his hand forwards, but, unintentionally, Alex redirected it so it smacked the wall with all its force. Unlike before, when he had stopped Arthur and his thugs from cornering him, this was deliberate. The bully released his grip on his victim as he howled in pain, clutching his aching hand, and fell back into his group of friends, almost treading over Thomas as the youth scuttled towards his triumphant friend. The thankful smile on Thomas' face told Alex that he knew he had used his powers to avoid the fight. Alex looked straight through him though, his emotions were still riding dangerously high. His eyes shone a magnificent green as he glared at the group of individuals who had caused him so much misery. His mind, being near perfect, recalled every single incident and the pain of each memory became fresh in his mind. Alex could hear the demon within him seeking to break free and crush his oppressors. In fact, Alex could not even consider it his demon, for he desperately wanted to smite Arthur for all of his wrongdoings. A small voice in the back of his head egged him on.

The anger within him was at an all-time high. Never had he wanted to exercise his powers so badly. So great was the urge to use his abilities that the lights in the room began to flicker, only ever so slightly. His brain seemed to be aware of the fact that Alex was trying to cover up any evidence of his gift. All examples of it so far could be explained as circumstantial. But there was no doubting that Arthur was suspicious, and Alex needed to be careful. With all his might he forced his anger back inside him and recovered his decorum. Thomas looked up at him as if in apology for his cowardice, with his mind now cleared Alex knew that his friend had done everything he could to help him. He just wasn't the brave sort.

Arthur, with his hand visibly red from its impact with the wall, shot a piercing glance towards Alex. "You think you can win the talent show with that?" Arthur laughed. "You'll be lucky to do a single trick before I send you crashing back down to earth! You can guarantee that I will not stop haunting you until your mind turns to mush and your body is broken from the continual torment I'll inflict upon it! FREAK!" He exclaimed. His threat was left hanging in the air as he ushered his companions to follow him to his lesson.

Alex watched Arthur leave knowing that from now on it would be all out war. They had had their Cuban Missile Crisis and the results were now going to lead to complete and utter annihilation of one side or the other. The second bell, to indicate the start of the lesson, rang with a somewhat lessened tone, as if it could sense the tension in the air and was being choked by it. Alex looked at his watch, giving himself a small amount of comfort and solace, and steeled himself for the rest of the day. Luckily his next lesson was psychology, the one thing he and Arthur did not share. So, with a somewhat improved mood, he began the walk to the psychology building and waited, with bated breath, for the day to draw to a close.

Chapter 5

Alex thought he had had the situation firmly under his control. He had the upper hand on Arthur, and all thoughts of Magnus had vanished from his mind as the talent show closed in on him. Then he returned. Alex rubbed his eyes with his hand in some attempt to wave away the tide of tiredness that had overcome him. It had been a long day since his conflict with Arthur in the common room and it had only gotten longer. During psychology they had been discussing the founder of the school of thought, Sigmund Freud. Alex found everything about his work deeply disturbing, but it only extenuated when he saw that man's face again. Magnus.

He had been a subject of Freud's for his theories on repression. No-one had recognised it was him though, for he had only been a child in this photo. His hair was noticeably shorter, and not styled in any real manner as it just sat naturally upon his narrow shoulders. His features were considerably less defined, as it often was with children, but the unmistakeable outlines of his cheekbones made it very obvious that this was Magnus. Alex supposed that they, in truth, did not look like the same person. There was no caption for the picture or no obvious adornments that confirmed his identity. One feature though made it quite apparent that it was Magnus. The eyes. His emerald eyes glowed just as brightly as they did on his adult photos, and yet no-one seemed to pick up on it. Even the four pupils that shared both history and psychology with him could not detect the similarities.

It had rekindled Alex's curiosity though. The state of his room was a testament to how engrossed he had become in his obsession with the deceased metalworker. Clothes were strewn about his room in such a mess that it could not even be called a form of ordered chaos. Underwear had somehow reached his highest bookshelf, socks had gotten jammed down the side of his bed, and his jeans were being used a doorstopper. Even his favourite shirt, a dark blue collared shirt with a thin over layer that allowed the collar to rest on top of it, was laying in an untidy heap in the middle of the floor.

Such was his current disengagement with the world that he had not even thought to speak to his family as he had come home, not that either of his siblings would be interesting in talking to him. One would be fanatical with a screen, the other with a page. He seemed to recall his mother calling up to him, but he had no idea why. Alex had bigger things on his mind, although he often would not talk to his mother as he never saw the need to. He preferred to deal with things on his own, something which his father understood, which was why he could confide confidently in him.

In lieu of talking to his family he had spent the entire afternoon so far looking up anything he could on Magnus. It was now evening, he gathered based on how numb his bottom was becoming, and he had not found a single shred of information. Not one iota. It was almost as though there had been a deliberate removal of Magnus from history. For some reason the powers that be did not want Alex to find out about him. Perhaps there was something unexplained about his disappearance, he thought to himself. It was a troubling notion, a man who could somehow avoid death. Alex laughed the thought aside, for almost no one on the planet could live to be over one-hundred and twenty, which Magnus surely would've been as he looked over fifty in his last photograph. He could not help but feel that it was somehow true though. Maybe he cryogenically froze himself? Alex self-concluded, or found some way of surviving in digital form without his body. Anything was possible in the modern world after all. Whatever it was, Alex knew that something was not quite right.

His search had left him tired and so he switched off his monitor and laid back in his rotating chair. He swayed gently from side to side as he contemplated the situation around Magnus Malum. There was little that he could do about it for the moment except wait. Charles had yet to write back to him and so he hoped, having mentioned Magnus to him, that perhaps his father would be able to answer his queries. Like an all-encompassing book, his father always held the answer, even when he did not mean to. It had been almost two weeks since he last wrote to his father, an unusually long gap. Comfortingly, Alex stared at his watch and sighed with a forlorn expression. The fact that Charles had not even phoned his mother for a few days made the situation even worse. Alex did not know what to do, and he needed his father.

Reminiscently he opened a small drawer that sat at the bottom of his bed, attached to the end so that underwear and socks could be placed within; although he had always used it for another purpose. He took the small container from its hold and placed it on top of his bed, as everywhere seemed to have been overtaken by the vast array of rubbish that was scattered about his room. Inside of the small lidless box sat a large stack of letters that had previously been sent to him by his father. He could remember reading each one, holding the paper between his fingers and taking in everything Charles had said to him. Regardless of the problem there was always one solution that he gave. So far it had not failed him either.

To overcome anything, we must push aside all restrictions and focus on those we love. Remember them, for when you need them the most, they will help you find your way. Those had always been the words both Charlotte and Charles had instilled in him since birth. Whatever the danger, and however far gone hope may be, family will always be there to support you.

Alex rubbed his hand over one of the letters with great fondness as he repeated the words in his mind. Although he often only confided in his father, he knew that his family would do everything they could to help him through anything. Even Steven, annoying and juvenile as he was, would go to great lengths to protect him; of that he was certain.

Almost as if on cue his brother appeared from behind his bedroom door. His footsteps had been so dainty coming up the stairs that he had suspected that it had been his sister, and so he had turned to greet her with a warm smile. When he saw that it was Steven though his smile faded and was replaced by an innate frown that he learned from dealing with his brother on a frustratingly frequent basis. Steven noted his change in expression and the atmosphere suddenly became very hostile between them, even though there had not been any single action which had set it off. In his hand his brother held a letter, which he had presumably been told to give to Alex sometime beforehand but had sat on it, probably literally, as he was engrossed with the television. It was a good act through Steven's eyes, as he was actually doing something that was asked of him, but Alex could not help feeling anger at his brother for delaying for so long.

The letter packaging was slightly crumpled and a small flap of torn paper told Alex that Steven had read his private letter. Alex could feel the familiar sense of anger building up within him. Yet, knowing that he needed to be calm for the sake of obscurity, he gave Steven a chance to explain himself before he flew into an uncontrollable rage.

"Steven…" He started through a thinly veiled layer of contempt. "Have you opened that?" He continued as he pointed to the torn letter. The answer was blindingly obvious, but he wanted his brother to do the decent thing and tell the truth.

Steven, who was not intimidated in the slightest by Alex's aggressive tone, raised the letter close to his eye as if to inspect it thoroughly, even though the damage to the packaging was apparent. Mockingly, he pressed his finger against the ripped paper and tore a section of it off, pressing it closer still. The tension in the room was palpable as Alex struggled to maintain his failing composure.

"Oh, I think I can see what you mean now…" Steven replied sarcastically, as if he were completely oblivious to the circumstances.

Alex let out a small sardonic laugh, the kind which he knew would lead to his rage bursting forth from him like a herd of stampeding elephants. He glared at Steven. One more chance, Alex told himself. One more.

"I won't ask you again Steven…" He let the end of his threat tail off for added emphasis.

There was a long and drawn-out silence, like you would find in a typical Hollywood film on the American West. Alex needed an explanation. He needed some reason that would explain his brother's intrusive actions. It likely would not calm him down, but he was desperate to try and keep his powers in check, and if Steven's answer did not sate him then he was certain the fury within him would be uncontrollable. Finally, as Alex was at his final thread of patience, his brother gave him what he sought.

"Yeah, I read it." He responded nonchalantly.

The simplicity of his answer was not something that Alex had wanted as he felt the pressure build behind his eyes. His gift was like a mad dog, just itching to be free and exercise itself. Worse still, with Alex watching, Steven brought the letter out in front of him, in plain view of his brother, and ripped it clean in half before repeating it time and time again. Alex watched the shreds of paper glide gracefully to the floor. He was not sure what he felt as he watched them fall. Part of him was completely incensed by his brother's blatant lack of respect and empathy for him. The rest of him though just sank into a dark depression that fuelled his desire to unleash his anguish upon the world. The only thing that was stopping him was the very thing that his brother had taken from him. Without his usual correspondence to his father he was almost completely alone, for Charles had been the only who had truly understood how he felt. As the scraps of paper finally touched the floor he knew that any solutions his father had given him were now inaccessible and he would have to struggle on with his problems by himself, unless Charles made a rare copy.

Anxiety rose within him. Arthur had warned him that he would never be able to win the talent contest, and thus the trip to the history museum which he so desperately desired to acquire a break from the usual burdens of his life, and now he was certain that he had no way of stopping the bully short of using his powers. Alex would not use his powers, he should not and could not, the repercussions for both himself, Arthur, and the world at large were too severe to contemplate. He would never be able to live with himself if he permanently harmed Arthur, despite the emotional torment he inflicted. The damage done to Arthur physically would probably be bad, but his psychological damage would be far worse as his mind was clearly already fraying as he battled his internal demons around Alex. If he did use his full force on Arthur then the world would know that they had a freak within them, a mutant who was different from the rest of them. Alex knew from history that different did not mesh well with humanity. He would be persecuted, or worse, he would be completely shunned as they cowered in fear from him. He did not want that.

His heart told him to hold back the tide of anger that he felt, to suppress it and never let it escape the bonds of its captivity, but his brain was less willing. Every fibre of his body was screaming at him to let out its abilities. Subtle thoughts began to creep slowly into his mind, once again it was as if his subconscious was independent of the rest of him; as though it were some kind of ethereal presence that lingered within him and twisted him to its logical will. Why shouldn't you use your gift? His devils told him, after all he had been blessed with these abilities, and what was the point in them if no-one knew he had them. Alex forced the thought back, but his subconscious was persistent, and yet surprisingly relenting. It tried to reason with him as he stared blankly across the room to Steven, who was laughing as loudly as he could in his brother's face. Why not use it in small doses? It negotiated, then nobody will know and you won't feel this itching urge all of the time. Alex admitted that it did sound tempting.

As his mind began to focus back into the room, almost as if his subliminal thoughts had released themselves, knowing that they had done enough to sway Alex before he himself knew it, the familiar feeling of total rage was within him. Alex would not give in so easily though. Yet, as he continued to watch his brother openly mock him, he knew that he had to do something. He was not certain of what, but as he charged at his brother like a bull towards a matador, a natural thrill took over him. For the first time he was experiencing one of the most typical traits of humanity, something he had never felt before as his only solution for his anger had been to exercise his powers. He had forgotten that whilst he was much more than human...he was still human! And he had never felt his humanity so purely as it pulsed through his veins and compelled him towards Steven.

Steven ran away with a smile on his face, he had clearly meant to provoke his brother into this action. Alex pushed his way through his room and tried to pounce on his brother as he turned to head towards the stairs. He missed by a hair's breadth. Steven taunted him as he slid down the banister on the stairs, hopping off at the end to avoid catching himself.

"Nice try second-place! But you'll have to do better, I mean what would Dad think if you couldn't catch me?" Steven laughed.

Alex followed his brother down the stairs but was quickly intercepted by Abigail as she was crossing the landing. She had only been curious to see why her youngest brother had bolted so swiftly out of the front door and into the street, but Alex had shouted at her to move all the same. Hopefully she wouldn't take it personally. He had no time to dwell on such things though as he sprinted out of the door as fast as he could, so fast that he almost went out into the road.

There was no sign of his brother. Steven was naturally quicker than him, due to his wiry build that allowed him to squirm away from many situations, and his brief hold up on the stairs allowed him to evade Alex. The eldest son held his hands up against his head, his anger was now seething through him with no outlet for it. He could feel the urge to use his powers building again. The tension was so high within his body that he could not possibly control it. That familiar voice, his subconscious, seemed to feel satisfied as Alex allowed the gift to flow over every atom of his body. His eyes began to glow bright green as they had done earlier that day, but with a much more noticeable hue and far greater intensity. As he felt his power flow through him he questioned why he had ever let it slumber, the feeling was phenomenal!

A rustling in the bushes some fifty feet ahead of him made him twist his head sharply. His senses seemed keener, his perceptions deeper. Steven hoisted himself out from his hiding place and, without staring at his brother, continued running down the street. As far as he was concerned the game was still going, but Alex had had enough. For a brief moment he had felt like a true human, but he knew that he was not. He was some kind of evolved specimen, the kind that would led the way and change the world. His power was unparalleled, his will unbending, and his aim simple. Steven continued to run down the street, his speed being aided by the gentle breeze that touched upon his back and propelled him forward, towards Thomas' house. Alex did not stop him immediately, part of him found thrill in wanting his best friend to finally see him utilise his abilities, after all Thomas had said that he wanted to see it. Alex was happy to oblige.

He allowed Steven to continue running for another few moments, he matched his brother's pace with ease but decided to go no quicker. The glow was so great from his eyes that he could see flecks of green amidst the bright yellow light emitted by the street lights above him. It pleased him. His brother seemed unaware that Alex was keeping pace with him, and even if he did register it he did not care as he continued to taunt him over their relationship with Charles. Without any regard for his own safety, Steven ran across the small road that led on towards Thomas' house. Thankfully no cars were coming in any direction. In fact, the street was silent as Steven found himself abruptly stopped outside of Thomas' house. He was confused at first, as he could not understand how the weather had turned against him so fast. His weak mind could not comprehend how it was possible that he could not physically move any further without being thrown back. The truth was actually very simple. Alex had stopped him. He was not sure how, but somehow Alex had used the wind, which had previously assisted his brother, to go against Steven so forcefully that he could not move against it, the only way was back towards Alex.

Steven seemed to sense that something was wrong about the situation, even his malnourished intellect could figure out that what was happening to him was not natural. He turned back to look at his brother, who was approaching slowly and in a calculated manner with his hands folded neatly behind his back. Now he noticed the difference within Alex. The green aura that surrounded his eyes had grown so powerful that wisps were forming and billowing away into the night like smoke. His gaze was fixed directly on Steven, and his brother returned it with a terrified expression. Desperately he tried once more to force his way through the wall of wind before him. It was to no avail. He merely stood where he was, as if running on the spot upon an imaginary treadmill.

"Look, Alex, I'm sorry…" He started his apology. Alex was not sure if he knew that he was causing the wind to go against him, or if fate had just gone against him instead. "You know I only joke around with you…"

Alex was not interested in hearing what his brother had to say. He did not want to harm him seriously, he just wanted to teach him a lesson that he would not soon forget. Alex stopped the wind from deterring his brother, he wanted to do this by hand. He gathered the wind behind his arm and used it to help him hoist his brother into the air by his shirt. Alex looked deep into his brother's cowardly eyes. Like the rest of the human race he was weak, slow to forgive and quick to forget, the familiar detriments that were attached to Homosapiens. Mankind was frail, but he was not. Yet, as he hoisted his brother into the air as far as his extended arm would allow him, he felt a very human sense of regret over his actions. His subconscious seemed to be focusing him back to earlier in the day when Arthur had held him against the wall with his arm. He was becoming like his bully.

Shocked, and completely disgusted with himself, he allowed his powers to subside back into his body, his arm releasing its grip upon the scruff of Steven's shirt. His brother fell the ground with a thud as his feet slipped, landing him on his rear. He used the opportunity to crawl around his contemplative brother and sprint off into the distance, back towards home. Alex felt abhorrent towards himself, he could not believe what he had done. He had felt bad about using his powers on Arthur on the two accounts before, but this was far worse. He had actively intended to harm his own family. The words of his father came flooding into his mind and he was crippled with guilt. Charles would have been ashamed of him if he had known.

The night air, surprisingly cold for the time of year, wrapped itself around him and intensified his horror. Alex continued to stare blankly into the distance, contemplating his hideous decisions. Of course Steven had always teased him, it had been that way since his younger brother had been old enough to talk. He had always gotten him in trouble for one thing or another, but that was all a part of the experience of siblinghood. Those small malfeasances did not warrant what he had had planned though. Everything that he loathed in this world he had become so close to mirroring. Alex thanked God that he had come to his senses before that unholy moment.

Just as he thought his mind would push him further into his pit of self-pity he heard a loud bang just in front of him. Alex's focus was snapped as he stopped glaring into his soul and fixed his gaze back into the real world. Before him, in a blue and fluffy dressing gown and some ill-fitting slippers, was his best friend. Of course, Alex thought, the whole event with his brother had occurred right outside of Thomas's parents' residence. That thought disturbed Alex even more. Not only had he wanted to harm his brother, but he had wanted to boast about it also. He dreaded to think what kind of monster lurked inside him just waiting to creep into the real world, like a bear huddled tightly in the back of its cave or a dragon that waits to waken from its slumber.

Thomas was eyeing Alex with a great deal of suspicion, and regrettably, apprehension. Alex did not want his best friend to be afraid of him, like Steven now would be. His friend began groping the air, as if to try and muster back the shield of wind that Alex had created in some vain attempt to utilise it for himself. Thomas had always been jealous of his gifts, but Alex knew that that would never again tear their friendship asunder. Like all friends they had had their trials and tribulations; they were stronger for it though. Indeed, Alex found it hard to imagine his life without Thomas in it, or any of his family for that matter. For someone who often considered himself so lonely and alone in the world, Alex realised that he had a lot to be thankful for. It made him smile.

"You alright there Alex?" Thomas said to him as he tried one last time to try and make sense of the wind wall.

"Of course I am." He responded indignantly, the last gasp of his anger finally escaping him as he said it.

"Come on Alex, we've known each other since we were little. Do you remember the purple tricycle? I do. You had it taken off you and given to Max remember? Because you were on it for too long…" Thomas stopped to laugh and Alex couldn't help but smile fondly at the memory. His only happy times seemed to be in memories. "When I walked, well more like crawled I guess, up to you and asked you if you were alright you said 'of course I am' and gave me that same scowling look you're giving me now. I know you Alex, you had tears in your eyes back then. It may not be the same now, but you feel the same."

Alex stared at his friend, he could not deny that Thomas was right. "I never meant to do what I did...I could say I didn't meant to hurt him..." His eyes welled as he tried to explain it. "I did though..."

"I'm no expert Alex, but on TV don't they tell you that you need to control it. If you don't try then I don't know what you'll do."

"Try?" Alex was immediately furious again. "You think I'd want to see this hellish side of me again!? I cannot and I will not unleash it!" Even as he spoke his eyes shone brightly again, like true emeralds. Thomas took a step backwards before Alex calmed down. "You see? I don't mean to do it, I really don't..." Alex pleaded.

Thomas continued to walk backwards towards his house, he was clearly uncertain as how to respond to Alex's behaviour. "If I were you Alex, I'd let your powers out a little bit each day. Hopefully that way you won't try and hurt anyone."

Alex tried to call after his friend but Thomas retreated back inside his house. The entire day for him had been an utter shambles from start to finish and so he decided to go home and hope that the next day would be better, or at least not as bad. He failed to see how anything could be as bad as threatening to maim your brother and intimidating your best friend into leaving.

He suddenly felt a sudden sense of anxiety as he began walking back. With a quick glance backwards though he knew that it was alright. Alex had been worried that people had seen his debacle with his loved ones. Luckily though everyone had either gone to bed or was busy watching television, the usual way to spend an evening in the developed world. If anyone had seen him though, he shuddered to think what the consequences might have been. Thomas accepted him for who he was, but that didn't mean everyone would.

When he walked through the front door he half expected to find a kind of twisted welcoming party awaiting him. His mother angry, his brother scared, and his sister disappointed. Yet everything seemed normal. His mother was sitting on the sofa with a glass of wine in her hand as she watched her favourite period drama. Abigail was likely asleep, she often went to bed early so that she didn't overload her brain. It was actually a self-imposed bedtime as Charlotte had never been one to force things upon her children, except family outings. Where his brother was though, he could not tell. He did not even want to ask. As far as he was concerned Steven deserved some time to himself to contemplate before Alex made his apology.

Familiarly he trudged up the stairs and into his room. Using his abilities had made him unbelievably tired. He could not even take his clothes off before his cumbersome head fell onto his soft pillow and his eyes fluttered shut, sending him into a deep and well needed sleep. As he began to dream though he wished he had never gone to bed.

His powers were the core element of his dream. The world around him didn't make sense, everything was as it should be but without certain details. He could not focus on any of it, it was all simply background. In his foreground he was experiencing an awful sense of familiarity as, in a reverse of the events of his school day, he held up Arthur against a wall. With a flash of his eyes he caused their surroundings to collapse as his bully screamed in terror, but it was not his scream. It was Steven's scream. Alex hated everything that he was seeing, it was an appalling nightmare that reminded him of exactly why he despised his abilities. Yet as he wielded them, and the power flowed within him, elation overtook hesitance.

In the background a small bridge was being formed out of nothing. A man was walking across it with a wide smile on his face, the rest of his features being hidden by a traditional style top-hat. Roles changed once more as the shade of Arthur faded away and Alex was the one with a sense of mortal terror as he realised who the man was.

He awoke with a blanket of sweat over him, and yet he was freezing cold. The image of that face, the last thing in his dream, was still haunting him. The image of that man that he so desperately wanted to forget. The image of Magnus.

Chapter 6

By all accounts he should be nervous. Everyone else seemed to be, and he supposed that he looked it as well from the outside. Inside though he was feeling a very different emotion than that of nervousness. He was feeling fear. The kind of icy dread that kept you frozen in place until you were swallowed whole by irrationality. Alex knew it was just that, it was irrational, but he couldn't help being petrified all the same. Every corner of his mind had been penetrated by the idea of Magnus Malum. That hollow figure that had approached him in his dream, he knew it to be that man. All he had done was smile and yet, even in that pure gesture, there was an unmistakable malice.

The events of the previous day had not pleased him either, but he could not bring himself to think upon them again. The memories were too fresh, and too painful. The other contestants in the talent show were busying themselves. Each one preparing in their own way. The singers were testing their voices, for no imperfections in tone could be allowed, especially when Simon Gartland was there to bring pride back to his master. The dancers were limbering up so that they could perform everything they needed to. Actors were practising their lines, even though they had a member who was designated as a prompter. There was even one comedian who was reacting as if the crowd were bantering with him. Alex thought they all looked too serious, as if they were trying it for a show, he saw it only as an opportunity for an interesting trip; obviously he had been practicing though. The school was actually allowed to pick three winners and so Alex had no idea why everyone was getting so worked up about it. Stage fright he guessed, something he had never suffered with.

They had been allowed to take the day off from their lessons, which Alex had been very thankful as it would have been an Arthur-filled day. Others had used the time to practice but all Alex had done was contemplate over what his dreams meant.

Those who had already gone were milling around the backstage expectantly, hoping that they had done enough to secure their victory. There was little to sit on, as the entire backstage seemed to be taken up with endless clutter from previous school performances that Henbane had simply neglected, and so they walked about around him. The incessant tapping of shoes upon the ground, the whittling and the whining, it was all driving Alex insane. He could not understand their extreme emotions. There was no point in getting worked up about something that had not happened. He could perfectly comprehend being upset afterwards, but to him it was just another reason why human nature was failing their species. There was no need for it. A gazelle doesn't get anxious about being eaten by a lion before it sees one. At least that was how he saw it.

A roar from the crowd erupted as one of the singing groups took a bow before leaving the stage, they were clearly favourites. Alex knew both members of the group and he could completely understand why they had done so well. The show was being judged on crowd reactions, and then decided by a panel of four teachers. These two, a boy who was known for being an improvised rapper and openly a part of Arthur's circle, Simon, and a girl who was innocent enough and had an amazing harmonious voice, would have the support of the school. He knew which one he preferred. Yet it was only because they had the backing of Arthur, who was undoubtedly the pupil that nobody went against, that their victory was assured. Even Alex's stand against him had not been enough to shake his tyrannical grip over

Henbane. Everyone, from the year sevens all the way through to the sixth-formers, obeyed his whim or stood well clear of him. Alex was the only one who dared to challenge him, and that was why Arthur hated him.

Act after act progressed and each time Alex had to wait before he could show the school his tricks. He was quite proud of them, having worked on several more than he had currently shown to anyone, and so was keen to show off. In truth he just wanted something to take his mind off of the horrible acts that he had committed the night before. No matter how hard he tried he could not forget without a distraction, regardless of how much he wanted to. As with all clouds there was light beyond it though as he no longer felt the incredible urge to utilise his abilities. The itching sensation had subsided. For the moment.

Alex looked across the narrow corridor where he was sitting and saw someone he had not expected to see. His friend Maxwell King, whom he had known just as long as he had Thomas, was sitting with his hands buried in his head. His legs were jolting with nerves and he was clearly distressed about his performance, which was obviously still to come. Alex hadn't really spoken to Max in years, he was one of these forced childhood friendships, the kind where your parents are friends and so you have to be with their children. Their parents had met when they were in nursery together, after Max had taken Alex's tricycle, and were still good friends, albeit if they fought quite often, and so he still saw Max a lot. The older they had gotten though the further they had grown apart, for they had nothing in common. Max was like Alex's antithesis. For the sake of his childhood though he felt the need to try and converse with him, to help him calm himself before he did his act. Thus, with a slight spring in his step, Alex walked over to him and sat on the floor beside him, despite the thick layer of dust that was upon it.

"You alright, Max?" He spoke with uncertainty in his voice.

Max was confused at first. He knew that they did not really connect anymore, but still he seemed relieved that he had someone to blurt out his worries to. "Just a bit nervous I suppose. Never really done anything like this before. You?" He replied with an indifferent expression.

"I am actually. I kind of need other people for my act so I'm used to seeing people react to it." He shrugged.

"I know, I saw what happened yesterday with Arthur."

Alex felt his back crawl. He hadn't really spoken to anyone from school since the incident. He expected it to be okay, as if everyone would've forgotten and moved on with their lives. Alex mentally slapped himself for his stupidity. Out of curiosity he swivelled his head around to look at everyone else who was still backstage. No-one would look him in the eye, yet as soon as he looked away they all stared at him. One of his worst fears was coming to life, they had glimpsed his real self and had made him an outcast. Even Max seemed reluctant to talk to him, like he was some kind of social pariah. Like the leper, Alex was now something to be despised. Max turned back to look at him.

"You've never been quite right. I was always aware that you weren't like the rest of us. You're like a mutation." He spoke coldly.

Alex did not have time to respond as Max was called to the stage. Despite what his old friend had said to him he wanted to end their conversation with the moral high-ground and so called after Max as he walked away. "Good luck Magnus." He shouted.

Max just looked at him strangely, as though he had just insulted his family, before storming off towards the stage with a greatly worsened mood. Alex laughed to himself, at least Max wasn't nervous anymore. Then he realised what he had said to him, he had called him Magnus. Thoughts of that insidious snake came flowing back into his head and suddenly, from nothing, Alex was reliving his dream again. The calculated walk Magnus made as he approached Alex when he was tormenting Arthur; his hideous smile sitting gleefully upon his face like some kind of painful contortion for him. Alex's mind conjured up a similar walk that Alex had done earlier that night as his brother had struggled to run away from him in fear, just as Alex had tried to do from Magnus. They were eerily similar. Alex did psychology though, he knew that the mind used experiences to create dreams and so concluded that that must have been what happened. The Magnus in his dreams was not real, he could not have been real. He was just a reflection of the darker side of Alex's personality. He had locked that portion of his being away, and in doing so hoped to banish all thought of Magnus from his mind.

Alex closed his eyes to banish the revenants from his mind, to cleanse himself from all of his deviousness. His mind slipped into a kind of tranquil state, like it had rebooted itself just as a computer would, and gradually the thoughts began to fade as he focused on the girl singer from the earlier groups. Verity. Alex could not say that he was infatuated with her, for he believed that you could never be sure and that was part of the beauty of it. Yet as he imagined her long and dark brown hair cushioned against his chest he could not help but feel happy. Her naturally green eyes, a different shade to Alex's, looked up at him lovingly and she smiled. It was all he wanted in life. He was alone, having never had a proper girlfriend of any kind, and wanted that to change more than anything. Whether that was with Verity or someone else, he did not care. For the moment though, he wanted her. He had not had time to think about her since before his obsession with Magnus but her effect on him was obvious. As he opened his eyes again he felt serenity and calmness, until he saw who was now stood before him.

"Hi Alex." Thomas said in a low voice, he was obviously still wary of being confronted by Alex again.

Alex was glad to see his best friend, he needed to explain things to him. "Thomas…" He began. "I am so sorry for how I acted last night, I-" He was cut off as Thomas raised a hand to gesture for silence.

Thomas simply looked at him, a kind of interrogation through the eyes. When he determined that Alex had genuinely not meant it he gave his friend a hearty smack on the back to indicate that all was forgiven. Alex smiled with relief, a smile that was shared with his best friend. He had convinced himself that Thomas, most likely like Steven, would never have forgiven him. He had acted in a disgraceful manner that he was deeply ashamed of, and yet he had received forgiveness. Now he only needed redemption.

"You did scare me a bit though I must admit." Thomas said with a titter.

"How do you mean?" Alex responded, his smile slowly decaying.

"Well, I saw what you did to your brother through my window…I was kind of worried that you might do the same to me." Thomas said seriously.

"Thomas, you are my best friend-" He answered as he was cut off again.

"And Steven is your brother…"

"I know, but I promise that you will never see that side of me again." Alex said with an attempt to lighten the mood again with another smile.

Thomas smiled also, his usual joviality returning to him as his cheeks filled with colour again. "So does that mean you'll use your powers every once in a while?"

"It means I'll find ways of controlling it more effectively." He replied.

"Yeah, that's what I said." Thomas retorted with a bellowing laugh.

The thoughts of Verity and the conversation with his best friend had made all of his problems disappear before him. Now he was focused and ready for the show. He wanted that trip to the museum and nothing was going to stand in his way. He was determined. Alex gave his friend a firm handshake as his name was called out by the four teachers who acted as a kind of panel for the contestants. Thomas trotted out through the back door as Alex steeled himself one last time before moving towards the stage. He suddenly felt nervous. Each step began to weigh a tonne and the room span around inside of his head. Gently, he placed his hand against the wall to steady himself, catching a piece of his blue collared shirt on a loose nail. As he moved away he heard a tear and felt a draft as a section of his shirt was left hanging on the wall. Silently he cursed to himself, but there was no time to get changed and no time to reconsider as he was the last act. What a wonderful start, he thought to himself as he felt his anger rise inside of him.

His name was called out once more and he stumbled onto the stage, blinded by the light as he stood in the centre with a hole in his shirt on the left side of his midriff. As his eyes adjusted he could see the plethora of people that were seated and ready to see his performance. They seemed ready to inflict hate upon him, as if they had been trained to despise him by someone. By Arthur most likely. Just as he thought of his tormentor he saw a hand raise itself in the front row. Alex looked down to focus in on the subject and saw that it was indeed Arthur. He was smiling maliciously as he held up his other hand to reveal a bag of tomatoes. They had not been opened and so clearly he had been saving them for Alex, regardless of whether or not he had liked or disliked any of the previous acts. Alex was at least thankful for the fact that there were teachers present, hopefully they would try to stop Arthur should he assault him with his vegetables.

He was familiar with all four teachers on the panel. Two of them were not his teachers but they were aware of who he was, as he was quite well regarded amongst the teachers, and the deputy headmistress herself who was seated at the judging table. That was one of the reasons why Arthur despised him so much, because he actually cared about his future enough to ask questions about what they were learning. The other two were his Psychology and History teachers respectively. He had no idea why any of the teachers other than Mr Barnes were on the panel, since he was a history teacher and the prize was essentially a history fieldtrip, but he did not complain as they all gave him a knowing smile before asking him to begin his act.

The crowd sniggered at him at first as they spotted the large hole in his shirt. Alex did his best to shake it off though as he started with his easiest trick, although he knew them all off by heart and so considered each one to be easy, so the audience could be gradually led in to his more convoluted illusions. It went down well. He had taken a member of the audience, a small year seven boy, as his participant and had rewarded him with a sweet for his assistance. That had done him wonders with the crowd and had completely quelled any who still saw him as some kind of master manipulator, much to Arthur's disgust.

There was no time to waste as he hastily reshuffled, which was in itself something to behold in the minds of the audience, and set up his next trick. He only had fifteen minutes in total and so had budgeted for five tricks in all, methodologically allotting three minutes for each one. That gave him one-hundred and eighty seconds to shuffle, set-up, find a participant and perform the magic. It was tricky, he laughed to himself, but Alex had always been a very scheduled person and so knew that he could do it.

His second and third illusions went down wonderfully, with each being lapped up by the audience as they asked for more. Alex felt much like Pavlov, whom he had learnt about through his psychology lessons, for every time he revealed his finished work the crowd would salivate with joy and hunger for more. People were actually wanting to be picked by him as, with each phase of his act, he called for a new assistant. Arthur seemed to be getting more heated with each trick. He knew that he could not unleash his tomatoes onto Alex with the crowd so firmly on his side as he would risk losing his vice-like grip on the minds of the pupils. Alex watched his bully as he sat in the front row fidgeting, he was clearly struggling to hold in his anger. No doubt he wanted nothing more than to seek revenge for his damaged hand, which Alex could see had some protective gauze around it. Arthur just needed the audience to turn on him.

His fourth trick worried him though. It was the one that he had performed only a day earlier in the sixth-form common room. The upper years would react in one of two ways. Either they would be elated to see that display of magic once more, or they would be wrathful at Alex re-using material that they had already seen. A thought occurred to him though that might help him avoid the dilemma he was in. As he shuffled his cards once more he pointed to the teachers' panel and beckoned for one of them to join him on the stage. They refused at first, believing it to be most irregular and possibly unfair on the other contestants. However, Mr Barnes, always keen to help out, rewarded Alex for his ingenuity in recruiting the teachers by lifting himself from his chair and sauntering onto the stage.

The crowd was waiting on him with tenterhooks, eager to see what Alex would do next. He hoped he would not disappoint them as he asked his history teacher to pick a card from the deck. When his card had been selected Alex picked one of his own and showed both of them to the crowd before placing Mr Barnes' hands on top of each other. Upon hearing a heckle from one of his peers he stepped to the side to address the crowd. His anger was beginning to rise again.

"I understand that some of you may have seen this before, only yesterday in fact, but this is for the benefit of those that haven't." He spoke clearly.

Arthur used this as his opportunity, calling out in a strained voice to mask his identity. "Boring! We want to see some new stuff!" He called out.

Instantly the crowd turned on him. They were distraught at the possibility of not being the first people to have seen this trick. They demanded something new from him for their time and patience. The teachers tried to subdue the crowd, yelling at them to be quiet and respectful. Evidently though it was not going to work as the crowd became increasingly hostile. Alex turned to Mr Barnes and shrugged as he had no clue on how to proceed in such a situation, but neither did his history teacher as he returned the gesture. Behind them the cacophony of howls, an ever growing din of displeasure, continued to assault his eardrums. Alex could definitely feel something within him stirring once more.

He turned back to face the crowd, his expressions determined as he attempted to get the crowd back on his side by performing very simple shuffling tricks. He threw the cards up in the air and caught them all in a kind of rainbow arch, pulling them back into place. The pupils did not care though as they ensued to shower abuse directly at him this time. That familiar itch crept back into his mind. Alex turned just at the wrong moment as Arthur threw a tomato at his face, and it succeeded in finding its target. Like a military coup, Arthur had taken control and was laughing heartily to himself amongst his friends as he passed each of them a handful of tomatoes to use against their victim. Alex was livid though, his blood felt like it was being placed directly on a hob as it boiled inside of him. Arthur couldn't let him have one day, not even one! Alex shouted internally, why did that scum have to ruin everything that brought some kind of solace to his increasingly dreary life?

Arthur and his crew stood up, tomatoes in hand, and flung them as hard as they could in Alex's direction. The teachers were powerless to stop them, simply shouting to try and convince them to cease fire, but Alex was not. Alex was prepared. With incredible ease he stopped the tomatoes in mid-air, no more than a foot or two before him, and held them in place. His anger was beginning to take over him until he heard the roar of approval from the crowd. Somehow he had gotten them back on his side, with them believing that his use of his abilities was just another parlour trick. Alex suddenly felt control flow back into his veins as he began to circle the tomatoes above of his head. The crowd went insane as he did so, their puny minds unable to comprehend what was happening.

Arthur turned on the crowd now, hailing abuse at them left right and centre. He had lost his hold upon them, never to regain it again. Alex allowed himself to laugh as he continued to manipulate the vegetable above him. His mind had been opened to a whole new world of possibilities where he could control his powers and use them for good. No more did he have to be ashamed of what he was. If he could control himself then there was no need to be afraid of what he was capable of. It was only in anger when he was most dangerous and so Alex vowed silently to himself, there upon the stage with the crowd firmly in the palm of his hand, never to bottle up his rage so much again. He did not consider himself to be an innately angry person, although he knew that he had a short enough temper, and so considered the task an easy one.

He continued to twirl the tomatoes about, sending them in and around the crowd, until his time wore out. The pupils were particularly overjoyed when he squeezed one of the tomatoes over the head of the sulking Arthur. The bully had truly lost every sniff of power that he once held and so stormed from the hall with his comrades in tow like loyal sheep to their shepherd. He slammed the door so violently that the glass within it cracked. No-one seemed to notice though as they applauded Alex for his abilities. Every single one of them, from the smallest year seven to the oldest year thirteen, stood from their chairs and gave him a rousing ovation the likes of which he had never thought possible in his wildest dreams. The school seemed much brighter for it.

Before he had seen Henbane as a mundane and functional establishment. It did what it was supposed to with no flare or colour added in. Yet now he could see the beauty behind it. The sprawl of blackthorn across the surface of the school, which had seemed to him to be nothing more than an infestation, now looked purposeful. The smattering of tall grey buildings had lost their attached miasma. No longer were they monotonous and dull, bringing the personality of the school, and those within, down. As he glanced at the school symbol and its grey backing he realised that the buildings represented uniformity, a cohesion within the school that brought all within it together. With Arthur's tyrannical regime over it had become clear to everyone that they could all now rejoice in their homogeneousness.

The crowd continued to cheer and clap for him for well over a minute, almost moving Alex to tears as he bowed appropriately and laughed and smiled with the rest of them. Just as their enthusiasm began to die down he watched Thomas, who was standing at the very back of the hall, run forward and up onto the stage. With great fervour he lifted Alex's hand into the air and roared, thus generating a second wave of applause which was no less impressive than the first. Thomas leant in to him as the crowd showered support and praise down upon him.

"I told you so." He said with a smile.

Alex did not need to respond as he laughed with such genuine joy. He had not felt this elated in a long time, not since before sixth-form when Arthur had been contented to stare at him malevolently from a distance. He wanted to enjoy every single moment of this, for he had no clue when he might get to experience such a moment again.

The teachers, who had also been cheering their pupil, restored order and the four panellists joined him on stage, although Mr Barnes was already there. All of the other contestants flowed forth from backstage, each with either a face of joy or terror, and created a crescent so that they could all be seen. One final round of applause greeted them all before the teachers got to the matter at hand.

"Well, what a wonderful talent show that was." His deputy headmistress began. She was a terrifying figure of authority, yet she also knew how to be subtle and how to adapt for the occasion. She beamed a smile at all of the contestants before she continued. "However there can only be three winners I'm afraid, and now it's time to announce them! Panellists…" She said as she turned towards the four allotted teachers. "Over to you."

"Well, in all honesty this was a very difficult choice, although there was one clear winner." Mr Barnes spoke, as he had clearly been designated as the orator for the teachers, which was understandable given his tendency to waffle on.

"Firstly…Maxwell King for his inventive and insightful recitation of his own poem."

Max stepped forward from the crowd to a small applause, most likely from his group of friends before standing to the side to indicate that he was a winner. Briefly he looked over to Alex and gave him a wink to show that he had not meant what he had said to him before. No doubt he would explain it as being manipulated by the cruel influences of Arthur, but that did not matter to Alex as it was always useful to have another friend, especially such a long-term one as Max.

"Secondly…" Mr Barnes continued with his booming voice. "Simon Gartland and Verity Lane."

The pair stepped forward with a much greater applause this time. Alex had expected Verity to do well and so was pleased to see that her talents had been recognised. He was less thrilled about Simon going on the trip and even more annoyed when he held her hand in his and raised their arms into the air. It was only a gesture of victory, Alex knew that, but that did not stop his jealousy rising. Barring any incidents, he told himself that the tomorrow was the day to ask her on a date, although he wasn't sure if being surrounded by war items was perhaps the right setting to do it in. With their applause finished, the pair stood by Max's side as they waited for the announcement of the final person to be joining them on the trip to the Imperial War Museum in London.

"And finally, I think we all know who the third winner is….Alex Manningley!" He shouted one last time as he pointed towards him with a broad smile.

Everyone erupted into a frenzy of cheers once more. Alex even thought he saw Verity smile and blush as he stole a glance in her direction. Thomas embraced him in a hug, possibly genuinely or possibly because he knew that each winner was allowed to take one person with them, to the symphony of blissful praise around them. Alex had done it, he had won, and, for once, he was happy.

Chapter 7

For the entire walk back home he had been in a complete haze of happiness, unable to focus on anything around him other than his own elation. Thomas had been jabbering to himself for the entirety of the journey as Alex relived the glory that he had experienced earlier in the day. It was all still fresh. The huge applause and cheers offered by the crowds. The disgusted face that Arthur pulled as he realised he had lost his was war. Most of all though his joviality came as he now knew what to do about his issues with his abilities, no-one else would get hurt because of him. Everything was finally favouring him and he could look forward to life again.

Even his senses seemed heightened in his state of joyousness. The trees had become sharper, each individual leaf seemed to possess its own distinct patterns, all as aesthetically pleasing as the next. The birds chirped happily in each piece of foliage, their sweet songs were literally music to his ears as he allowed them to tweet harmonious melodies towards him. Even the acrid stench of humanity was uplifting his nostrils as he walked by. An old lady was cooking dinner for her husband and the wondrous aroma of baking pastry permeated his nose like a euphoric miasma. Thomas finally noticed his entranced state as he stopped talking and poked Alex hard in the chest. He did not mind though as he turned towards his friend with a raised eyebrow and smile.

"What's up?" He asked Thomas.

Thomas laughed a little. "You haven't been listening at all have you?"

"Not really." Alex responded with a laugh of his own.

"Well, I was saying why don't you use your powers more often now? We've seen that they don't have to be associated with bad stuff, even if they have been before."

"Thomas…" He began.

"I know what you're going to say…" Thomas spoke, interrupting Alex before impersonating him as best he could. "Oh, I don't ever want to use my amazing powers…" Thomas said in a depressed voice to mimic his best friend. "If I were you Alex I'd use my powers as often as I could."

Alex laughed some more at his friend's terrible impression, although it could've been described as quite accurate. "I know you would Thomas, but you're not me. You have no idea of the responsibilities that come with my gift."

"Enlighten me then." Thomas said coldly.

Alex turned to look at his best friend with an inquisitive eye. Normally he was the one who brought the mood down as Thomas was often one of the cheeriest people he knew. "Tom, I know you're jealous but-"

"Jealous?" Thomas laughed sardonically. "Of course I am!" He shouted. "I would give anything to be you Alex. You're courageous because you know nothing can hurt you! Whereas me…" He looked away in shame. "I'm just a coward."

Alex tried to reassure his best friend. "No, Tom, you're just not a fighter."

"When Arthur had you up against that wall…any normal person would've helped. Yet he ordered me to stay back and I did! Like some housetrained mongrel! I'm craven Alex…so of course I'm jealous. If I had your gifts things would be different." Thomas concluded with a venomous hiss.

Alex had not seen this darker side to his chum before. He still knew exactly what to say though. "That fire Tom, I've never seen that before. I let mine show…you're stronger than I could ever be."

Thomas turned back towards him, his tear-filled eyes showing remorse. With a single sleeve he wiped away his sorrow and smiled at his friend once more. "You are kind Alex, despite everything." They both laughed again. "Perhaps one day I will have a chance to prove my worth."

"Knowing you, you'll probably get yourself killed." Alex responded with a smile.

Heartily they both laughed and comforted one another. It was strange for he and Thomas rarely fought. Even when they did, as he could clearly prove, it did not last long. With their friendship renewed they continued the final leg of their journey back home in a contemplative silence before parting ways. Even though it was a Friday he would still see his best friend the next day, as he had chosen Thomas to accompany him to the Imperial War Museum in London. Thomas had leapt at the opportunity, even though he surely knew that Alex was going to take him anyway.

Alex walked up the small steps at the front of his garden, taking a moment to stare lovingly towards the headstone of his old best friend, and placed his keys in the lock. Before he could even turn them the door flung open and his mother embraced him in a loving hug. His sister looked on with a proud smile also. Steven did not look so pleased as he scarcely looked up from the television. He had seemingly calmed down since the incident, but that didn't mean that he had forgiven Alex.

"Oh Alex!" Charlotte said as she kissed him on the cheek, much to her son's embarrassment. "Your father would be so proud!" She said as she kissed him once more.

"Mum…" Alex blushed with a smile. "It was only a talent contest."

"Exactly!" She replied just as enthusiastically.

"How did you even find out?" Alex asked, seeing as both Steven and Abigail went to a different, considerably better, school.

"Apparently Abi has a friend at Henbane and she texted her." Charlotte explained.

"How did she know it was me though?"

"I guess you're just famous now Alex!" His mother exclaimed with the same unwavering support. "Now, to celebrate my son being so special we're going to have a cheat night."

Alex heard Steven scoff at the idea that his brother was unique. "So no foliage with my dinner tonight?" He joked with a merry smile.

"Nope, we can have anything you want." Charlotte said as she beamed at him. She was clearly eager to forget about her diet for one night.

"I really fancy a nice curry?" He suggested. "If that's alright with everyone else?"

Steven barely twitched, a sign of his assent. Charlotte nodded fervently. Abigail looked up, for once she was actually paying attention to the television and not a book.

"Did you know that originally the sauce in curries was used to mask the fact that the meat was rotten?" She spoke with gumption.

"Well thanks for that Abi…" Alex replied as he laughed along with the rest of his family, barring his brother.

They waited anxiously for their meal to arrive. Since they rarely ordered takeaways, unless Charles was back, the wait seemed to take an age. The tension between himself and Steven was palpable as they vaguely stared at each other, not willing to focus their entire attentions on one another. Eventually though their food arrived and they took to it as if they had not been feed for days, eager to devour every last morsel as if would somehow slip away from them if they did not eat it quickly enough, like fish to bait.

Alex lifted the lid from the metal tub containing his tikka masala. He took a moment to inhale the wondrous aromas that it conjured up. The bubbling sauce offered to him its light spice and carefully balanced flavours and he could not wait to tuck in to it. Many would consider him boring for such a typical sample of 'Indian' cuisine, even though it was created by the British, but he loved the simplicity of its design. Unlike other foods it was not so hot that he was likely to pass out whilst eating it, yet at the same time it left a slight zing in his mouth that made his savour every bit. When accompanied by his rice and other sundries it became the perfect meal when laziness and elation are at their peak.

His sister picked at her dinner daintily, like a true educated lady would, despite her evident want to shovel into her mouth as quickly as she could. Steven did exactly that as he relentlessly assaulted his food until it had disappeared. He made no attempts at communication with his family throughout, choosing to ignore all of them and focus on obliterating every smidgeon of his lamb bhuna. When he had finished he went and sat back down on the sofa, content with his contempt. His mother had taken a more tactile approach, mediating somewhere in between her children as she made vague attempts at conversation between mouthfuls.

When everything had been finished, and leftovers had been wrapped up for use the next day, they packed everything away and bundled the dirty crockery into the kitchen. Alex volunteered to do the washing and so filled the sink up with a mixture of hot water and washing-up liquid before dealing with the cups, then the cutlery, and then the plates. When all of it had been cleaned he went to grab the tea-towel that was held against the side of the sink unit by a bar. As he moved his hand across he heard his mother enter the kitchen, the sound of her slippers scuffing against the tiled floor being a blatant giveaway, and turned around to see what she wanted.

"Yes mum?" He asked politely.

"I just wanted to say how proud of you I am." She replied emotionally.

"Thanks…" He responded with an awkward smile.

"I know I don't pay you much attention, and I'm sorry for that. You've always been so independent though, I guess I always thought you didn't need me." Charlotte continued as her eyes began to well up with tears.

Alex drew her into a close hug to comfort her. "It's okay mum…I know you don't mean to, and I always have Dad since your busy with Steven and….well, just Steven actually." Alex retorted with a laugh.

He gave his mother a kiss on the forehead and retired into the living room. His brother was busy sitting in front of the television, as per usual, with his mobile phone in his hand and his eyes lazily listing between the two screens. Alex stared at his brother for a while, trying to judge his mood. Of course he still felt guilty for what he had done to Steven only the night before, but he had wanted his entire family to enjoy the evening, and that included his brother. Steven eventually focused his gaze on Alex. His eyes, full of a mixture of malice; fear; and false manliness as he tried to remain unintimidated by his brother, fixed unwaveringly upon him.

"You…" Steven said emotionlessly. "I don't know what you are…but you're different. You're not one of us, and you're not a part of this family…". He continued before getting up from the sofa and flinging a brown envelope towards his brother.

Alex had been hurt by his brother's words. He knew that he had affected his brother in a bad way through his accidental wrongdoings, but he had not expected such a genuine display of venomous animosity. There had been no emotion in his words, and that made it all the worse. He was not saying what he said to cause Alex emotional torment, he was saying it because he genuinely believed what he spoke. Steven had witnessed Alex's abilities first hand and now he knew Alex was not like the rest of them.

Alex looked at the letter sitting in his lap and saw that the writing on the front was his father's. He did not open it straight away like he would any other time, especially since

Steven tore up the last one his father sent only the day before. Fortunately Charles sometimes sent two copies of each letter, if they were important, and left one with their local post-office depot, since he knew how petty his youngest son could be in certain circumstances. Evidently his mother had gone to pick it up and left it on the small coffee table in front of their sofa, which had obviously been why Steven had been able to get his grubby hands on it. Alex was intrigued though as to why he had not torn the letter up just as he had before. Perhaps it was because he knew that when he had ripped apart the letter he was wrong in doing so. Although Alex suspected that the real reason was that he didn't want to see his brother's dark side again, something which Alex could very well understand.

His heavy heart still burdened him over his actions. In an attempt to comfort himself he flicked his wrist towards him to gently rub the glass surface of his watch. It gave him solace, and helped him remember better times. Charles had always been the kind of man who relished sayings and he remembered yet another one of his father's as he stared at the moving hands of the watch, and the mechanisms underneath which powered them.

"As long as this works, you'll be safe. As long as it works, I will come back to you. Time is key, it is the answer to many riddles. Hold it close, and keep it safe."

Time is key. Alex kept that thought with him as he motioned to open his father's letter. Before he could though he felt a familiar presence behind him. She was like a fairy in the shadows, ever watching over him and guiding him towards the light. Abigail seemed to have a kind of sixth sense about her as she always knew when he needed her comforting words. An old head on young shoulders; which was how Alex had always seen his sister. Despite her youth she could always offer words of wisdom and heart. Daintily she glided over to him and planted herself on the arm of the sofa, looking lovingly into his green eyes.

"You know, being different isn't always a bad thing." She said with a smile before she bounded off towards the bathroom, or so he assumed since it was still relatively early.

It was a very simple piece of advice, yet it still worked perfectly on Alex as he smiled at his sister's immeasurable astuteness. She always knew exactly what to say to cheer him up, much like a gifted clairvoyant. He did not even need to consider her words as he was aware of how correct she was. Alex had been different all his life, not just because of his abilities. For some reason he had only recently begun to let his obscurity bother him. It was mostly Arthur's fault for isolating him so obviously, and so publicly in front of people he considered to be his friends. A small part of him still blamed himself for allowing such low-brow comments to upset him. None of that mattered anymore though, for he had won his skirmish with the bully and he was now one of the most popular pupils at Henbane. How long it would last though, he could not tell.

With his mood improved, once again by the magical guile of his sister, he tore open the tip of the envelope to read his father's letter. The paper was of a much worse quality than the ones he used to send to his father, but he could not blame him for that since he was in a war zone, and since Steven had ripped up the better quality piece. Each marking on the paper was very distinct, almost un-joined, giving the letter a typed looked despite the fact it was very clearly hand written. Alex read through the contents carefully, wanting to absorb every detail of what Charles had to say. It was not quite so important as it had been the day before though, since Arthur had been largely dealt with. Nonetheless his father offered some useful advice on how to deal with the bully should he continue having issues with him, but Alex did not suspect that he would.

Further into the letter, as his father began to discuss his own issues, Alex began to feel a familiar insidiousness as the image of Magnus reappeared in his mind. Charles had found something, a strange piece of metal that had almost led to his own men killing him for no good reason. Alex breathed a sigh of relief when he read that his father had locked away the object to keep himself and others from harm. That relief did not last long though as he read the final paragraph that his father had made before ending the letter. He had been seeing a strange face in his dreams.

It was strange. Charles had been seeing an ominous man in his dreams for several nights, a situation that was eerily similar to Alex's own. He remembered seeing Magnus' face the night before, only for a brief moment, yet it had terrified him all the same. From what his father was saying though he had seen this strange face for several days, and for most of his dream on each night. Thus Alex decided that the man in Charles' dreams could not be Magnus; but it was still odd.

It was nice of his father to share such intimate details of his life with Alex. That was why he loved receiving letters from him as he got to see a side of Charles that neither of his siblings had experienced. Letters were personal, and within them emotion was displayed within every word. Only lies are spoken, his father had once told him. Everyone had some kind of façade to maintain that coloured their words accordingly. It was truly a rare thing to find someone who actually displayed what they felt, Alex could not claim that he was so brutally honest and nor could anyone he knew. Perhaps it was only those who joined the services, having any insubordination or lies straightened out of them, who were able to be so objective.

Alex decided to think no further on the matter and so went up to his room to retire for the evening. It was still early, but he felt a sudden heaviness in his eyes that almost bade him to go to sleep, like it wasn't entirely his choice. He made no attempts to argue as he shouted goodnight to his mother and sister, both still keenly awake, and dragged himself up the stairs and into his room.

Before collapsing into his bed he undressed himself and stared down at the hole in his shirt. He remembered the anger that he had felt in that moment, and yet he had been able to stop himself from using his gifts. It made him feel even more hopeful knowing that he did have the willpower and mental stability necessary to stop himself if he needed to. The thought worried him also, as that would mean that he actually meant to use his powers upon his brother the night before. Or perhaps it was his subconscious, he considered to himself, which stopped him using his abilities in anger in front of every pupil of the school, and thus exposing himself to them. Every single one of them had been enamoured with his gift, probably thinking it nothing more than a complicated illusion. Part of Alex wanted it to stay that way, but now that he had seen he could be adored because of his powers the rest of him wanted to display himself further. He knew he could not though and so retired into his bed.

It had been a long time since he had been able to fall asleep quite so quickly without having to have brief insomnia over his issues with Arthur, and more recently Magnus as well. It had been a very good day for him though and his brain seemed to congratulate him as well by allowing him to quickly slip into a deep and blissful slumber. Until he began dreaming.

It was almost the same dream as the night before. Arthur was slowly crawling away from Alex in fear, his face etched with terror. The bitter stench of urine filled Alex's nostrils as he continued walking towards his prey with his eyes glowing intensely. The wisps of green flare coming from his eyes had their own power as they touched the imagined world around him and sent objects flying into the void and out of his dream. They were in his history classroom. Books and what few posters that remained cracked and ripped apart as they were embroiled by just the periphery of his powers.

Arthur, whimpering as he tried to find a way out of the classroom, desperately managing to grab hold of the door handle. Alex did not allow him to open it though as he evaporated the handle with his mind. The bully utilised his physical superiority by smashing through the dreamed door and into the corridor of Henbane. This is sport, Alex thought to himself as he glided out of the classroom and after his target. When he reached the corridor he could see Arthur standing at the end of it before he screamed in fear and tried to find the stairs that led to the lower level of the school. Alex had not done anything though so he had no idea why Arthur retreated from him so hastily.

A sudden tingling filled Alex as his body began to fill with horror, even in reality he began to sweat a cold perspiration that told of his fear. He ignored it, even though he knew what was behind him. It had been there before, and he had no intentions of seeing it again if he could help it. Thus he resumed his chase upon Arthur, who was now frantically running and vaulting down the stairs to try and reach the open spaces of the outside world. Alex followed. He lifted himself from the ground with his abilities, harnessing the breeze that was blowing in from a conveniently open window. He hovered above the balcony of the square staircase, looking down upon Arthur as he swore to himself. He allowed the wind to slip from beneath his feet and fell to the bottom of the stairs, gathering the breeze once more to cushion his landing as he stood in front of Arthur with glowering eyes.

He felt like Manningleyman, the superhero persona of his childhood. The world changed around him, as it always does in dreams, as his mind swapped from a supposed reality into a fixed memory. Alex and Thomas were playing happily in the park near their homes, pretending to fly as they swung as high as they could on the swings before jumping off. Alex, seemingly looking at himself, still remembering the short numbness in their legs as they landed back upon the ground. It was a time when there was no such things as sadness as every aspect of life was a new avenue to explore. Everything was one grand adventure. Even this happy memory was spoiled though as that feeling behind him of dread did not cease. He could almost feel breath upon his nape.

The world around him changed once more, back into the school scene as Alex regained control of his dream body. Arthur was smiling now, even in his dreams he could not help being arrogant. With a wide grin he opened the door to the main hall, where all assemblies, and performance such as the talent contest, were held. Deftly Alex chased after him and reached the room before the door could even close. This was not the hall that he was familiar with though.

It was like being in a horror film, and there was no sign of Arthur any longer. The hall was full of every single pupil, barely illuminated by the lack of lighting on the walls. They were all seated as they had been when he had won the talent contest, and they were staring at him now with inhuman smiles. Their eyes bulged to the greatest extent possible and their nostrils flared. It was harrowing to look upon. Thankfully, within a moment, they twisted their attention towards the stage and began rhythmically clapping as a lone figure stood at its centre. Alex's body, both in mind and physically, renewed its petrification. He stood rooted to the spot as he was gripped by the sudden realisation that he had not been hunting Arthur as his dream had supposed. Arthur had been the bait to lure Alex in.

The little light that was present in the room suddenly extinguished itself and Alex was left in complete and utter darkness. The never-ending abyss before him was like his very worst nightmare. Suddenly his antagonist appeared before him, no more than an inch away, and screamed at the top of his voice!

Alex awoke from his sleep with a scream of his own, alerting his still awake mother to his predicament. Quickly he assured her that he was fine and so she returned to her room. He was not fine though for he knew the face within his dream all too well, and it had not been just a split-second image this time as it had the time before. He had been stood behind Alex for the entirety of his dream, leading him into his trap so he could confront him. Magnus Malum.

Alex wasted no time as he turned on his computer and began composing an email. He knew that he had to explain everything to Charles and he could not wait for the postman to spend half a week delivering it. Arthur was not the issue any longer. Arthur was a pawn being utilised by the true mastermind behind Alex's miserable existence, Magnus. Alex had now convinced himself that Magnus was not dead, not if he held such power of the mind over someone living. Hastily Alex scribbled down everything he could about Magnus, and his company Malum Metal Industries, in the vague hope that his father would be able to use the information to help protect his son. When he finished he checked over every detail before sending it to his father and falling back into his bed just as the sun was beginning to rise. It was a new day.

Chapter 8

He was glad that the Colonel would be coming by to see him at the next inspection as the behaviour of his troops had not changed. Ever since they found that accursed artefact not a single one of his soldiers had been quite right. There had been times when they regained themselves, unable to comprehend that anything was wrong as they continued on like normal. Cassandra had been acting out of turn as well. Charles' theory that perhaps it was something in the water could still be held true, but then he did not understand why it had not affected him also. He could not deny that there were times when he was not himself, yet he was always able to maintain control of his body. The others though, they became like zombies, unable to assert any form of authority upon their own being. It troubled him deeply.

Not only that but since the chunk of metal had been recovered he had been having some very strange dreams. Every night for over a week, without fail, the same man had been standing in the background. It was almost as if he was observing Charles' dreams, trying to discern their meaning and significance. He did not consider it something to be deeply troubled over, as he was no stranger to nightmares; nevertheless it was still odd. Charles could not even truly consider them nightmares actually. The man never did anything. He never threatened Charles' life or crippled him with mental anguish, he simply just stood there. Night after night after night, just standing and watching.

He did not know whether or not he should talk to anyone higher than himself about the strangeness of what was occurring around him. It was almost as though a thick miasma was upon them all and Charles was the only one not inhaling the toxic fumes that permeated the cores of the others. There was no-one he could tell really, at least not within his own camp as everyone else seemed to be affected by it. They had not even been able to train properly or run basic field tests because the situation had been so precarious at times that Charles had not wanted to tempt the zombies into doing something unsavoury towards him. He still remembered, vividly, having private Wazid point a gun at him, especially since it had not been from afar, where his details could have been understandably mistaken for another's. The troops were still under armed guard for having threatened an officer.

Charles was just glad that the Colonel would be arriving soon so they could get everything sorted out. There would be no doubts about what would happen to those that threatened him as they would be dishonourably discharged without pay, and possibly with further punishment issued also. That still did not fill Charles with confidence though since the others were acting just as interdependently, and neither he nor the army as a whole could risk losing the amount of men he had under his command. So he had made the decision to be exceedingly careful until the Colonel and his reinforcements arrived, even if it meant losing some valuable time in the process.

Due to the odd complications of his situation Charles had been mostly filling out paperwork in his quarters for over four days straight. Obviously he had taken breaks here and there were he had gone round inspecting the squaddies to make sure they were doing what they were supposed to, and more often than not they were not. He even went to investigate the artefact once a day, just to make sure that it was still there. Still, he needed a break from the dull monotony that sat upon his desk. He felt like a hiker climbing Everest, with each piece of paper that he triumphed over another would take its place, and another after that and another one after that one. With a slight groan of exasperation, a sign that his days as a soldier really were coming to a close, he pulled himself from his chair and stretched out his cramped limbs. It was a wonderful feeling but he did not drag it out any longer than necessary as he pulled his boots on and laced them up before heading out into the open.

There was never much going on in their camp, since it was considered a fairly small military base, but as he stepped out Charles literally saw nothing. Nothing and no-one. Not a single man; woman; or child was in sight. Not one of the local children wanting to try and play with the soldiers, pretending to be one of them. Not one of the local envoys delivering food and drink to excuse the troops from their pitiful excuse for rations. That was a pleasant thought to Charles as his stomach rumbling in protest at not being fed for several hours. Since there appeared to be nothing for him to inspect, and Charles did not want to risk his life again by trying to root out his squads from whatever they were up to, he decided that he would go to the mess hall. Perhaps his troops would be there, he thought to himself.

The sun was at its zenith and its midday burn was scalding his body as it often did. For the first month or so that he had been stationed in Afghanistan he had been almost constantly sunburnt before his body adapted. Now he walked across the scorching sands with little discomfort, even the beads of sweat dribbling slowly down his back did not bother him as he had become so accustomed to feeling their presence. They were irritating, but there was nothing he could do about it and so he tried his best to carry on. The nights offered no relief either as bitter colds swept through their camp and chilled every single one of them to the bone, as was common in such intemperate countries.

As Charles continued his walk across the camp he could still not see a single person, it was as if the need for their presence had ceased overnight and he had been the only one to not know of it. He hoped that the cook would be in the mess hall at least. Even if it was only basic foodstuffs he still needed something to satisfy his deep-seated hunger. Charles did not like it though. If it was something to do with the strange behaviour of the soldiers then it had reached new levels of concern. It was only ever a few at a time who were affected, never the entirety of his unit. Perhaps it had something to do with the artefact, he thought aloud. Charles convinced himself that he was being ridiculous as there was no such thing as mind control. He supposed instead that something had happened that had peaked the interest of his troops and they would soon be back to how they were normally. Not that their recent behaviour could be considered normal.

Charles still did not see a single person as he made his way through into the loose structure that they called the mess hall. Unlike his own quarters this was an actual building, which they had repurposed for the use of supplying the British Army with serviceable food and satisfactory drink. It was slowly falling apart though. The concrete around the outside was old and parts of it had been chipped away, either from natural decay or from gunfire in the rare skirmishes that were centred in their area. The metal wires underneath, that held the shape of the material in place, were beginning to show themselves and allowed natural light to seep through into the otherwise gloomy and dreary mess hall. The one single window that sat at the far end of the structure shone light upon the kitchen area, thus keeping the food warm, at least, if it had been out for a while. Whilst it was probably a positive point Charles personally did not like it as it meant that any meat products would go off far quicker than they normally would otherwise, and he was a firm believer in not wasting anything since they cherished what precious little they received in the army.

Charles pushed open the flimsy door that led into the mess hall, which was normally open when somebody was inside it and so he already considered it a bad omen, and strode in. He was not quite sure what he had wanted to expect, but certainly something a bit more lively would have been preferred than the scene that greeted him. Not a single living soul could be seen besides one of the locals they had hired to help cook them some tasty meals with the ingredients they had. He was a middle-aged man, almost bald, with an untrimmed beard and a sinewy figure. Charles had not taken the time to get to know him personally but he had seen him around many times before. The man waved at Charles to come forward and so the Major smiled politely and stepped towards the small canteen area that served as their kitchen.

"Five minutes." The man said with a thick local accent, holding his hand just in case Charles had not quite understood him.

The Major suddenly felt his head become clouded and so he perched himself upon the nearest table and decided it would be best if he sat down as he waited for his food to be ready. Charles had no idea what was on the menu but he considered anything vaguely edible to be welcome. Since he had become acclimatised to the Afghani palate he knew that he would thoroughly enjoy whatever the man was cooking for him and his troops. Charles hoped that someone would join him soon, since it was just after midday and no doubt some of the patrols and squads would be retiring for lunch soon.

As he waited though he sat in solitude. Even the cook ignored him as finished preparing a tray of food for the soldiers. The minutes ticked by, each one agonisingly slow as he had nothing to occupy himself with. The only thing that gave him something to focus on was the far end of the building where a distinctive chunk of concrete was missing, exposing the metal wires underneath. He could recall how it happened almost perfectly, such was the brevity of his existence. It was all going too quick for him and he feared that he was missing out on some of the finest moments his life could offer. That being time with his family.

Charles missed all of them sorely. Abigail, so clever and so wise, taking after her father in that respect, he thought to himself as he chuckled aloud. Steven, he was somewhat troubled but Charles knew that he had a fire inside of him that would find him success in whatever avenue he pursued in life. If he could be bothered to try that is as he was well aware that his youngest son was, more often than not, incredibly lazy. Alex, he could not deny that he had the closest connection to his eldest son out of all of his children but that was purely because he had been present for Alex's formative years. He regretted not being there for Abigail's or Steven's, but he knew that Charlotte was raising them as best she could. Ever since he met his wife he knew that she would be instrumental in their children's lives as his job dictated that it needed to be so.

He missed Charlotte most of all. It seemed like only a few weeks beforehand when they had first met back in the Adam and Eve. Every moment away from her was another moment in which his heart broke further. He tried to phone her at least once a day but even that was not enough. Modern technology made it possible to physically see her, but the connection was so dreadful where he was though that there was little to no point as the line would completely break once every few minutes. It made him want to leave the army all the more so that he could return home and hold her in his arms once again. But Charles was a man of duty and had to wait for this latest call to arms to be completed. Something told Charles that there was still a great war to come, he only hoped that he lived through it so that he might spend time with his family and grow old next to the woman he loved.

Charles ceased his selfish thoughts as the cook called over to him to come and get some of what was ready. It was a traditional Pashtun dish that he'd sampled many a time. He was welcome to see it all the same.

"Pilaf." The cook called him to as he continued with whatever else he was making.

Charles took three full ladles of the dish and planted himself back down upon the table where he had been sitting. He raised the steamed rice to his nostrils and inhaled its aroma before taking it into his mouth. There were many variants to Pilaf but Charles was glad to see that the cook, probably unknowingly, had included some of the Major's favourite ingredients to it. Alongside the fluffy, separated, rice was shavings of carrots and onion, chopped pistachio nuts and almonds, a few raisins and chunks of some kind of undiscernible meat. That did not bother Charles though as any kind of meat was welcome.

As he was tucking in to his meal he heard the door to mess hall creak open and through it stepped his Lieutenant. Charles was glad to see a friendly face and pointed towards the Pilaf tray as she looked at him. Cassandra seemed to ignore his hallo as she grabbed herself a plate of food and sat by herself. It was almost as if he were transparent, although he suspected that the blame was on her side of things and not his own. Quickly, Charles wolfed down what was left of his food and handed the plate back to the chef so that it might be cleaned, offering thanks to him at the same time for his delicious food. He then walked over to where Cassandra was busy picking at her food, like it was something to do rather than something that would keep her alive.

"Cassandra…" He said cautiously.

She stared at him for a while as though she didn't know him. Eventually recognition flickered in her eyes and she switched into her normal self. "Major, I didn't see you there."

"How can you not see me?" Charles spoke, hoping to probe for some details around the strange illness that had inhabited their camp. He was aware of the dangers posed by this mind-altering infection but he trusted Cassandra and believed he was in no danger from her. "I was only sitting over there." He continued as he pointed to his table. "And even when I came over here you blanked me, like I was nothing."

"I'm sorry sir, I just haven't been myself lately." Cassandra's eyes almost welled up as a thought occurred to her. "You don't think?" She asked pleadingly, trying to gain some kind of reassurance from her superior.

"No, I don't think this is your mother's disease. It's happening to everyone else as well." Charles replied as he placed a hand upon his Lieutenant's shoulder. "I have no idea what this is." He conceded.

He spent the next half hour trying to reassure Cassandra that she had not inherited her mother's disease, Huntington's Disease, as the Lieutenant had become convinced she possessed the genetic defect. As they were talking, and the conversation gradually shifted onto a much more cheery subject, the matter of their service history together, Charles still could not help noticing that they were the only ones in the mess hall. He stole a quick glance at his fog watch, an anniversary gift from his wife that was almost a decade old, which he kept in his pocket at all times. He only really looked at it when he needed to as he preferred the day to progress naturally without having to worry about how long he had left for a training exercise, or some food as the case had been. It was nearly two in the afternoon. Charles had been in the mess hall for over an hour and the only person he'd seen in that entire time was his Lieutenant. That raised two immediate questions in his mind. First of all, where were all of his troops? Secondly, and much more important, who was looking over them? He and Cassandra were the only commissioned officers within the camp, and with both of them in the same location it led Charles to suspect that something of ill repute was now taking place.

"Lieutenant, is there anything you've noticed?" He said to her. She quickly grasped what he was thinking about as she gasped and placed her hands over her mouth. "What were you doing this morning?"

"I can't remember." She answered truthfully.

"Damn it!" He snapped in anger. "Well, where was the squad you were with?"

"I...by the storeroom." She said.

In a rage Charles stormed from the mess hall and back out into the open. He could not even take in his surroundings as he pounded across the camp grounds towards the storerooms, which sat at the south-east corner of the camp as this was closest to the helipad. Cassandra struggled to maintain his seismic pace as she faltered behind him. As they got closer to the

125

stores the gap between them increased. Charles looked backwards for a moment to see Cassandra holding her head, she appeared to be in a great deal of pain. He did not even hesitate as he marched back towards his Lieutenant, hoisted her upon his shoulder, and carried on. She had a well-toned, but lean, body which made her quite, but not completely, unburdening. He did not let that show as each step was filled with the same fervent ferocity that the ones before had also possessed.

Before he could even reach the storeroom he was met by a complete blockade of soldiers. There was no formation to them; they were not standing guard. They were just a solid mass that stared through the metal gates and towards the artefact which sat in the middle, as this was the only place it could fit. There was no way Charles was going to get through them without turning their attention towards him. Gently, as she was still not well, he placed Cassandra down and took out his pistol from its holster upon his belt. Of course he did not intend on shooting one of his men, he just wanted to gain their interest. He loaded the chamber, pointed the pistol towards the sky after checking no birds were in harm's way, and fired a single shot into the air. Not a real shot obviously, as they were only allowed to carry rubber bullets around the camp so that they could incapacitate someone without truly harming them. Although they often left a nasty bruise.

Instantly, and quite scarily, the soldiers all turned to face him. Their eyes were glazed, just as that squad had been before when he had had his life threatened, and their mouths were left slightly agape. All they needed was some rotting flesh and their zombification would be complete, Charles noted; though that the smell coming from them was not dissimilar and he wondered how long it had been since some of them had washed. Their gaze did not release for a few moments, it was as though something inside of them was judging the Major before it decided against taking hostile action towards him. Once it did they all stared at their superior with confused expressions, not a single one of them was sure what had happened to them, and neither was Charles. He was angry though, angry that something was taking his troops, those he trusted and was entrusted with, and turning them into mindless puppets. Be it disease or person he did not care, he simply wanted everything back to the way it was and he knew that it was in some way connected to that cursed object they found in the desert.

"What is the sodding fascination with this thing?" He murmured to himself as he silently pushed his way through the crowd of soldiers and opened the storeroom using his key. Swiftly he closed and locked it once he was inside to save them swarming the small area should they become odd again.

"What is the obsession with this thing?" He repeated to himself.

Gently, he kneeled down in front of the artefact, hoping to discern whatever its mesmerising trick was. He could detect nothing out of the ordinary though. So far as he could tell it was just an ordinary piece of British iron. British, he thought to himself. Being the lover of history that he was Charles was well aware that the way it was made was something indicative of early twentieth century England, so what was it doing in the middle of Afghanistan? He could not think of an answer himself and was perplexed as to how such an object could've ended up where it did.

Carefully he put a hand out to touch it. He was wary, almost as if he was expecting some kind of response from the metal as flesh touched its surface. There was. As Charles placed a single digit upon the metallic claw he heard a kind of muttered laugh, like it was something in the far distance and only barely within hearing range. The response from the soldiers was much worse as they all began to shout towards their Major. With heated anger they pounded upon the metal mesh that acted as a barrier between them and their beloved object. Charles paid no mind to them for the moment, though he was aware that such weak metal would not hold them back for long, as the voice continued to whisper into his ear. It guided his attention towards the base of the piece, where the metal was noticeably thinner but was still no leaner than two foot on any of its sides. It almost made the claw look like it was some kind of stand, or that it could stand at least, which was impressive considered it was no smaller than ten metres in length.

He glided his hand down the base of the structure. His mind was not entirely his own as he did so, but he could still see everything clearly, unlike the other times when his brain had been clouded for brief moments. Charles still felt every touch and it was his mind that compelled him forward towards the base of the artefact, but he was not sure that it was his will though. It was almost as though someone had taken control of his body but allowed his mind to stay as it was, like they wanted Charles to see whatever it was they were directing him to do.

His hand reached the very bottom of the object, where there appeared to be some very old dirt and dust which he scraped off, causing great pain to his finger in doing so. Underneath the grime was a symbol. It was two 'M''s of slightly different font which joined in the middle where an 'I' sat, making the symbol very much like a pitchfork, or like some kind of hideous tripod creature with a ridiculously slender frame on top. Underneath that read the words 'Malum Metal Industries'.

Charles' heart stopped for a brief moment as his mind was taken back to the frequent dreams that he had been having for the past few nights. His mind raced back to something he had read in a letter from his son. Alex had been worried about a man called Magnus Malum who had lived around a century ago. Charles had thought nothing of it at the time, and indeed was still partially trying to convince himself that it was all circumstantial, and that it was just some kind of disease or infection that was ruining his troops. Now though there was a tapping in the back of his head as his brain kicked into top gear, everything was linked somehow. He did not know how. He had received no word from his son about the matter progressing, but that did not mean Alex had not been communicating with him as Charles knew that, in extreme situations, his son would occasionally send an email to get his grievances quickly aired.

Hurriedly, as Charles seemingly gained full control of his body once more, he made for the exit to the storeroom. The whispers in his mind disappeared with a maniacal laugh as his troops became their usual selves once more. They allowed their Major through without hassle this time, not knowing of course that they had done anything wrong before. They shouted after him for orders but he was too busy to give any and so quickly delegated to Cassandra instead, since the Lieutenant knew very well how to organise a camp efficiently. Charles liked that about her, that willingness to adapt, which was why he was going to elect her as his replacement upon the Colonel's visitation.

There was only one place within the camp where he would be able to check to see if his son had contacted him, the communications centre which had one free computer within it, and so that was where he was heading. It was not that they did not have to the technology to have more, as they most certainly did, but the connection was so poor that it simply was not worth it. As he expected, the small office-like building was empty when he entered it and so he booted up the computer himself, being forced to wait the eternity it took for the technology to load itself. Eventually though, with a great deal of patience and a single smack to the side of the device, he was in and quickly logged onto his professional email address. Alex would have sent anything there if it was urgent. As the browser loaded, once again taking an age to do so, he contemplated what everything meant.

If the metal leg was something related to the same man that Alex was worrying about then strange circumstances were upon him. Worse still, he could not deny that the odd behaviour of his men was not in some way linked to that object, meaning that this man Magnus was a very gifted orator. He was manipulating the minds of his troops as though it were child's play, and he had likely been dead for over fifty years! What's more, Charles suspected that the man in his dreams was none other than this man Magnus. He certainly dressed appropriately for the time period with a big, and heavy, jacket; a top hat; and a three piece suit complete with Italian loafers. The profile of wealthy businessman certainly suited him.

Charles opened his emails and hoped to see his inbox completely empty, if only to alleviate his concerns. Sure enough though, at the top of the pile, was a message from his son with the subject line of 'Urgent', it had also been flagged as important in case his son had not quite gotten his point across. Hesitantly, like he did not want confirmation of his suspicions, he opened the email and pawed through the information within it. It was everything he had feared, and even more still. Within the first line of the email was the word Magnus, and his heart sank. Alex had been seeing the same character, and he had arrived at the same conclusion that Charles was now reaching. The man from his dreams, from their dreams, was none other than Magnus Malum himself. Somehow he was managing to invade the minds of those he cherished and cared for; not just his child but his troops as well. It angered Charles as he had no way of stopping it. It terrified him also.

Alex too was afraid. In his panic he'd supplied his father with everything he needed to know. Malum Metal Industries was the company of the Malum's, from which Magnus was clearly descended. They had been iron manufacturers since the time of the Industrial Revolution, which explained why Charles had found a piece of English metal. What it didn't explain though was how it managed to find its way to Afghanistan. He supposed that he had no way of knowing and so decided to focus on what he did know, sharing it with his son as he drafted a response. Alex needed to know about the artefact, perhaps it would help either of them in some way if more people knew about it.

As he finished the email and returned it to his son he heard footsteps behind him. Normally that would not bother him, however he had good reason to be worried and so darkened the brightness of the computer monitor so that he might see the reflection of whoever was behind him. Much to his relief he recognised the figure, and trusted her despite her strange behaviour.

"Orders received and understood sir." Cassandra said with a salute.

"Very good, nothing else to report?" Charles responded, expecting there to be some strange report of his soldiers attitudes.

"Nothing sir."

"Good." He replied whilst slightly confused.

If Magnus was somehow behind the odd behaviour of his men then he expected that they would also have seen him within their dreams. It made no sense just for Charles to see when everyone was affected by the dead man's trickery. Although he did not understand why he was not quite affected in the same way that everyone else was. Perhaps that was also part of Magnus' manipulation, perhaps he needed someone to question and to find out about him to increase his presence. Charles brushed aside such nonsense quickly. Even despite the strange circumstances he could not bring himself to the absurd conclusion that a dead man was haunting the minds of the living. There was one way to find out though, he thought to himself.

"Lieutenant…" He waited until he had her full attention before continuing. "Have you been having any weird dreams lately?" He asked.

"What do you mean by weird?" Cassandra queried.

"There's a man…" Charles began, he did not need to probe any further as he recognised a spark of realisation within his Lieutenant's eyes.

"With slicked back black hair and high cheek bones…how do you know about him?"

"Wait, so you see him as well?"

"As well? That implies that you've seen him?"

"Every night for the past week and a bit, he's always there."

"Same for me, he laughs when I dream about my mother, like he finds it funny." The memory was clearly a traumatic one for Cassandra as she struggled to hold back a tear. "What does he do in your dreams?"

"He just stands there. He inspects, but never interferes. Like a silent vigil."

The rest of the day passed quickly, and without incident, as he went around inspecting his troops whilst they worked. Casually, almost like he was inspecting a rumour, he would ask a single soldier from each squad if they had been experiencing nightmares. Several times their eyes flickered, like something was eavesdropping on their conversation from within, before they lied to him. Each time the answer was a no, but Charles did not believe them. Perhaps they thought they would be medically discharged if the Major thought them mentally unstable, which they would be under normal circumstances. Charles honestly did not know what to do with them. In all of his years of experience and his countless training courses, he had never been taught what to do in such a unique situation. He only hoped the Colonel would have a solution for him upon his visit.

After the trials had been completed he retired to his bed and instantly fell into a deep slumber. His dream was not a usual one. It did not form from one of his memories or experiences, or even one of his thoughts. It was like it had been created to cause him distress.

The settlement next to their camp, the town over which he was guardian, sworn to protect any and all within them, was completely ablaze. He could see no bodies, there was no blood on the streets and no bullet holes in the walls. In fact, there was no-one. Charles could hear screams in the distance. He pulled his SA-80 out, from where he could not tell, and raised it so that he was ready for anything. A figure appeared at the other end of the street he was on, and he recognised the person instantly.

"What do you want with me?!" He shouted to Magnus.

The figure stared at him, un-responding and unyielding. Charles had had enough of such silly games and so opened fire upon his target. The bullets had no effect. They dropped short of their target as Magnus merely laughed at the feeble assassination attempt. Charles found himself unable to move, his feet unwilling to budge even an inch. Magnus laughed at him, a low maniacal laugh that showed his malice. Slowly he advanced towards Charles, repeating the same phrase with each and every step.

"I'm getting closer. I'm getting closer. I'm getting closer…"

Chapter 9

After all of his worries, his various trials and tribulations that had kept him stunted for weeks on end, Alex was finally glad to have one day where he would be allowed to leave them all behind. Even in such a relaxed state though he found it extremely difficult to do so. The thoughts of Magnus, and his hideous master plan, if there was one, always found a way back into his mind. It was as if his subconscious would not allow such thoughts to be pushed aside, like Magnus posed some immediate danger that Alex needed to be warned about every waking moment he had.

As they crossed into London though he did his absolute best to rid himself of such thoughts, fiddling with the cards in his pocket as he often did. Today was meant to be a day of history after all, and that was exactly what Alex was trying to see Magnus as. He looked around the small minibus to see what the others were thinking about it, half-heartedly hoping that one of them was just as worried as he was. Maxwell was busy listening to some music in the back with such loud volume that it was being imposed onto everyone else as well. Alex considered himself a fan of most music, but whatever it was that was emanating from Max's music device could not be considered anything other than loud screeching. He did not have a problem with Max listening to it, as everyone had various tastes, but he would've preferred it if it wasn't quite so obnoxiously loud. Alex smiled briefly to himself at the thought that perhaps you could turn it up further and rid Alex of any traces of worry that were still mulling about inside his head by replacing them with that incessant racket.

The others were all staring out of the window, a typical way of spending time when travelling long distances with little to do. Simon Gartland was tapping his finger irritatingly upon the side of the window in his impatience. It struck Alex as odd that he was even going on this trip as Simon did not do History, and he was quite certain that the tall youth had never been interested in it, not even in the slightest. The girl clinging to his arm though gave Alex all of the information he needed as she was clearly his guest, and obviously had a deep love of history if her giddiness was anything to go by. Alex allowed himself to smile once more as Simon rolled his eyes at his partner's happiness. Seeing that Simon was a crony of Arthur's, and openly aided him in his torture of pupils, Alex was glad to see that he would have to endure a day of suffering himself.

Then his eyes came to rest upon Verity, completely ignoring the fact that she had not brought anyone else with her. Immediately he was at a loss for words as he stared at her immeasurable beauty. Her brunette hair rested delicately, just below her shoulders, against her as she sat with a hand placed against her head as she read. Alex could not see the book but he was almost certain that it was some kind of crime thriller or mystery novel, as he had noticed that that was all she ever seemed to read. He'd tried to read several himself so that he might use it as a conversation point between them. They were not really to his taste though as he found the plots overly predictable and often disjointed. He preferred a good historical novel, or perhaps some fantasy or science fiction. Anything where death and destruction were assured he enjoyed reading.

Alex found himself mesmerised as she removed her soft, silk-like, hand from her forehead and used her index finger to gently turn the page of her book. Every action she performed, no matter how trivial, was something to behold in his eyes. The situation with Magnus had almost completely derailed his intentions towards her, and still held him back in truth, but he needed to think about her as well. He needed to be reminded of why he fought so hard against Arthur and the general oppressive nature of the world. Of course his strong sense of morality guided him, but like his father it was always a woman who was behind everything he did. Behind Charles stood Charlotte, his father's beacon of hope that kept him moving and daring to be extraordinary, and behind Alex was Verity, even if she might not feel the same way about him.

He had lost himself so much in thought of her that he had not realised the pair of magnificent green eyes staring back at his own. Immediately Alex's face turned red and he was forced to look away out of shame. Surely she knew about his feelings now, if she did not before, but he was still not ready to ask her on a date, not yet. They both shared a passion for history and so he hoped there would be ample opportunity to psych himself up to the moment over the course of the day. Quickly he stole a glance in Verity's direction and saw her smiling. Whether that was because she found his affections humorous, or because she too felt that kind of elated embarrassment when you stare into the eyes of someone you care for, he did not know. He did not care either, for as long as she was smiling then he had something to be cheerful about.

As he turned to the left he noticed a familiar face mocking his affections. Thomas was staring at him with bulging eyes brimming with sarcasm. He then grabbed a hold of Alex's red polo shirt, something he had worn specifically so that he looked presentable in front of Verity, and puckered his lips to a ridiculous extent. When Alex cocked an eyebrow in question they both laughed before Thomas proceeded to look out of the window again with his hands raised against it. He was probably the most excited of all of them to be going. Ever since he had told Alex about the competition it had all been a part of his master plan, he was like a low-level criminal mastermind. Alex looked on, slightly worried about his friend's mental health as Thomas pressed his face against the glass as though it would somehow get him there quicker.

Alex had not been able to look at Thomas the same since the day before. His best friend had openly told him that he envies the life Alex has because of his abilities, and nothing he could think of would convince Thomas otherwise. It was clear that his friend felt robbed, cheated somehow, of a higher status, and that his comedic personality was mostly a façade designed to hide his innermost jealousy. Alex could not blame Thomas for thinking like that as he supposed he would feel exactly the same way in such a situation, after all it was a part of the human condition to feel greed and lust for something someone else has that you do not. It was exactly Alex's powers though that had led him to think that he was not human, at least not like the rest of them. That had been a point his brother had made loud and clear the night before. He was not one of them, no matter how hard he tried to be.

As the negative thoughts began to seep back into his mind his subconscious flooded him with concerns for Magnus once again. Desperately he tried to deny that there was any real danger, that it was impossible that such a ludicrous scenario could ever take place. Magnus could not come back, he told himself without actually believing it. By all accounts, by the very laws of nature, Alex should not exist. Yet he did. So if something as abnormal as himself can become a reality then why was the thought of Magnus returning from the dead so ridiculous to him? Nobody knew what happened to the villain after all. Perhaps he managed to evade death and was simply biding his time, Alex thought to himself.

As much as he was afraid, and he was terrified, Alex was also curious about Magnus for he possessed the same eyes as himself. Perhaps that meant there were others like Alex within the world who chose to keep themselves hidden. I should do the same, Alex thought to himself. Maybe Alex was simply an example of the next form of evolution for mankind, an elevated level of being that had developed so far as to control the elements themselves. It was all up in the air though, and nothing was certain. There was nothing he could do but continue to wait, no matter how agonisingly tormenting it was to him. A part of him even wanted Magnus to return just so that he could be rid of such conflicting notions within his mind as they threatened to engulf every aspect of his life, like they nearly had to Verity. For a long time he had been enamoured with her and yet Magnus had almost completely pushed her from his mind. If he truly was human, in some form, then he needed to feel the emotion that defined humanity. Love.

His subconscious seemed to realise that Alex was trying to shy away from the possibility of such an evil as Magnus returning to the world as it pressed the thoughts even harder into his mind with such force that he actually felt pain and anguish. Images flooded into his mind, like precursors for coming events should he not take them seriously. Destruction and death filled the streets as a great blaze of fire swallowed everything in sight. Magnus was in the midst of it all, laughing maniacally, just as he had in Alex's dream. His subconscious was forcing Alex to see that Magnus was a very real threat, but Alex would not lose himself to such thoughts. He was human! Why burden his mind with such troubles when everyone else seemed unbothered? He could not understand why he had been ladened with such heavy responsibilities. Each day it grew worse, and his fears with it, like Magnus was becoming stronger and his presence within the world was oozing into reality once more. He just wanted it to be over.

Alex suddenly felt the gentle touch of a hand upon his shoulder and his mind readjusted back into the world. He did not realise that he must have been showing signs of physical pain and exertion as the bus had stopped, pulled up along the slip-road of a motorway, and everyone was staring at him. Simon and Max did not seem to be bothered, but the others seemed genuinely concerned about him. Thomas had a look of deep worry upon his face as he knew how his friend could get, especially as of late. Even Verity, the person he had hoped would not see him in such a weakened state, was anxious as she held a hand to her mouth in

uneasiness. It was not her hand that he had felt upon his shoulder though, it was Mr Barnes'.

His history teacher stood over him with a look of confusion more than anything as he hoped

to understand what was going on with Alex.

"Alex, are you alright?" Mr Barnes asked.

"Yes…" He replied. "It's a…" Alex struggled to think for a moment before he found an

excuse. "Just a flash migraine, I get them sometimes."

"Are you going to be alright today? Or do we need to take you back? Do you have

medication for it?" His teacher was asking hastily, no doubt eager to resume their journey

quickly.

Everyone looked to him for an answer. Some were distraught at the prospect of having to

return to Henbane without having been to the Imperial War Museum, whilst others like

Simon were noticeably overjoyed at the idea. Alex could understand why the school were

being so protective, but they had no reason to worry.

"No, I'll be fine. They only happen once in a while." He reassured everyone.

Simon let out a moan as the journey continued, almost in complete silence. Verity could not

return to reading her book, he noticed, as something was putting her off it. If he did not know

any better he would have thought that she was concerned for him. Then again that had always

been his problem though, thinking too much and looking too deeply into things. He could

never be happy with what was. Even if she came up to right then and there and blurted out

affection for him he would not be able to convince himself that it was so. Still, he tried his

best to carry on as Thomas yanked at his arm to grab his attention.

"So, what kind of stuff will there be at this museum?" He asked.

"You mean the Imperial War Museum?" Alex retorted.

"Yeah." Thomas responded as he obviously failed to grasp the jest.

"So you're wondering what kind of exhibits will be at the Imperial WAR museum?"

"Oh." Thomas simply said as he realised.

They laughed heartily together until the minibus pulled up outside the museum. One by one they ejected themselves from the vehicle before the driver sped off again, no doubt going to somewhere to relax for a few hours before he needed to pick them up. Together, led by a very enthusiastic Mr Barnes, they walked up the long pathway to the entrance where huge white pillars greeted them. Monstrous artillery guns were positioned just outside, they were far bigger than any kind of weapon he had ever seen. The grass was kept neatly trimmed with barely a blade out of place anywhere along its body. Shrubberies and bushes surrounded the building, and the paths, and gave the whole place a feeling of welcome, or would have had it not been for the massive artillery. As Alex stared at it all and glanced up at the dome upon the roof, that was reminiscent of something you would find in Rome, he could not help but feel awe-inspired.

Mr Barnes gathered them in a small semi-circle so they could figure out timings. They were only given four hours to roam to their hearts content, certainly not long enough to see everything. Alex determined that he would focus on the things he liked, namely anything concerning the First World War. Such a horrific and brutal harrowing of human kind had never before been experienced and such intense trench warfare told of how unprepared everyone was for it. Alex liked it because of the trauma and emotion it brought, and because it was deep in the past and he believed that studying it would keep it that way. Surely no human who know of the horrors of the Great War would ever try and replicate it. Nobody except Magnus, he found himself thinking.

They set off in their groups to their respective interests. Simon was being half-dragged towards the outdoor area, which contained various vehicles and planes, by the girl who was accompanying him. Alex still found it hilarious. Max, like Verity, had not brought a friend to accompany him, for whatever reason, and rather annoyingly was heading in the same direction as his crush. He did not believe that his former friend was after her though, and besides, he held a small candle of hope that Verity was infatuated with him. No matter how small that hope was he needed to maintain something to keep himself from being overwhelmed by the numerous dark thoughts that swirled around within his mind like sharks surrounding their prey.

Alex felt joy fill his heart as he entered the museum as he was surrounded in his element. History had always been his favourite subject but the only times he ever got to go anywhere actually historical were when his father was with them. Charlotte had never been a fan of history, always preferring to live in the present and disregard the past. Alex supposed she needed to in order to cope without seeing her husband for long stretches of time. Still, it meant that he never got to enjoy what he loved, or at the very least it took a great deal of persuasion, and he was not prepared to go to such extreme lengths.

Everything around him was fantastic. From every small piece of memorabilia to every weapon and uniform, every single detail was perfect and magnificent. Alex had thought that he knew almost everything about the turmoil and warfare of the twentieth century. Yet within a few moments of looking around the museum he suddenly became aware of how little information he actually had. There were medals that he never knew existed. Uniforms that were completely unknown to him were out on display as if they were common knowledge, which they were now. The weapons were so diverse and unique that he found it hard to imagine so many being needed for the same act. It made him think of all of the differences in warfare, so many methods which all led to the same result. The best part of it was, for Alex at least, that it was all authentic. Every single item was an original either bought by the museum or generously donated by the families of those who owned the objects.

Thomas walked around with him. His best friend was intrigued by every single item as he had never experienced anything like the Imperial War Museum. Alex found it slightly annoying that with every single exhibit his friend would ask about the context behind it. He liked it as well as he felt like an authority on the subject, since he had learnt about most of the periods covered by the museum within the last month. It was all a fantastic experience regardless of any agitators.

Together, they continued to trudge through the museum, taking a small detour through the outdoor holocaust exhibit as Thomas wanted to see how truly awful it had been for the victims. Once again Alex found it difficult to believe that human beings were capable of inflicting such damage upon one another. Humanity had always had an obsession with making others out to be the monsters and the pestilences that destroys their world. In truth though there was no greater plague than humanity, as they spread quickly and viciously across the world and stripped it bare of all resources, maiming and slaughtering everything in their path that threatened to stop them. Sometimes Alex felt ashamed to be a part of such a brutal species, even if nobody else considered him as their kind.

Finally they made their way around to the section that Alex wanted to see. Of course he was pleased with all of it as his love for history covered almost every period and every topic, but now he was truly in his element as he stared at a replica of a trench from the First World War. It painted a horrific picture but Alex could not help being enthralled by it. Every minute detail helped to portray the appalling conditions the soldiers had experienced during war. Poor communication; poor conditions; and poor rations all made the scene seem like something out of the dark ages. It was a reminder of how lucky everyone was to have what they did.

All in all Alex had had a fantastic day and he was disappointed to see it drawing to a close. Thomas talked his ear off throughout the day but that did not bother him as it had been a rare opportunity to break the monotony of his usual weekends. On a standard weekend he might go to the cinema, or a walk if the weather permitted it, but did little besides this so he was glad for the opportunity to do something refreshing. Perhaps he would visit the much larger Duxford Imperial War Museum, he thought to himself. His father had been there many times but it had been almost a decade since Alex was last there. He was in no doubt that it had greatly changed since he was there last as major renovation works had occurred at the museum a few years beforehand.

With a somewhat heavy heart he began to trek back towards the entrance to the museum as Thomas ran off in a desperate attempt to absorb more information with the small amount of time they had left. Alex smiled at his friend's enthusiasm, considering it often tended to lean more towards tawdry superhero films and crime dramas. It was nice for Thomas to be invested in the same passions as him for once. Still, they needed to leave and so Alex could not chase after his friend. There would undoubtedly be other opportunities to return to the museum, no matter how infrequent they might be.

Alex was just about to cross the threshold of the entrance, with many of the others already waiting, including Verity who gave him a beaming smile that lit up his heart, and his cheeks, when Thomas came running down the corridor and grabbed him by the arm. He was pulled away from the others with an awkward jerk and found himself unable to stop his friend's momentum for a few moments as he struggled to maintain his balance whilst being pulled along by Thomas. Within a few more metres though he was able to regain his stance and forced his arm free from Thomas' grip. Alex wanted to know what was going on.

"Thomas, why are we running through the museum? We have to go soon." He protested.

"There's something we missed, you need to see it!" He said in rapid response, struggling to catch his breath from a mixture of running and excitement.

"Why?" Alex asked to try and probe for further information.

"Just come on!" Thomas replied stubbornly as he once again took hold of his friend's arm and pulled him across the museum.

They stopped in the outdoor section of the museum, next to the famous T9171 Mark V 'Devil' tank. Alex did not understand. They had taken the time to examine the tank earlier in the day, something which Thomas surely remembered as he was obsessed with its rhombic appearance. The Mark V was used during the closing months of the First World War and Alex could see why the war did not last much longer, with such destructive machines being introduced. The evolution of the tank was an area of modern history that he was particularly interested in, as was Thomas clearly as he dragged his friend to witness it once more. He could still not understand though why his friend had brought him back to see something that they had already seen. As he turned to speak to Thomas though he found his friend staring at something behind the Devil tank. It was a large exhibit with a long glass case, covering around ten metres in length, which was around a metre in diameter, if not larger.

Somehow they had missed it earlier on. As Alex stared at it though the synapses within his mind made the connections and Alex wondered how he could ever miss something so vital. Before he could even begin to think about what he was staring at he had to ask Thomas a question, a question so important that it could determine the fate of the country, or perhaps even the entire world.

"Thomas, what made you lead me here?"

"What do you mean?" His best friend replied dumbstruck.

"I know you. You like tanks and guns and weaponry. What led you to lead me to this hideous deformity of metal?!" He asked again.

"Well I…" Thomas said as if to reply. Yet as his friend thought about it more the more it became clear to Alex that the thought had not been his own. "I just needed to, like it was some kind of compulsion. Like…"

"Like it wasn't you at all?" Alex suggested.

"Yes…" Thomas responded with a shiver of fear. Alex could tell his friend wanted to run away and hide, as was his nature, but there was nothing to run from. He knew the culprit well enough though.

"Thomas, why don't you head back and tell the others I'll only be a moment. I want to get a closer look." He said with a smile to throw Thomas off of his true feelings.

His friend obliged his request and moved towards the entrance where the others would be waiting, holding his head as he went as a sudden headache had obviously just come on. This gave Alex the opportunity he needed to focus upon the object before him. It was undoubtedly the same type of object that his father had described to him in his last letter. Everything was as Charles had described it. The long piece of metal was like a claw, or an upper joint like the human thigh, made of pure black iron so seamlessly welded together that it seemed like a single giant ingot that had been sculpted perfectly. The shape and flawlessness of the object was not what concerned Alex though, the logo was. At the base of the object sat two 'M's with an 'I' between them, making a trident-like symbol, and beneath it the words 'Malum Metal Industries' haunted him.

No matter where he turned, no matter what avenue of life he took, he was there. Like a fetid pestilence Magnus had invaded his world and would not relent until he seeped into every part of it. Alex felt nauseous with anger as he realised just how out of control of his own existence he was becoming. He had less and less decisions he could actually make as Magnus preoccupied his every waking moment. Alex could not even have a simple day out at the museum without Magnus forcing his way in to ruin everything and take centre stage once again. He could not even ask Verity out on a date because he now had to find a way of dealing with Magnus' influence. At least that was the excuse he was now giving himself.

For whatever reason Magnus was not only controlling his life, and that of his father's. It was like the villain knew that Alex was looking into his life and he was now doing everything within his power, however much a dead person could have anyway, to push himself into their minds. Everyone else seemed to be oblivious to the dangers that Magnus posed, although Alex himself was still not certain on what exactly the dangers were, or at the very least they believed the evidence to be so circumstantial that it was not worth worrying over. Anyone could have bad dreams, but not a single one of them was able to make the connections that he had made.

Alex's blood boiled as he thought about the ignorance of everyone around him, that is if they were also experiencing dreams involving Magnus, which he suspected they were as it was difficult to imagine that he and his father had been singled out. They were simply the only ones who had the intelligence to feel fear over such an invasive presence from someone who had most likely been deceased for the better part of a century. His mother, normally a perfectly capable woman, had not sought to ask about her son's troubles. His sister, despite her intelligence, completely disregarded his worries as irrational as she retreated back into her private bubble. His brother was too stupid to understand what was going on as he was only concerned with wasting his life in front of a television screen. His best friend, normally so attuned to Alex's personality that he could tell exactly what was going on within his life, could not see the dangers before him or he surely would have cowered like the craven fool he was. Even Verity, his sweet Verity, whom he saw as just as intelligent as himself, could not connect the dots.

In his anger, deep-seated within him and rising to the surface, he didn't realise his eyes were glowing so heatedly that green flares were sparking out of them and hitting the walls around him, evaporating upon contact. He could hear murmurs behind him as his abilities began to surge within his body and the very ground began to shake slightly in his anger.

Before he even knew what he was doing the object had lifted up from its plinth within the glass case. With fervent rage he slammed the object down without moving a muscle and the people began to move away and out of the museum. With his anger exercised he regained control of his emotions and cursed himself for his ill judgment. Even if the object had belonged to Magnus at some stage in history it was still reckless of him to risk being exposed. He hoped that they simply thought he had smashed the glass case himself, even though his fists had been clearly bunched by his sides in anger with his fingernails digging into his palms. The human mind would adapt in any way it could to logically reason with the impossible. Alex could not help but think of his dog, whom he had accidentally killed with his abilities, and was reminded of why using his powers always led to trouble. Even in winning the talent show, a joyous experience, the consequences were being felt now. You reap what you sow, he thought to himself. Instinctively Alex rubbed his watch to give him comfort as he remembered his father's words. As long as it worked, he was safe.

He heard footsteps behind as two voices, one male and one female, were communicating with someone else via their walkie-talkies. Alex felt like a common criminal thug as he did not even try to resist their calls to go with them. The looks he was receiving from people made him feel sick though. They all judged him, each one with a different variation of disgust etched upon their faces. The human race, as ever, were quick to judge without realising the context or witnessing the evidence. He was trying to help them for he knew that Magnus posed a serious threat to each and every one of them. They could not see it though. All they saw was young man who was clearly 'troubled' and needed to be disciplined.

"Alex!" He heard a shout from behind him.

Within seconds Thomas was standing next to him. He did not understand why his friend was being led away by the museum security. In fact, when Alex told him what had happened, he didn't have any knowledge of the metal leg at all or any recollection of dragging Alex around the museum to see it.

"I need to let this out of me Thomas, I thought I'd dealt with it." He told his friend as he harkened back to the day before when he had won the talent show. Obviously though it had only temporarily dealt with his urges.

He was taken to just outside the museum's security office where he was forced to wait until Mr Barnes had been summoned to address the situation. Unfortunately he brought the other students with him, including Verity, to witness his shame. For what seemed like an age the security officers droned on about the seriousness of the situation as if Alex was completely unaware of the severity of his actions. He would not be prosecuted, it was not quite as bad as all that, but he would undoubtedly be made to pay a fine by the school. It was even possible that he could be excluded from Henbane, or at the very least put on report. That did not matter to him though, for there were far bigger things at stake now then some letters and numbers on a piece of paper. Alex was now completely convinced that Magnus was going to return as there was no other explanation for what was occurring. His thoughts were broken as Verity smiled comfortingly at him, and it was only then that Alex realised his history teacher was addressing him.

"I really didn't expect this from you." Mr Barnes exclaimed. "Well Alex? What do you have to say for yourself?"

"Obviously I didn't mean to." Alex explained. "I will face whatever punishment is put upon me…but it doesn't even matter anymore."

"Oh, why doesn't it matter then?" The female security guard enquired.

"Because Magnus Malum is returning." Alex muttered in response.

The reply from Mr Barnes deeply worried him. "Who's Magnus Malum?"

Chapter 10

Magnus was returning. That was the one thought he could not wipe from his mind and there was nothing he could do about it. It was like every aspect of his life was being used to draw Magnus closer, like they were linked. Alex was at a crossroads. He knew that something had to be done but yet, at the same time, there was nothing he could do. Magnus was creeping closer, threatening to burst into existence once more. Nothing else mattered anymore. Not school, nor his family; nor Thomas; nor Verity. Even his past troubles, with Arthur and his brother, were now completely irrelevant as this new hazard took shape.

He had read his father's return email, and he did not like what he saw within it. Somehow, he had no clue as to how exactly, something from Magnus' factory had been discovered by his father in the deserts of Afghanistan. Even when Charles had described the object to him in his previous letter, and when Alex had seen its counterpart at the museum, he had not wanted to believe it. This email confirmed that Magnus' reach was encroaching around his life like a fire, threatening to swallow everything with its burning tendrils. It was a startling revelation, and one he wished he had never heard because now it seemed all but certain that Magnus would return. Everything was falling into place, and there was nothing he could to delay it.

He needed to find a way to stop him from coming back. Alex's mind was left blank though. A vast chasm within his mind, which should have been full of creative and exuberant ways to dispose of the menace of Magnus, was completely void of all signs of life. It was obvious though that conventional weaponry and warfare would not work against such an individual as Magnus Malum, for the way in which he presented himself was most unconventional. Alex knew that it would have to be him, or someone else with his gifts, if such a person did exist. There was no other option left open for him. His destiny had been preordained and Alex had to follow it.

As he stood in the kitchen, with his hand holding the fridge open as it had been for the past few minutes, he could not help but feel a certain hope. Perhaps the path of his life was strewn before him, but he would decide which path he would take. More than anything he wished, childishly, that his father was with him to help him choose. If Charles were there then he would know exactly what to do, shielding his family with one hand and brandishing Magnus' destruction in the other. Alas, Alex was not a child any longer. He could not rely on his father to fight his battles or wage his wars for him, not that he ever had, but still Charles' face would have been a most welcome sight.

So distracted was he by his thoughts of Magnus that he had not even noticed his mother come into the kitchen and close the fridge door, with his hand still placed upon it. As he shifted back into the real world Charlotte was standing before him with a surly expression and a raised eyebrow. Alex smiled at his mother to try and cover up his worries, but it did not have the desired effect. As mothers often did, although perhaps not his own mother quite so frequently as others, she knew that something was amiss. Judging by the fact that the shopping, which she had obviously just returned with, was still not unpacked he could tell that his mother would not leave until he addressed her.

"Sorry mother, I was just a bit preoccupied." He tried to explain.

"You have been 'preoccupied' a lot lately Alex. What's going on?" She asked with genuine affection and worry over her eldest child.

"It's nothing…" He responded half-heartedly. He did not want to give Charlotte any cause for concern.

"Alex, I'm your mother. If you can't talk to me about it then who can you talk to? I want to be there for you." She replied with a smile. "And then there's this whole business at the museum…" Alex rolled his eyes at the mention of it. "Don't think I don't know about that Alex…I don't even know what to think anymore. Is there something driving this behaviour? It's not like you Alex, I want to help you…" She concluded.

"Thanks mum. I don't mean to be so distant, it's just that…well…there's nothing you can do to help me." He spoke truthfully with a voice filled with lamentation and sorrow.

Charlotte embraced her son in a loving hug and gently kissed his forehead as she had done when he was an infant. Normally Alex was not one for such displays of affection, but right then he needed it. There was something soothing about it that suggested everything was going to be alright. He knew it would not be though and he savoured every moment of their embrace, not knowing if they had long left for such times. Alex cursed Magnus for even threatening to put an end to it all.

Timidly, and slightly embarrassed, he pulled away from his mother and began to help her unpack the shopping. He could not help spying a chocolate gateau within the frozen items, since it was his favourite dessert. In all of his worries he had forgotten that it was a Sunday, a wondrous day for food. Normally his mother would prepare a well-cooked piece of meat, chicken mostly since it is healthier than many darker meats, for their roast dinner complete with roast potatoes; vegetables; stuffing and several giant Yorkshire puddings to encase it all before it was drowned in gravy. For all of his mother's health obsessions Alex had to admit that his mother knew how to make good food, just like that honey-roasted ham they had eaten before. Something so simple, and yet so elegant and delicious. He was very lucky to have what he did. He realised that now more than ever as the threat of it all being wiped away grew with each passing minute Magnus was allowed to manifest himself within the world.

Magnus, Alex pondered to himself. Why was he aware of the man's presence when everyone else seemed oblivious to him? Even Mr Barnes, despite not having the best memory, was still an expert in all of history and he could not recall the man. Alex placed the tin of soup he was holding within the appropriate cupboard to the side of the sink and turned to his mother. This would settle it.

"Mother?" He called to her.

"What is it petal?" She responded, using Alex's least favourite name she had for him.

"Do you know who Magnus Malum is?" He asked tentatively. His entire body was on tenterhooks waiting for the answer.

"No, can't say that I do." She responded truthfully as she placed a pack of smoked bacon within the fridge. Alex breathed a sigh of relief. "Is he the one that's been troubling you?" She asked in return.

"Never mind that, I was just curious." He spoke as he placed some detergent in the cupboard underneath the sink. His curiosity spurred forwards within him though, compelling him to question his mother further. "He has quite a long face with high cheek bones and thin cheeks, almost a gaunt look I would say. He dressed in a suit with a waistcoat and thick trench jacket like you would see in Victorian times…"

He did not need to describe the man any further as a look of absolute terror overcame his mother. She stood petrified to the spot as the jar of raspberry jam she was holding fell to the floor and smashed into innumerable pieces, covering the floor in the substance and making it look like a murder scene from some second-rate police drama. Alex responded in kind with a look of utter despair. She knew who Magnus was, everyone did, he concluded, but they forgot about him, or repressed any memory of him, as soon as they woke, as though he were just a bad dream.

"Silly me!" His mother said frantically as she picked up the dustpan and brush from the hook it was on by the back door and began to brush up the residue of her accident.

Alex needed to be sure. "Mum, who's Magnus Malum?" He asked once more.

"No idea petal, why do you ask?" She replied with genuine forgetfulness. She had no idea who he was.

"No reason…" Alex said with fear gripping his vocal chords. "I'm not feeling very well mum, do you mind if I go and sit down?"

"Of course not, I can manage the rest."

Alex did not feel ill, but he needed some time to think. The threat of Magnus was real. Everybody could sense the impending doom he would bring but their minds blocked him out of it, probably a defence mechanism to shield themselves from his horror, Alex mused to himself as he put what he had learnt in psychology to good use. Why then was he allowed to remember when all others were permitted to block Magnus out? He would prefer to not know about the monster so that he could enjoy his life. All other elements of negativity had been removed from his life, Magnus was the only thing stopping him from being truly happy, or content at the very least. Why was he the one who had to suffer such crippling fear every waking moment? He did not understand. He just wanted to be normal.

Alex moved towards the sofa to try and distract himself with television, as there was nothing he could to prepare for the inevitable. He hoped to calm himself by carrying on as he normally would. As he sat down upon the solid piece of furniture that they laughably called a 'sofa', struggling to find the comfortable spot on it, he did indeed feel a sense of normality returning to him. The world had not ended yet, and until it did he intended to act as though it would not as he pulled his cards from his pocket and began to systematically shuffle them.

Perhaps not the soundest strategy, he considered, but it was the only option open to him. There was no way he would be able to prepare against Magnus, and besides, he did not know how to.

The usual litany of drivel was present on television, but that did not matter much though as he only wanted it for background noise as he shuffled. He skipped to the documentaries to see if there was anything to keep him sane and grounded. In the end, after flicking through every conceivable channel, he settled on a programme about the myth surrounding sea monsters such as the Leviathan. Of course it had no real roots in history, and so it was pointless watching it, but he had always found such conceptual programmes to be highly entertaining. The idea that terrifying monsters of colossal proportions might have once existed was not a comforting one, but he found it amusing to see so called 'experts' present their evidence. Human nature, he supposed. It was a part of their conditioning that they challenge old views and present their own, no matter how ludicrous they might initially sound. Of course Alex did not firmly believe in such nonsense, although he did hold true the notion that there is no smoke without fire.

Just as he was getting enthralled about the legend of the Kraken, and its links to the now known colossal squid, his brother came bundling down the stairs to join him upon the sofa, much to his aggravation as he placed his cards back into his pocket to keep them safe. Steven was just an innately annoying person, he did not even need to try. Immediately his brother snatched the controller from him and turned the programme over onto something that he would enjoy. Alex glared at his brother in the hope that it would intimidate him into giving it back. Alas, he had no such luck as his brother turned to him with a mocking smile and a laugh.

"You alright there?" He asked sarcastically.

"You know damn well that I'm not alright." Alex responded.

Steven just laughed his usual, contemptuous, laugh. "Good, because you don't ever deserve to be happy." He said scornfully. "When everyone finds out what you are they will despise you and you will lose everything. Dad, Mum, even that girl that you like so much, they will cast you out into the cold and leave you to rot! And do you know who they'll turn their affections to then? ME!"

Alex instantly felt his anger rise within him and so quickly moved up from his seat and stormed out of the door. There was a small woods not far from his home that few people ever ventured into, as it held little significance to anyone and the park itself was more appropriate for runners and dog-walkers, that he needed to go to in order to calm himself down. He could feel the intense glow of his eyes burning bright green like the very hottest flame. It swirled within him like a parasite, eating away at his self-control and willing itself into the world.

Steven had no right to say what he did! Alex thought to himself angrily. Why should he, a pathetic worm of a creature, live in happiness whilst Alex is subjected to every kind of torture mankind could throw at him? No, he would not lose everything. He would not let it happen. Steven would never dare tell anyone about what he was, because he knew the consequences that would befall him would be far greater than the smug satisfaction of seeing his brother exposed.

He could not even concentrate upon his walk as he mind kept diverting onto displeasing topics. His father, always so supportive and loving, was turning his back upon his son, branding him as a freak and declaring no love for him. Alex did not have his watch with him and so had no reassurance that it would be otherwise. His mother silently wept over the monster she had created. Then there was Verity, the object of his affections. Disparagingly, and without hesitation, she rejected him in favour of his greatest living rival. Arthur laughed at him, the final battle was his. Alex would lose everything.

No! Enough! Alex screamed internally at himself. His rage had never been so high. Steven, and Magnus, had reawakened the slumbering giant within him. He needed to find a way of exercising his powers quickly or someone would get hurt, something he did not want to ever happen again. So intent was he, on reaching the woods, that he blocked out everything around him as though it were nothing but a distraction. The swaying of the trees in the gentle winds. The glaring sun upon his back. The twittering of the birds on high. It was all just white noise to him as it was consumed by his anger.

He did not care if people saw his fury. Almost subconsciously though he moved with his hands half-covering his eyes so that they could not see his abilities. Despite everything he knew that nobody could find out about what he was, or Steven's jibes could very well become reality.

The woods were only a short walk away and yet it seemed to take him an age to reach it. The long main roads stretched further than they ever had before, doubling or even tripling in length within his mind as his thoughts and rage surged through him. Finally he reached the small country lane that led to the small wooded area. He was very fortunate to live relatively close to one of Leicester's several parks. Whereas others had to put up with the constant humdrum of the city he could freely escape it if he chose to. Alex needed that escape now more than he ever had. Never had he felt such power flowing through him as he did now, not even when tormenting Arthur, and it was searching for any conceivable way to be released. At least here, by the trees and the rocks, no-one would be in harm's way. That was all he could hope for.

He took one quick look around to see if anyone was lurking and saw nothing, not even a single rabbit or squirrel; it was like they could sense the danger that Alex posed in his anger. He allowed his body to ready itself before lifting several rocks from the ground and holding them like he had the tomatoes beforehand. It was not enough though. His mind seemed to laugh at him as it pressed forward its urges once more. Alex knew he had to let it all out.

Without thinking he raised his arms outwards and began harnessing his energy into what he was about to do, no matter how stupid it was. He projected his thought into lifting everything around him. The trees and the roots, the bushes and the grass, even chunks of earth. It was unbelievably painful at first as his mind struggled to maintain command over the objects he was now possessing, which must have numbered in the thousands. Never had he commanded such majestic power before. His anger turned to pride as his body gained control of the objects around him. With powers like this he had no reason to be afraid of people, but they most definitely had a reason to be afraid of him. Even if the objects were not sapient, as he had made sure not to focus on the insects and anything that could control its own actions, he was still amazed by his abilities.

As he lifted the objects from the ground, with the trees desperately trying to hang on to their roots before they too were uplifted, he began to laugh hysterically. For so many years he had shied away from using his powers out of fear, but there was nothing to be frightened of.

Suddenly Alex became aware of what he was thinking. He was once again allowing his ego to swell over common sense. His powers should not be used in such a way. His subconscious directed him to Muffin, his very first best friend, and the memory of his death. The low whimpering of his final moments, even when he looked towards him with forgiving eyes, was enough to drive Alex back into the realisation of what he was doing. The land around him was no longer green and pleasant, it was a shallow pit of earth as everything on top of it floated some ten feet in the air above him.

With a howl he dropped the objects, too upset with himself to set them back as they had been. The trees smashed into one another and combined with the dense surfaces of the rocks as everything flopped onto the ground in a disorganised heap, like a child who was building a den from the ruins of old foliage. Alex prayed that no-one saw his display of arrogance and foolishness. Despite feeling such fury with himself though Alex could not help but feel quite relieved. Not only had the urge to exercise his abilities subsided once more, for the moment, but now he knew that there was something he could to combat Magnus, should he return. He needed practice though, and lots of it, to control his abilities. Even still, with the weight of the world upon his shoulders, he could not find it within himself to give in to his powers. There was still that nagging sense, deep within the back of his mind, which told him it was unethical to wield such powers.

That nagging almost seemed to take a shape as he heard the voice of a young girl behind him, a very familiar voice that turned his stomach to ice. If she had seen what he had done then it would mean the end of everything he held dear. Alex walked towards the rubble he had created and placed his hands upon it. He was resigned to his fate. Behind him the small pitter-patter of tiny footsteps became louder, they heralded the end for him. Each step developed like a bellowing drum with more and more sounding at each moment. There was nothing he could to stop it, to stop her.

"Alex?" She said to him as she placed a gentle hand upon his shaking shoulder.

Alex turned around to face her. She reminded him so much of their mother. The same dark brown hair that fell to just below the shoulders. The same oceanic eyes that seemed to swirl like the ebbs and flows and of a great sea. He could not bear to look into those eyes for shame of what he had done. Alex turned his head away just in time as he noticed one of the trees he had felled, which had landed upright as it was propped by a small trunk which was now giving way, was leaning in towards them. The towering body of the tree, assisted by gravity, fell in their direction and Alex was left with no pause to think about his actions this time. Instinctively he raised his arm to protect himself in case his powers failed him. They did not, as he instantly gathered wind around him which pushed the massive frame of the tree to the side where it fell harmlessly into the soil. There was no hiding what he was now.

Once more he turned to look at his sister, this time making no effort to avoid her eyes so that she might see that, despite everything, he was still the brother she knows and loves. Much to his surprise, and happiness, though, all she did was smile. A pure smile of affection that told Alex that Abigail thought no differently of him. Humans feared what they did not understand, but he knew that his sister, being as intelligent and perceptive as she was, understood it perfectly, or at the very least was aware that Alex presented no danger to her. He embraced his sister in a loving hug, pulling her as tight as he could without constricting her, and nestled his head gently upon her shoulders. Steven's prediction would not come true.

"I always knew you were different." Abigail said as she pulled away from her brother and wiped down her thin blue jumper as she noticed a grass stain upon it.

"Really?" Alex said with genuine surprise. "How?"

"Your eyes." She responded simply.

Alex laughed at just how clever Abigail was. Something that he had only realised a short while ago his sister had picked up on with little difficulty. A sudden thought occurred to him. If she was aware of the correlation between his eye colour and his abilities, and, presuming she had been having the same dreams as himself and their parents, and probably everyone else, then she knew who Magnus was. Even if she did not then, if he told her, she would know how much of a threat he was as she had only just seen exactly what those who possessed the gift were capable of. He needed to find out.

Alex did not even need to ask the question though as, almost as if she had been reading his thoughts, she raised the topic herself.

"Your eyes are just like Magnus Malum's." Abigail said nonchalantly.

"So you know who he is?" Alex asked eagerly, and yet with trepidation also.

"No." She responded, much to his bitter disappointment. "But I've seen you researching him, or I think I have anyway. It's all a bit fuzzy actually." She explained in a clearly frustrated tone.

"It's alright." Alex reassured her. "You're doing far better than anyone else." He wondered why that was.

Another, equally complex, theory occurred to him. Both he and his father had been exposed to elements of Magnus' life in some form whereas no-one else had. They had just been experiencing the nightmares, which no doubt would just be shrugged off as something simple like eating cheese before going to bed. Even Mr Barnes, normally a very astute man, would likely have forgotten everything they had learnt in his lesson when he returned home. For all of his benefits it had to be said that his history teacher did not hang around for very long when the final bell rang. Abigail must have absorbed some of the information that Alex had researched, even though there was almost nothing on him as it was, and made the link to the man in her dreams. That was why she could partially remember!

Alex could almost envisage the round of applause he would be given if he had presented such a theory. He was becoming delirious with his ideas as new knowledge was being poured into him. Knowledge was power, and now he was beginning to gain the power necessary to stop Magnus. He stopped short of celebrating this small victory though as he saw the look upon his sister's face. She was almost in tears.

"He's going to come back isn't he?" She asked.

Alex could not lie to her, she would have seen through it in a heartbeat even if he did. "Yes, I think so." He answered bluntly. "But I promise, on my life, that I will not let any harm come to you or mum, or even Steven." He said with a smile in an attempt to cheer up his sister. It seemed to work as she smiled in return. "Speaking of which, can you not tell Steven about this...he resents me enough as it is."

"He doesn't resent you, he just…dislikes you…" She said coyly.

"Oh thanks." Alex retorted with a laugh.

With all the nastiness sorted out they returned home. He gave her a piggyback ride most of the way as Abigail had grown tired, or so she told him. He was not so sure himself. Alex himself was equally as worn out from the exuberance of his abilities and the realisation that there might be a way to prevent the impending darkness that threatened to swallow them all and drag them deep into the bottomless abyss.

When they got back he placed his sister gently into her bed, even though it was still the afternoon, and decided to take a nap himself. He hoped that in her slumber she would forget everything that they had discussed for he did not want her to needlessly worry over something that she could do nothing about, like he had to. Within seconds of laying back onto his bed, even with the sun still shining, his eyes began to flutter until they closed and he fell into a deep sleep once more.

The dream was not as it had been before. Alex could not control his own thoughts as he floated above a lone figure in the middle of a desert. There was no sign of Arthur, or himself for that matter, there was just this single person shrouded by darkness. Alex did not need any light to know who it was as his spectral view of things shifted downwards, like a camera on a dolly. As he shifted his focus he noticed a shimmering in the background, almost as if he was inside some kind of egg-timer, or prison. The man raised his hands, as though he was inhaling the freshest air after having been taken away from it for so long, and laughed as Alex spotted a small crack in the glass prism.

"Close. So close." Was all Magnus kept uttering.

Chapter 11

Abigail seemed to have no recollection of the previous day. She could remember what happened in the woods, as anyone would, but she could not even recall the name Magnus Malum. It gave breath to the idea that something, or someone, was deliberately trying to remove the villain from history. Magnus seemed to be growing stronger every night though, there was no stopping whatever it was that he was planning. Whoever was trying to erase Magnus, it would not matter soon enough.

Everyone at school had heard about what happened over the weekend at the Imperial War Museum. His wave of supporters seemed to have swelled even further when they found out, thinking he was some kind of bad-boy for his 'rebellious' behaviour. It was all a farce of course, but now he was respected by everyone and Arthur's repute had fallen even further. The fact that the incident had put him on report, a form of behaviour monitoring, with the school only bolstered this. Even Thomas had been enjoying some extra fame, much to his delight, purely through association with Alex. Everyone seemed to want to be his friend. Everyone except Verity. She had been distant from him lately, as if she actually believed that he had changed. He would give up everything he had worked so hard to strip from Arthur if it meant that she saw him favourably.

As he sat in history once again, with Arthur going to every conceivable length to distract his attention so that he could glare at him, he could not help but feel absent. If Magnus truly was returning then there was no point to any of it. No, Alex thought to himself, history was full of the mistakes of the past, mistakes that they could learn from and use to make themselves stronger. Even with Magnus there was something to be learned from his story, despite his history seemingly being merged into the present. The other pupils seemed to pick up on his unwillingness to learn and were goading him into doing something stupid, assuming that he would do it without hesitation. He merely raised an eyebrow at them and turned to look back at the board with his pen in hand. Boring though it was, something he never thought he would hear himself say about history, he needed the information to gain qualifications, or so the school kept telling him. Alex supposed that all Henbane was concerned with was their statistics.

He considered it strange how perceptions can alter like the flick of a switch. He had always seen Henbane as a dreary place full of despair. For one shining moment though it had become the pinnacle of education within his mind, like its real image was hidden by the grey visage surrounded by the school. Yet, now that it did not seem to matter any longer, it had returned to that bleak outlook. Its brief allure had vanished. As he turned to look at Verity though he could not help but see some colour seep back into his surroundings. When she returned his gaze though he could not face her, not when she thought what she did about his behaviour.

Instead Alex looked down at his watch to examine the time, as he was desperate to see the lesson end. He knew that school was important, despite all of his groaning and complaints, but that did not mean that he wanted it to last longer than it should. When he looked down though he was horrified by what he saw. It was broken. A crack, almost exactly like the one Alex had seen in his dream, had appeared somehow. When he had placed it upon his wrist that morning it had been fine with barely a mark upon it, barring some minor scuffing to the leather strap. So how had it broken? And, more importantly, why did it look like the crack from Magnus' prison, or prism, or whatever it was! Alex could not think straight. His mind was filled with the most awful realisation as he looked up at the clock above the whiteboard, for it too was broken in the same way.

No! Alex screamed internally. It was too late, there was nothing to be done. Magnus was returning! Almost on cue he saw the villain appear before him. He was not in a corporeal state, no, it was more like a vision of the man whose ethereal nature gave him the appearance of a ghost. His long features were unmistakable and his repulsive mouth was drawn out into a malicious smile. He was back.

A sudden wave of pain inflicted itself upon him, a kind of mental anguish that physically made him sick from hurting. Instinctively he grasped his head with both hands in some kind of effort to stave away the pain as Magnus' blood-curdling voice filled his head. He had never heard something so terrifying in all his life. The man repeated the same words over and over again to drive home the fact that he was now in control once more.

"I'm back!" He kept saying as he laughed maniacally.

Alex fell to the floor in his agony, which left him dazed and so momentarily blocked out the horrors of both seeing and hearing Magnus at the same time. In his brief moment of respite he looked across the classroom, expecting everyone to be alright as they stared at him in fascination, and saw that everyone was clearly afflicted with the same vision. Some were blinking madly, as though it were some trick of the eyes. Others grasped their heads as he had, as the pain was too much for them. Even more still were crying, for they were the people who had never experienced such terror in the entirety of their lives and it affected them the most. Verity was one such person and he could not take the sight of seeing her in tears.

Mustering what strength he had, and using his powers slightly to gather the wind behind him so that he could lift himself from the floor (as it did not matter now who saw him, they would witness Magnus' powers soon enough), he moved over to where she sat. The use of his powers seemed to blot out most of Magnus, but he was still there in the background, like white noise, causing him anguish.

It was clear that Verity was in no fit state to walk as she did not respond to his attempts to hail her. He could not leave her as she was though, there had to be something he could do to protect her from the malice of Magnus. A thought, hazy though it was, occurred to him and so he scooped her up into his arms and began walking towards the door. With every step the pain seemed to intensify, but he could tell that Magnus was feeling it too. The image inside his head seemed to be visibly pained at exerting himself so. Hopefully he would not be able to keep it up for much longer.

As he carried Verity towards the door he could hear another person rising from their seat as it crashed into the table behind. He knew it was Arthur. Alex had no time to deal with him though as his priority was the woman in his arms. Using his powers once more he pushed the door open, since he had no spare hands, and made his way out into the corridor. His destination was on the floor below him and so he desperately tried to quicken his pace as he felt his strength being zapped from him. As he reached the door to the stairs he heard an almighty bang behind him. As he looked back he could see that it was Arthur. The bully's physical prowess was making him able to withstand the punishment Magnus was inflicting, and, like a shark attracted to blood, he could sense that Alex was weak. Now would be the time to regain his throne.

Alex continued to the foot of the staircase. He knew that he would not be able to outrun Arthur with Verity in his arms and Magnus in his head, and so he did the unthinkable. He looked at Verity and believed that he saw trust in her eyes, although it was difficult for him to tell through her tears. Suddenly she seemed to be slipping out of consciousness, the pain was too much for her body to take. He could see Magnus' face nearly screaming within his head as the agony was unbearable for him too. There had to be a point to what he was doing. Still,

Alex had no time to wait for Magnus to relent his grip upon them all. Trusting in his powers, he dropped her over the edge of the banister! Thankfully though he was able to push the wind underneath her in time to make sure she was gently placed upon the floor. He could tell that she was in a great deal of pain, as was he. Using so much of his energy had almost taken him out.

Arthur thrust open the door to the stairwell and smiled, it was a mixture of happiness and agony though as he stopped for a moment to clutch his head. Alex took the opportunity and vaulted over the banister onto the floor below. He did not have enough energy within him to use his powers at that moment and so he took the ten foot drop on his legs, although with bent knees to avoid shattering anything. Alex howled in pain before gingerly picking up Verity once more and proceeding through the lower-level doors into the detention area. He could hear Arthur slip behind him as he tumbled down the first set of stairs and landed a short distance from the second. It did not seem to deter him though as he looked directly at Alex and began to crawl after him. He was like a man possessed.

Alex pressed on to the detention area where he could see his destination. At the far end of the hallway was a room marked 'Isolation Unit'. It was a soundproofed room that ill-behaved students had to sit in when they had been extremely bad. Alex had never had to go in there before, but now his entry into that room was all he was counting on. With the finish line in sight he sprinted towards it with his hopes held high. Quickly he rammed open the door and placed Verity, who was still struggling to maintain consciousness, on the ground before firmly shutting the door again. His plan came to fruition almost immediately as he saw Verity blink, as if she had been asleep, before she smiled at Alex. It was the best outcome he could have hoped for.

Like it was some sort of sick plan to torment him for as long as possible, the vision of Magnus disappeared from his mind. He called to Verity to stay where she was though in case the image re-emerged. He would come back and get her when everything had been sorted out.

With Verity now safe he could deal with Arthur. He had not been running from him, as the bully believed. He had simply been biding his time. With Magnus now gone from his mind he could focus upon the anger within him, anger which he would use against Arthur. Suddenly Thomas came bounding out from the Geography room, which was adjacent to the detention area, as he had clearly heard his friend's voice.

"Alex!" He shouted. "Did you see-" He could not finish his sentence as he collapsed, whether from exhaustion or pain Alex could not tell. Luckily he managed to break his fall, mostly, by using his powers once again. Thomas would wake up with a headache, but it was better than smacking the floor.

Unlike the others, Arthur casually pushed the door to the hallway open as he knew that he had his 'target' cornered. Like anything when cornered though, Alex was going to fight. He did not want Verity to see what he was about to do, what he had to do to alleviate the year of torment that he had suffered at Arthur's hands. With this in mind he turned left towards the abandoned classroom, which was now only ever used during exam periods as a venue. The setting was definitely eerie, but undoubtedly appropriate as he harnessed the darkness inside of him. Arthur did not hesitate to follow him in, like a lamb to slaughter.

"I've got you now Manningley!" Arthur roared gleefully.

"Oh do you?" Alex responded calmly, hiding the burning rage within him.

Alex was stood at the back of the classroom examining some stains upon the whiteboard from years past. Such fleeting instances were common among humanity, for they were determined to leave their mark upon the world. The victim approached him slowly, confidently, as he believed he had the situation in hand. Suddenly he found himself unable to move though. It did not matter how much he willed it, he would not move again until Alex allowed it.

"Do you remember me saying to that you would spend your life in emotional torment for what you did to me?" Alex said coolly as he turned to face his prey and walked slowly towards him.

"No!" Arthur replied brutishly as he tried again to free himself from Alex's grip. It was of no use though, his superior physique would be of no benefit to him here.

"Of course you don't, because people like you never listen." Alex used his powers to propel him forward so that he stood no further than a few inches from Arthur's now petrified face. "Well listen now!" He hissed in an angry whisper. "I'm going to make a slight amendment to my statement. You won't live in emotional torment because of what you did to me, no…it will because of what I am about to do to you!" He shouted as he flung Arthur against a wall.

There was a loud thud as the victim connected with the surface. He had not done it hard enough to cause Arthur permanent damage but it would have certainly taken the wind from his lungs. Arthur fell to the floor and curled up in pain, revealing a large crack in the wall behind him which would no doubt need repair work done to it. Alex was not finished yet.

As soon as Arthur turned to look at him he outstretched his arms and began to push everything to the side with great force. Tables and chairs smashed against the weak frame of the building causing scratches and surface damage on one side and shattering the windows on the other. Alex was glad that Verity was in the soundproofed room, and that the school would still be preoccupied with what had just occurred, as he did not want her to hear what was happening lest her previous judgement of him be deemed correct. Arthur whimpered, like a scared child, and made a desperate dash upon all fours towards the exit. Alex did not stop him, but he did lock the door with his mind. The strong youth tried frantically to get out before resorting to his usual method of violence, shoulder-bashing the wood in the hopes that it might give way. Eventually, when he realised that there was no hope, he fell onto his knees and turned towards Alex with sympathetic eyes. Alex was not going to forgive him though, not until he had exacted revenge.

Alex hoisted Arthur up, no doubt putting an unbearable strain upon his legs, just as the bully had done to him before. Posters were scrapped from the walls, and his victim's clothes became ragged and torn, as Arthur reached higher and higher until his head was touching the ceiling. Like a deer caught in headlights, he did not know what to do and so simply allowed what was happening to take place. Alex was slightly disappointed that his fun was being ruined so easily.

"Do you know how much suffering I have had to put up with from you?!" He shouted. "You have crept into my mind and broken it down from within! People who didn't even know me were judging me! You forced me into believing that I wasn't even worth scrapping off of the bottom of your shoe…" He allowed his words to linger before he committed his final atrocity. The very thing that had caused him to forsake his powers would now become his catalyst for revenge. "You invaded my mind, now I will invade yours."

Without hesitation he willed himself inside of Arthur's head with no shame or compunction. He was shocked by what happened next, aside from the searing pain that was coursing through him. He was not just seeing through Arthur's eyes, he had his memories as well. Alex could see everything from Arthur's life, and it gave him a whole new perspective upon the bully.

One memory was of Arthur, only a couple of years younger than he was now, talking to his father, a well-built bald man, about some trouble he was having at school, something he thought would never have happened to Arthur. He was a scrawny boy, not like the intimidating presence he gave off now. Even his home was relatively unkempt. Every aspect that he could see of Arthur's life helped to create pity for him, and heart-breaking shame for

Alex. The words of advice that came from his father's mouth had shaped his child's future ever since. He told Arthur that he should never let people step over him, he should be the one stepping over others as though they were insects and he was a boot. Arthur had taken his father's advice to heart and began to transform himself into the man that he had become.

Alex suddenly felt quite awful for what he was doing. Arthur had not always been a bully. He had once been the victim and, as a response, had been driven into changing who he was to protect himself. No doubt the power he had gained had corrupted his mind, driving him into the Arthur that had continually tormented Alex for the entire year. The metamorphosis of Arthur Cressing was not unlike what was happening to him, an obvious comparison that even Alex could not deny. Yet even still, even aware of what he was doing to both himself and Arthur, he could not bring himself to release control of Arthur's mind, not after everything that the bully had done to him. Suddenly, like his subconscious knew that he needed to find himself again, the words of his family came into his head.

"To overcome anything, we must push all restrictions aside and focus on those we love…" He heard himself uttering with the echo of his father's voice. "Remember them, for when you need them the most, they will help you find your way."

He released his grip and relinquishing control of Arthur's mind back to him.

Alex had never felt so appalled by his actions. When he killed Muffin it had been an accident, a misunderstanding as he did not know how to handle his abilities. Even with Steven it was much the same, he did not know what he was doing or what he was capable of. But this, this act of terrorism, had been completely of his own volition and he knew exactly how much it would hurt them both. Perhaps he needed this experience to evolve and adapt past the primal need to exercise his abilities. It was no excuse though. There could be no excuse for his horrendous actions.

Arthur, having fallen to the ground once again when Alex released him, collected himself and looked up at Alex. There was no fire in his eyes, no burning hatred or palpable need for revenge. Arthur had been completely subjugated. Alex had won.

Yet he still felt awful, worse than he had ever felt. He knew that an apology would not set things right, nothing could, but it would be a start. Alex extended his hand to help Arthur to his feet. His victim did not reciprocate the gesture though as he scrambled onto his feet and pinned himself as tightly as he could against the wall. His collar was ruffled, his jeans ripped, and sweat covered every inch of him. He looked awful, and it was all Alex's fault. Why was it that the victim appeared ruined when the victor, standing untouched with his blue jeans and neatly ironed polo shirt, was left without a mark? That was not justice. He had to do something to make it right.

"Arthur…" He began his apology, and stammered as he was unsure of how to continue.

The former bully did not give him time to go further though as he seized his opportunity and sprinted out of the door, no doubt hoping to never enter that room again lest he be reminded of the horrors that Alex committed within. Alex had no means of redemption now, he was completely without hope, as Arthur had been. His father's words echoed in his head once more, and he did not know where else to turn. He reached into his pocket and pulled out his mobile phone, which would be considered inferior compared to some of the modern smartphones. He looked through his list of contacts, which only consisted of family and Thomas, and found the several numbers that he had for his father. This was an emergency, for he was losing sight of who he was, and so he could not wait until Charles was off duty for him to answer his mobile. Thus, with a great sense of trepidation, he phoned the base that his father was stationed at, along civilian communications of course. There was no connection. The tone was dialling but no-one was picking up.

A horrible thought occurred to him, as it often seemed to in such troubling times. What if everyone there saw Magnus as well? His father had found the metal leg, perhaps the villain had managed to penetrate their minds as well. Out of desperation he rang his father's mobile, as it was now the only way of reaching him. Much to his delight he heard the call connect. But before he could even begin to get his troubles off of his chest his father uttered something that made Alex's heart sink with complete despair.

"Alex! Did you see him too?"

Chapter 12

Charles put down the phone with a sense of impending disaster that he had never before experienced in his life. His entire adulthood had been spent covering his back and making sure that his troops survived every possible threat. Skirmishes; full on battles; bombs and Improvised Explosive Devices; guerrilla warfare, all of them dangerous with the obvious threat of death attached to them. Yet these things had never given him this intense feeling of helplessness like Magnus had. There was no preparation that could be made for a man who could invade minds and tear them down from within.

He seemed to be the only one affected by the vision of Magnus though. His soldiers were still stood exactly as they were, exactly as they had been when the noble-featured man appeared within him like the image of a ghost. It was like they had accepted his presence as a fact, as if Magnus had been known to them for some time. That would certainly explain their unusual behaviour, Charles thought to himself.

They stood now transfixed, in their regular positions on the parade square, like nothing happened. If Magnus had taken control of them again then his life was in danger, based on their aggressive behaviour before. Although Charles found it curious that they had not tried to murder him already, given that they had had ample opportunity to do so. Yet, they seemed as if they had no recollection of these events. If Magnus had released them then he needed to know why. All too often in the world were henchmen terminated when their use had come to an end. Magnus' return heralded only one thing, death.

Charles was at a loss. He feared for his family, for his friends, and for his troops. There could be no doubt that Magnus had somehow found a way to cheat death for decades, and now he was back. There was no way of knowing where, and no hope of ascertaining this information. For the first time in his life the situation was out of his hands. He felt grateful that the weight would soon be lifted from his shoulders, or so he hoped, and he could concentrate on protecting his family.

As he thought it he heard the rotating blades of a helicopter sounding in from the distance. Charles removed himself from the storeroom, where had had been staring at the metal leg they had found since Magnus had appeared within his mind, and locked the door behind him as he checked his pistol, an LA106A1 German-made weapon, was still in its holster. His men still stood, as one would expect from a perfect soldier, on the parade ground with unfaltering correctness in the blistering midday heat. Charles walked across the desert grounds towards the helipad with a kind of childish glee as he knew that his sense of pressure was about to be greatly relieved.

The helicopter, a Puma HC1, was carrying the three staff that needed to operate it as well as six passengers. Three of them were bodyguards, one an analyst and one a translator. Charles, as harsh as it sounded, did not really care about them though as it was the man who accompanied them that concerned him. The helicopter gradually descended and sent up a haze of sand as it blew away everything around it. The crew, consisting of a pilot; a weapons systems officer and a regular crewman, were trained to deal with all kinds of terrain and so this did not seem to deter their descent, even if it did hinder their vision. A deafening roar accompanied the aircraft as it touched down upon the crude concrete markings of its target.

Charles made sure to maintain his distance throughout this to avoid having sand in his eyes and wind in his ears.

The blades ceased rotating and the figures from within emerged into the sunlight like heroes on return from a mission. The truth was much less glamorous though as they came into clear sight and Charles could see the one amongst them that he was interested in. He was dressed exactly as Charles was but on his chest was the crown and double pip that indicated his rank. The Colonel.

He appeared to be a well groomed man with not a single hair out of place, not that there was much hair if his thin sides were anything to go by. A small scar was visible above his right eye, as it made it not quite open fully, although there was no sign of damage on the eye itself, which stretched to just below the orbital bone. His uniform was neatly pressed and the creases were amplified as nicely as if the kit had only been bought a few days beforehand. He was clearly a punctual and regimented man, not unlike Charles himself. The Major raised his right arm in open salute, with his palm facing outwards, in respect of his superior.

The Colonel walked straight past him. There was not even time for a single word to be uttered as his superior marched his way towards the parade ground. The Colonel was a man of action it seemed. Charles was grateful that that was at least one duty he could be relieved of for a while. He checked his phone to see if Alex had rung him again, as his son was just as terrified of Magnus and the danger that he posed as he was. There was nothing though and Charles had to carry on with the painful thought of Magnus running amok in his home country whilst they floundered about in a territory that was largely civilian and had little risk of insurgency. Obviously not that small, Charles pondered to himself, otherwise there would be no need for the Colonel's presence. The army was always taught to expect insurrection from the locals, but never from their own troops as Charles had experienced. The hasty nature of the Colonel told Charles that the military brass was taking this situation very seriously indeed.

He turned to follow his superior and found himself lagging behind at the Colonel's surprising speed. He was some ten paces behind him when Cassandra rounded the corner to his right and met up with him. She saluted her Major but was unable to do the same for the Colonel as she paced herself next to Charles and walked alongside him.

"Is that the Colonel, sir? She asked.

"It is." He replied plainly.

"Did he say anything?" She continued.

"No, not a word." He responded just as bluntly.

"Are you alright?" She enquired. When there was no reaction from her superior she tried again with a more personal touch. "Charles?"

The Major stopped where he was and pulled his Lieutenant to one side. He glimpsed the Colonel looking back to where he was briefly and shaking his head indignantly, as if Charles was some sort of slacker. He let it pass and answered his subordinate's probes.

"No, I'm not. I'm worried."

"About what?" She spoke as she gently placed a hand upon his shoulder and smiled at him to alleviate him of some worry. "You know you can talk to me."

"You're a loyal friend Cassandra, and you always have been." He said as he thought upon her upcoming promotion, which he would discuss with the Colonel, so that she might replace him and he could retire to be with his family. "What do you mean 'about what'?" He suddenly thought. "You didn't see him?"

"See who?" She retorted innocently.

"Magnus Malum."

The very mention of his name seemed to root her to the spot, since she had also been affected by the metal leg that they had found. Her short black hair almost stood on end and her face paled, but there was no recognition of him within her eyes. It was like her body knew who he was but she did not.

"You can't remember him can you?" Charles asked. "In fact, I'll bet there are huge chunks of your day that you just can't quite recall anymore...am I right?"

"No." Cassandra replied with a croaking voice that was blocked by fear. "I mean no I don't remember him...and yes...you're right, there are hours that just seem blank to me." A sudden look of horror was etched on her chiselled features. "You don't think..."

"No..." Charles stopped her. "This has nothing to do with your mother's disease. There is something far more sinister and infinitely more powerful at work here. I thought nothing of it at first, thinking that some sort of virus was spreading through the camp, but now I see the folly of my unwillingness to believe what was really at stake."

"And what is at stake?"

"The world." He exclaimed before he brought himself back onto the main stretch of road that ran through the camp.

Cassandra followed hot on his heels as they quick-marched to the parade ground, where the Colonel was no doubt already getting acquainted with his soldiers. Charles just wanted to get it all over with so that he could announce his retirement to the Colonel and be with his family. Being such a longstanding member of the British Army, and being of significant rank also, meant that they would give him his life back as quickly as they could. He would live comfortably off of his pension for the rest of his life, as well as significant earnings which he had kept. Not that any of that mattered at the moment. All that mattered was finding out where Magnus was, only then could he decide his future.

Much to his surprise, as he glanced out across the never-ending sea of golden sand that extended before him, the Colonel was stood at the back of the parade ground, some fifty feet from the front, where his men stood with him patiently with their arms folded behind their backs. It was customary for the leading officer to stand to the left of the troops, Charles' right, so that he might be given information by his subordinates before inspecting the men individually. This was no ordinary inspection though, and the Colonel was clearly no ordinary officer.

His superior gave him a single nod to indicate the start of the parade. Charles stood with his own arms placed firmly behind his back, shaking slightly, and with the Lieutenant next to him as he dispensed with the formalities, putting the men to 'ease'. Only then did he commence his speech.

"Listen up!" He shouted. "We have with us the Colonel today, who came all the way from Camp Bastion just for this, and so I want you to be damn near perfect!" The troops were clearly confused as to why the highest ranking officer in their region was standing behind them. "He is here because of your appalling behaviour lately!"

He could not continue any further. The sudden image of Magnus appeared within his mind once again, causing him a great deal of mental anguish. His soldiers were clearly perplexed by what was happening as they muttered to themselves. Charles could not chastise them and neither could the Colonel as he too appeared to be affected by the hideous vision. Cassandra, strangely, was not though and she leaned in to the Major and whispered in his ears.

"Are you alright?" She echoed from earlier.

His answer had not improved though as he witnessed Magnus' face contort in agony as he placed his hands in a pulling motion, despite not touching anything. The energy he was exerting was clearly monumental as sweat ran off of his brow and fell into the sand at his feet, which was being pushed around him as he struggled. Suddenly it became apparent what was happening though as some glass, that seemed to be situated above Magnus and already had a crack running through it, began to pull apart to reveal a tear big enough for the man to slip through.

Magnus, pulling a handkerchief from the lapel of his waistcoat, wiped his brow and fell to his knees with a deviant smile that stretched from ear to ear. "Finally, I return!" He yelled before the image was suddenly removed from Charles' mind, gone just as quickly as it had arrived.

Charles fell onto his own knees from exhaustion. When Cassandra asked about him again he waved her away and instructed her to check on the Colonel. Unwillingly she stepped off of the small concrete patch that they had been standing on and ran through the sand towards the Colonel, kicking up a bucket of the substance with every stride. Before she could even get halfway though there was an almighty shake around them as a bright light began emanating from Charles' left.

He turned to look at the light and saw the vague outline of a shape emerge from it. At first he thought it must be car headlights on full beam, but then he noticed that the light had a shape to it. The shaped was exactly the same as the one that Magnus had just made out of the glass. Charles felt an unfamiliar sense of fear within him that made his back crawl as the figure came into view. It was clearly a man who was dressed in a suit with a waistcoat. The golden chain of a fog watch could be seen from the lower right hand pocket whilst the lapel sported a white handkerchief with the initials 'MM' written in gold inlay. In his hands were a top hat and a fur coat that had obviously been removed to cope with the dry heat of their surroundings. There could be no doubt about who this man was. It was Magnus.

Cassandra, and all of his troops, raised their weapons towards the intruder, who did not adhere to their requests to cease movement. He carried on undeterred until he reached the concrete road that ran through the camp. Delicately, and deliberately at a slow pace so as to induce fear, he placed his hat and coat upon the ground before rolling up the sleeves of his white shirt. His leather shoes, Italian loafers if Charles had to guess, sounded his approach as he walked across the concrete towards the parade ground.

Magnus was not an ugly man, like you would expect from such a grotesquely repulsive individual, as aside from his pointed nose, he could be described as having a handsome appearance that extenuated his noble features. He was clearly aware of his 'look' as he made sure his slicked back black hair was placed firmly behind his ears so that no loose strands obscured his vision. It was his eyes that Charles noticed the most though, as much as he did not want to. They were a piercing green just like his son's, and now they were glowing fiercely like something within was trying to escape.

"I said stop!" Charles heard Cassandra shouting as he struggled back to his feet.

"Ah, my minions." Magnus said casually in his well-accented voice. He was clearly from the heartland of England, most likely Hertfordshire, or possibly Buckinghamshire or Oxfordshire. "This is the problem with humanity, so fickle."

"Stop talking!" The Lieutenant commanded.

"Insolent whelp!" Magnus spat back. "But of course, it is just like humanity to ignore the majesty of those greater than yourselves. You would rather bury your heads in the sand and ignore the blindingly obvious than actually believe…well…" He smiled maliciously. "You may have your wish."

Without warning, and without Magnus moving a single muscle, the dunes around the soldiers lifted high into the air to form a canopy over them all, covering those underneath in darkness and quashing any hopes of survival that they might have had. Cassandra gave him a single look, filled with a single tear, before it came crashing down upon them all. It was unlike anything that Charles had ever experienced. In war there was always a way to wound your enemy, but there was nothing his Lieutenant could do about the huge volumes of sand that had fallen upon her. No bodies were left, it was as if they never existed.

Charles screamed in anger and drew his pistol from his hip, firing several rounds in Magnus' direction. They fell short of their target. Somehow a weapon that could fire up to a mile in length had dipped over five feet within the space of a few metres. Magnus turned around to face him with a cocked eyebrow, almost as if he was amused by Charles' ill-fated attempt at revenge.

The Major's arms were suddenly outstretched and his legs were clamped together, holding him in place, as he was lifted a few inches from the ground so that his entire weight was placed upon his feet, causing him a great deal of pain from his efforts. He could not move. As Magnus was focusing on him Charles spotted, from the corner of his eye, movement at the back of the parade ground. The Colonel had survived the assault along with two of his bodyguards, the others had clearly been too slow-minded to evade the devastation, and was now sprinting back towards the helipad. Magnus lifted himself from the ground and followed them as he glided through the air as gracefully as a bird, as though it were second nature to him.

The Puma was equipped with machine guns, which the bodyguards mounted, flares and missile warnings. There could be no warning for what Magnus was about to though, and there was no stopping him as the bullets seemed to curve around him and fall harmlessly into the sand, as if there was a barrier around him. Charles watched as the Colonel strapped himself inside the machine to protect himself, but it was no use. Magnus, just as he had before, raised the dunes around the airspace and brought them heavily down upon the helicopter. There were no flames and no explosion, it had simply been buried beneath him. In the blink of an eye Charles had watched everyone around him fall to the powers of this madman, and yet he had been left alive. Once again his anxiety flared within him as he feared for the safety of his family, now more than ever.

Casually, as if he had done nothing wrong, Magnus walked back towards Charles and smiled as silence reigned in around them. Desperately he struggled to free himself from the man's invisible grasp, but it was to no avail. He could move his eyes, his hands and his feet; he could blink; he could swallow and he could breathe, but he could not move. It was as though shackles were being placed upon his limbs and midriff, like an invisible form of crucifixion.

Charles was disgusted by the man who so gleefully smiled. He killed without mercy and he gave no quarter. Charles had killed, but not without good cause, and a mountain of shame and regret. Yet Magnus seemed to be enjoying himself. The man stretched out his limbs as he continued approaching the Major. With every lean the villain groaned slightly and let out a sound of relief, as if he had not been able to do so for years. Within a second, before Charles could think further upon his abhorrence for Magnus, the man was before him. Clearly he was able to propel himself in any direction he wanted to with little to no effort.

"Why am I alive?" Charles asked honestly.

"You are strong, I can feel it. A man of wisdom. A man whose words would carry weight. You will tell them for me." He spoke clearly.

"What do you mean? What should I tell them? And who's them?"

"Questions!" Magnus laughed. "I knew you were an astute man, for only the wise ask questions, whilst the sheep follow blindly. I have observed this 'modern' world and I know that you can communicate as freely as you like with anyone with little effort, a disgusting advancement that I will not sully myself with." He spat upon the floor to show his disdain. "I could do it myself but it would bring further pain unto me…and I must rest, and plan my attack…" He said slowly. "You will tell them, your superiors I mean, that I am Magnus Malum, and I have returned!"

Chapter 13

He knew it. In truth he had known it for weeks, but had done absolutely nothing to prevent or prepare for Magnus' return. The phone call with his father had confirmed that the villain was back in the world of the living and Alex had a horrible feeling that he would stop at nothing to complete his conquest of the world. There had been no sign of him though. Magnus had returned and yet the sun had set and risen as it would on any normal day. Magnus was hidden.

Alex had rushed home as soon as the visions had ceased. Arthur vanished after the turmoil that he had put him through and Verity too, much to his horror, had retreated. When he left school everything seemed to have been exactly the same as when he had left his home that morning. People returned from work to their loving families to recount the stories of their day without a single hint of the horrors that were about to be unleashed upon them. There was no fire raining down from the heavens, no screams of peril of despair, no signs that anything at all was out of the ordinary. His family had been performing their usual activities and had greeted him in their regular manner. Dinner occurred as usual and television programmes remained uninterrupted by emergencies. The only thing that had changed was Thomas' attitude towards him. His best friend had taken to ignoring him for his actions, even though it was Thomas that often encouraged him to use his abilities. When Alex had questioned him about it though he made it very clear that he had never meant for Alex to abuse his abilities, believing instead that they should be used for good to protect and help people. Alex had so far only used them for his own selfish reasons.

Thankfully, though, there had not even been a nightmare for him that night. To Alex, however, that was the biggest indication possible that Magnus was amongst them once more, like a God descended from on high to wreak havoc upon the world of man. Clearly there was no longer any need for him to push himself into the minds of the living, not when the atrocities could, and most assuredly would, be experienced first-hand. So far as Alex knew he was the only one that could stop him. He had no idea how though.

Despite all of this, the only thing that concerned him at that moment was the bitterly disappointed look that Charlotte had in her eyes as she looked at her son with tears welling. She simply could not believe that a child of hers would be so destructive and seem so remorseless. Even Arthur, who was present in the room, was not taking any enjoyment out of the punishment that Alex was facing from the headmaster. He was still too traumatised.

Alex took a moment to distract himself from the ceaseless tirade of spit and anger that was emanating from the mouth of the leader of his school. The headmaster's office was not very impressive for someone of his standing. A pretty accurate synonym for the entire school, Alex found himself thinking as, in the end, it was just bricks and mortar. It could easily fall, just like the world.

The room itself had very little to it barring a nice oak desk and a small plasma television attached to the wall behind the headmaster's head, presumably so that he could check on the news without being distracted by it. Everywhere else, in an erratic mess, sat files for every conceivable aspect of the school and its students. One in particular caught Alex's eye as it read 'expelled students'. He could not help feeling that he would soon be joining that ill-reputed list. Not that it mattered to him though, he just wanted to make sure that his mother would be able to forgive him before their lives were put in perpetual danger.

Alex's mind focused back into the room as the headmaster was filling the air with his spittle. Of all the people that Alex had seen enter and leave the leader of the school's office, he had never thought that he would be one of them. The deathly stare of the middle-aged man's sinewy face had broken down many pupils, but Alex was not fazed by it. He was still too preoccupied and just wanted to get home.

"Alex?!" The headmaster shouted at him.

Alex did not respond as the leader had expected. He simply inclined his head towards the man and raised an eyebrow. He did not even care if he was about to get expelled for his apparently appalling behaviour. Charlotte registered his lack of empathy at his situation and broke down into tears once again, actually believing that her son was a monster. Perhaps I am, he thought to himself. After all, even though he deeply regretted it, he had invaded the mind of another purely in the name of vengeance. He had inflicted severe mental tortures upon Arthur that could not easily be forgiven, and it was only the latest offence in a string of hideous behaviour. These instances had only occurred because he had hidden himself away, but now there was no reason to do so. If Magnus had returned then it was his duty to do everything he could to stop him, and yet he was wasting time in a small office whilst having abuse shouted at him and guilt driven into him by his mother.

"How could you act like this Alex?" His mother asked him. "Your father and I raised you to be better than this…"

Alex suddenly felt his heart crash. He could not deny that she was right for he had acted absolutely shockingly. His father would be ashamed of his actions, and it was quite clear that his mother already was. He hadn't meant to behave in such a manner though. It was driven from a mixture of fear and anger, fear from the obvious return of Magnus, and anger from the scared teenager in front of him who was seated next to the headmaster.

Alex looked at his watch to try and comfort him. There was nothing but a cracked screen though, and even the gears underneath had stopped working. Charles had told him that as long as that watch worked he would be safe, and his father would come back to him. Due to its current state he had never felt more vulnerable in his entire life. Everything around him was crumbling and Magnus had not even shown himself. His father was not responding to his mother's phone calls, as they often checked on each other daily. His brother despised him. His best friend was not speaking to him because of how he had treated Arthur, as even he did not want to see a person put through what Alex had done to him. Even Verity most likely could not stand him, as everyone now knew of what he had done to Arthur.

"Do you have any explanation for your shocking behaviour towards Mr Cressing?" The headmaster bellowed as Alex snapped back into reality.

Alex shook his head indifferently. Of course he cared deeply about what he had done and wanted to make amends, but it was blindingly clear that such a reprieve was not possible and so his shame turned to ambivalence. It was at this point, much to Alex's chagrin as this was exactly what he did not need, that Arthur spoke.

"You looked inside my mind..." He said with a shaky voice that was indicative of his hidden rage and fright. "You strolled about inside as if it was your own. How?" He continued with a glassy-eyed expression. "How is that possible?"

The headmaster, yet again to Alex's surprise and ultimately his shame, interjected. "Don't be so utterly ridiculous Arthur!" He snapped. "Walked inside your mind indeed!" He scoffed. "That's what bullies like him do!" He shouted whilst staring at Arthur but pointing a finger squarely at Alex's chest. Alex did not appreciate the accusation. "They get inside your mind to tear you apart from within..."

"NO!" A suddenly angry Arthur shouted. "It was real…He took control of my mind and tore apart that old classroom without touching anything!" Arthur prostrated.

"What rubbish!" The headmaster retorted, seemingly forgetting that it was in fact Alex, not Arthur, who was the one in trouble. "Did anyone else witness this miraculous feat?"

"Well…Verity Lane was in the room next door…" Arthur tried to retort, and Alex physically winced at the mention of her name.

"Did…anyone…see it?"

Arthur shook his head indignantly.

"That's because it didn't happen." The headmaster exclaimed with his victory.

"You saw him as well sir." Alex spoke, finally deciding to try and defend himself despite his horrific behaviour.

"Him? Who's him?"

"Magnus Malum." Alex said softly.

Everyone in the room froze with irrefutable recognition of the man. Even the very walls of the building, grey though they were, seemed to grow paler as if in fear of him. Henbane itself shuddered. Charlotte and Arthur had sudden expressions of terror etched across every feature of their face, albeit if it was only for a brief moment before they regained their respective composures of disappointment and angry resignation. Yet, the headmaster, being a more rational man, simply shook his head as though he were attempting to deny the man's existence. Sure enough, just as Alex thought it, the school's leader spoke up to try and dispel Alex's suggestions.

"Nonsense, pure nonsense…it was just some sort of contaminant in the water supply…happens all the time."

Alex did not try and protest, as he knew it was pointless to do so, but that did not stop the headmaster acting as though he did. With an air of authority he raised his finger to his mouth to indicate silence. Charlotte, as if she herself were a pupil at the school, fell into an obedient quietness as the headmaster issued his punishment.

"The bullying alone, considering your previous, and shockingly recent, destructive behaviour, is enough to have you expelled." He paused for a moment and shot a glance towards his mother as she broke down into tears again. "So, not only will you be taken away from this school but, to further your shame, you shall pay for the damage done to this school. You should be expecting a bill of no less than a thousand pounds when the work gets sorted out."

Charlotte turned to look at her son with a hideous mixture of abundant rage and disappointment. Not only did she have to suffer the horrendous shame of having her son expelled from Henbane, and thus leaving him with no other options locally to do his A-Levels, but she also had to magically conjure up a four figure sum of money. The tension between them was palpable as Alex stared into the eyes of his mother, hoping to convey some sense of regret and praying for forgiveness in return. She was not interested though.

Suddenly Alex's mind turned him towards the television situated behind the headmaster's desk. It was not switched on, but that did not matter as the screen came to life with little effort from himself. The headmaster did not seem to notice that there was noise in the room that was not coming from himself as he continued his rant about Alex's abysmal behaviour and his apparent lack of remorse. Alex did not care though as he focus was now completely on the television.

"You are a complete and utter disgrace to this school! And to your family!" The headmaster shouted at him. Alex did not take his eyes off of the screen. "How can you just sit there? Say something boy! Ah, but you won't, bullies like you are happy to pipe up when there's a victim nearby. Let me tell you something…" The headmaster whispered angrily as he leaned over the desk towards Alex and his mother. "You'll not find a victim in me my lad, and you will answer in full for what you have done! You should be thankful that the authorities haven't been alerted and yet all you can do is sit there and stare into the distance at…" Words failed him. "At what exactly?"

Alex did not need to respond as his mother also turned to look at the catastrophe unfolding on the television screen.

"Oh…my…God."

The headmaster, now instantly worried, turned to face the screen were words failed him again. There was nothing that could be said that could adequately describe the carnage being displayed before them, although the field representative for the channel was doing his best.

"You join me here in Leeds!" The reporter shouted above the hideous groans that the monstrous machines let out as they slammed their gigantic metal rods firmly into the ground. "There are machines of terrible proportions literally tearing down the city as they move through it!"

People were screaming and running in every direction, creating a tremendously inharmonious cacophony of shrieks and bellows that befuddled any who were trying to listen to the report. The reporter clearly realised as he turned around to survey his surroundings and was forced to cover his ears to blurt out the undying din. Dust covered the streets as people furiously sprinted towards him, and thus away from the destructive force that was upon them, and he was thankful that he was wearing his contact lenses rather than his glasses. He didn't know right now whether to consider his job a blessing or a curse, quite probably the latter at this moment in time. The reporter knew that all hope of his coverage was lost in the chaos and so decided to make sure that people would at least have some idea of what was happening.

The cameraman was fixated on the reporter, desperately trying to avoid looking at the devastation that was unfolding a mere one-hundred or so yards in front of them. The reporter noticed the folly of his colleague and tried to direct his attention towards the monstrosities.

"Robert!" He screamed. "Point at the machines!"

The cameraman, suddenly shocked back into reality by his yelling comrade, turned towards the towering machines, not daring to open his eyes for fear of what he would be looking at. They were behemoths in stature, standing no smaller than two-hundred feet each, with one nearly twice the size of the others. Their numbers were not great, as there was only five in total, but that was all that was needed. Their four legs, arranged in an 'x' pattern about a third of the way up the main frame of the machine, slammed into buildings and brought down entire chunks whilst leaving themselves unharmed. The cameraman winced as the one closest to them, now some seventy odd yards away, raised its centre piece, a giant slab of metal that reminded him of an ancient pillar, although made of metal and clearly designed to rise and fall. The metal came crashing into the ground, the plate at its bottom slamming tremendously and razing the damaged buildings around it with a sickening screech of metal against metal. The minute seismic activity it created was clearly too much for the already weakened structures. Great swathes of the sites began to shake loose from their foundations and fall towards the ground like an almighty meteor shower, or gigantic hailstones. The buildings collapsed inwards, fortunately for the reporter and his colleague, and so any who had not managed to break away from the assault would no doubt be lost. All of this happened inside a few seconds, the efficiency of the destruction clear for all who were watching.

Alex stared at the machines in complete horror. His mind cast back to the metal leg that he saw at the Imperial War Museum in London and realised that it must have been from one of these behemoths that he was now witnessing. This meant this his father had encountered the same thing, how far had Magnus' power spread? Alex thought to himself. How far would it stretch again?

Suddenly, from behind the machines, a lone figure appeared to be descending onto the field of carnage, floating down like an angel. Though it was impossible to tell from such a distance, and through the lens of a dusty camera, Alex knew that it could only be one man. The cameraman gasped as he watched the man creep closer towards them with his arms deliberately outstretched to draw attention to himself, shattering any glass remaining on the damaged buildings and sending its dust-like remains onto the fleeing townspeople below; Alex was thankful that was out of shot though. As the man came into full view of the camera his identity was confirmed. Dressed in an old-style suit with a waistcoat and slicked-back dark hair, and with rolled up sleeves that somewhat highlighted his incredibly skeletal frame, he was clearly of the old world where class systems determined success in society.

The reporter had already started backing away from the scene slowly as he shuffled towards an alley that was only some twenty feet from where he stood. What he saw next confused him, for he did not know whether to run away as fast as he could; stay rooted to the spot like a piece of petrified wood; or make a quick dash for the narrow alleyway before him and thus remain in check with his original plan. They all had their drawbacks and he could see no positive options for himself; the safety of his cameraman had not even factored into his decisions.

The lone figure, stopping around fifty feet above them and in front of them, whirled the small licks of fires that were present from the chaos and turned them into swirling infernos, miniature suns so large that he could feel their heat even with the distance and height between them. The reporter could not believe his eyes. Everything else was possible, improbable and completely manic, but possible. Yet this, he struggled to find the words, was like magic.

"Tim…" Robert tried to gesture but found himself unable to. "I can't move!" He said with a clear sense of horror that the audience could understand.

Before he had further time to try and rationalise the situation in his mind the madman sent the fire sprawling into the streets. In a split second he dashed towards the alleyway and just managed to dive into it as the flames licked at his heels. He could feel the hairs on his leg singe off as the skin underneath was beginning to turn red from the small amount of contact it had had with the flames. Gently, he propped himself up against the wall of the building he had just been standing on front of him to inspect the damage to his legs.

Alex watched the unfolding display with a kind of morbid fascination that made him feel sick, after all it was a truly impressive display of the kind of power that Alex could one day wield. Magnus clearly felt no remorse for his repugnant behaviour as he descended the final few feet onto the ground just in front of where the camera was positioned. The others in the room had previously been unable to identify Magnus, but now his face was clearly in view. Arthur screamed as he noticed who it was, clearly remembering that it was the same man who had appeared in their minds the day before. His mother kept silent as she struggled to comprehend the irrational behaviour of the man who had haunted them all. The headmaster kept muttering the same phrase under his breath, wanting to maintain his rational presence of mind despite the clear evidence that not everything was immediately explainable.

"It's not possible." He kept chanting, almost like a mantra.

The reporter watched the man land around the corner from him and quickly snapped his head back behind the wall. He prayed to God that the man had not seen him, it was too late for Robert though, or so he kept telling himself. There was nothing he could do to help anyway. He let out a small sigh as he resigned himself to hiding in the alleyway, until he turned his head to the left that was. Shockingly he noticed that the alleyway was no more than twenty feet long before it ended, and he had no other alternative routes to take. The only way out was through the way that he had come in. With arms raised, he looked up to the blue sky to see if there was some sort of answer as to why he had been condemned. His world was quickly coming to an end, yet the earth continued as normal, quite happy to see its occupants snuffed out in an instant.

Gingerly he placed a hand upon the cement corner that slightly jutted out from the wall, highlighting the shoddy workmanship, his fingernails only just passing its edge to avoid the threat of detection. It did not appear to work though as the man wielding such destruction like a toy was already glaring at him with piercing hawk-like eyes as his own eyes dared to look out into the road. Desperately, with his presence now known, he broke into a run to try and escape the burned streets that this villain stalked.

"Pathetic." Magnus spoke. "Typical of humanity."

Alex did not see what was happening, all he knew was that Magnus had prematurely ended the life of yet another innocent. All it took was a simple outreach of his hand, which was also purely just a way of showcasing his power since it was obviously not required, and a spark of his green eyes for the person's existence to be extinguished. His power was awe inspiring, dreadful in every sense of the word, but awe inspiring all the same and that was something that Alex could not deny despite his burning hatred for the man.

Robert did not want to look to his left, given what occurred only a few seconds before. Instead he focused on the man in front of him, the cold-hearted killer who now threatened him also. The devastation that he was capable of causing was already clear to see from the scarred buildings. The machines had stopped tearing them to pieces but their skins were burned black from the waves of flame that had licked up against them. What had appeared new only an hour beforehand now looked ancient, as if time itself had enclosed around it but left the rest of the city untouched. The same could be said of the occupants who had rapidly transitioned from life to death in a matter of moments. Not that Robert could see them, any trace of their existence had been burnt to cinders, like they were only a dream or a story.

"Why did you do that?" Robert asked from behind the camera, his face remaining unseen but his fear obvious to all through the tremors in his voice.

Magnus shot a piercing stare through the camera to its wielder, although it gave the impression that he was staring at those watching this particular report. He did not seem to understand the question, as though he could not fathom the idea that human life might be worth something. His reply was equally as cold and calculated. "He was not needed." He answered simply. "Now, is this contraption working as programmed to?"

The cameraman uttered an obedient 'yes' in such hushed tones that it was almost imperceptible. Magnus nodded his understanding before speaking a damning sentence. "Then neither are you." Was all he had to say before the camera jerked slightly as its holder was detached from the machine, his condition unknown to the audience.

Alex felt uncontrollable rage inside of him. Even though he was right in front of him, for thousands to see, he still could not believe that it was real. The slaughter had truly begun. Magnus peered deep into the camera so that his features were clearly visible and Alex almost broke the television in his rage, only holding back because he wanted to see what it was that Magnus had to say.

"People of the world...I am Magnus Malum." He stopped for a moment. "Some of you may recognise me..." He said with a terrible grin that oozed malice. "You have witnessed the trail of destruction that I have left in my wake in only a matter of minutes. Soon, very soon, the fate of this city shall be the fate of you all. The human race..." He laughed heartily to himself with an unmistakeable tone of superiority. "You decrepit species, laughable, every single one of you. Only the elite amongst you, those who possess the same abilities as myself, will survive my oncoming purge, provided you do not resist me of course...For seventy years I have been locked away, like a secret that you desperately tried to forget, but now I am free to finish what I began so long ago. It is one of my own that I have to thank for this, I know his features, I see them in my mind even now…but I know not his name."

Alex knew that he meant him, it was the only possible explanation.

"Step forward, my brave minion, and claim your reward." Magnus continued, although clearly not genuinely. No doubt if Alex chose to reveal himself to Magnus then he would be killed in an instant, he was the only one that could stand against the villain after all. Alex was not even given the chance to respond.

"Any who do not join me, included my kin, will face the same fate as these evolved monkeys!" He said venomously. "You shall be first Britain, and any who try to interfere shall soon find themselves my next target. Think wisely before you choose to act against me, for you will not like the outcome." It was more of a statement of fact than a threat. "Leeds has already fallen, and soon, so shall the world."

With those last words he knocked the camera to the ground, where it landed looking towards Magnus' monstrous machines in the distance. The man in question stepped into view once more, for only a brief moment, as dust gathered around him before he shot off into the air and out of sight. The transmission ended as the behemoth closest to the camera restarted its function of levelling the city. Only white noise was left. The presenter for the station, clearly lost for words, erred in lieu of speaking as he was unable to string together a coherent sentence. Alex switched the television off with his mind, seeing all that he needed to know that nobody was safe from Magnus.

With a look of urgency he turned towards his mother, who had obviously realised that there was some sort of connection between Magnus and her eldest son. There was one course of action that he immediately needed to take.

"We need to get Abigail and Steven…now."

Chapter 14

His sense of urgency had been greatly diminished as his mother drove them furiously back to their home. It had started with a mad rush, assuming that everyone would be struggling to rush home to their families ahead of the coming apocalypse. It had not been so though. Instead everyone had continued to act as normal. Hubris, humanity's greatest flaw. Perhaps, Alex considered, because of the ridiculous amounts of scare-mongering within the media that never quite fulfilled its promise of world annihilation, mankind believed that it would soldier on in a typically obnoxious manner. After all, Leicester was far enough from Leeds to not have a military presence within it at that moment in time. The focus had immediately been on the centres around the now ruined city, with Manchester; Doncaster and Sheffield all being defensively upgraded with the impressive might of the British Army. It would all be futile, Alex knew, but in the minds of the people it gave them enough reason not to worry, for the time being at least. They would carry on with the typically British stiff upper-lip, not allowing their fear to show itself.

Alex knew better though and was deeply troubled by the events that had unfolded at Leeds, a harrowing foreshadowing for everyone. His family were safe, even his brother whom he still cared about despite everything. He did not know about Verity, and that alone was enough to drive him insane with worry. Thomas had seemingly evacuated his home, without his family, and so he did not know about him either. But at least his family were safe.

He looked out onto the greenery of the wooded areas by his house, a place that held both good and bad memories, the latter being more recent. The area that he had mutilated was now covered in police tape, as they suspected arson but could find no evidence since he did not actually touch anything. The ground was still bare and the trees had clearly lost much of their colour as their last supplies of water shrivelled up within them. He was sat only a few feet from the incident, but he could still see the beauty within it. Insects had already taken the new ground as their home, and so presumably had a herd of rabbits as Alex watched one hop into the centre after briefly examining their intruder. There was always a light to shine through the darkness, and so would there be with Magnus. He was scarily powerful, and capable of acts beyond the comprehension of the ordinary person, but there would be something or someone to stand against him. Alex just hoped that it was not him.

Perhaps it was pure selfishness, an unwillingness to try and climb such insurmountable odds, or perhaps he just did not want such power thrust upon him. Once he got involved there would be no going back. There would be no chance of a normal life with someone like Verity, no wife or children, no quaint family home with a couple of pets and annoying neighbours. No garden to tend to and no family to visit. He would be an outcast, either the hero who saved the humans or the embodiment of their failed hope. If he fought against Magnus then there would be only one way in which the conflict would end. Death. Either his or Magnus', it did not matter either way as the world would be forever changed.

Yet, still to Alex's amazement, people did not consider these eventualities. They only saw what was immediately in front of them, like the end of the working day and the prospect of going home for a relaxing night of dinner and television. Strangely though Alex felt the need to preserve them, like he was their protector. As he looked over the land around him, and those enjoying its beautiful splendour, he knew that there was only one course of action. I need to fight, he told himself, or I'll lose everything anyway. He would not be so foolish as to outright challenge Magnus though as the latter's power was far superior to his own. No, he would found out his weaknesses and work against him, undercutting him at every moment before taking the fight directly to him.

Alex's mind focused onto a group of people crowding onto a nearby bus out on the main road, which was clearly visible from where he was sitting due to the lack of foliage covering that side of the park. They appeared to be excited about something, and at the same time he could not mistake the vague spark of fear that was flittering about also. It was a kind of panicked motion, as he could tell from the tapping of legs and jittery movements of their hands, that immediately made Alex's spine crawl. Something was not right.

"Where's everyone going?" He found himself casually asking a man who was jogging past him.

"There's something happening at the edge of the city, I don't plan on going to see what the fuss is about, need to keep myself focused, you know what I mean?" He replied with perspiration dripping down his forehead, and a wide smile to indicate his passion.

Alex nodded politely. "So, whereabouts exactly?"

"Do you know where the A6 intersects with the A46? At that roundabout with the Ibis hotel?" The man asked.

Alex nodded again and gave the man his thanks, allowing him to continue his exercise. Everyone seemed to be using public transport to get to the centre of the commotion, but Alex had another means of getting there. He had never used his powers in such a huge way before, even with recent events, and so he was uncertain of how he would be able to accomplish what he had in mind. Even if he did there would be no way of being able to conceal himself, he would be out in the open for the entirety of Leicester to see. Alex laughed to himself with his realisation of how needlessly perturbed he was being. The world already knew that people like him, if there were any more beyond himself and Magnus, existed. There had been irrefutable proof put before all of humanity only the day beforehand.

Alex steeled himself as he looked towards the green grass that swayed so delicately in the wind. As he pooled the elements around himself he saw the strands get pushed back into the ground by the increasing force. Like rotating helicopter blades the pull only got stronger as Alex became more confident in his own abilities. He could not watch as he lifted himself from the ground with his arms held tightly into his body, as if they would be cut off. As he dared to open a single eye he beamed a smile of such genuine happiness and purity that it threatened to outshine the very rays of the sun. It was like a dream come true for him, a childhood persona fulfilled, and something that would no doubt make every other person on the planet jealous of him.

The wind that he had gathered was still around him, pushing up into the soles of his feet and into his sides to keep him afloat and steady. He was flying. Never, in his wildest imaginings, had he even thought that his powers would be so strong as to help him defy the laws of gravity. He was only a foot or so from the ground, but the capability was there for so much more as he lifted himself further to reach the height of the trees. Even from such a low height the views around him were enhanced to highlight the magnificent beauty of everything from the smallest birds to the tallest skyscrapers, although Leicester did not really have any buildings that were that large.

As he propelled himself higher people began to notice a lone figure in the sky. At first they seemed to be frightened, perhaps terrified that the horrors they had witnessed on their televisions the day beforehand were about to become a reality for them, but soon their fears turned to amazement as they noticed that the world was not turning to cinders around them. They pointed and cheered at him, fuelling his courage with their support. Maybe they realised that there was someone who could stand against Magnus as their protector, if they were even aware that they needed one.

With his powers well within his command he began to push himself forward rather than up. He was not certain on which direction he needed to go, seeing as he had never flown anywhere before, and so he looked around for the Highcross area. From his height it was easy to spot, and so, utilising his skills as vastly as he could, he sped off across the landscape as quickly as he dared. Within seconds he had passed the Leicester general hospital upon his right side, sparing a thought for those within as he zoomed further into the city. The buildings blurred around him and cars seemed like nothing more than spiders scuttling across the ground as he peered down on them.

Alex had never felt so ecstatic. Nobody could possibly imagine the joy of being able to move around as freely as you liked without the restrictions of winding roads and seemingly unending traffic. A group of blackbirds appeared to his left and flew alongside him in the glorious sunshine, they were not bothered that he should not be up there with them as they darted and danced in the sky for his amusement. Alex laughed as loudly and heartily as he ever had, momentarily forgetting about the enormous uncertainty surrounding the future, and cheered with genuine happiness. It was such a rarity for him to feel so elated. Despite the unnatural state he found himself in it almost felt like a primal instinct to blurt out his joy with a blaring roar; an ear-to-ear smile and twinkling green eyes.

His target approached him quicker than he had anticipated and so he eased the wind pushing into him to allow him to float gently once more. The Highcross centre was directly in front of him and with it he could see the road that he needed to take to move towards the incident. Just as he revved himself up again he noticed a figure waving at him from the Leicester Cathedral, as he was up in the spire and so was not much further down than Alex himself. Alex returned the wave but did not go over to the man. Instead he built the air behind him once more and headed north towards the National Space Centre with a far greater speed than he had before, as he was determined to test himself as much as he could. There was no time to stop and so he sped past that as well as he continued along his path. Even from the distance he was at it was clear that there was something not quite right.

In the distance he could see two distinct masses on either side of the roundabout that the jogger had mentioned. They were not actually on the junction itself as they were placed just to the left, along the A46. On one side were the clearly distinguishable people of Leicester and its surrounding areas, gathered around on the edge of the deserted road. Alex looked around for signs of disruption, some indication as to why the road had suddenly been shut down. He spotted those responsible at about a mile long interval that blocked off access from the roundabout. The Leicestershire fire service, no doubt from their station that was very close to the standoff, even though it was completely blocked by abandoned cars, had cordoned off the road. Along with them a great many police units were now positioned around their vehicles, which were attempting to hold back the crowd, as they clearly had no idea how to respond to the other mass of beings across the road. There was roughly a thousand or so of them, around about the same as the human numbers, with each gleaming in the sunlight to create a kind of solar mirror that made Alex's eyes hurt as he looked at them. It was so bad that he could not distinguish anything else about them, only that they were made from some kind of metal and were no doubt not just positioned there to look intimidating.

Alex set himself down away from the main crowd of people that were gathered to watch the army that was situated upon their borders. He decided that behind the fire station would be best, since presumably the firemen were all out by the road on call. His happiness was immediately deflated as his feet touched solid ground once more and the reality of the situation struck him like a blow to the head. Magnus was an intelligent man, and thus his creations would be imbued with his genius, and he did not feel like being spotted by his minions and carted off to live the rest of his life in extreme pain and discomfort, as it would surely be so.

Gingerly, he stepped out from behind the concrete mass of the fire station, which thankfully did have nobody in it after all, or at least nobody that he could see. Just as he thought it he heard the sirens sound from the building and so quickly leapt around the corner so that he would not be spotted, as it would surely raise some questions when everyone else was gathered by the roadside. One of the final fire engines stationed at the building came blaring out with its lights and sirens on. Much to Alex's surprise though it did not go towards the coming calamity but instead moved off towards the centre of Birstall, the small town they were in that was attached to the outskirts of Leicester. With everything that was happening Alex had forgotten that the world was continuing as normal, even though England was currently preparing for war. The rest of the world would remain unaltered by his nation's civil dispute, since Magnus had warned them off quite effectively with his malevolent display. Alex had seen on the news that the Americans were planning on sending a Division of soldiers in to assess the situation, but when or where that would be he did not know. He did not even know if it would actually be of any help to them.

Alex moved himself around so that he was facing the road before setting off towards the large group of people. They did not seem to notice anything around them as they stood staring into the distance to try and gauge some understanding of the creatures positioned no more than a hundred metres from them. Alex reached the back of them with little difficulty, but he could progress no further as the solid mass of humanity before him did not move an inch. He still could not tell what the machines were. As Alex tried to get a better view, without resorting to his powers as he was still not keen on being targeting by Magnus' machines, he noticed a familiar back of head to his left.

"Thomas!" He called, with no response. "Thomas!" He shouted again.

His best friend turned his head to see who was calling his name and spotted Alex walking towards him. The two smiled at each other and gave an awkward wave as neither knew what the other was doing there.

"Why are you here?" Thomas asked him.

"Why do you think? I should ask the same of you." He retorted.

"What do you mean?" Thomas responded sheepishly, pretending not to know what he meant.

"Come on Thomas, if something goes down how will you get away?"

"I should ask the same of you!" He said with a smile, and they both laughed. It was not a true laugh though. Rather than mirth there was sardonic tones as they both knew the seriousness of the situation, probably more so than everyone else who was gathered. "I brought my car…" He finally answered.

"Thomas…" Before he could continue he noticed a figure with cascading brown hair standing behind his best friend.

Alex discontinued his thought and pushed past Thomas, not stopping for anything, including a familiar face that he needed to make amends with, as he moved towards the figure. As he approached she seemed to notice that somebody was coming towards her and turned to face him. There was one unmistakable sign that this person was exactly who Alex thought it was. As he looked into her naturally green eyes his heart was filled with a mixture of elation and grief. Alex had not seen Verity since the incident with Magnus appearing within their minds, and he believed that she thought him to be some kind of monster. Now it seemed that he would never get the chance to correct that view as the danger around them mounted.

"Verity…" He began before he was interrupted by her as she embraced him in a loving hug.

Immediately all of Alex's worries seemed to melt. All he could think about was the warmth of her body upon his, the feel of her arms wrapped around the back of his neck, and the low laughter she emitted to indicate her joy at seeing him. As she pulled away from him he could not help but feel embarrassed, his cheeks flushed red and she let out a beaming smile to reassure him. Any negative thoughts he had about her view of him had dissipated, leaving only happiness and the prospect of a bright future in their stead. Now there was even more reason for him to fight against Magnus, regardless of the consequences it brought upon himself.

"I thought I would never see you again Alex, I wanted to thank you for helping me the other day." She spoke genuinely and clearly did not disapprove of his methods.

"Well, it didn't really matter much…" He said as he tried to play down his heroism.

"It's the thought that counts." She responded as they shared a laugh.

Alex had never thought that they would connect in such a way, and he needed to make sure that nothing jeopardised that. With that in mind he decided to ask her a crucial question. "What are you doing here?" Alex enquired protectively.

"We needed to escape after what happened to Leeds, and what's been happening here. Everyone else just seems to ignore it like it's nothing!" She exclaimed.

Alex felt like hugging her again at that moment for her unwavering brilliance. Whilst everyone continued with their normal lives she had come up with a plan of action to try and combat the coming catastrophe. In a world of ordinary people Verity was proving to be quite extraordinary. His joviality was obvious as she blushed in response and looked towards her feet.

"So why come here?" He asked again, desperate to gain more insight into her reasoning.

"My auntie and Grandparents live in Nottingham." She answered. "Believe me it wasn't my idea." Verity continued as she noticed the confused look in Alex's eye, since that was closer to Leeds than Leicester was.

Before they could continue their conversation there came a shrill scream from the front row of the crowd, quickly followed by others. Chaos quickly ensued as the front ranks turned and knocked into the rest of the crowd, who were still unsure about what was occurring. Alex knew though, even if he could not see. The machines were attacking. The crowd suddenly surged towards him and Alex was quickly knocked to the floor by an elbow, from a largely built man, which he was unprepared for. His head smacked the dry grass and grazed most of his face, filling his nose with the smell, and his mouth with the taste, of decaying greenery. There was little time to wonder what had happened as the crowd continued to press back towards their vehicles. Instinctively he used his powers to form a protective bubble around himself from the wind that pushed out in all directions, to stop anyone from treading on him and crushing him to death. Still people climbed and clambered all over him, unwilling to notice that they did not actually connect with anything beneath their feet despite the obvious presence of his body.

"Alex!" He heard Verity scream.

He looked up to see the object of his affections trying to break free from the hold of her parents as they ushered her away from the crowd so that she was not brought under the stampeding herd of humanity like several others surely were. To calm her Alex placed a single thought within her mind to let her know that he was alright. He did not know how she would respond to such an invasion of her privacy, but it seemed like a good idea. Much to his relief Verity seemed to receive his message and stopped trying to resist her parents as they sprinted back down the road towards their car.

With Verity safe Alex twisted his head around to see if he could spot Thomas. Thankfully his best friend was exactly where he had been before, his stocky build making him easy to spot and difficult to knock down. Still, he was in danger and so Alex made sure that there was a protective barrier around him as well, momentarily losing control of his own to do so. People were pushed around him without the faintest idea of what was happening as they continued along their paths, intent on making it out of the assault. Alex had still not been able to see what was happening, or even what the machines looked like, but there was no time to think about it as he noticed something terrible. Both Thomas and Verity had stopped moving.

Despite his message Verity had turned away from her parents and broken free from them, and she was now sprinting back towards him. Thomas, in his fear, simply could not move and was at great risk of becoming a victim if he did not do so soon. Quickly Alex renewed his message in Verity's mind, with more force this time, to try and deter her before he was forced to make a hideous choice.

Alex did not know how to choose. If his friend were not such a coward then there would be no choice at all. Unfortunately he needed to make a choice. Verity was already some fifty feet away whilst Thomas was still rooted to the spot as those in the front ranks were being taken down by the mysterious machines. One was his best friend, a man that he had known since near infancy and who understood him better than anyone else. They had shared so many experiences together and Alex did not know if he could bring himself to allow Thomas to be knocked unconscious into uncertainty. Yet he did not want that for Verity either, someone with whom he hoped there would be many experiences with in the future. She had begun, reluctantly, to run away though and would more than likely make it much further than Thomas and most of the other civilians, since she was towards the back of the crowd.

Alex, still with a deep throbbing pain in his head and a small trickle of blood running down his face from a small cut just above his forehead, braced himself for the pain that was about to come. With great strain upon himself he invaded Thomas' mind and focused purely upon making him run for his life, as he hoped to avoid another Arthur incident where he discovered things that he had not meant to. Thomas seemed confused at first and desperately tried to resist as he found his courage, like an animal backed into a corner and forced to turn aggressive. Even then he would not move, and the machines were only getting closer. The pain burning within Alex's head was so intense that he had to release his control momentarily for a very brief respite.

Alex tried again, willing himself in once more and having to break down several barriers to stay inside. Eventually, after almost peering into Thomas' mind, he succeeded and began to motion his friend's limbs towards the people now fleeing the scene and getting back in their cars to head into Leicester once more.

Thomas had passed his driving test a couple of months before everything and so Alex searched frantically for his best friend's car so that he might flee with everyone else. As he searched he noticed his friend's brain become much calmer. He had suddenly become aware that it was Alex within his mind and so accepted that he was just trying to help. His mind focused Alex onto a silver Ford Fiesta in the distance and they both recognised it immediately, owing to the fact that Thomas had named his car and so would recognise it from the others. Through all this time Alex had remained on the floor with a small protective bubble covering him, but time was running out. Within moments the machines would be upon him and he was not certain that his powers would be able to withstand any kind of assault from Magnus' minions.

He started to make Thomas move to the car with a speed that belied the chubby nature of his best friend. He had lost sight of Verity and so he dearly hoped that she had managed to get away quickly enough, which was not difficult to imagine since their car was surely towards the very back of the jam. After all, she had surely arrived later than both Alex and

Thomas since he noticed her last of all. His doubts seemed to have crept into Thomas' mind as he stopped moving, despite Alex's best efforts to keep his momentum going. Thomas' thoughts mingled with Alex's and the latter immediately knew why his friend was now moving at a snail's pace once again. He did not want to leave his best friend. The man that Alex had accused of cowardice, and who had, by the mountain of evidence stacked against him, always been slightly craven, could not bring himself to move away. Alex tried to convince him to move forward again, exhausting his willpower to make him see sense, but he could only do so for a few moments as his mind was drawn to matters by his own body. The machines were upon him.

Swiftly Alex withdrew himself from Thomas' mind and hoped that his friend would have the sense to retreat towards his car and move back towards Leicester. The relief he received as he released his grip made him realise just how exhausted he had become. His excessive use of powers within the last couple of hours had completely drained his energy from his body and left him as little more than a husk, a tortoise that had lost its shell.

With the machines now clearly within his field of view he was able to determine exactly what they were, and it made him feel sick. Just like something out of a science fiction movie, they were clearly a mixture of metal and glossed flesh that told Alex everything he needed to know about Magnus and his hideous intentions. For the most part they were purely machinery, the same kind of iron as the tower-sized machines, which obviously came from Magnus' old factory in Yorkshire. In places though, presumably where it was impossible to create semi-collapsible limbs, something which the larger machines did not require, there were elements of human flesh that were covered in some kind of see-through plastic so that the skin could be protected but still seen. Knees and elbows were on show, as were shoulders and ankles, and so was much of the face, although it had been heavily distorted as only the eyes; nose; mouth and ears were displayed. Each of these was also covered in the same material, although Alex suspected that a bullet would easily shatter this protective plastic. They seemed perfect in design, which highlighted how disgusting they were.

Alex did not know how to respond to the hideous nature of these creations. On one level he could not help but feel sympathy for those poor people whose skin, and possibly other features beneath the surface that he could not see, such as a brain which he assumed would be required in order for them to be possessed by Magnus as they were, was being used to complete this synthesis of machinery and humanity. He also felt fear, that the same fate could befall himself or any of his loved ones. Then there was the most overpowering feeling of all, repulsion. Everything detail about them, down to the rivets that held the metal plates together, gave him an almost unbearable feeling of abhorrence. Their amalgamated design was simply wrong, a stark contrast to everything that represented humanity.

There was no time to think about the hideousness of their design though as Alex, still not recovered from the pressures he had exerted upon himself, scrambled to his feet to avoid being picked off by these monsters. Just as he did so, and the ground crunched beneath his feet, the machines lurched forward again into those immediately surrounding him. Presumably, since Alex had not made it obvious, they had no idea who he was since they did not seem to focus solely on him. He was thankful for that at least. The machines used some kind of rudimentary propulsion system, tiny in design, in the soles of their cold metal feet, to push themselves from the ground and launch through the air, reaching around ten yards with every leap. Their quickness seemed to directly contradict their heavy frames and made them all the more dangerous.

Alex, still stunned by the sick and malicious nature of these creatures, watched as one of the monstrosities pushed itself onto a young man, perhaps no older than Alex himself, and knocked him out with one swift punch. It was executed perfectly so that there would be no damage or risk of concussion, yet still rendered the victim temporarily unconscious. Alex could not help but admire the complexity of Magnus' designs, terrible though they were, and they showed Alex the true enormity of his mission. The way he was at the moment, with no energy in his already shattered body, he was not sure if he could resist a single one of the machines and so decided to run away with everyone else. Unfortunately for him, everyone was already in front of him, making him a prime target for one of the machines when it spotted him.

As soon as he turned around to retreat he was identified by one of the hideous creatures as it twisted its metal head towards him and removed itself from its unconscious prey. Alex's half-run turned into a full sprint as he desperately tried to escape the creature that was now pursuing him. Yet he was already being outpaced by his pursuer as the machine bounded ten yards for every two that Alex could manage. In desperation he turned towards the fire station in the hope that the machine would no longer be able to track him. For a moment Alex believed that it had worked, as he was unable to see the creature for a few seconds. Beyond the concrete world, mixed in with patches of greenery and foliage, there was nothing.

His hope did not last long though as a loud thud behind Alex forced him to roll away out of instinct. Clumsily he botched the landing and fell onto his knees, clutching his mildly injured right arm as the pain throbbed. The machine pulled back its own arm to deliver the knockout blow. Alex closed his eyes as he did not want to see what was about to befall him. Somewhere though, in the last drips of his reserve energy, he was able to muster the ability to force himself inside the machine's mind. He expected it not to work, and for a moment he believed that he had not as there was no pain or mental anguish this time. Yet he had the opportunity to open his eyes, something he did not think he would be afforded. Much to his amazement, the machine was no longer positioned to strike as it stared down at him. Alex would never get used to looking at himself through the eyes of another.

Casually he made the machine extend a hand to help himself up and found that it did so without trouble or even the slightest hint of resistance, it was completely compliant. Alex laughed to himself, though not too loudly, as he realised that he was able to control these machines of Magnus', although he did not know how long for or even if he could possess more than a single one.

To make sure that the other machines did not try anything he allowed himself to go limp as the machine that he controlled picked him up and placed him upon its fleshy shoulder. Alex was still revolted at the sight of the monster, but now he had a means of getting back to his family. With that in mind he positioned the machine to face back the way he had come as they set off for his home. Alex just hoped that Thomas and Verity were safe.

Chapter 15

It was a strange feeling being carted around his city by a contraption that was somewhere between a human and an automaton. Alex only knew one way back to his home through the city, down London road, and so it had taken far longer than he would have liked, and therefore increasing the likelihood that his family were in grave danger of being taken by the machines. Even worse still was that one of the building-sized machines had arrived at the edge of Leicester, it was only the one though and it did not seem to be destroying the buildings of the city. Clearly it had been issued forth for a different purpose, one Alex did not wish to find out. What intrigued him more was how the machine had got there. He had not seen it during the assault and yet it had somehow materialised outside the city. Alex could not even begin to understand the power that Magnus wielded.

It had taken them almost an hour, even with the machine bounding ten yards with every pace, to reach the Highcross centre again, although this was in part due to Alex's generally poor sense of direction, at least by foot anyway. The building had been almost unrecognisable when they had approached it. Unlike Leeds, Leicester's buildings had not been brought low by the monstrously destructive behemoths, but their surface damage made them look just as bad. Presumably people had panicked when news of the attack reached the city, making the machines work harder for their prey. Alex had no doubts that looting had played an abundant role in the damage dealt as well, as the inhabitants desperately tried to cling on to anything they could. To make matters even more repugnant, the Cathedral had also been looted, and there was no sign of the man who had halloed him as he travelled earlier that day. It made Alex sick that humanity was capable of such deplorable acts when they should be banding together against the evil at their door.

They had paid dearly for it though. Alex had seen no end of people being taken as he slowly made his way through the city, the machines none the wiser to his actual state as they believed the creature that he controlled to still be one of them. He had had to think of the bigger picture, and so he needed to leave them behind. His family came first, regardless of the terrible consequences that brought for other people. Alex did not like it, and he was not sure he could stop himself from feeling the guilt that was pouring into his soul like a black pit of corruption, but it needed to be done. That was what Magnus had done already, and he had not even encountered the villain yet. Desperation forced him, but to be a hero he needed to transcend all moral boundaries. He did not feel like a hero though.

It still felt outlandish to see the world through someone, or something, else's eyes. Everything was blurred around the edges, like there was a piece of dirt or an eyelash in the way, although Alex knew that that certainly would not be the case with the monstrosities that were all around him. He could still feel everything that was happening to himself as well. Every springy jump, and every harsh landing, knocked his vulnerable flash against the metal who was resting upon. Each time he received a sharp burst of pain unto his midriff, but so far he had been able to fight through it. After all, he did not want to compromise his family's safety simply because he needed to stop to alleviate himself of his agony. Thus, with his chest burning in protest, he carried on.

Even without the hideous events that were being inflicted upon Leicester, his family had already suffered a great deal. His mother had quickly fallen into a deep depression. She now understood why Alex had been expelled from Henbane, even if the headmaster was still adamantly refusing to believe there was anything extraordinary about the offence, but that did not make it any easier on her. That, coupled with the fact that his father had not contacted her for over two days, and they normally talked everyday if Charles was given the time, had taken her happiness from her. Alex tried not to worry about his father, as if there was anyone whom he would place a wager on to overcome any obstacle, it was his father. Charlotte clearly could not think the same way though. She had not even been able to enjoy her favourite program on the television, as her mind was no doubt preoccupied with trying to figure out how she could have led Alex astray. He had tried to talk to her, but there was nothing that could be said. He needed to save her, and his siblings, to prove to her that he had not fallen into the depths of despair and degradation that she thought he had.

A sudden vehicle caught his eye as they were travelling through London road. Unsurprisingly, the traffic had come to a standstill as the entire city frantically sprinted towards whatever exits they could find, and that included those who attempted to hide within the city after retreating from the initial attack. There, within the array of cars that were spread across the tarmac roads and the concrete paths, was his best friend's vehicle. The silver ford fiesta would have blended with the crowd quite easily had it not been for its unique number plate which had given it its name. It was positioned adjacent to the station and so Alex held out some hope that perhaps he had been able to get away from the city to somewhere a bit safer, although he did not see how anywhere could think they were safe from the travesties that Magnus was inflicting upon the nation. There was no sign of Verity either, and, just to add to his growing anxieties, he could not recall what her family's car looked like. He had no way of knowing if she was safe.

Before the machine he controlled could move more than a single further bounding step he spotted something that he wished he had not. In the distance he could see a figure that was unmistakable to him. His portly build and dirty blonde hair told Alex that it could not be anyone else. It was Thomas. His best friend was slumped upon the shoulder of one of Magnus' creatures, like Alex himself, although Thomas was obviously unconscious. His head lolled from side to side as the machine strode towards Alex and his own automaton. He determined that they had to be moving towards the tower-sized machine that was encroaching upon the city and had now reached the space centre.

Alex would have tried to grab him there and then, but he had no idea how the machines would react. He needed to be tactical about it, so as to not raise suspicions against himself. To that end he decided to be cautious about every moment and take everything one step at a time. The machine that was carrying Thomas was moving at a snail's pace compared to them and so it was easy to match its speed, which was good as it meant that Alex did not have to work very hard to manipulate his machine. He was still amazed that he felt no pain from possessing it, as he had with Arthur and Thomas, and even Muffin to a much lesser degree.

Alex made sure they continued stalking the machine carrying away Thomas until he was certain that it was safe to move a closer distance to it. Every so often he would increase the speed of the creature that he controlled, to move just a little bit closer each time. It was infuriating having to take so long to accomplish something so simple, and painful as well as each step continued to bounce Alex up and down upon the metal shoulder of the machine he was slumped over. By the time he got close enough to the other machine for his own to reach out and grab Thomas they were no more than fifty feet from the behemoth that was progressing through the city. It had stopped around the Parish Church of St. Margaret, and there it had sat lifelessly for around ten minutes as Magnus' soldiers bounded towards it, their purpose unknown.

Just as Alex was about to grab his best friend, through the eyes of his controlled monstrosity, the machine leapt into the air and rounded the corner between them and the behemoth. Alex cursed to himself, silently of course, and casually slid down off of his creature, feeling his midriff for any signs of permanent damage. Out of despair he placed his hands upon his head and let out a long sigh, unsure of how to proceed next. He looked around the corner to see if there was any sign of the machine that was carrying Thomas, but there was none. In a flash it had disappeared and left Alex alone in the world once more. He had delayed ten minutes to retrieve his friend. He almost sobbed to himself at the thought that it had all been for nothing as Thomas, and now potentially his family as well due to his loyalty, had been carted off like cattle to the abattoir.

Alex was so engrossed by his failure that he did not notice several of the machines, approaching from the other direction and each with cargo of their own, speed off towards their larger counterpart. They landed at its base, where the metal pillar was positioned against the floor rather than in the air as he had seen it. To his amazement a door seemed to open from within the structure and the machines stepped inside, with their prey still upon their shoulders. The pillar could have been no more than five yards in diameter, roughly half the size of the centre circle on a football pitch, and so Alex realised that it must have been a very tight fit inside, not that the creatures would be bothered. I need to get inside, Alex told himself.

He turned back to his machine and saw it completely lifeless, it was unable to function at all when he did not command it to do something. It truly was an example of a robot, developed well before its time, incapable of actual thought yet programmed to respond to its master's every whim. Carefully he made the machine pick him up and place him upon its shoulder again, bracing himself for the last few final jolts of pain to his abdomen. The concrete below them cracked as the machine forced itself forward towards its towering relative. A familiar feeling of weightlessness came over him as they flew towards their target, before it abruptly came to an end a moment later with a loud thump as his body rammed against the metal plate once again.

As they stood at the base of the machine, with the sun thankfully out of his eyes for the first time that day, Alex felt a sense of awe. The behemoth was terrible in design, yet flawless at the same time. It instilled a kind of tyranny over him. He despised it and every action it took, but he could not help but feel overwhelmed in its presence, like he was acknowledging that it was a far greater being than himself. Of course, it was no being at all though. Unlike its smaller brethren this machine seemed to possess no human characteristics and was not even capable of responding to demands, it was a machine designed to be operated. Alex did not know by what, or indeed how, though.

The door opened as the creature in front of them stepped through it and into the black spire of metal that was within. Regimentally, as he was trying to copy the movements of the others as best he could, he pushed through with his own machine. It was very poorly lit inside, the only light coming from places where rivets and bolts had been neglected and rusted slightly. From the outside the machines looked imposing and indomitable, but on the inside their age clearly showed as further rust lined the edges and crevices of each piece of separate metal. Alex supposed that they were originally built during Magnus' early years, which made them around eight decades old. It was a testament to Magnus' skills that they had remained standing for that long, since there would have been no-one to tend to them.

A small spiral staircase wound itself up the inside of the pillar, sticking tightly to the edges so that there was still room for people to stand within it without getting in the way, it was a very efficient design. That was not all that was inside. Upon the walls were manacles, for hands and ankles, positioned around the stairs so that anyone walking up would have to look at those who had been taken. Alex suddenly realised why the machines were taking victims inside the pillar. Several faces, all of which unconscious, could be seen through the dim light that entered the pillar. Their bodies were limp and their chests rose and fell quickly to cope with the physical demands required of them as they hung like dried slabs of meat against the wall. There were men, there were women, and, to Alex's eternal disgust, there were even children. People from all walks of life decorated the walls and made it seem like some sick trophy room. Alex could only imagine the pain they would be in if the behemoth was using its primary seismic function.

Thomas has to be in here, he told himself to keep his hope alive. He pushed past over a dozen people on the first level, each one moaning silently to themselves as they threatened to wake up from their induced slumber. Alex thought it strange that so many had been taken when relatively few could be stocked within the behemoth.

The pillar was what made the machines so humungous and so Alex did not know how long it would take him to find Thomas, considering there would be about twenty levels to it. Still, he pressed on, driven by his determination to retrieve his friend and return to his family to protect them. Each level he checked carefully, looking for the chubby cheeks and dirty blonde hair that would identify his best friend, before moving on to the next. The machines around him seemed not to mind his presence as they shackled up their prisoners before leaving the machine again. They would be able to fit around two-hundred and fifty humans just in this one machine. A harrowing fact.

As he reached the fourth floor the jarring he faced on every step became too much and so, after checking that everything was clear and none of Magnus' minions were in sight, lowered himself onto the floor once again. A sudden low-pitched whine came from behind him and Alex turned around to see that one of the victims had woken up. He was a young man, roughly of a similar age to himself, with a tall and lean body that no doubt made it extremely uncomfortable to be shackled against the wall in such a way. Alex gasped suddenly as the man propped his head up to face him. He knew who it was. Simon Gartland. Alex could tell that the youth recognised him as he whined again for help, but he could not move his hands to gesture this. Alex shook his head silently as he knew that he had bigger priorities. He had thought it before and now it became apparent that the hardships this conflict with Magnus was bringing were not going to come to an end anytime soon. Alex felt atrocious, even though he had been one of the prime bullies of the last year, but he could not help him.

When the man realised that he was being refused help he suddenly found his voice again as he screamed an order at Alex to be released, still thinking that he held power over him. Desperation creates anger, he thought to himself. The man continued screaming at Alex for his help, which quickly drew the attention of the man's captors. Alex pulled his hands together in prayer, pleading with Simon to be as quiet as he could, hoping that perhaps he would remember that they had once been friends. He did not stop though and Alex knew he only had seconds before the bailiffs were upon them. Without a second's hesitation he made sure that his automaton picked him up and placed him on its shoulder for a third time. A moment later one of the other machines, which had obviously been dropping of its cargo, descended and landed on the stairs just above Alex and his machine.

Alex froze. Simon was still shouting, although now it was about how Alex was somehow manipulating one of the machines. He told the machine looking at him to take Alex and not himself, as if bargaining with it would somehow improve his situation. It was the typical hubris of humanity to betray others for self-preservation. Alex was not truly worried though as he already knew that the machine was not capable of its own thought, and so could not be swayed by sweeter options, as it had no concept of them.

The response to the man's cries was typical, but that did not make it any nicer or easier to hear. Rapidly the machine cocked its metallic hand back and drove it forward into the man's forehead, knocking him unconscious once more. Alex shuddered at the thought that the situation could have reversed, with him on the receiving end of that knockout blow. With that small debacle concluded, Alex continued up the pillar to try and find Thomas.

As he climbed the levels his situation became increasingly dire. There was no sign of his friend and he was now on the penultimate level, or that was what he guessed at least. The presence of the machines had increased with each level as they strapped in their victims and sat dormant upon the stairs, pushed against the side and stored like cardboard boxes. Alex knew that he did not have long, soon they would be at capacity and they would leave the city; or so he theorised. One thought continued to persist within his mind though. Why Leicester? He asked himself. It was not even remotely close to Leeds. The only reason he could surmise was that Magnus somehow knew that he was the one that he wanted, and that had led the villain to his home city. It was his fault these people were about to be taken away, that was why it was crucial that he saved his family; and Thomas; and Verity. He needed to help all he could. The sacrifices the nation were making would not be forgotten, he ingrained into himself. Alex just needed time, and a great deal more than he was being given.

Finally, he found him. On the second-to-last floor he was just about to be chained against the wall to join the others in their misfortune of becoming part of whatever plans Magnus had in store for them. His head was still slumped against his chest, which indicated his state of wellbeing, and he was in no shape to resist his attacker. What worried him more was the person next to him. He was definitely beginning to think that God was playing some kind of cruel trick upon him to test his abilities. To the left of Thomas sat a young girl with long and flowing brown hair, her manacles already in place. Her head was rested against her raised shoulders and so he could see her beautiful face in full, even in captivity she retained an aura of elegance about her. Alex had hoped Verity would have gotten away, as he had certainly given her the opportunity. Alas, it had not worked as anticipated as she sat next to his best friend in the same state of unconsciousness.

After all the effort that he had put in to making sure that his best friend and his love were safe, it had all been in vain. He had grossly underestimated the speed and power of Magnus' machines, and those that he held dearest were about to pay for it. Each thought became darker than the last one. Quickly, he found himself questioning everything that had been so unfairly thrust upon him in the first place. He did not know how he was going to beat Magnus if he could not even defeat a single one of his foot-soldiers. Alex needed to save them quickly, now that the machines were clearly preparing for departure, before he returned them safely to their homes. Only then could he check on his family. He trusted that Abigail, with his extreme levels of perception and intelligence, had managed to keep them all safe in his, and Charles', absence.

Alex could not lament on his failure though, as action was needed. The machine that had shackled Thomas was still there, standing as if it could suspect that something was wrong. Alex felt a tremendous sense of fear fill him at the thought that Magnus was directly watching him, perhaps even that he was aware of who he was. A lack of anything from the minion before him though got rid of these anxieties as he slowly and methodically moved his machine towards the wall where the prisoners were shackled. Closer and closer he crept towards his quarries, thinking only of their safe return and good health and little for his own protection, and yet the machine did not move like the others. Alex wondered for a moment if it was broken before discarding the thought as Magnus would never have allowed it to 'live' if it had any kind of imperfection.

With only a foot or two to go the machine suddenly decided to resume its duties. It made sure that Thomas was secure, much to Alex's chagrin, before it took its place upon the wall along with the others, although it still seemed like it was watching him. Gingerly he commanded the machine to slump him down against the side of the pillar, as if preparing him for capture, before looking at the restraints that held his best friend, and his crush. They were made of the same iron that everything of Magnus' was made of and seemed to be clamped together with no particular key or security system in place. Judging by their thickness though Alex surmised that no human would be likely to pull them apart, making them perfect in their simplicity. Magnus had never anticipated that someone would be able to take control of his machines though.

With ease Alex made his machine rip open all fours locks on both Thomas and Verity, the rusting metal squeaking in protest as it was done, which made them fall to the floor like a sack of potatoes. Both of them were still unconscious. Casually, as though it was a part of its routine programming, the machine picked up all three of them and place them upon its bulky shoulders. Alex was amazed at how absentminded Magnus' creations were, they literally served no other purpose than to carry out their basic function. Alex even doubted that Magnus was fully possessing them, as they did not seem capable of any kind of act outside of their programming.

With just as much ease, Alex made his machine carry all of three of them from the pillar just as it began to lift into the air, obviously ready to leave now that every space within it had been filled. He opened his eye from on top of Thomas' body to look back at the behemoth as it simply began walking in the reverse direction to which it had arrived, it's four legged design making turning around nonessential. With the threat diminishing he deemed it safe to finally step down from the shoulder of his machine, almost pulling Thomas off with him as he scrambled over his body. As he turned his head towards the direction of home he could have sworn that a single black mass descended from the behemoth as it began to retreat. He thought nothing of it though as he made sure that both Thomas and Verity were also placed safely upon the ground, although he did not want to wake Verity up just yet as he needed to know where she lived so that she could return home.

Alex sat beside her limp body upon the chilled and dirty ground, doing everything he could to delay the process he was about to initiate. He needed to though, and so, with a sense of trepidation, and regret, he went inside her mind to find the information he needed. He tried to avoid looking through her memories as he sifted through them for information, but a certain memory caught his eye and his curiosity got the better of him.

Verity was sat beside her bed with her parents calling her down for dinner. She looked exactly as she did now and so the memory was very recent. Her cascading brown hair was brushed delicately over both sides of her shoulders and her beautiful green eyes were reflecting within the screen of her laptop, which was positioned fittingly upon her lap. A book was positioned beside her, clearly a favourite of hers since the pages were quite worn down and yellowing. Its place upon the shelf was empty, except for some dust which confirmed how frequently she looked at it. It was peculiar; Alex had never imagined her as a reader of romance, but it was quite clear that she was.

The rest of her room was as anyone would expect of a teenage girl. A smaller shelf held makeup and perfumes whilst clothes seemed to spring forth from every conceivable space within the room. Alex laughed as he looked at it. Pictures of friends graced her walls, but there was one particular picture that Alex could not believe he was seeing. Even then it was positioned in a clear place of priority above the headboard of her bed. Alex was astounded that here, in this place of pride and affection, was a picture of himself.

He remembered the day well, as it had only been a short while since it passed. There he stood, upon the assembly stage within Henbane, with the crowd cheering him on. It was from the moment he had been declared the third winner of the talent contest. Alex remembered the time fondly, especially so since Verity had given him a beaming smile of approval which had reddened his cheeks. He was flabbergasted to think that Verity looked upon the moment with the same affection as himself. It gave him hope.

Verity's parents were still calling her and so, with a final look upon the social networking website that she was on, she closed the browsing window she had open. Alex had hoped he would see another picture of himself upon the background of her laptop, but there was no such image. Instead there was a short poem which summed up her views on life in a few short sentences. Strangely he had not heard of this poem, but it touched him all the same to know that his crush was such a profound individual.

She rushed down the stairs with a spring in her step and moved towards the back of the house where the dining room was located. Alex had never experienced the sensation that he was now as he could feel and sense everything that Verity could, although not as profoundly as an emotion of his own. It was more like a memory of an emotion, an attempt to remember the feeling of a feeling. Of course, he could do this with the machine, but that was in reality and this was a mere memory. Verity sniffed loudly to inhale the aroma of her dinner, and yet Alex was the one who could experience it, although he sensed it was his own memory that allowed him to smell the sweet fragrance as the delicious scent of a roast dinner wafted into his nostrils.

Just as Verity was about to eat her father beckoned her and her mother to join him in the living room to see what was on the television. For the second time in his life Alex was subjected to watching the assault on Leeds as Verity was looking at the same report that they had been when it had occurred. Clearly it was too much for Verity as she rushed outside her front door for some fresh air. That was all Alex needed to see as he recognised the street that she lived on, and thankfully it was not too far from where Alex himself lived, which was curious to him as he had never seen her upon the bus back from Henbane.

He did not wish to see anymore of Verity's life, as it was so easy to get lost in a single thought, and so he withdrew himself from her mind and placed himself back in the real world. Around him he could see people staring from windows and behind bushes, within which they had clearly hidden during the attack as their clothes were ruffled. They were very skittish, like cats, not daring to come any closer as they stared from a distance. Still, Alex was relieved to see that the machines had actually taken relatively few people compared to the city's population. That only means that they have plenty more stock to choose from, Alex reminded himself.

Without even thinking about it he made his machine place Verity and Thomas upon its shoulders once again as they set a slow pace through the streets, as he did not want to frenzy the public into another panic, since they were clearly wary about his companion. They clung tightly to whatever was around them as they passed, as if Alex would try and detach them to bring them to the behemoth that was now curiously out of sight. Alex waved to a few of them to try and reassure them that he was not an enemy, but this only pushed them deeper into their shells out of some fear that it was a trick. He had no idea how many were watching him, but he could feel an infinite number of eyes burrowing into his back as he continued his slow and methodical walk towards Verity's house. Alex needed to pick up the pace.

Before he knew what was happening a crowd of people had gathered in front of him, their stance undeniably aggressive. Alex cautiously turned his head around, as he wanted no sudden movements, and saw that another, smaller, audience was at his rear. They slowly encroached around him, like he was somehow the villain in all of this, with their intent obvious. Alex did not have time to deal with them though and so commanded his machine to leap into the air, like a giant metallic kangaroo, as he lifted himself from the ground and flew over the crowd. He only set a slow pace, but seeing a person hovering was too much for the gathered mass as they scattered in their individual directions, no doubt believing him to be some kind of associate of Magnus'.

The crowd may have dissipated but Alex saw no reason as to why he should slow down and take it easy. The behemoth was gone, and with it the creatures, and so he was in little danger of exposing himself to Magnus' all-seeing eyes. The wind riffled through his hair as he sped through the city towards Verity's parents' home, birds moving away from him cautiously at the unexpected sight as if they too were also nervous now. Some fifty feet below him his machine was bounding along at ten yards a pace, it speed lessened by its continual need to propel itself with each step. Together they trekked through the city undisturbed, with no-one daring to come forth to challenge them again, and reached their location in no time.

Alex was familiar with the location as it was not too far removed from his own abode, and was easily accessible from the centre. Alex and his quarry came to a sudden halt when they reached their destination, the jolt clearly a little too much for Thomas as he audibly groaned in frustration and pain. Alex descended rapidly to check upon his best friend, having been careless enough not to consider how painful the journey had been for Thomas and Verity. He physically winced as he still felt the potential bruising around his own midriff.

"Thomas!" He yelled as he approached his machine, which he had just commanded to place Thomas gently upon the floor.

His best friend groaned once again and complained about being disturbed, making Alex laugh almost uncontrollably. It seemed that the machines truly left no damage upon the bodies of their prey as he pulled his friend to his feet and saw no signs or markings of punishment. Alex was glad that he had made it to him in time.

With a grogginess that Alex found amusing, Thomas stumbled and swayed upon his feet as he struggled to adjust his eyes to his surroundings. It took a few moments for his haziness to wear off before he recognised where he was, and who he was with. No words were exchanged between them as Thomas ran forward and clasped his friend upon the shoulder, giving him an appreciative look that his words could not express for him.

"Where are we?" Thomas asked, clearly still unfocused.

"We're by Verity's house." Alex replied bluntly.

"Verity?" Thomas said confusingly, clearly having not noticed that she was still slumped across the shoulder of his machine.

When he spotted the creature he recoiled in fear and hid himself behind Alex. When he noticed that Alex was not afraid himself he regained himself and looked towards his best friend, noticing the permanently faint glow of green around his eyes from the continual use of his abilities. It took a few moments for Thomas to realise.

"Holy moly!" He exclaimed dumbfounded, whilst obviously attempting to avoid using expletives. "You're controlling that thing aren't you?" Thomas continued as his tone changed to one of excitement.

Alex shrugged as if to suggest that he had no idea what his friend meant. Thomas ecstatically bounded towards his follower and waved in front of it. To humour his friend, Alex returned the wave and made the machine pat Thomas on the head. His best friend seemed beyond words as they exchanged several other gestures that were unique to their friendship, proving beyond doubt that Alex was the one controlling the machine. With his curiosity satisfied Thomas turned back towards Alex and placed his hands upon his hips questioningly.

"So, why are we here?" He asked.

"To bring Verity back safely." Alex responded truthfully, not expecting the tirade that was about to be blown in his direction.

"And what about our families? Have you checked on them?" Thomas probed, suddenly very angry. Alex shook his head. "So you put HER before my parents! Before your siblings! Before your mother!" His venomous tones surprised Alex as he had never heard his friend like this before, but he knew that he was right. He was risking everything to save a girl that he had barely gotten to know. A fool's decision.

"Well you're the one that's been prancing about with a machine for the last few minutes!" He shouted back, equally as enraged by his friend's lack of understanding.

Thomas raised his hands to try and quell the argument before it spiralled out of control, like it almost had before when Thomas had discussed his distaste for Alex's lack of using his abilities. Alex nodded and turned towards the house that was Verity's, looking to calm himself down before he spoke again.

It was a large house, three separate floors in total, with a small, but well kept, front garden and a brightly coloured red door that made it distinguishable. Trickles of vines covered parts of the house, giving it a natural feel whilst not ruining its rustic aesthetic. The tiles upon the roof betrayed its aging image as they were completely clean of moss and other foliage, showing that they had only recently been put in place. The brick chimney that sat on top of the home restored the image though as the tarnished surface made it clear that the house had been in use for quite some time, like the houses on either side of it that it was almost attached to. The windows were typically square, with one patio-style window that allowed light to flood into the living room. Alex could see within, where two pairs of eyes were staring at him. Alex almost turned red when he realised that these must have been Verity's parents.

Swiftly, Alex made sure that the machine he controlled could not been seen, as it gingerly placed Verity upon the ground for Alex and Thomas to scoop up. She was still unconscious, yet, even in this state, Alex could not help being mesmerised by her beauty. It seemed almost a shame to disturb her, but he knew that he had no time to admire her and so he beckoned Thomas over to him so that they could place her arms around their shoulders. Her shoes were being tarnished slightly as they dragged her across the concrete road, with loose chunks of stone and gravel being caught against the fabric, but it did not really matter as they pushed open the small wooden gate that led to the entrance of the home.

As they approached the front door it suddenly flew open and Verity's father was stood in front, ready to receive his daughter, with her mother stood behind him with tears coming down her face. Alex had no idea how they would react to him, since it was probably his fault that they were separated in the first place. Thankfully though her father did not seem to be concerned with Alex as he picked his daughter up and placed her in his arms, delivering her to the sofa within the living room before returning to the door. It seemed there was to be a conversation, whether Alex wanted it or not.

He stared into Alex's eyes, his deep blue penetrating into Alex's colourful green, as his greying hair swayed across his ear and his loose-fitting tie leaned forward with him. Verity's mother, who had just recaptured her place in the corridor after checking upon her daughter, seemed equally as intense. Her brown hair was frizzy in places, having not been styled, and her eyes seemed wide and wet from the tears she had been shedding. A handkerchief was held in one hand, visibly damp from soaking up the moisture of her grief, and a fist was in the other as she stifled her emotions as best she could. She placed a hand upon the shoulder of her husband, he turned to face his wife with a knowing nod. It seemed like he was about to deliver a harsh speech towards Alex, as his eyes focused on him once again, before his eyes softened and his naturally frowning face creased into a joyous smile that told of his love for his daughter, and his appreciation for her saviour.

"We owe you our thanks Alex!" Verity's father said as he embraced Alex in a firm hug with tears of gratitude streaming down his face. Alex was surprised, and overjoyed since Verity must have told them about him, that they knew who he was as he had never met them before. "I thought I would never see her again when she went back for you." Mr Lane continued, just as emotionally.

At least I'm alright with the in-laws, Alex laughed to himself. "It's my pleasure Mr Lane, I couldn't have left her there."

Verity's father pulled away from him and noticed Thomas in his company as well, but thankfully not the machine, whom he had made hide behind a bush so as not to upset anyone. "I see you saved Mr Gordon as well…you truly are a hero young man. Your father must be so proud of you." He said with a smile, but all it brought to Alex was sadness.

Alex had not given much thought to his father since the attack, but now it seemed to consume him and his need to find his family intensified. He had left them to the devices of Magnus' creatures for longer than he would have liked. He did not even know if they were safe anymore, although he tried to reason that they were since he had not seen them within the behemoth that had intruded into their city. Regardless, he needed to find out quickly to belay his worries, and so, with Verity safe, he quickly said goodbye to the Lane family before taking Thomas to one side.

"I'm going to take a shortcut back home, I think we'll be safe enough now." Alex told his best friend.

"Are you sure?" Thomas replied sceptically as he was clearly worried that more of the machines were waiting in the shadows.

Alex nodded and gave his friend a firm tap on the shoulder to encourage him before ordering his own machine to meet them where they stood. Even though he still felt safe he could not deny that his machine would come in handy should they ever run into Magnus' minions again, which they most assuredly would. He had never tried to lift anyone other than himself, but thankfully he did not live far and so he did not need to sustain his powers for such an extended time as he had done before.

Just as he lifted off from the ground he could have sworn that he saw the same shadow that had descended from the behemoth as it had left the city. Had it been stalking him the entire time? Quickly, hoping to use speed to outrun his purported chaser, he raised the three of them into the air. He was quite surprised about how light a load he was carrying, given that one of them was almost entirely made from metal. It was only a few moments, filled with adrenaline and haziness as they sped through the skies, before they arrived at a familiar road, he just hoped he was not too late.

He was home.

Chapter 16

Alex had never been more pleased to see his home in his entire life, now all he needed was for his family to be inside. He looked around the street with Thomas by his side. Around his house the world seemed essentially unaltered, with not even a single blade of green grass out of place. Yet the further down he looked the more he could see the damage, as it was closer to the centre. It was almost like Magnus was testing Leicester to try and find him, and, like his life were a film, the villain had stopped inches short of uncovering his target.

Street lamps were bent and shattered glass littered the ground, although the reason behind this destruction was unclear. Perhaps the machines believed the humans would not try to run away if shards of glass were likely to penetrate the soles of their feet with every step. The pavements too, almost every slab, was cracked in one place or another with obvious signs of struggle. It was like looking at two different world as, only two doors down from his own abode, the damage stopped and his road regained its prestige look. Stones remained resolute and lamps retained the faint glow of early evening, not quite ready to grace the roads with their glimmering protection.

Thomas clearly recognised the damage as well, and for a moment Alex did not realise the consequences this would have. Then, suddenly, Thomas tried to dart forwards to reach his home, but Alex physically held him back. He was much stronger than Alex would have anticipated, and he found controlling his friend's blind panicking to be a difficult task.

"Thomas!" He yelled to try and calm down his friend, but he would not stop struggling as he gripped viciously onto one of Alex's arms. "I didn't choose Verity over our families you idiot, I chose to save you! Now don't throw it away!"

Thomas stopped squirming. He turned to look at Alex with eyes that pleaded for forgiveness, which Alex took to mean that he was sorry for the way he had acted. Yet, in reality, he was apologising for what he was about to do. With a quickness that once again astounded Alex, he sunk his teeth into the forearm of his friend to make sure his grip was released. The pain shot through Alex's body like a bullet wound, Thomas had even drawn a small amount of blood from him. Whilst he withdrew his arm instinctively his best friend had seized the opportunity and dashed off towards his home. Alex desperately tried to call after his friend, not believing it to be safe after that shadow he had seen around Verity's abode, but Thomas would not listen. He dashed off towards his house with extreme fervour, with Alex quickly in tow as he held his injured arm.

A sudden thump in front of Thomas caused him to fall backwards in fear. A machine had descended from over the houses. Alex realised straight away that the shadows in the distance had not been a figment of his imagination. Clearly Magnus had sent it to investigate why one of his machines had turned against its owner, and that meant Alex and his family were in grave danger. He could be upon them anytime of his choosing.

With that sense of urgency in mind Alex propelled himself forward, with the power of the low wind pulled together behind him. The closer he got the more he regretted his irrational decision as his fleshy shoulder collided with the metal of the machine. Even with a small elemental shield protecting him the impact pained him greatly, but he achieved his aim. The machine tumbled to the ground with him, obviously unprepared to resist such a burst of energy from a mere human. It did not seem deterred though as it literally threw Alex off of it and quickly got back to its feet, grabbing Thomas by the scruff of his shirt. As his back cracked against the floor, and Alex looked up in agony, he realised that this must have been the machine that had taken Thomas in the first place. It was here to complete its mission.

In a way Alex felt relieved, as it meant that Magnus was not necessarily aware of what was going on. Yet, he still needed to protect his best friend and so got back to his feet, with a hand upon his back to try and relieve the pain he had received from his sudden impact with the cracked concrete path.

"MAGNUS!" He shouted towards the creature.

The machine turned to look at him with an almost befuddled expression that allowed Thomas to slip away from his captor and continue his journey towards his home, leaving the scruff of his shirt behind as it was trapped in the closed fist of the machine. It was like Magnus himself was peering through it. Thomas was almost at his home when it realised that it had lost its target and tried to move towards him once again. Alex needed to make sure that Thomas was alright, but he could not do it with the machine blocking his every attempt, and there was only so many times that he could surprise it with his unnatural strength. Alex needed to think fast and so drew his own machine into the fight as he chased after his best friend. He did not stop to see what was happening behind him as he could see it with his own eyes, projected in the back of his mind.

Unfortunately for Alex, as he reached Thomas's house, the machine still had to be controlled by him in order for it to fight, and that meant that it had Alex's fighting skills. Like something from a movie, he raised the machine's arm above its head to deliver a massive punch to its opponent, but, unlike in films, this did not work. With its arm raised it was unprotected, and therefore open to attack. Magnus' minion swiftly delivered three successive blows to the midriff of his machine which knocked it back several steps, creating a sufficient gap with which his opponent could escape. It tried to turn back towards Thomas' house but Alex made sure his machine gripped it by its fleshy ankle, cracking its protective casing with its powerful grasp.

Alex rushed through Thomas' front door and called out for his friend. There was no answer. He proceeded through the small corridor and into the living room to see things in a state of disarray. Everything had been tossed about, whether from a struggle or a blind panic to clear everything out quickly, he did not know. Most of the electrical equipment, such as the ancient television, had been left behind, but that did not surprise Alex given that Thomas' parents were fairly old fashioned in how they ran their home. They believed in more traditional family outings and reading over sitting in front of a computer screen, which he disagreed with considering he used his own frequently to write with. Although, he could understand, and even respect, their love of the older ways of doing things, as he preferred it also in terms of communication. Other things, like the books and photographs, had been snatched away, or at least were no longer in sight, and so Alex believed there was no reason to give up hope yet.

He heard a noise upstairs. Carefully, as he briefly peered into the raided kitchen with drawers and the fridge-freezer thrown wide open, he moved back into the plainly coloured corridor and placed his hand upon the acorn-shaped banister that ran up the length of the staircase before him. Alex knew that there was no reason to be afraid, but he was not sure if Thomas would want him intruding in such a time. Thankfully, much to the relief of his indecisiveness, his best friend appeared at the top of the stairs with a picture held in his hand, cradled like a child or precious object. He looked towards Alex with eyes moist with tears.

Back outside, the machine was now pounding down upon the metallic wrist of Alex's own minion to try and get it to release its grip. They were made of the same material, they possessed the same strength, but in such a position Alex knew that his machine was at a distinct disadvantage. The metal began to cave in as his enemy's foot came down time and time again, like a pickaxe rhythmically mining a valuable ore, although the machine undoubtedly cared little for what laid inside its traitorous brethren. Alex needed to be quick.

Thomas stood at the top of the stairs, almost numbed by his sadness, as he stared at the image held in his hand. Alex twisted himself around to place himself upon the first step, uncertain whether to progress further, as he looked for some kind of recognition from his best friend. None came and so he tried his best to console him with words.

"There's still hope Thomas." He said.

"Hope…" His friend replied blandly and without mirth. "They're gone Alex."

"I don't think so." Alex replied sternly to try and persuade his friend to his line of thinking. "Everything important to them has been taken, maybe they left in time." He suggested with the anticipation that it would raise his friend from his dark depths of depression.

"Without me." Thomas responded with the same sadness.

"Is there no way that you can get a hold of them?" Alex asked. Before Thomas could answer he clarified his statement. "I know they don't carry phones with them, and there probably wasn't time for a letter, but maybe they left some clue?"

That comment seemed to spring Thomas back into life as he bounded down the stairs and past Alex with great enthusiasm, turning into the living room so fast that he almost smacked into the door. Alex followed him as he rushed towards a fruit bowl that stood atop an oak chest of drawers to the right of the television, just before the patio-style doors that led to the kitchen. It was empty, but judging by the ecstatic look upon Thomas' face Alex guessed that that was a good thing.

"They're gone Alex!" He reiterated, confusing Alex at first.

"I know…" Alex began to respond before Thomas shut him off.

"No! I mean the keys, to my grandparents!"

Alex spoke back with similar enthusiasm. "So where do they live?"

"Cambridge! They must've gone to Cambridge and expected me to follow in my car!" He said excitedly before realising that his car was sitting in the city centre, with a roadblock all around it from other abandoned cars.

Alex was about to tell his friend that he would take him there before he heard a scream, not through his own eyes as it was inaudible, but through those of his machine. It was the scream of a young girl, and her voice was unmistakable. It was Abigail. Alex darted from the home with the power of the wind behind him, taking the side off of the front door in the process. Thomas, not knowing what to think, tried to follow him out but by the time he got outside Alex was already only a second away from the two machines.

Alex's machine had finally released its hold upon its opponent, the strain almost taking off its hand as the metal was now crushed and warped out of its formerly perfect human imitation, and now struggled back onto its feet to chase after Magnus'. The villain's minion had sensed that it would not be able to take its intended target and had now settled upon the first thing in its sights, his sister. The machine grabbed her by the arm and forcefully placed her upon its shoulder with the same arm cradled around her so that she could not escape. Thankfully, Alex was so close behind that it did not even have time to deliver its signature knockout punch.

Alex had been furious before, but that was nothing compared to the enraging urgency within him that willed him to bring his sister back unharmed. He sped through the air so rapidly that he had to force himself to slow down as he approached the machine now darting away with Abigail. He did not want to accidentally harm her, and he knew that he was fully capable of doing so when using his powers. He heard a call from behind him, coming from his house, as his mother screamed at the thought of her youngest child being taken away. That meant they knew about his abilities, if they could see well enough to spot him from the distance he was now at, with his machine closely following behind him.

Alex could barely see through the green wisps of anger that flew away from his eyes like stardust, he had never experienced anger like this. He put everything he could into forcing his arm down onto the fleshy shoulder of his sister's, and best friend's, captor. The protective seal broke from the pressure put upon it and the machine crumbled under the force of Alex's hand squeezing down upon its vulnerable area. Abigail was sent flying through the air as the machine released her, screaming as she feared for her life. Alex had planned ahead though, even with his anger, and the machine that he controlled darted forward and caught her gently with its hands, both of which were still obviously functional, supporting the small of her back so that she would not come to harm. Quickly it turned towards Alex, who was now standing, not floating, over his prey like a successful predator. The machine twisted onto its front, momentarily displacing Alex as he stumbled two steps away from the centre of his hate. His minion was quickly upon it though, with its foot placed firmly upon the exposed shoulder to discourage it from squirming away like its cowardly master had done.

Alex was grateful that his abilities extended as far as they did, because at least he was able to protect those that he cared about, no matter how frantically they shied away from him at first. His sister was no exception as she struggled to escape from the grasp of his minion, but Alex did not worry about that for the moment. He had to deal with the disgusting monstrosity, in act as well as appearance, before him.

The machine did not try to struggle frantically as a human would, as it knew there was no hope of overpowering its turncoat brother without being permanently impaired. It did not whimper or make a cry. It felt nothing for its acts as they were just a part of its existence. It was the pure and vile evil of Magnus embodied in a monstrous concoction of flesh and metal. Yet, Alex could not help feeling sorry for it. He could not bring himself to end this being in front of him. His eyes were glowing green with anger, their wispy flares dissipating around him, but he still could not pull the trigger and end it. With a roar to release his rage he made his machine launch down and punch the machine square on the nose, rendering it the equivalent of unconscious. It would live to fight again though, and Alex needed to live with whatever consequences that brought.

Alex turned towards his sister, who was still positioned in the arms of his minion, and took her into his own arms to embrace her in a loving hug. She fell against him, completely exhausted from her struggles, and attempted to wrap her arms around his back. He had never been so pleased to see her before, and he always enjoyed her company anyway, and was overjoyed that he had managed to save her from harm. Alex had spent so long worrying about his family and what had happened to them and now he knew that they were safe, regardless of the part he played in this safety he could not help but feel proud.

He took a slow saunter towards his home with Abigail held in his arms, like a returning hero. His family clearly did not feel the same though as Charlotte pushed Steven behind her and stepped back inside, closing the door behind her. This was what Alex had feared. She could see what he was, in the flesh, and now she could not decide whether or not to reject her son for being a freak. Steven already knew and so was easily willing to follow their mother in their shunning of him. Or that is what he thought. As he strode quickly towards his house his mother called out to him and it became clear that it was not Alex she was afraid of.

"What is THAT thing doing here Alex?"

Alex was instantly relieved that she had not been retreating from him, for that was what he had always believed would happen when they found out what he was. Although she clearly still did not understand the extent of her son's abilities, despite the machine she charmingly referred to as 'that thing' being responsible for the safeguarding of her daughter; which was surely a good indicator.

"It's alright mum, it's safe." Alex tried to assure her.

"What do you mean?"

"I control it…I used it to save Abigail."

He heard a soft whimpering from his mother. "Abi?" She called through the door.

"It's okay mum, Alex saved me. He's…a hero."

Charlotte was about to respond when Steven burst into the conversation with his usual mixture of bravado and irrationality. "Get away from him Abi! He's dangerous!"

"Steven…" His little sister replied calmly. "He saved me."

This small insult was clearly enough to enrage Steven to new levels of courageousness as he threw open the door and stared deeply into his brother's eyes, his own welling with tears as he struggled to contain his emotions. "So why did he try and kill me then?!" He whispered angrily.

"Steven…" Alex tried to begin his apology but quickly found himself without the oratory skills to convey his remorse.

"You don't even know what you've done to me do you?" Steven continued in his low tones, his nostrils flaring with anger. "I don't just mean your freaky abilities! You've always pushed me down, even if you didn't mean to. The golden boy." Alex tried to interject but he could not. "How am I meant to compare to you? All mum ever talks about is how proud of you she is…her gifted child, while I'm left to fall in your shadow." Tears were now actively streaming down his face, silent in their story of sadness. "Dad knew you were something special as well…" He began to laugh sardonically to himself. "Do you know, I'm even jealous of those stupid letters you send each other? At least they're something personal, all I ever get is a quick minute or two to talk to Dad when mum's finished! I can't even imagine how Abi feels, she barely even knows that she has a father!" If the comment was meant to affect his sister in some way, or turn her against her eldest brother, she gave no indication that it worked. "And now you save her and turn HER against ME as well?" Steven was barely able to contain himself now. "How am I meant to live when I have no family?"

"Steven…I am so sorry for what I have done to you…" Alex began his apology with tears of his own forming. "I never meant to-"

"Hurt me?" Steven interrupted. "That's not what it looked like…you've always wanted to get rid of me!" He said spitefully.

"That's not true!" Alex shouted with green wisps of anger flowing from his eyes. Steven suddenly began to pay attention. "You annoy me sometimes, well, most of the time…" He said with a smile, which he was glad that his brother shared. "But you're my brother, I would give everything to help you, just like I would for Abigail; mum; dad; and even granny and granddad all the way in Australia." He carried on with another warm smile.

He did not need to carry on any further as his brother ran forward and hugged his chest as he sobbed heavily. Charlotte as well, overwhelmed by the emotions on display, rushed forward to embrace her sons as both of them wept over the catharsis from their past conflicts. Abigail held her eldest brother's hand, but did not cry, and gave it a light squeeze. She had always been quite awkward in such situations, believing such emotions to be counterintuitive at best. She could not resist breaking down and crying though as Alex pulled her in closely. Just like at Henbane, every sense seemed to intensify as he grew to appreciate every colour and smell that the world had to offer. He knew it would not last though, but that made that moment all the sweeter.

Alex was so happy at resolving every issue he had, and at not having to hide who he was any longer, that he was lost for words to express how elated he felt. That was, until he realised that he could no longer see through two sets of eyes. In his happiness he had endangered everyone around them. He had released control.

Chapter 17

Alex shoved his family back inside from the hulking mass of metal that was now beyond his control. Before closing the door he shouted at Thomas to run, which caused his friend to panic with confusion. The machine rounded upon his best friend and appeared to glare at him, its intent unknown, but Alex needed to think about his family first. With them safely inside, and thus behind a door that would potentially be difficult for the machine to break down, especially if Alex used his powers to reinforce it with wind, he pushed himself through the small slither left in the door. Swiftly he brought up a weak barrier of wind to separate himself and Thomas from the machine. With equal deftness he then grabbed his best friend by the wrist and propelled himself back towards his home, shutting the door before letting down the barrier that was holding back his former minion.

"What was that about?" Thomas asked as he held onto his arm in the spot where Alex had grabbed him, as it clearly pained him.

"I let go of it accidentally." Alex responded as he peered through the spy hole in his door.

"Well go out there and get it back." Thomas retorted.

Alex turned towards his best friend with an inquisitive eyebrow. "Thomas, what do you think I'm talking about?"

"I don't know! Keys? Wallet? Something you would keep on you I guess."

"No." Alex replied bluntly. "I let go of the machine."

"Well what does that mean?" Steven chimed in angrily.

"I'm not controlling it anymore."

"So who is?" Abigail asked astutely.

Alex gave off a worried look that instantly sent the same expression to his best friend and sister, whilst his brother and mother seemed oblivious to the obvious threat that was now before them. Since Alex no longer controlled the hideous monster that awaited outside their door that meant that someone else could, and Alex was almost certain that Magnus would want to reclaim his property. Then he would realise that someone had taken it from him, and it would not be long before he actually found out who he was. Fear is a powerful motivator after all, Alex thought to himself.

"It's that man isn't it Alex?" Charlotte asked. "The one who destroyed Leeds?"

Alex nodded, almost sagely.

"Who is this man?!" She said, fuming with the injustice that Magnus wrought. "What gives him the right to take life and deliver death? Who is he Alex?" She asked again.

"I don't know who he is, not really. He used to own a metal industry in the north, which is probably why he's able to make those hideous things that you saw. I'm fairly certain he tried to do this once before, but he was stopped before he could try."

"Stopped by who?" Abigail probed.

"I wish I knew. If I knew then I might be able to find out a way of stopping Magnus."

"Why do you have to stop him?" Charlotte said as she pushed through her other children to cup her son's cheek in her hand. "Why can't you stay here with us?"

"You've seen what he can do, and who else can do what I can?" He said with a wry smile.

"But-" His mother tried to continue, but Alex cut her off.

"Mother, if I don't try and stop him then he could take over far more than a city."

"I know."

Before they could continue any further there was a loud knocking at the door. They had forgotten about their guest. Quickly Alex raised a shield up against the door to stop the machine from smashing it down through sheer brute force, but its attacks did not increase in strength, or speed. They continued with the same rhythmic knocking that they had begun with. A rasping of three knocks, followed by a three second pause before the knocks resumed. It was curious that the machine was not being aggressive, but Alex still did not trust it and so told his mother to bring some items to jam the door with.

Together they pushed the small coffee table towards the door, which slotted perfectly into the quite narrow opening that laid in the corridor. It would not stop the metal hinges from snapping under force, if the machine decided to become more vigorous, but it should provide a suitable doorstop. Alex made sure that the downstairs windows were closed as well in case it tried to force itself inside that way, even though it was obviously capable of smashing the glass with little effort. Throughout all of this, the knocking continued. The incessant noise rang in Alex's ears like a persistent taunting, drilling deeper into his mind and driving him insane. Even without Magnus being present the villain was still finding a way to get the upper hand on his enemies.

They tried to sit down in the living room to avoid it, yet even the squishy cushions upon their sofa, and mind-numbing television, could not distract them. The knocking droned on and on, covering up the tweeting of the birds and the meowing of the local cats, all having forgotten the commotion that had caused them to flee earlier. Alex, having had enough, removed himself from the sofa and walked to the door, moving the coffee table back towards the staircase so that he could gain access. Annoyed, he placed his eyes into the spy-hole to see what the machine was doing. It was just standing there, like a normal person, as it knocked against the door. There was no hint of aggression in its posture or its actions, it was almost like a neighbour coming round to chat.

Something within Alex told him to open the door, reassuring him that Magnus must not have regained control of the machine, although if that was the case then he had no idea who was possessing it as he certainly was not. He looked towards his family, who were still on their sofa watching a program about housing auctions, and considered them for a moment. If he opened the door, and it turned out that the machine's docile behaviour was part of an elaborate ruse to infiltrate their home, then they would be in danger. He could go from having everything, after painstakingly making sure that his family and close friends were safe, to having nothing all within the space of a few hours. Yet if he did not then the irritating knocking would continue, possibly indefinitely, until he did. Thus, for the sake of his own sanity and despite the warning bells ringing in his head, not that he could hear them through the frequent rasping upon the door, he pulled the latch back and placed his hand firmly upon the handle.

"Alex?" Charlotte called. "What are you doing?"

Alex did not respond. His grasp was still firmly placed upon the handle of the door, his hand now beginning to shake with his indecisions. He could not take the knocking any longer, and so, without further hesitation, he pulled open the door.

"Alex don't!" He heard Thomas yell, but it was too late.

The machine did not react though, Alex was not sure if that was a good or bad thing. It did not raise its fist in violence or extend its hand in friendship, it simply stood and stared back at Alex with an expression that could not be read, which was not surprising considering that it did not have a full face. It still disturbed him to see the combination of metal and flesh, especially since all the features of a human face were still present, although they were stretched and withered beyond recognition.

Its mouth tried to stretch, opening slightly, as if it was trying to speak, but it could not form any words. It looked visibly distressed as it struggled to find the words it was searching for and raised a hand towards Alex, not in violence, which told him to wait for a moment. After a moment or two some low noises were beginning to resonate from within it and Alex instinctively backed away, as though it were a bomb in its final stages of detonation. He was still cautious, yet it still showed no signs of aggression towards him or his family, who were now huddled together in the living room, except Thomas who he suspected was hiding around the corner. Alex could not blame them, for the machine had the potential to turn on them at any moment and catch him by surprise.

Eventually, the low noises turned more into metallic gargles, like the machine was clearing its throat. It took it another minute or two before a great ball of dust erupted from inside it, no doubt collected from the decades of inactivity. Then it was silent. Its position remained unchanged as it stood fixed at his doorway. Alex wondered if it had somehow deactivated itself when attempting to speak, if that had been what it was trying to accomplish. A small voice from behind him answered the question for him.

"It's not broken, it just has no function." Abigail said.

"How do you know that?" He asked, before realising there was a more important question. "Actually, why are you here and not with mother, Steven and Thomas?"

"Actually…" His best friend mimicked as he peered around the corner. "It's just your mother and Steven."

"Well, why are you both here then and not hiding in case this thing turns rogue?"

"Because we know it won't." Abigail answered.

"We've seen these things up close, both of us, and this is not acting like one of them. I don't think Magnus is controlling it." Thomas replied honestly.

"How can you be sure?" Alex probed as he was still not convinced.

Abigail simply waved a hand towards the machine. Alex expected no response, or a bad response, but much to his amazement the machine waved back, and even partially smiled with its deformed mouth. It seemed that Magnus was not influencing it after all, as, judging by what Alex had seen of him, he would not choose deception over brute force.

"Why aren't you trying to harm us?" Alex asked it.

"Why should I?" It replied in a heavily metallic tone.

Thomas hid around the corner again as it spoke, his fear renewed with this new horror. Alex widened his eyes in astonishment. Abigail merely smiled contentedly to herself, as she had clearly known that it possessed the ability to speak. Alex raised an eyebrow towards his sister and smiled, her intelligence proving once again to be greater than his own, even though he was several years her elder. Alex looked back towards the machine, with a large sense of trepidation, and continued his questioning, as he realised that this was a very unique opportunity.

"Well, because Magnus created you." Alex answered.

"He did, but you freed me of his influences. I no longer follow his directives." The machine answered truthfully, having no reason to lie.

"So you only received orders from Magnus, he did not directly control you like I did?"

"Magnus did not see through me as you did. He controls thousands of Matella and so seeing through each one would be like looking through a never-ending hall of mirrors. He thought it far more productive to maintain a small amount of control over us, so that we do his bidding, without individually ruling each of us." The machine explained.

"I see." Alex answered, unsure of where to take his questioning, before the obvious struck him. "Matella?"

"That is what Magnus calls us." The machine replied bluntly.

"And the huge city-destroyers?"

"Animus." It retorted just as nonchalantly.

Alex nodded. "Wait, wouldn't it cause him pain?"

"No. We are all like shells, or vehicles needing to be piloted. We have no free thought and we know nothing of life outside of Magnus's world."

"But you're talking to me, so you must have free thought?"

"It is not free. I have cognitive function, due to the fact that the brain is still preserved inside of this metallic exoskeleton, but I can make no decision for myself. None that I am aware of anyway."

"But you refer to yourself as 'I'…" Alex persisted.

"Indeed. Perhaps I retain some semblance of personality from the flesh that was welded to create this body."

"So, why are you able to think of your own accord now?"

"I have no outside influences interfering with my actions, any thought or action I give is my own." The Matella answered.

Alex laughed to himself, believing to have the machine in a trap with his contradictory questions. "So you do have free thought then?"

"No. I am responding to your questions, I am reacting out of necessity."

"This is infuriating!" Thomas yelled in the background.

"I think it's hilarious." Abigail contributed with an angelic laugh.

"Fine." Alex conceded. "So you follow my commands then?" He probed tentatively.

"No." The machine replied bluntly.

"Oh for goodness sake!" Thomas yelled again as Abigail let out another chuckle.

Alex himself released a small irritated breath. "So why are you responding to my questions and queries?"

"I have no other active function." It retorted. "You released me from Magnus' control, and also your own, thus I hold no mode of function any longer. I will go where you go." It spoke, almost loyally, although it was hard to tell through the heavy metallic tones that it used to speak.

"So, you'll stop Magnus with me?" He asked, aggravating himself with his continuous bombardment of questions.

"If that is your goal." The machine spoke plainly, again.

At this point Steven re-emerged, leaving his mother by herself within the living room, and so prompting her to come forward also. His brother was clearly irate with his decision, judging by his huffing and fuming. With his cheeks reddened in fury and his nostrils flaring with rage. He widened his eyes as he examined the machine up close. He had clearly never been so close to one before and blatantly struggled to hold back the bile building in the pit of his stomach from the disgusting sight of it. Alex had been with it for almost no time at all, only a few hours, and yet the initial repulsion that compelled him to vomit at seeing the monstrosity had evaporated. It was now just another creature to him, another being that had been subjected to Magnus' twisted will.

"Are you really thinking about taking this THING with you to…to what exactly? Save the world from this Magnus bloke?" Steven shouted as he turned towards his brother.

"That's exactly what I was thinking." Alex replied with a half-smile, now that he was guilt-free in ridiculing his brother again.

"But, what if it turns on you?" Steven protested.

"It's already had plenty of opportunity to do so." Alex said confidently, believing his new companion to be a loyal ally. "So if you're quite finished?"

Steven stepped back in another huff of anger, as he often did when provoked by his brother, although without his usual counter remarks. Instead, before Alex could ask the most vital question of all to the Matella, his mother came forward again and laid a hand upon her eldest son's shoulder. Even with tears in her eyes, and despite it going against her own wishes, she realised that she had to let him go.

"You do what you have to Alex." She spoke softly.

Alex nodded to his mother with an affectionate smile before turning back towards the machine. "So, what can you tell me about Magnus?" He finally asked.

"I can tell you many things, but not everything." The machine answered, being unintentionally cryptic in its wording.

"What do you mean? Either you know something about him or you don't?" Abigail responded for him.

The machine ignored his sister, after a brief glance at her, and addressed Alex instead. "It is difficult to describe…" It stopped speaking for a moment as it worked through appropriate metaphors to use in its explanation. "When those with your abilities possess something you can see through their memories if you choose. You are aware of this. But, when you possess an empty shell like myself the connection become like a bridge. It can be accessed from two sides." It exclaimed.

"I don't understand." Alex answered truthfully.

"When you possess a being like myself you leave your own memories inside, whether willingly or not, as there is nothing to replace the memories with. In a normal person, their own memories would take over yours. But I have no memories of my own…I do have some of Magnus' though. When you displaced his possession over me the memories remained, but Magnus knows about this and so sealed off many memories to protect their secrets from being learnt." The machine concluded, to the disappointment of Alex, and no doubt the others as well. "However…" it continued. "I have access to roughly ten percent of Magnus' memories, mostly relating to his childhood and events he regarded as insignificant. There is much that you could learn from some of these."

"So I should be able to access these memories from my own mind right? Since I possessed you." Alex suggested.

"No. Your own memories stopped them from entering your cerebral cortex." The Matella replied with yet another crushing blow to his morale.

"But I remember things from the others, from Arthur and Verity."

"That is because you directly possessed them and saw through their minds, thus creating a memory of your own which contains theirs. You would need to actually possess Magnus himself in order to see what he has already seen."

"I have to go through you then? Since you have these memories?"

"Correct. I will attempt to guide you to the memories that contain useful information regarding Magnus and his pursuits." The machine clarified. "It will not be like possessing a person though. You may take control of me, as you did before, but to see into my collective databanks you must focus. It will be difficult, and I cannot assist you, I can only guide you to the correct memories when you are inside, and even then I may become lost within myself."

Alex nodded and steeled himself for the task ahead. Even though the machine had told him that it would not hurt, he still braced himself for the sharp agony that possession had always given him, except on Muffin for the most part. Alex closed his eyes and intently focused, lingering on no thoughts and fixating only on the darkness around him.

Alex had invaded minds before, but this was different. He was not trying to access the memories of the person in front of him, as he had been before. This was like trying to grab hold of specks of dust appearing from the rays of sun shining through a window. Not only that, but it was Magnus' memories that he was trying to access and Alex had no doubt that the villain would have placed some kind of countermeasure so that this did not occur. A thought appeared within his own mind as he continued to try. What if it's a trap? Alex told himself. If Magnus allowed Alex to access his memories then Magnus could reach into his own and know exactly who he was.

The machine seemed to sense his trepidation as it spoke to him again in its raspy tones, the exertion of speaking clearly difficult for it. "Relax yourself Alex, I am not Magnus' anymore and he cannot see through me as he could before. You may find it difficult, and many memories may be lost to you as they are to me, but you can do it. This is your chance to understand him, and to find a way of eliminating him."

Alex kept his eyes closed to focus as much as he could. No matter what he did though all he could see was darkness. Unlike before he was not able to produce images from the memories of the possessed. It was like staring into a black abyss with nothing else in sight. He could not do it. He opened his eyes to yell at the machine for giving him false hope, but stopped when he realised what was happening. Everything around him was still black, the darkest colour he had ever seen, but he was standing within it. In the distance he could see small specks of light that reminded him of distant stars, still worlds away. As he focused upon them they rushed towards him and revealed themselves to be portals, or gateways, into the memories of Magnus. Many of them were shut off, blocked by seem unperceivable force, but he expected it to be so and thus waited for the machine to silently guide him towards the correct experiences.

As he waited he looked about to see if there was any indication of who the machine had been before its horrific transformation, but there was nothing. Suddenly, Alex began to understand. He was in the machine's mind, with everything of who it once was now lost, and it had no memories or feelings of its own. It was hollow. That did not matter though as now he had a way of understanding Magnus, and a better chance of finding his weakness. He could fight back.

Chapter 18

Alex was deeply confused. He had no idea which memories he was supposed to be looking at, and that was even out of those that were available to him. He trudged around the empty space that was the Matella's mind for what seemed like an eternity, every second turning into years in his own mind from the tediousness of his activity. The piercing black that surrounded him did not help matters either, as it made feel as though he were asleep and so he could not be certain on what was truly happening. It was all like a blur, with each moment merging into the next.

Alex gesticulated in frustration, kicking an imaginary football to try and relieve himself of the stress. The machine had not been seen or heard from since he opened its mind and yet it had promised to guide him through its collective memories of Magnus. Just as he began to curse the Matella for its lack of loyalty he suddenly felt a tap upon his imaginary shoulder, a strange feeling to say the least. He turned around inside the black chasm to see the equally dark machine staring back at him, its iron exoskeleton so dark that it barely stood out from its surroundings.

"You scared me." Alex said.

The machine did not respond. Instead it pointed towards a fleck of light in the distance, which was clearly Alex's first target. Just as he focused in on it, like a hawk upon its prey, the small speck hurtled towards him with a ferocious speed. Instinctively, Alex ducked to avoid the beams of lights. It stopped just before his prone body and held an image, almost like a stationary window, into the world of Magnus. Judging by the surroundings Alex assumed that it was from the villain's childhood, as the factory looked positively bustling with work, and not at all like the shell that Magnus had made it under his regime.

Alex struggled back to his feet and peered at the image for a moment, as he was uncertain of how to proceed. The Matella, still present, remained silent by his side and offered no help, its gait unchanging. It simply touched the screen and stepped away again, beckoning Alex to do the same. Once again he felt an extreme sense of apprehension as he moved his hand closer to the static wall of light.

"I can't believe I'm doing this." He muttered to himself.

As he touched the gateway nothing seemed to happen, and he found himself continuing to doubt the validity of the Matella's words. A second later though, the gateway, whilst still connected to Alex's hand via his fingertip, extended to surround everything about him. Suddenly, Alex was no longer in the black chasm that was the machine's mind as he saw himself looking into a completely unknown world, through strange eyes. Machinery could be heard all around him, the hammering and smithing that indicated a time that had long since passed. The putrid stench of fumes filled the air and infested his nostrils, an acrid reminder of the stench that humanity produced. So toxic was its thickness that Magnus found himself stifling a cough, as he often did.

Alex stopped. He had not even realised it, but he was looking into Magnus' mind. No, he thought to himself, it's more than that. Before, when he had possessed Arthur and Verity, he had not truly felt like he was inhabiting that person. Rather, he was ordering them about and guiding them, or peering into things that they had experienced but Alex could not. Yet, with Magnus' memory, he not only saw as he saw, he felt as he felt and smelt as he smelt. Every emotion and sense was tingling within him. Alex was still very much his own person, able to separate his thought from Magnus' on demand, and yet, he was somebody else entirely. He was Magnus.

He was only six years old and the world was a continuous mystery to him. The laborious work of the employees, if they could even be called that based upon their scraggly appearances and dirty grimaces, did not make sense to him either. Magnus was a privileged child and, unlike many other children only slightly older than himself, some of which his father employed, he had never been subjected to a single moment's work. Neither had his father for that matter. Yet these disgusting, dirt covered, peasants worked almost twelve hours every single day and had nothing to show for it. It was not fair. In fact, the young Magnus thought to himself, it was downright unjust. He loved it though, and, as one of the workers looked up at him with a face full of sweat and positively aching with exhaustion, he knew that he belonged on top of these people.

His father had always told him that only the strong could survive. He had not meant physically, otherwise the workers would be in control. Peter meant that power, real power, came through manipulation and intimidation. The brain far outweighed the bicep. As Magnus looked around the ramshackle hull that was his father's main workshop floor, he found it very difficult to disagree with the concept.

The thin metallic roof, that covered the underground workstation, rattled in the low winds that often swept through rural Yorkshire and threatened to unravel itself. His father had never prided himself upon the appearance of his factory, which was a good thing considering it looked awful, and that was evident from the state of the roof, with various leaks pouring onto the red-hot factory floor, but nobody could doubt the exceptional grade of machinery that he put out into the market. Magnus watched the workers apply the finishing touches to the latest line of artillery, a complete set of a dozen Gatling guns to be immediately used, each well-oiled and perfectly shaped. He found it amazing that his father could create such fines objects but still refused to remodel his factory to reflect their more than modest earnings. Magnus did not complain though, since it meant that more money would be given to him upon his father's death.

He leaned in closer to the small rail that stopped him from falling over the edge, although so miniscule was its size that he could already peer over the top of it. Before he could pull back a familiar hand grasped the back of his neck and forced him to look down the fifty foot drop. Magnus tried to resist but the grasp was firm and held him in place.

"Look at it Magnus!" His nanny angrily whispered into his ear, her heartland accent giving him chills. "You know your father and me have become very close lately…all I need is to nestle in a little more and his fortune will become mine!" She continued as she tightened his grip. Magnus let out a low whimper but she took no notice. "And if you dare try and stop me then you'll be taking a short, and yet very long, tumble. Such a tragedy that would be for Peter, to lose his only son."

"Why would you do that?" Magnus asked with small tears filling his eyes as he peered down the platform onto the factory floor.

"I told you to look you stupid child!" She shouted back as she clouted him on his ear. "Look around you….these pathetic cretins waste their lives away for pittance. Well, not me. I will take everything I can, and I will not let anyone stand in my way, no matter who they are. No matter if they're children…" She replied chillingly.

Magnus did as he was told and looked out over the factory floor, taking in the stinking mass of humanity that tainted his nostrils. They would scramble for such amusingly low amounts of power, beating each other to death if need be. As Magnus felt his nanny's bony fingers digging into his neck, rage and pain swirling within him, he vowed that he too would do whatever it took to stay unimpeded on his journey to the top. That meant eliminating Ethel.

Without even thinking, just like before, he had yet another outburst of rage towards his alarmingly violent carer. He did not move though. His eyes, their luminous green blazing so brightly that Magnus thought his eyes might jump away from him or bubble into nothingness, flared and his nanny wailed behind him. It was only a small act, of bending her fingers back so that she released her grip upon the nape of his neck, but yet he had willed it to happen. This was just the latest example of him forcing his will onto others, something which the other children, measly and dull as they were, could not manage to do.

He had not meant to, and now he feared the repercussions of his actions. His anger had clearly gotten the better of him and now he was about to pay the price. With tremendous strength, for such a scrawny woman, his nanny slapped him around the face with all her might. The red mark that was instantly emblazoned across the area of impact stood as testament to his ill behaviour. Tears welled within his small eyes again, glistening his orbital bones and wetting his cheeks, but for the first time Magnus felt no remorse for his actions, even if he had not meant to commit the act. He only felt burning anger, and a loathing so deep that the fires of hell itself could not compete with its bitter intensity. Magnus did not know how much longer he could contain this rage within him.

He turned to look at his nanny, eyes still containing a mixture of tears and daggers, with a challenging stare, almost daring her to strike him again. Her willowy features, her pale complexion and light brown hair, complete with blood red lips and very tight skin, gave her the look of a ghost, somewhat ethereal and yet still very much present. Her white dress, the usual attire for nannies, completed the image. Magnus was not afraid though. He continued to stare deep into her eyes with the same bravado, just waiting for an excuse to let loose his anger upon her. It would be incredibly easy, especially since it was such an easy place to take the long fall down onto the factory floor. Nobody would be any the wiser.

Ethel seemed to register the young master's strange intent for harm and so deftly regained control of the situation by using the one thing that he feared against him. "Just for that insolence...we're going to see your father! And by God will I tell him of what you've done!" She threatened. Except, it was no threat, as she was deathly serious.

Forcefully, she grabbed Magnus by his right hand and held him tightly as she pushed towards the end of the raised platform, which was actually on ground level due to the strange sloping geography of the area. At the very end, behind a heavy glass door with obscured mirroring, so that nobody could see inside but he could see out, was his father's office. On the door itself the words 'Peter Malum: Owner and Proprietor' were etched on it in thick black letters. Magnus, already terrified, tried to turn away and run, but Ethel's continually surprisingly strong grip prevented him from doing so. Alex could feel every emotion inside of the young villain. His anger, his sadness, his pain, and his fear. They all swirled about within him, each one fighting for a crowning place above the others.

Before Magnus could try anything else his nanny knocked politely, very uncharacteristically, at least in his own experience of her, upon his father's office door before hearing the barking command to enter. Magnus, now realising that there was no escape, looked down as he entered his father's domain, as it was rude to look your elder in the eyes without their permission.

"What is it?!" Peter shouted towards Ethel as he looked at the headlines of his morning paper.

"It's the boy, sir. He's behaved most ungentlemanly."

"Bloody awful..." Peter replied and Magnus feared that his other cheek would soon burn with pain. Little did he realise that his father was looking at the newspaper, and its main headline. "A whole group of soldiers, just terrible..."

Magnus could not help looking up to see what his father was so intrigued with. The headline of the newspaper, dated to 26/01/1897, read 'The Benin Massacre' and went on to describe a horrific humiliation for British troops that would no doubt cause havoc to be unleashed in revenge. Peter put down his paper quicker than it took Magnus to react, and thus caught his own son displaying an act of rudeness. Magnus could almost see the anger boiling off of his thinning, yet thick, hair as his skin visibly shook.

"What have you done now boy!" Peter yelled at his child.

"I promise that I have done nothing father!" Magnus hurried in reply as he returned his head to its former position, with his eyes focused firmly upon the tiled ground.

"You will look at me when I speak to you!" Peter shouted, even louder this time as he raised himself from his chair.

Magnus could not see it, even as he raised his head so that he was looking into the bloodshot eyes of his father, but he knew that his nanny was smiling. Her plan was coming together. It angered him that someone such as her, with no entitlement to his riches whatsoever, was squirming her way into his fortunes. His father may raise his voice on occasion, but he was a fair man all in all and would no doubt leave everything to his son upon his death, as he rightly should. Once again the intense green flares of fury rose from his eyes and all he heard was a loud snap and a scream shortly following it. His father had not even blinked through it until he heard the audible cries of Ethel as she wailed over the state of her, now, bent and broken fingers.

"FOR GOODNESS SAKE ETHEL!" He bellowed. "Don't you dare show weakness in front of me, be gone from my sight!"

Ethel left the office, with great difficulty owing to the fact that her fingers were now nothing more than a grotesque and twisted mess, and now it was Magnus who simply could not help smiling to himself. It felt good to have some leverage of his own. Peter, still with the same eyes that told of his belligerent rage, resumed the conversation that he had been having with his son. Whether he genuinely had not seen what had occurred, or refused to acknowledge his son's genetic enhancements, Magnus did not know.

"So, why were you brought in here boy? Answer me truthfully or so help me I'll smack the fear of God into you!"

"Well…" Magnus began, quickly having to think on his feet now that he was able to deceive his father. "I noticed a worker slacking on the new line Gatling guns and I didn't mention anything." He continued, quite satisfied with his fabrication. "When nanny noticed she told me off for not informing you straight away."

Peter stared at his child for several agonisingly long moments before his features relaxed slightly and his expression became one more of justness than anger. He sat back down in his chair and folded his hands into a triangle, as if in contemplation, although Magnus already knew how he would punish this worker.

"What did this man look like? Would you recognise him?" Peter asked him.

The sudden question threw Magnus off guard as he considered the possible options that his father could be considering. He knew he could not wait for too long though and so gently nodded to his father.

"Excellent, then you'll come with me whilst I issue some discipline." Peter spoke, almost cheerfully.

He did not touch his son and lead him to their destination as his nanny would have, as he did not need to. Magnus followed his father obediently, like a puppy being trained, as they went down the winding staircase, at the far end of the walkway just pass Peter's office, which led onto the factory floor. His black leather shoes reverberated off of the metal and announced their approach to every single one of the workers, as it was a sound they were always wary of. Neatly, like a troupe of dancers, they separated to allow smooth passage for their boss, and his son as he followed one step behind with his arms folded behind his back, just like his father.

It was eerily silent as they walked. No hammers were rounding metal or fashioning other shapes. The furnaces produced no loud hiss as water poured into the boiling metals that now sat in moulds, ready to be turned into anything their owner desired. Even the breathing of the employees, which was no doubt heavy and laborious considering the terrible conditions in which they worked, could not be heard. They too walked silently as Peter waited for his son to point out his victim.

Magnus spotted his chosen target after walking past a few, very nervous looking, workers. It was the same man who had stopped to look at his betters as he had been up upon the walkway with his nanny. Thus, his story was not a complete fabrication since the man had technically been slacking for that brief instance.

Peter moved towards the man, as the small crowd of employees parted to reveal him like a traitor in their midst, with a deliberate pace that sent chills up the spines of the workers, his face set in stone and his step ringing loudly.

"Are you sure this is the man?" Peter asked.

Magnus looked towards the target, who was now shaking his head towards him in a desperate plea, and nodded. Before Magnus could even blink the punishment was being issued. All Peter had to do was produce one small coin and a heavily built employee snatched it up and turned towards his colleague with greed in his heart. Magnus could not watch the man's sentence being carried out though as his father gently placed a hand upon his shoulder and led him back towards the metal staircase. The wails of the beaten man were ringing in his ears, a beating that he was only receiving because of Magnus' word against him.

"Remember boy…" His father said. "Only the strong survive, and here…" He gestured at the walls to indicate his meaning. "We are the strong."

Magnus was led up the stairs before his father returned to his office and left him outside. Before he closed the door and turned to look at his son with a puzzled expression as he clearly could not understand why Magnus was still in his presence.

"Go play! Or go do whatever it is that you do." He commanded before slamming the door shut to leave him to his privacy.

Magnus suddenly felt quite hurt that his father did not want to spend time with him. It was nothing new of course, but he thought that their recent experience would have bound them together in their collective enjoyment at the punished man. He had not even given his son a thanks for his help in reprimanding the culprit. He did not want to show any sign of weakness in front of his father and so, without his nanny to stop him this time as she was still no doubt reeling from her horrible wounds, left through the exit at the other end of the walkway that led out into the woods that surrounded his father's factory.

The fresh breeze upon his face felt good and helped nurse his lungs back to life, since they were continually exposed to the horrid conditions within the factory. There was little scenery to enjoy though as the trees, with decaying limbs and brown leaves, were evidently dying from the pollution that his father was spewing forth into the world. It made Magnus sick that humans were destroying the beauty of the natural environment, for he had always loved wildlife. To him, it enforced the idea that humanity, for the most part, was a terrible blight upon the planet's surface, and one that needed to be sterilised or removed before the earth was irreparably damaged.

His emotions flared inside him again, and Alex felt the huge resurgence of his anger over both his father and his father's business. If only Magnus had a way of doing what he wanted, then he could shape the world into what he wanted it to be. With a shrill shriek he pushed his hands out to the side and screamed with his eyes flaring, brighter than they had ever been before. The low winds suddenly turned into hurricanes as the mighty winds easily knocked over the trees surrounding him. The horrendous creaking and cracking, as their roots

stubbornly remained in the ground, was a terrible cacophony.

Slowly, after the damage had been done, Magnus opened his eyes to witness what he was

capable of. He had always known that he was different, that he was meant for great and

dreadful deeds, but now he could see exactly the tremendous power that had been given to

him. The results were disastrous. Cracked wood and timbers now scattered the landscape, the

rotting limbs finally snapping off to reveal what little fresh wood was left. The leaves had

fallen off to create a hideous brown covering over the floor around him, some of them

breaking and disintegrating with the low blows of the wind.

Magnus could still feel the power swirling within him, like a mighty storm, and so, without

even thinking about it or breaking a sweat, he lifted the snapped trees from the ground and

slammed them into each other to knock off any of the dead wood that was still attached. The

noise was just as hideous as it had been before, sending shivers up his spine; but it excited

him. The now bare trees were stripped to their cores. With his other hand, not that he needed

it, Magnus grabbed several stones of considerable size and began to chip away at the base of

the wood, thus forming multiple stakes within only a few moments. Such sharp and powerful

objects could destroy everything, he thought to himself. The thought consumed him for a

moment, turning his soul into a torrential black pit, before he considered how irate his father

would be.

Angrily, he trusted his judgements over his emotions and drove the stakes into the stumps

that they had left behind, creating a rather strange looking piece of art. No doubt everyone

would have heard the commotion that he had made, although possibly not over the

horrendous noises of machinery. That did not matter to Magnus though, he did not care if the

whole world knew about him, because then they would fear him.

"Only the strong…" He muttered. "Only the strong…"

Chapter 19

Alex retreated from the memory, having learnt enough from it. Magnus had started using his gifts at six years old, and to a far greater power than Alex could muster even with his ten year advantage. The machine was waiting back in the eternal darkness that was its mind. It did not speak to him, it did not even move, it simply stared at him and expected Alex to proceed to the next memory. Alex had no idea what to do though, no idea of how to locate the next piece of information that would help him take down Magnus, or at the very least help him to understand the villain and his motives.

He walked about inside the abyss for a while, hoping that the memory would just unveil itself beside him. It did not. The never-ending black was spotted by only a few specks of light in the distance that Alex inspected as he willed them towards him, having gotten the hang of accessing memory from within the Matella. Each time he looked to the miniaturised machine for some kind of hint to see if he was looking at the right memory portal. It gave nothing. Thus, every single time, he pushed the mirror-like flecks of light away from him to try and find the specific access point that he was looking for.

When it became evident that Alex was struggling the machine leapt off into the distance. Alex presumed that its aim was to guide him and so he followed it as best he could. He could not fly like he did in the real world though as, here, in the black void, there was no wind to help keep him stable and push himself forward with the same ease that the Matella was experiencing. Quickly the machine got too far ahead and vanished into the night, leaving Alex by himself. He did not call after it, for he did not even know if sound travelled in such a place of non-existence. Instead, Alex waited.

It seemed like an age had passed before he got the slightest hint of what he was supposed to do. Just like before, a speck appeared in the distance, nothing more than a distant star. Unlike earlier though he did not need to pull the memory towards him as it came speeding onwards with a pace greater than anything he had seen. He did not even have to time to duck like he had before, and he could not raise a barrier against it as there was no wind to manipulate into a force-field. Alex flinched instinctively, although stood his ground, as the mirror passed through him and came to a sudden stop. It did not hurt him at all. As Alex smiled at his fortune he noticed the silent figure of the Matella leaping back towards him before it too ground to halt just in front of him.

"You could've warned me!" Alex angrily whispered to it, hoping that it might convey some kind of reaction, or even acknowledgement of what he said.

The Matella stood silently once more. It gestured towards the mirror behind him, its edges fraying to indicate its fragile nature, something which Alex could understand since the memories had obviously been within the machine for more than seventy years. Alex looked at the portal and stared into its contents, almost hoping for some kind of sneak peek that he could get without actually stepping back into the eyes of Magnus. His mixture of rage and fear combined to create a harrowing experience for Alex that he was not looking forward to going through again. He needed to though, and so, with his hands shaking and his stomach in his throat, he gently touched the portal and allowed Magnus' world to surround him once more.

Magnus, now a man in his mid-twenties and with hair that matched his father's from all those years before, albeit if it was black rather than silver, stood before a familiar gravestone that he relished visiting fortnightly. His fur coat ruffled in the winds and his hat threatened to remove itself, moving slightly astray before Magnus gently corrected it with his gloved hand, delicately brushing the piece of slicked back hair that had fallen forward when it was displaced. His face was still as stern and unforgiving as it had been all those years beforehand and now resembled the features that Alex had been tormented by, even if there were less wrinkles and bore fewer bags under his eyes.

Magnus stared at the gravestone that was situated by his, now almost two decade old, artwork. The once fresh wood of the broken trees was now withering, and was far darker in colour than it had been beforehand. Aside from that though the wood was in perfect condition, with no animal markings or loose splinters upon it, as Magnus had given it his personal protection. It was the very first display of his powers, and it was something worth keeping for it would be a monument in his world. The first sign that the age of humanity was drawing to a close.

Gently, he bent down and placed a single gloved hand upon the marble headstone that was almost immaculate in its presentation. Like his art, it was a reminder of everything that he had accomplished without the repression of his brutal nanny. Her headstone was the only thing that her quest for power and greed had led to, for she had not understood the dormant power that had lain within him. He would not go the same way as her.

As he ran his hand along the top of the grave, patting the ground with the other as if to alert the deceased nanny, he decided that an amendment had to be made to the epitaph, after all her family in Hertfordshire would not care considering that they had allowed her to be buried so far away from them in the first place. With a single finger he wiped across the word 'beloved' and a fine crack appeared through it to cut the word in half, making it almost eligible, although still recognisable. It now read 'Ethel Bridges, 1854-1898, housekeeper, rest in peace.' Magnus looked upon his work with a smug sense of satisfaction. Why he had not defaced that wicked woman's tombstone before he did not know, for he had always hated her with scornful fury.

With his work done Magnus got back up into a standing position and turned to walk away, after brushing off loose pieces of dirt from his left knee. He could not stand to have a single aspect of his appearance out of place, for it made him look shabby, and if he looked shabby then he would be perceived as weak and fragile. Appearance was everything. Every time he walked through the factory floor, with his fur coat and hat removed, and his shirt rolled up tightly to the sleeve and pressed to leave no creases, he struck fear into the workers' hearts. Thus, it had to remain just so. With his appearance corrected, and the same strand of hair brushed back under his hat to fall neatly into place, he turned away from the grave and muttered the very words that drove his life, and his ideals, forward.

"Only the strong…" He murmured as he remembered how frail his nanny had been upon her premature death. "Only the strong…"

Magnus, with a very macabre spring in his step, walked back towards the factory to see if there were any workers he could terrorise. His father did not believe in chastising when it was not necessary, but his father was weak willed and did not know what was needed to maintain order and discipline. Whilst he lived though, he dared not go against his father, for it was a horrendous sin to commit an act of violence against a parent. The world was already moving beyond the notions of an almighty being, but Magnus needed to be careful anyway, for he did not know if his father had left everything to him, and it was vital that he gained the resources at his father's disposal. Plus, as much as Magnus was ashamed to admit it, he still feared what his father could do, even if he lacked the incredible gifts that Magnus had harnessed and nurtured across his life.

His father's health had been steadily getting worse though. His age was catching up to him and now he required a cane to move himself around his ever expanding factory. The workers could see it, their faces were continually etched in fear every time the old man bent over to retch. They knew. They knew that once his father died Magnus would be free to take the factory and impose any rules upon it that he saw fit. He had already forbidden them from fighting in the Great War, which had unfortunately cost him a pretty penny, and they loathed him for the social pariahs they had become, which made their lives almost unbearable when combined with their laborious working days. His father was a fair man, punishing only when required, but Magnus felt no remorse in admitting that he was not. He was a villain, with a heart as black as coal and no soul to redeem himself.

As he walked the small distance back to the factory, across the now browned grass and with no trees to better the view, he considered what it would be like to control such a titan of industry. On a certain level he abhorred the thought, after all, humanity was a blight upon the earth and was quickly turning it into a hideous wasteland with nothing left of its original state. He despised humans for their toxic pollution. Yet, almost ironically, he needed the factory to fulfil his aims. It would take many years, and he did not want to raise suspicions prematurely, but eventually he would be able to tear down the factory and crush any who stood in his path. He would save the planet from its inhabitants, and then, only the strong would be left standing with him as their leader.

He heard a story, passed down from the centuries, of the very first man that been gifted with the abilities that Magnus cherished so dearly. Yet he had squandered his abilities, using them to engage in a petty rivalry with a woman whom he clearly outmatched. After that, he had vanished into thin air, allowing humanity to evolve into the world eaters that they had become. No matter how much research he did, he could not decipher what had become of the old man, or his great nemesis for that matter. Magnus would not make the same mistakes as them though. He would use his abilities for the good of the planet, like a cleansing plague, before attaining immortality in the hearts and minds of his subjects. He would not fall into degradation like those before him.

With his heart hardened he pushed open the doors to the balcony which overlooked the factory floor. His father, Peter, was standing against the railing with his arms over the edge to steady himself as he read his newspaper, his cane propped against it also. Magnus almost found it a shame that his father had chosen to increase the size of the railing some years back to stop any further 'accidents' from occurring. Magnus casually looked at the subject of the paper and rolled his eyes upon seeing that there had been further bloodshed, and the war had not even been raging for a year. Even the very title '25/05/1915-Festubert Fighting' made it clear that there would only ever be one outcome from this war. He did not care for the loss of life, but the horrendous state in which they fought this 'Great War' was ruining the landscapes of everywhere involved. It was an atrocity to believe that anyone was in the right in this conflict, although his father clearly stood firmly upon the side of the British.

"Can you believe this?" Peter shouted towards Magnus as his son's boots tapping upon the metal, with every step, heralded his approach. Alex was momentarily taken back again by the thick Yorkshire accent with which Magnus' father spoke, as Magnus himself most definitely had a southern accent, much like that of his nanny's. "Another sixteen-thousand of our men killed at Festubert! This whole war is appalling! Thousands upon thousands of brave young men dying for king and country week after week! And that bloody idiot Haig cannot see the sense in using this new machines that we've devised! What a ridiculous man!" Peter raved. "Here, take a look at this."

Peter handed the paper to him. Magnus glanced over it with a vague show of interest, although in truth even that was a disguise to give his father the impression that he actually cared about the war. Alex could feel his own feelings separating from Magnus' at that moment as his heart split in two from the grief. It was as if he was actually there. Of course, as was to be expected, he had learned from Henbane about the impact of the First World War, but he had never experienced the enormity of its consequences. Yet, through Magnus' merciless eyes, he could see the devastation that it had wrought, and it made him sick to know that Magnus did not even have a shred of decency within him to spare a thought for all of those who had fallen. He just did not care.

"Truly awful." Magnus said with half-hearted effort, as he knew that his father would not really be paying attention to his reactions.

"Humanity makes me sick!" His father continued, and Magnus rolled his eyes once more as he prepared himself for the tirade. "People wonder why God doesn't give us evidence of his existence, ever since bloody Darwin! I know why…He's seen what we are and he left as quickly as he could. We're a plague, and only the strong deserve to live! Only those who fight for glory and justice! And where are they now? Face down in mud and water. Disgraceful!" Peter finished, with every vowel producing spittle from his mouth which dripped onto his silver stubble.

His father bent over to retch and Magnus contemplated upon his father's words. Perhaps he had underestimated his father, as he seemed to think more like him than he realised, albeit if he was clearly prejudiced towards the British, something which Magnus could not understand as they were just as poisonous as every other nation. At least the Germans have some kind of order to themselves, Magnus laughed inwardly. It did not end though as his father recovered from his coughing fit and pointed, with a shaking hand, towards their newest creations.

"You see them down there?" Peter asked his son.

"Of course, father." Magnus responded calmly, even though he wanted to shout at his father for such a stupid question. Of course he could see them.

"They're what make us strong…what make us great! Everyone is looking for a way to end this war, and I have the ultimate solution." Peter boasted.

Their latest creations were around twenty foot in height, with four legs arranged in an 'x' shape to allow maximum mobility. The main body was comprised of solid iron plating, capable of reflecting a great many bullets before its hide would eventually be penetrated, and that was only after having it bent and warped beyond recognition. It was almost like an egg on a stand, with the rugby-ball shaped top having a single seat in for the driver and a hatch underneath for a gunner to shoot from.

It was essentially a means of pushing the frontlines back, but Magnus saw so much potential for it. He could not help thinking how much more impact could be made from changing the oval shaped top into a long pillar for disrupting the earth around the soldiers. The only problem was the size. At the height it was the plating would last a suitable amount of time, but for his designs it would be insufficient. It needed to be much larger than what it was, and then the devastation wrought by them would be magnified tenfold. Magnus conceded that his designs would take significantly longer, probably years for a single contraption, and even more to extend the factory floor to a suitable level to match these technological leviathans, but it would be worth it for his ultimate aims. He could not tell his father about such modifications though, no, he had to make his father believe that he had created the ultimate war-machine.

"They are truly impressive father." He lied, only able to see his own image of what the contraptions could become. Perhaps I could even replace soldiering all together, Magnus thought to himself, his imagination running wild with the possibilities.

"Indeed they are." Peter agreed with a warm smile, something he had never given to his son.

"Perhaps you could allow me to take one so that I might study it?" Magnus casually suggested.

"And why, in the name of God, would I allow such a preposterous notion?!" Peter shouted in incredulity.

"I thought perhaps that it could be a belated gift." Magnus replied with an equally sour tone as he struggled to control his anger over his father's short-sightedness.

"Why?" His father continued, deliberately irking his child.

"Because father you know damn well that it was my birthday yesterday!" Magnus finally exploded. Peter did not respond. A single eyebrow was raised in question at the surprise of his son's outburst and Magnus was immediately forced to apologise. "Sorry, father, I didn't mean to shout."

Peter nodded, although with the kind of expression that suggested he would not allow it to happen again. "I have left you a gift anyway." He said coyly.

Magnus tried not to show any peaked interest, but he realised that he must have been grinning inanely like a moron over the prospect of a mere present. His father had never been one for gifts, unless Magnus suggested and bought them himself, and so he could not help being genuinely enthusiastic for his surprise. Desperate to hide his glee, he turned back towards the railing and leant on it, with his head twisted away.

"I've decided to leave the company to you, my boy." Peter said nonchalantly, as if it meant nothing at all. Magnus turned to look at his father with a mixture of genuine bewilderment. "I know I don't treat you fairly sometimes, and, in truth, its because I can never forgive you for what you did to your mother…" Magnus looked down again with his head held low.

Peter did not speak of the incident as he continued to rant about how bitterly he regarded his son for ruining the best part of his life. Alex could see it though. A single image was burned into Magnus' mind, a projection from his subconscious to remind him of how terribly awesome his powers were.

"I know you were only an infant, but I saw that look from your eyes. Your mother knew about it too, drove her to madness to know that she had bred a freak of nature." Peter stopped for a second as he struggled to control his emotions. "But…you are my son, and it is only fair that I allow you to lead your life the way God intended it, I am not the man to question the will of our Lord."

A normal person would be brutally crushed to hear such awful things about them from the mouth of their own parent, but not Magnus. Magnus did not even seem to mind as he instantly thought of something that made Alex's stomach churn with renewed disgust at just how vile this villain truly was. Magnus was imagining possessing his father, like he had done to so many others over his years, and forcing the old man into taking his own life as his frail body flopped over the railing and plummeted onto the floor below. To everyone else it would look like a tragic accident, and there would be no proof against him. Magnus would be free to take hold of what was rightfully his.

Before he could think further in his scheming though a man, holding a flimsy-looking camera, walked through the main doors, at the other end of the walkway, and came towards them and extended his hand. Magnus looked at him as though he had some sort of illness before his father explained.

"I contacted The Times yesterday to inform them of my decision. I want the whole country to know that my legacy will live on! And with a title like 'Titans of Industry, The Malum Legacy continues', how can we be seen as anything other than just that! Titans of Industry!" He laughed heartily, before coughing loudly and violently as huge chunks of spit flew from his mouth. So aggressive was this attack that he needed to steady himself upon the rail, and even that could not sustain him as his body collapsed under its own weight and his father fell to the floor with the photographer quickly by his side to give him what aid he could offer.

Magnus simply smiled. "Only the strong…"

Chapter 20

Alex withdrew himself from the second memory with relative ease. Throughout both he had felt as if he was Magnus, feeling and experiencing everything that the villain felt and experienced. That last moment though, as Magnus contemplated killing his own father to take control of the business, had completely separated him from his unwitting nemesis. Such a hideous and violent thought went against every value and ideal that Alex strode towards and lived his life off of, and yet to Magnus it had been his very first thought! Alex realised now, if he held out some hope of coercing Magnus before, that there was only going to be one end to this conflict. Magnus had to die, but Alex was not sure that he could do it.

As Alex contemplated his only remaining option, in the familiar surroundings of the dark nothingness that was the Matella's mind, he saw the machine dart towards him with a small speck of light held within his hand. Clearly it had decided to save time by bringing the memory to Alex. It had not spoken to him beforehand, but Alex hoped it would speak to him now to help him realise just how Magnus ended up being the monster that he was.

"What made him like this?" Alex asked.

The Matella did not answer.

"How can he think he is doing the world any good?!" Alex probed again, this time more irate.

Still, the machine did not respond.

"How far did he go?"

The machine did not answer itself, but instead it showed Alex the speck within his hand. It opened into a horrific scene that was blurred beyond recognition, but the sound from it was still clearly audible. Alex listened to the horrendous cries of people, who were clearly Magnus' workers, as their bodies were desecrated and welded with metal. Or so he guessed. Everything that they were was lost as they were ripped apart to provide the flesh for the vital parts of the Matella. It was not a case of encasing the body with metal as Alex had hoped, because then something of the old person would be left. The cadavers were pulled apart and harvested, before being placed into the readily made exoskeletons. Alex was thankful that he could not see this hideous process unfold, as the memory was damaged, but it was still something that he could envisage within his own mind, and it was harrowing to say the least. Alex looked towards the Matella with renewed sympathy and asked one last question.

"So how do I stop him?" He enquired, trying a different tactic.

As if by magic, a memory window appeared behind him, signalled by a whooshing noise which indicated that it had travelled from wherever it was from within the Matella's mind. Alex was beginning to understand. He needed to know what he wanted in order for him to find what it was that he needed. Before, when he was in the dark, the silent machine had guided him, but now he knew what information he required, and he could attain it at ease.

"Thank you." He said genuinely to the Matella, despite it never actually responded to his questions.

Alex turned to face the window with a renewed enthusiasm for finding some kind of weakness in the impenetrable wall that Magnus had built for himself. From the still image that represented the memory he could see that Magnus looked like he did now, as his reflection was shown in the well-polished marble of the grave that he was looking at. So much time had passed for Magnus in such a short span of time, and yet, seventy years or so later, he looked exactly the same. Alex, hoping that this would supply all the information he needed, placed a finger upon the frame and, once again, felt the seamless transition into the world of Magnus.

Magnus felt the gentle winds brush against his air as he was bent next to the familiar gravestone. It was newer than Ethel's, and much cleaner with a finer grade of marble to make it truly spectacular, even though it was still just a headstone. It had been some years since his father had died, his 'illness' finally getting the better of him, but he still felt the need to come and visit his final resting place, as if his father would rise from the grave and strike him down for his insolence if he did not. He would be even more outraged with him if he knew what he had done to his memories of him, if he knew what he had reduced him to.

Magnus smirked at the grave of his father, his plans being so close to fruition that he could almost envisage what his world would look like, as he got back onto his feet and turned to walk away. He gave a quick look towards the first display of his abilities, now blackened by the continual release of smoke from the factory, and smiled inwardly at how far he had come, and how close he was. His assistant, a very young man whom he hoped would follow in his footsteps, almost like a son, gave him a quizzical look as he clearly did not understand the strange expression that Magnus had etched across his face. Magnus placed a hand upon his shoulder and uttered the same phrase that the young man had heard an untold number of times previously.

"Only the strong, Ben…"

"I know sir." The young man responded coolly, his blue eyes unwavering.

"Is that the paper?" Magnus asked.

"It is sir." Ben replied as he handed it to his master.

Magnus seized the paper firmly and looked at the article on the front page, as it often told him all he needed to know about the contents. More often than not it was full of things that he simply did not care about, but today's headline somewhat amused him. It read '21/05/1943-Nazi Massacre at Warsaw'. It tickled him to think that the world was so preoccupied with the war, when they should be worried about what was to come when they finished weakening one another. It did not matter who won, for they would all fall before him.

Ben noticed the smile that Magnus was wearing and could not help question him, as surely no person so could be so sadistic as to laugh at such a horrendous affair. "Why are you smiling sir?" He enquired, his limbs visibly shaking from attempting to contain his rage.

Magnus neatly placed the paper within the back pocket of his trousers, so as to not litter the area, before placing his hands upon Ben's cheeks, cupping them uncomfortably. He chuckled again. Ben was a man with a soft heart, but Magnus aimed to slowly change that by making him understand that no good was coming out of the world.

"These people think that Hitler is the vilest think to come forth from hell, yet even he pales in comparison to myself. Whilst he continues his assault, all of the attention is taken away from me. The government are willing to look past all the disappearances because I'm not the immediate threat. They think Hitler is evil, but just wait until they see what I have in store." Magnus chuckled.

Ben looked absolutely horrified. His mouth was completely agape and his face was almost white from the shock of what his employer had just admitted to. Magnus gave him a stern look, but realised that it was to be expected since Ben was not aware of how putrid humanity was. "Oh Ben, my Ben Vire. You need to understand…" He stopped, unsure of how to persuade his ward. "But now is not the right time."

"Then when is sir?" The youth probed.

"Even I, in all my glory, cannot tell you that. You will know soon though, I can promise you that."

Ben, obviously still not convinced, nodded his assent and Magnus gave him a friendly pat on the shoulder to indicate that all was well. His assistant did not smile back. Alex was disgusted by Magnus' view of the world and he was beginning to understand that perhaps this young assistant was the key to defeating him, since he was so obviously against the plan that the villain had set in motion, although Alex did not know how yet. Alex could not even tell if Ben would last much longer, if Magnus' current emotions within this memory were anything to judge by.

The villain almost skipped back to the factory with his happiness, the increasing winds not bothering him as his assistant shielded his eyes as best he could. He knew that his time was drawing ever closer and it was killing him to hold it off for a moment longer. Of course, it had been years since he had started his endeavours but now that the moment was almost at hand every single second felt like an eternity. Ben clearly did not share the same enthusiasm as he trudged alongside his master with an apparent deep loathing. But, he had not seen the wonders which he had created and laboured over, only then would he understand.

Magnus thought about his options for a moment as they opened the doors to the monumental factory that fell over two-hundred and fifty feet, not that the depth could be seen as it was bathed in complete darkness. Blissful silence greeted them as it always did. There were no sounds of industry and sighs of hard work, as there had always been until only a few months beforehand. He looked towards the massive elevator that he had made, which now sat in the middle of the unaltered, although repaired, walkway, with a great sense of pride. It could support even the biggest of his creations, even if he had not created a separate exit for them outside of the factory. He stole a quick glance towards the old office which had fallen into ruin, but still stood as a reminder to everything that once was, and a symbol of how even the mighty can fall.

"So what's in store sir?" Ben asked as he closed the old, and creaking, factory doors that led out into the vacant areas beyond.

Magnus, confused, turned and looked at his ward with a puzzled expression, his eyebrows raised in misperception. "Pardon?"

"You said that the world would think Hitler was nice compared to what you have in store." Ben continued before Magnus muttered a quip to himself.

"Well I didn't quite put it like that."

"I was just wondering what it was you had in store."

Magnus did not answer for a moment as he stared at his father's office. All the memories from within it were ones of pain and misery, every moment with his father was connected with sorrow. He recalled the time his father gave him the back of his hand for his ungrateful comments. So strong was the memory that Magnus touched the same cheek with his hand and could almost feel the strong burning sensation that had christened it, even through his black glove. Ever since he had not dared do anything against his father's wishes, or even dared to speak against him at all, but if he could see what was waiting in the depths below then Magnus knew that he would feel the sting of his welt.

He turned towards his young assistant with a flare in his eyes. Perhaps it was time that he knew what was coming, Magnus thought to himself as he stole one more glance towards the abandoned office. Without warning, which gave his ward no time to prepare, he grabbed hold of Ben and lifted him off of the floor using the wind from the open windows to hold him in place.

"Sir?" Ben questioned with a worried tone.

"I want to show you what I have in store, but we won't be using the elevator." He said chillingly as he lifted himself from the ground as well.

Ben looked terrified as Magnus floated towards him and joined him as they looked down into the black abyss that had no end in sight and only one source of light in the south-west corner, where the furnace burned as brightly as the sun piercing the dark of space. Together they began to descend and were swallowed by the sea of darkness that surrounded them. Ben could barely contain his fear as his master disappeared from sight, his heavy breathing through the thick smoke the only thing that he could hear.

"Why are you taking me down here sir?" Ben asked, trying to cool his emotions as best he could, although it did not help that he could not tell where the answer came from.

"Are you ready Ben Vire?" Magnus hissed.

"Ready for what?" Ben replied with the same horrified expression and tone.

"To witness the instruments that will bring about my new order."

"Your…new order, sir?" The young man probed.

There was no response as they continued to descend at a slow pace, the dim lights of the walkway growing ever fainter as they descended into the abyss. Magnus did not want to give away anything, hence the darkness, so that he could judge his ward's genuine reaction to his creations. Only then could he judge his character, and deem him worthy of a place in the new world. The furnace only gave off the faintest outlines of his creations, making them appear more like shadows whose size was greatly exaggerated by the cast of the fire. It was not. As they touched the bottom, by the leg of one of his machines, the area was faintly illuminated and the edges of his creations could be seen, but still nothing more than that. Ben was still unaware of what was with them in the depths of his father's factory.

Magnus released Ben from his control and allowed him to regain some semblance of himself as the young man looked about the room for some of the answers to his many questions. Magnus intended to oblige and so, with a quick deftness, he gathered a long thin strand of flame from the furnace and slowly brought it out into the factory floor. So narrow was this strain that its glow did not light up more than a foot on either side of it, leaving his machines in the dark. Slowly it trickled past Ben, who was unflinching in its presence, and made its way to the far end of the room. Magnus branched the flame out to several braziers that were waiting, ready to be lit, throughout the area. Gently he allowed the flames to touch them. Immediately the room was illuminated as gigantic metal legs sprouted out of the dark, with the main bodies still shrouded in the abyss, for the most part. Ben gasped, and Magnus smiled.

"May I introduce, my Animus!?" Magnus said with pride. "City-destroyers reaching two-hundred feet into the sky. More than enough to wipe away anything that humanity has built." He moved over to Ben and whispered into his ear for the next bit, as if it were something shameful to have help of any kind. "Admittedly, it was my father's idea first..." He spoke quietly as he peered towards the walkway again. "Although, he was never the visionary that I am. He always thought too small."

Magnus looked upon his work with eyes that burned with ferocious ambition. Dozens upon dozens of his Animus', although in reality there was only one controlling the drones, were stored in the expansive warehouse that his father's modest factory had become. Alex's own emotions got the better of him as he gasped at the sheer number of city-destroyers that Magnus had within his command. He had had almost thirty years to gather such a force, and the world had only seen but a fraction of it. No matter what information Alex found here, he simply could not put faith in anyone ever defeating such a ludicrously powerful army. Their only hope was to cut the head off the snake; if Alex could eliminate Magnus, then everything would be put right again. With that in mind he focused back on the memory to try and figure out this puzzle.

Ben opened his mouth to answer, but Magnus quickly interrupted him as he rushed the thin tendrils of flame backwards to ignite further braziers that illuminated his foot-soldiers. Once again Magnus stared at them with a sick sense of pride and achievement. Ben could not look upon the creatures with the same mixture of amazement and befuddlement. The instant resentment he felt for the machines was so strong that he vomited onto the factory floor until there was nothing left in his stomach, and even then his retching did not cease for several moments. Magnus looked towards his assistant with a troubled expression. He hoped that the young man had enough strength within him to see beyond the aesthetically unpleasing qualities of his creations, for they served a far greater purpose. Ben was beginning to understand, but Magnus needed to explain it as clearly as he could.

"It seems that the time to explain it to you has come sooner than I would've liked, you're weak nature has forced my hand." He said bluntly as he approached one of his Matella and touched it gently on its fleshy face. It was his very first creation. "This is the only way that humanity can have a place in my world. Without my guidance they are left to destroy themselves, and this ever degrading world. I will not allow their stupidity and selfishness to overlook common sense." He turned back towards Ben. "Nor will I allow your morality to impede my progress. Humanity is a cancer upon this world, a blemish which needs to be contained…and then removed." He smiled, despite trying not to, at the thought. "Only then can this world become the verdant paradise that it once was." He now walked towards Ben with a hint of anger in his tone. "Yet you, and all those like you, you cannot see what I am trying to accomplish! You respond with revulsion and hatred of that which you cannot possibly comprehend! The hubris of humanity! You cannot see that you are the problem." Magnus' expression then changed to one of sadness for a moment. "The workers could not see it either, but they had to die all the same. Well…" He smiled again. "I say die…" He lightly laughed as he turned and patted the shoulder of his first creation.

Magnus could hear Ben struggle back to his normal state after the initial wave of sickness had evaporated, and he knew that Ben would find any angle he could to question his motives.

Magnus did not mind though, for the more his young assistant probed the more he would understand.

"You speak of cleansing this world...but you enjoy it..." Ben said with a clear sense of disgust.

Magnus did not look towards his ward, and the authority with which he spoke made it clear that he still regarded himself as the better person. "It is the privilege of those with power to revel in it." He claimed nonchalantly. "Do you think the mighty Roman Empire ever questioned their morality as they sought to bring order to the chaos that surrounded them? No, because they knew that there was a higher purpose to their plans and because of this they took great pride and joy in their actions. As it was with them, so it is with me." He stated proudly. "If I am to rescue the world from the brink of destruction, then why shouldn't I be entitled to some enjoyment?"

He had hoped that that answer would have been enough to sate Ben's curiosity, and bring him around to his master's way of thinking, but the young ward had one more question that he wanted answered.

"And how close do you think you are to being ready?" Ben asked with obviously feigned interest.

Magnus smiled, genuinely, as now Ben was clearly trying to see his point of view and get on his good side. He did not think that the young man had come around to his way of thinking, but it was obvious that he wanted to judge whether or not to align himself with the winner.

"It's only a matter of days now before I begin my assault upon the blight that is humanity. With the whole world at war they will be no match for my creations...my children." He smiled. "It's all functional of course, I've already tested them out individually."

"Then that's all I needed to know." Ben replied brusquely.

Before Magnus could face his ward he saw, in the reflection of one of his Matella, a massive whirl of fire coming towards him from the direction of the furnace to his south-east. The swirling fireball hurtled towards him at tremendous speed that almost caught him off-guard. Nothing could though, and so he was prepared with a shield around him that protected him from the scalding heat of the fire. Magnus allowed the flames to run their course, their heat licking up his back but not causing him any damage. When he turned around to face the culprit he was surprised to see his young assistant Ben with green flares emanating from his eyes before they resumed their supposedly natural blue pigmentation.

"I knew that you were evil…he told me so. But never, not even in my wildest dreams, had I imagined that such a horror could ever befall the world."

"Ben?" Magnus said with a smile as he ignored his assistant's jabs. His joyous giddiness was overwhelming. "How did you learn to do that?"

Ben smiled back, although mockingly. "I needed to blend in. You would've noticed my abilities if my eyes were like yours…well, they are." He said as he switched his eyes back to their natural green.

"Ha! I knew I could not be the only one left with the Evolutis Mente! Are there any others like you?" Magnus asked, desperate to not be the only survivor in his new world.

Ben shook his head. "Not that I know of, or they would be here by my side, as any decent human being would."

Magnus shook his head with visible disappointment, choosing to ignore the last part of the comment. "You still haven't answered my question about your eyes."

"We all have our strengths, I prefer a more tactile approach to your methods of sheer brutality." Ben said disdainfully.

"So, you infiltrate my company and gain my trust just to betray me?" Magnus probed before laughing hysterically to himself. "I can't say that I didn't expect it. You're too soft, but I admit that I held out some hope of you seeing my perspective." He chuckled again. "You know you cannot defeat me, Ben. Nobody can." He said deathly seriously. "Soon my army will spread to every corner of the globe…and I still offer you a chance to join me."

"You think yourself immortal! But I need not defeat you…I only need to contain you." Ben retorted cryptically. Alex's imaginary ears picked up at the remark.

"And do you think your power is sufficient enough to keep me at bay?" Magnus chuckled again, openly mocking his opponent's audacity. When he noticed Ben's intense stare, and how serious it was, he tried a more logical approach to give his ward one last chance to reconsider his actions. "Even if it is, how long do you think you can hold me? An hour? A day perhaps? Or mere moments as my majesty overwhelms you and you become nothing more than dust to be swept away by the wind."

Ben gave him a menacing look before he answered. "I promise you that I will not hold back."

"A challenge then-" Magnus tried to respond before he was interrupted.

"If you have your will then there will be no world left. It is us, the inhabitants, that make the world what it is, and to remove us is to leave nothing but the earth behind."

"My dearest Ben…" He spoke jokingly, as his vehement hatred for the boy grew with every insolent rejoinder offered by the youth. "You speak to me as if I did not know this….I do. I just don't care." He roared. "You think that I want anyone left on this world? The inhabitants are the problem! Humanity is weak…but we are strong, and only the strong will survive."

"There is only the one cancer upon this planet, one source of venom that needs to be purged from its surface…and I'm looking at him."

Magnus smiled sardonically and savoured the environment around him. The lack of sound as his machines silently watched on, and the dim lighting illuminated only the faintest of features, was a moment that he would treasure forever, for his powers were about to be truly tested for the first time in his life. Or so he hoped. With one great breath he stretched out his arms and exhaled so powerfully that the cobwebs, many feet above him, rattled with their occupiers scuttling into the nearest crevice. Alex could feel the palpable sense of impending death from every living thing as Magnus harvested their fear and used it as fuel for his fire. The entire world seemed to stop as it was aware of what was about to happen, a monumental occasion that had not been seen for centuries. Magnus was ready.

"Very well." Magnus simply said as he pushed open the doors of the factory, allowing the strong winds to swell inside the building, and prepared himself for the ultimate battle.

Chapter 21

Alex withdrew himself, not just from the memory, but from the dark chasm that he knew to be the Matella's mind. It had been quite an experience to peer inside the memories of another, completely feeling what they felt with every twinge of emotion emanating through him. At the same time, because of this catharsis, it had been hellish. Alex had been angry at times, and downright furious at others, but never had he experienced the seething rage that Magnus had fuelled inside of him constantly. He was so angry with humanity and Alex knew that he would never stop in his pursuit to cleanse the world of what Magnus thought was the problem.

Slowly, as if he feared the world would not be his own but one of Magnus', he opened his eyes and looked out into the corridor by the front door of his home. The Matella was where it stood before, its eyes and facial expression revealing nothing of what it was thinking. Alex could not tell how long he had been inside the mind of the machine, but, judging by the posture and position of the Matella, which had not even moved a muscle, if it even had muscles, he imagined it had not been long. Even though, to him, it seemed like an eternity. The metallic twang rang hollow in its throat as it prepared to speak.

"I'm sorry I could not help you." The Matella apologised with what seemed like genuine sympathy, although it was very difficult to tell through the heavily metallic voice that it spoke with. "The memories were difficult to find, they were lost to me as they were to you. It was not to be unexpected after being dormant for more than seventy years."

"There was a version of you in there though, but it was silent. It guided me." Alex replied.

"That cannot be right." The machine responded matter-of-factly. "I have no personality, and no free-will, and thus no subconscious. There is no way that I could assist you, for I cannot enter my own mind." It explained. "I tried to find the memories for you, but that was all I could do."

"Perhaps there is more to you than meets the eye." Alex suggested with a smile.

He could not tell how the Matella took his comment as it simply stared back at him, yet he could not escape the feeling that it was blushing. It hid this well though as it continued to speak like it was nothing more than a machine.

"It was a ghost, nothing more than a deformed remnant of the person I once was." It explicated, hoping to satisfy itself.

"Or perhaps, now that you have been liberated from Magnus' control, you are truly a free being once again." Alex smiled again, and it did not respond.

"Alex?" A small voice squeaked from behind him.

Alex was so ingrained with his experience that had forgotten to talk to his family, and now that he remembered, he did not want to. He knew what he needed to do, what he had to know in order to find a way of defeating Magnus, and it would tear him from them. His heart would surely break at such a separation, especially since the likelihood of danger was high. Alex wanted to keep them safe though and this was the only way that he could guarantee that whilst still attempting to save the world from the villainy of Magnus.

Alex, hesitantly, turned around to face his family; doing his absolute best to cover his sadness. They smiled back at him, even Steven who had obviously put any petty arguments they had had behind them, and arched their eyebrows quizzically. Alex could not help but chuckle slightly at the odd family trait that he was just detecting before he realised that they were actually seeking answers.

"Well?" Steven asked, typically rudely, although probably unintentionally.

Charlotte gave his son a playful, yet stern, slap on the top of his arm and looked at him with an aghast expression before turning back to Alex. "What Steven means is-"

"How does it work?" Abigail interrupted inquisitively.

"Abi!" Charlotte gasped jokingly at the sudden, and uncharacteristic, interjection.

Alex laughed again as Abigail tried to make sense of it. "I think you must have advanced forms of mirror neurons which allow you to manipulate anything you see."

"I don't know how I do it, I just do." Alex explained bluntly, but with a smile as he tried to assure her that the science behind it was not important. "It's not about the logic behind everything. It's about the experience." He remembered soaring through Leicester and feeling the wind rushing through his hair as the birds chirped alongside him. It was a very fond memory. He could not maintain it though as his powers came with burdening responsibilities. "And then you come to realise that it isn't as great as it seems." He smiled sardonically.

"So, did you find what you needed?" Charlotte asked tentatively.

Alex nodded, which should have been a happy action, yet it was full of sadness. When his family noticed his expression their own one's changed to match his. They did not know what it was that he had to do, but they could tell, almost telepathically, that it would take him from them. No words needed saying as Charlotte's eyes filled with tears, as did Abigail's, while Steven tried to remain as neutral as possible.

"I know what I have to do." Alex spoke gloomily. "Although I have no idea if it's even possible." He continued with a sudden awareness of how ill-informed he actually was. "Excuse me for a moment." He said rudely as he turned away from them and faced the Matella. "Thomas, with me." He ordered without even looking towards his friend.

Obediently, his best friend followed his instructions and tailed behind him. Alex gestured a finger towards the kitchen and beckoned for the machine to follow them, leaving his family completely in the lurch as the trio swerved around them and closed the door into the kitchen once they had passed through it. Alex wanted to make sure that his family did not hear his plans, as they would only worry and try and stop him, or worse, come with him, and so he turned on the microwave to cover up any noise they were making. He would tell his family in due time, but not before he finalised exactly what it was that he was going to be doing.

With another depressing gaze he shifted his attention to Thomas, knowing that what he was about to say would greatly upset his friend. "We have to leave."

"Well, Cambridge isn't all that far, I'm sure we can be there in good time." Thomas tried to reassure him, not realising what Alex had meant.

"No Thomas." He replied gently but sternly. "I can't take you to Cambridge."

"But...my parents..." Thomas tried to protest. "My grandparents..."

"I know, but I can't risk it. Magnus would spot me in an instant if I flew you there, and we certainly don't have enough time to walk." Alex explained.

"What about by car?" Thomas tried desperately.

"Thomas, you know that we can't. Your car is stuck in the middle of the city and I assume transport will soon be banned, or at least strongly prohibited, given the current crisis, and I don't think they'll see your situation quite as sympathetically as myself. Besides, how would we acquire a vehicle?" Alex asked, trying not to crush the hopes of his best friend but at the same time realising that it had to be done.

"Alex is right." The Matella agreed non-subtly. "Magnus will hunt down any he perceives as a threat, and Alex is the biggest threat to him. He must remain hidden and be protected at all costs if Magnus is to be defeated."

Alex nodded to the machine with gratitude. When he looked back towards his friend he could see the tears building in Thomas' eyes as he realised that there was no joy to be found in his pursuits, no hope of achieving them at this moment in time. Silently, a sign of utter despair, he let out the tears and adorned an expression of extreme bleakness. Alex did not know how to respond in such situations and so took a moment to allow Thomas to calm himself before he went to his friend's side and placed a single arm upon his shoulder, patting it lightly to offer some kind of comfort. Alex could not tell if it worked, since Thomas continued weeping for several more moments before he regained his composure.

"Sorry." He stifled through his overpowering emotions, a feeling that Alex knew well.

"You have nothing to be sorry for." Alex reassured his friend, gently patting his shoulder again to emphasis his support.

"I do, we can't afford to be selfish in these times…even if we want to be."

"Sometimes we need to be selfish." Alex replied.

"But this isn't one of those times." Thomas smiled, trying to inject some humour and comradery into the conversation. "I am going with you though." He smirked.

"Thomas, I can't-" He tried to protest before he was disturbed.

"Give over you annoying bugger!" Thomas laughed. "There's no way I'm leaving you to fight that madman all by your lonesome, and if you think I'm going to let you die without taking me to my parents…" He deliberately tailed off for comic effect.

They laughed together and suddenly the world did not seem so dark, not now that he had someone to keep him company. Every hero needs a sidekick, Manningleyman thought to himself as he looked over at Gordonovich.

"He will be a burden to us, and a weakness to use against you." The Matella spoke harshly.

Alex turned towards the machine with fire in his eyes. "So, if you consider him a weakness then you must be aware of what I have planned?"

"Of course." The Matella replied simply. "There is only one course of action that is logical."

Alex continued his tirade. "Why not just tell me what I need to know then and save us all the trouble?!" He raved.

"You have given me no directive to do so." It responded.

"For goodness sake!" Alex fumed, beginning to get irate by the machine's lack of understanding and humanity. "I do not control you, you do not need an instruction from me to do something. You are a free thinking being! You have your own will!"

"Incorrect." It stated, still wanting to believe it was nothing more than wires and metal.

"Then why did you rudely butt in to our conversation?" Alex questioned. "As I gave you no such instruction to do so."

Once again, defeated, the machine did not respond and Alex took that as a sign of meaning that it had given in to his idea of having Thomas accompany them on their journey. Before they could go anywhere though he needed to find out some information on their target, or the whole adventure would be pointless. He needed to find out what he could about Ben Vire, and the Matella was the best person, or thing, to ask; especially since it had basically just told Alex that it had the information he required.

"We need to find Ben Vire. That much is obvious." Alex mused.

"Yes..." Thomas nodded "Why? Who's Ben Vire?" His best friend questioned when he realised that he had no clue about what Alex was talking about.

"He was Magnus' assistant until Magnus disappeared. I was about to watch a battle between them when the memory I was looking at was cut off..." Alex explained. He had a contemplative expression etched across his face. "He must have managed to defeat Magnus somehow. If I can find him..." Alex got ahead of himself before he realised that he was assuming Ben was still alive. He was only fifteen at the time of his confrontation with

Magnus, even younger than himself, albeit if it was only by a single year, but that would still put him in his mid-eighties if he were alive. Unfortunately few make it to such an advanced age, Alex thought glumly, and even if he were alive then he would no doubt not be as powerful as he had been in his prime. Alex needed to try though and so looked directly at the Matella, still not knowing if he had the creatures' attention.

"I need to know about Ben Vire." He said boldly.

"Unfortunately there is little I know. The memories were Magnus', not mine, and I have never attempted to access them myself."

"Well tell me what you can!" Alex implored the Matella.

"The only thing I know is where he lived, and I only know this because Magnus visited his home when he returned to see if he still lived…" The machine deliberately stopped speaking, bringing yet another crushing blow to Alex.

"And?" Alex asked cautiously, not wanting to hear the answer he knew was coming.

"There was no sign of Ben Vire, or any spouse or offspring he may have potentially had." The Matella said, somewhat glumly.

"Does that mean he's dead then?"

"No." The machine replied, bringing back a single ray of hope which it was about to snuff out with further evidence. "But the home was overgrown and looked ruined, almost uninhabitable, on the inside."

Alex got the sense that it was leaving some information out on purpose. "What else?"

"There was a grave in the back garden." The Matella spoke softly, as if trying to lessen the blow. "And it was marked Ben Vire…It says he died eleven years ago."

Alex almost cried with the enormity of the failure that was imminent. Without Ben they had no way of knowing how he defeated Magnus seventy years beforehand, and without that knowledge Alex had no hope of doing it by himself. He turned his sadness into rage as he questioned the machine's theory, desperate to find any kind of weak point in the armour that Magnus had built for himself.

"How do you even know this?! I released you from his control!" He barked.

"This was before he attacked Leeds, and thus before Leicester and our meeting. He also made no attempts to cover this memory, through lack of time or not believing it to be necessary, I do not know, which allows me to access it." It explained. "Furthermore…" It added, rubbing the salt ever deeper into Alex's wounds. "This memory is fresh, and not seventy years old, and so I was able to find it with little trouble."

"So where does he live?" Alex asked irritably.

"There is no mention of the name within the memory." The Matella spoke again. Once more Alex wished it had not. "However I know the place to be Burn, a small village to the south of York. Judging by the position of the sun within the memory and Magnus' approach to the house it seems that it is the only house on the south side of the village." The machine explained matter-of-factly.

"How do you know where it is?" Thomas questioned, but, when the machine ignored his enquiry. It was dropped without answer.

"So what do you suggest we do?" Alex investigated.

"Nothing, it is evident that Ben Vire has perished."

"I thought you said he wasn't?" Thomas questioned again, with no response.

Alex was beyond annoyed now and his eyes burned with green intensity as wisps of his anger flew out of them. "So what if he is?! Don't you understand that he is our only hope of vanquishing Magnus? Even if he's dead I still need to go there! I have to try!" He shouted. "All it takes is a scrap of paper, some loose note of what he did…"

"What are we doing then?" Thomas chimed in.

The Matella, despite its face still remaining expressionless, relented to the indomitable will of the pair. "I would advise moving on foot. If you use your powers then it is certain that Magnus, or his forces, would spot you before you got within fifty miles."

"Maybe you could propel us there?" Alex tried. "It would certainly be quicker."

"Different methods, same result." The Matella bluntly retorted.

"What about by car?" Thomas suggested again, obviously not keen on the idea of walking across half of the country. "If we move quick enough then we could make it."

"Unlikely." The Matella responded firmly. "We would probably be the only ones foolish enough to use a car that close to Magnus' centre of power. We would stand out, and then we would get taken."

"Alex could fight any of YOU that come near us!" Thomas roared with enthusiasm, drawing an audible gasp from the living room as they could obviously hear what was going on.

Alex, after piling wind against the door to make the room soundproof, as evidently the dull hum of the microwave was not enough to stop his family from eavesdropping, was not quite so confident in his abilities. "I'm not sure I could. The only reason I was able to fight them off before was because I was focused on saving my family…and you of course." He added when he saw Thomas' slightly disappointed expression. Of course, he had done it for Verity as well, but they were all safe now and he needed to move beyond such primal instincts. There was more at stake.

"Well, if you think about, you still need to save us Alex…all of us. It all rests on you." Thomas spoke sincerely with a beaming smile, and a hidden expression of jealousy.

Alex nodded his thanks to his friend and dashed out of the kitchen, past his family who quickly tried to grab his attention by bombarding him with questions, and into the living room. Immediately his eyes came to rest on the magazine rack, behind which sat various maps and atlases. Frantically, like time was against him, he rushed through them to find the maps he needed and darted back to the kitchen, ignoring his questioning family again and closing the door decisively behind him.

Thomas and the Matella looked towards him expectantly as he spread the map out on the kitchen surface before grabbing a knife to pinpoint the route they would take to the home of Ben Vire. Together, they gathered around the kitchen island and looked over the details of the two maps that they needed. One detailed the journey from the Midlands towards the North, with the other being a more intimate map of the latter which detailed even the small villages that the larger maps would ignore. Alex confessed though that he had no idea what he was looking for, as geography was not his strong suit. It was Thomas' though.

"Thomas, what do you think is best?"

"Give me a minute." Thomas requested as he looked over the maps. It took several minutes in fact before he gave up his hypothetical route. "Well I presume we want to avoid the major cities?" He asked as he looked towards the machine, which nodded, almost sarcastically. "Well then we should take the A46 out of Leicester until we reach Newark-On-Trent. It's a fair sized town but it shouldn't be a prime target and we'll only be brushing past it anyway." Thomas explained as he borrowed Alex's knife to indicate what he meant. "From there…" He thought again for a moment. "We should take the A1 around the edge of Doncaster until we reach Knottingley." Alex could tell that his friend was enjoying the limelight he was receiving. "Okay. Then we take the A456 directly east until we reach the A19, which will take us straight to Burn." Thomas smiled as he concluded.

"And how long do you think that would take?" Alex asked.

Thomas shrugged as he did not know the answer. Fortunately the machine, being a methodological thinker, was able to give a rough indication of the distance. The journey, going along their route, would be just shy of a hundred miles, but that gave little indication of how long it would take. Thankfully, due to Alex's love of ancient history, and particularly the Romans, he was aware that the legionnaires were able to travel roughly thirty miles in every day. Obviously though he was aware that his company were nowhere near as physically fit as the typical legionnaire would be.

"I think, if we cover twenty miles a day…" He saw Thomas grimace at the thought. "We could do it in five days."

"That seems accurate." The Matella agreed.

"Yes…" Thomas added, clearly still not taken on the idea.

With the plan decided they needed to gather resources and so they left the kitchen. Thomas, not paying attention to Alex's family, bolted out of the door, almost stumbling over the coffee table which had been propped up against it beforehand, and back towards his own home, probably hoping to pick up some vital bits before they headed off. If his parents had not taken everything that was. The Matella stood where it was, not needing anything to function for five days, which left Alex to tell his family of what needed to be done. They had gathered around the open space within the living room, with Charlotte placing a single arm around each of her younger children. The two girls looked mortified, as they surely knew what was about to happen, and even Steven looked depressed. Alex did not even need to speak.

"Can't we come with you?" Charlotte said with tears in her eyes again, obviously never quite accepting that her son would actually leave, despite giving him her blessing only a few minutes beforehand.

"Magnus came here, to Leicester, because of me. He knows that someone around here has the same abilities as him. When he finds out that it's me he'll go to whatever lengths he can to hurt those around me. I owe Thomas a debt, but you're my family and I need to make sure that you're safe. I will not let him get to you. As soon as we find out where Dad is…" He stopped himself to get rid of any false hope. "If we find out where Dad is, then he can keep you safe…but I can't."

Charlotte pulled her son in close for a tight embrace with tears streaming down her face and her hair parted in an array of emotions. His shirt quickly became wet with the glistening, but he did not mind. Alex could not help silent tears of his own, as he was stepping out into the world for the first time, at only sixteen years of age, before he pushed his mother gently away.

"It's alright mother, remember our words." He said with a comforting smile, to which she nodded.

Suddenly, there was a vibration in his pocket. Quickly he pulled his mobile phone from his jean pocket and looked at the flashing screen. Somebody was trying to ring him, but he did not recognise the number. Alex considered ignoring it for a moment before an important thought hit him. Father. Nobody had heard from Charles since Magnus had returned, a worrying thought, and although the number was private Alex had a feeling that it was his father trying to contact him.

"Dad?" He spoke expectantly, waiting on tenterhooks for an answer.

"Alex!" Came the response from a familiar, and most welcome, voice. "He's back Alex, that man! Is everyone alright?"

Alex was not sure how to respond. Everybody was alright, well every member of their family anyway, and yet half of the city, and all of Leeds, were in ruin and were no doubt soon to be followed by other major urban centres in Magnus' personal crusade. He decided that the truth would be best and so drew in a deep breath to deliver the shocking news of the world's imminent conflict.

"Leicester's been attacked." He spoke softly, in some attempt to try and break the news gently. "But don't panic!" He added swiftly. "Everyone is fine. These monsters though…"

He looked towards his own companion with an apologetic face for using the word, although the machine remained blank in expression. "Part-machine and part-flesh, they took so many people away."

"What do you mean? What for?" Charles probed, obviously confused.

"So you haven't heard then?" Alex asked.

"I've only just landed son, and I went straight to the nearest phone that I could find." Charles said with a deep sense of fatigue. "I was attacked by that man, he killed everyone but me...even Cassandra. They're all gone."

"That doesn't matter now Dad, what matters is stopping him before he kills anyone else." He said coldly, but truthfully.

"No. What matters is getting your mother and siblings safely over to Birmingham, that's where the Army has set up their new command." Charles ordered his son. "Take them to the fields around Great Glen and I'll get a helicopter to come and pick you up."

"Okay Dad, I'll make sure they get there."

"What do you mean they?" His father picked up perceptively. "Where are you going?"

"I have to try and stop him Dad. You know...you've always known, that I'm not like everyone else." He laughed cynically. "The entire family has blue eyes, and yet mine are green. You noticed it as soon as I was born."

"I know." His father admitted. "And I'm so proud of everything you have become..." His father sounded emotional, almost close to tears. "But I cannot bear the thought of my son going into battle...I don't want you to die son." He said crying.

Alex was struggling to hold back the tears himself, hoping to lighten the mood with a terrible joke. "I don't want me to die either...I have to try though Dad. I think I've found a way of beating him, and I need to at any cost."

"What do you mean Alex?" His father asked with a clearly worried tone.

Alex could not respond though, the conversation was too emotional to carry on.

"Alex?" Charles asked again, the worry clear in his voice.

Alex could barely reply as the emotion grabbed hold of his throat and held the words within him. "Goodbye Dad…" He managed to let slip out as his eyes welled with tears again. "I love you." He finished as he ended the phone call and turned towards his family.

Charlotte, obviously realising that now was the time for emotional goodbyes, rushed forward and hugged her son once more. Alex could not allow his emotions to spill out again though, for it would only make it harder to leave. Gently, he pushed his mother back and cupped a hand to her cheek to comfort her.

"You need to drive to the fields around Great Glen, that's where Dad will pick you up." Alex told his mother.

Charlotte was clearly still not happy about the prospect of leaving her eldest son behind, but, even still, she nodded her assent. "Wait…" She thought quickly. "You said it wasn't safe by car."

Alex gave his mother a knowing look, a sarcastic teasing for her eavesdropping on the conversation between Alex; Thomas and the Matella. "I did. You're driving south though, further away from Magnus. You should be safe."

"And what about you? Will you be safe?"

"No." He responded bluntly, not wanting to lie to his mother. "But that's the point."

Charlotte almost protested before accepting that it was the way things had to be. "You had better make sure you're prepared then!" She tried to say jovially, although it only came across as awkward. "I'll gather you some stuff."

Like a typical mother, Charlotte began rushing about in the kitchen cupboards, making sure that he had enough supplies to keep him going for the journey. Fortunately, through the various failed diet programmes that Charlotte had pretended to be interested in, they had plenty of dried foods that could be boiled in a few minutes. Soups, cans, pastas and rice were all dumped into his rucksack, even things that he did not like were packed. He could not afford to be fussy though and so left his mother to it as his siblings looked about sadly and slumped into the furniture. They were not yet ready to say goodbye.

"Make sure to leave some for yourself!" He called to his mother. Charlotte brushed off the comment as she knew that, with any luck, they would be safe with his father within a few hours.

Thus, with his family in safe hands, Alex rushed upstairs and began to pack his things into one small sack that could hold no more than a few days' worth of supplies. His pack of cards, stuffed into his pocket for safekeeping, some clothes and toiletries was all he took with him from upstairs as he needed little else. He would gather food shortly. He looked at the foiled packet fondly, which had been in his room since before Magnus unleashed his horrors, and placed it back upon the computer table. Alex realised that, with a heavy heart, he no longer needed to practice magic tricks as he had something else to aspire to. The thing which he had seen as his ultimate curse was now going to be the salvation of the world, or so he hoped. So much had changed in such a small amount of time, and his forced maturity made him see that his abilities were nothing short of a miraculous gift.

Alex could not help thinking of all of the horrible things that he had done with his powers. Threatening his brother. Possessing his bully. Killing his dog. His mind came to rest upon the memories he held of Muffin and how many memories he had lost due to his immaturity and inexperience. Yet now he had the ability to change those memories into lessons. Magnus would not stop until the entire world was extinguished under his oppressive boot, like the tide washing away a sandcastle. Only Alex could stop him, but first he needed to find Ben Vire.

Once he had gathered the supplies his mother had left for him it was time to say their goodbyes. Abigail did her best to hide her emotions, but, in the end, Charlotte had had to force her into the family car so that they could leave. She might be upset now, soon though she will realise that I was keeping her safe, Alex thought to himself. She was exceedingly intelligent and perceptive after all. With his mother and sister already dealt with it left only his brother. Steven looked around awkwardly, and thus so did Alex. Curiously, the other Matella that had been left unconscious could no longer be seen. That worried Alex deeply. When Steven finally began his farewell Alex had to cut him off, to warn him and make sure he did what Alex could not whilst they were separated.

"Alex, you are my brother-"

"Save it Steven." Alex interrupted rudely. "I don't need your apology, I already know, and don't worry, I forgive you so long as it's mutual." He looked towards the spot of the formerly unconscious machine. "I need you to keep them safe. That creature that I stopped might still be out there, and I need you to stop it if it turns up."

"How am I supposed to do that?" Steven protested.

"Take your cricket bat. I'm certain it will be weak from its fight with me, but, if you see it, just hit it in the fleshy spots. It should go down without a fight then."

"And what if I can't do it?" Steven gestured again.

"You can brother." He said confidently. "You're stronger than you think you are." They shared a rare smile together. "Keep them safe."

Steven nodded and turned towards the gate that led into the back garden, obviously going towards the shed to retrieve his bat. Whilst Steven was gone he moved out into the road with the Matella and was quickly joined by Thomas, whose rucksack was almost overflowing from the things jammed within it. It was getting more and more difficult to leave with each passing moment. Abigail looked longingly out of the back of the family car, her eyes moist with tears, and Alex knew that he needed to say a proper goodbye to her. Without effort he pushed a thought into her mind, simple in its message and yet as powerful as the strongest waves of the oceans.

"Be careful, be just, and, above all, be magnificent. I will always be with you." Was all he said, but it seemed to work as his sister smiled as Steven gathered himself into the car, with his bat in hand, and they set off into the distance with one last toot of the horn.

Alex was left to stand on the street with his strange entourage. Nobody else had dared to come forth from their homes and so it gave the entire road an eerie feeling which crept up his back and made his spine shiver. Alex looked towards his home, and the plaque in the front garden, one last time as he did not know if he would ever see it again. It was time to let go of the past though, all the guilt and responsibilities, but also the friendships and the ties that kept him grounded. His destiny was ahead of him.

"It all rests on you now Alex." Thomas said with anticipation rich in his voice.

"No." Alex replied. "It all rests on Ben Vire."

Epilogue

Slowly he regained consciousness, unclear of what had caused him to lose it in the first place. All he could remember was the screams of the crowd as they struggled to get away from the attackers. He could visualise them now, as he remembered pushing others aside to try and escape their mechanical grasp. They had been a hideous concoction of metal and flesh, an ungodly combination that physically repulsed those who looked at them. He had been so desperate to escape them.

As he fixed his gaze around the room he struggled to discern any notable features. From what he could tell it was an empty room. A sudden pain emanated from his arms, the feeling only just coming back to them as he regained his senses. Horror gripped him as he realised that they were chained against the cold metal wall, holding him in place and putting great pressure upon the rest of his body to hold him up. He just considered himself grateful that he was as well built as he was, as it enabled him to withstand the torment for a great deal longer than most other people. That did not stop him panicking though as he gave a sharp tug upon the chains to try and loosen them, but it was no use. They would not budge.

Resigned to his fate, he decided to reflect upon his situation, a rarity for him. Everything that had happened to him over the past few weeks, every low point within his life, had been down to a single person. Alex Manningley. No doubt he was involved with his predicament at the moment. Maybe he was inside his mind again and this was all a projection that was being used to torment him. No, he thought to himself, there was no pain this time and everything seemed like it was real. If he could pinch himself to test this reality, then he would have. Instead, he was left hanging, his body open to any kind of punishment that his captors thought was needed. He could endure it though.

He wondered what his nemesis was doing, or if he too had been captured by whoever was holding them. He remembered the destruction they had witnessed on the television, and the fear that it had evoked in everyone, even Alex. As much as he hated Alex, he could not blame him for what was happening. Although, Arthur was aware that the youth knew more than himself, given the special nature that he seemed to share with the madman that they had witnessed completely and utterly destroy an entire city.

I need to get out of here, Arthur thought to himself. The more he thought of that man, the more he was sure that he was in danger. His face was the picture of perfect evil, gaunt features and piercing eyes with hair straight from a morticians. The way he walked, so purposeful and calculated. It made him that much more menacing. Even his clothes helped his aura of malevolence, for they were so old, and yet barely worn, creating an uncomfortable impression for people who look at them. I need to get out of here, he repeated.

With all his force mustered behind him he pulled as hard as he could upon the chains that held him in place. His face turned red from the exertion and sweat instantly glistened his body. Arthur's straining muscles continued to pull as hard as his body would physically allow, but it was to no avail. The chains did not even move, it was like there was some kind of barrier keeping them in place. Arthur relaxed his tired arms and realised the hopelessness of his situation. He screamed as loudly as he could as he knew that there was no hope of escape. No hope of seeing his father again, and no hope of fulfilling his dreams.

Somebody obviously heard his cries as the doors to his small prison opened, allowed artificial light to temporarily blind him, since he had been without its presence for a while. Arthur closed his eyes to avoid the horrible brightness of the torches and did not dare open them for fear of what might be in the room when he did. Eventually, once he had dispelled his irrational phobia, he opened his eyes to look around his room, properly, for the first time. When he did, he realised that he should have kept his eyes shut.

Standing around the room were several of those machines that had taken him captive, and others he could not see he assumed. Their fleshy joints combined with the metallic exoskeleton almost led him to vomit upon the floor, the hollow slits that made up their eyes, complete with human, or seemingly human, eyeballs, were enough by themselves to make him retch nigh uncontrollably. When he regained himself his heart almost leapt out of his chest as he noticed one of them standing less than two feet to his right hand side, and another to his left. He would have screamed, but he knew that it would only exacerbate his situation.

Arthur was ready to give in to whatever fate awaited him, until he saw the figure that had appeared in the dimly lit doorway that led to his prison cell. Even from a distance he could tell that it was the same man who had sacked Leeds and terrorised Leicester, his pompous bearing making it blindingly obvious.

Arthur squirmed in position as the man moved closer to him, the faint smelled of leather drawing nearer as the villain's gloves and boots squeaked with authenticity. The rhythmic bounding with which the man moved made it all the more unsettling as each step was timed for maximum effect. Arthur tried to loosen the grip of the chains once more, using all of his strength and not caring about how much he damaged his body in the process. Once more, it was to no avail and so he slumped forward and silently wept. There was no way out.

With great force he was pushed back up against the wall, without being touched, and his head cracked against the metal, making an audible, almost comic, twang. He was not even allowed to wallow in grief in peace. Instinctively, he closed his eyes to avoid the gaze of the villain, but this too was also taken from him as his eyelids were forced apart. He could not even move his eyes as they too were forced into staring at the man who was now no more than a few feet before him, with his features still obscured due to the terrible lighting.

Arthur was beyond feeling trapped, and the overwhelming sense of déjà vu was making him nauseous as he recalled the abandoned classroom where his mind had been invaded and played about with like a cat messing with yarn. Arthur flinched again as a small ball of flame zoomed towards him, stopping just shy of his face so that it did not burn him, although the swirling mini-sun still felt uncomfortably hot against his bare cheeks. Now he could see the face of the man and was shocked to see that, for such a horrendous person, he looked perfectly normal. His features were quite lean, and gave clear evidence of his wealthy upbringing, but were easily recognisable.

Without warning the man forced himself into his mind and wrapped himself around Arthur's memories, becoming a part of them. Arthur screamed in pain, for it was truly agonising, much more so than when Alex did the same, and struggled as much as he could as his life was being examined from the inside. He could not even blot out the horrors of it, as his eyes were jammed open by the sorcery of this scoundrel. Thankfully, it did not last long as he was relieved of the pain and free to save what memories there were that had not been tarnished.

The man scowled at him with disapproval, although Arthur had no idea why this was so. Slowly, in a calculated manner, he moved his face in closer to Arthur's, so that their noses were close to touching. In a low, and evidently furious, tone the villain asked a single question.

"Where, is Alex Manningley?!"